Legends of Vietnam

ALSO BY NGHIA M. VO AND
FROM MCFARLAND

Saigon: A History (2011)
The Vietnamese Boat People, 1954 and 1975–1992 (2006)
*The Bamboo Gulag: Political Imprisonment in
Communist Vietnam* (2004)

ALSO EDITED BY NGHIA M. VO

*The Viet Kieu in America: Personal Accounts of
Postwar Immigrants from Vietnam* (2009)

Legends of Vietnam
An Analysis and Retelling of 88 Tales

NGHIA M. VO

McFarland & Company, Inc., Publishers
Jefferson, North Carolina, and London

LIBRARY OF CONGRESS CATALOGUING-IN-PUBLICATION DATA

Vo, Nghia M., 1947–
    Legends of Vietnam : an analysis and retelling of 88 tales / Nghia M. Vo.
        p.   cm.
    Includes bibliographical references and index.

    ISBN 978-0-7864-6846-1
    softcover : acid free paper ∞

    1. Legends—Vietnam.   2. Tales—Vietnam.   I. Title.
GR313.V59 2012
398.209597—dc23   2012017529

BRITISH LIBRARY CATALOGUING DATA ARE AVAILABLE

© 2012 Nghia M. Vo. All rights reserved

No part of this book may be reproduced or transmitted in any form or by any means, electronic or mechanical, including photocopying or recording, or by any information storage and retrieval system, without permission in writing from the publisher.

Front cover image © 2012 Shutterstock

Manufactured in the United States of America

McFarland & Company, Inc., Publishers
  Box 611, Jefferson, North Carolina 28640
    www.mcfarlandpub.com

*To Maggy, JD, Christina, Mya, and Taylor.
To the Vietnamese and those who
try to understand their culture.*

Table of Contents

Preface   1

Part One: The Vietnamese Cosmos   5
   I. Introduction   6
   II. Spirits and Religions   7
   III. A Tale of Division   16
   IV. Legends and Folk Stories   23
   V. The Making of Vietnamese Legends   28
   VI. Asian Legends   35

Part Two: Northern Legends   43
   VII. Introduction   44
   VIII. *Việt Điền U Linh Tập*   47
   IX. *Lĩnh Nam Chích Quái*   57
   X. Other Northern Legends   77

Part Three: Southern Legends   88
   XI. Introduction   89
   XII. Southern Legends   96
       A. Historical Legends   96
       B. Animal Legends   125
       C. Traditional Legends   148
       D. Social Legends   185
       E. Ethnic Legends   232

Table of Contents

XIII. War and Postwar Legends   234
XIV. A Tale of Deception and Failure   245

Chapter Notes   249
Bibliography   259
Index   263

Preface

Legends have always fascinated people, from antiquity to modern days. They began as a form of media—although people did not know much about media at that time—to convey news about and reaction to the surrounding world, which indeed could be strange, brutal, and powerful, yet interesting and refreshing. Simplistic in the beginning, they became more sophisticated as civilizations became more advanced and structured. Transmitted orally in the early stages of civilization, these stories were then collected and written down for future generations to read.

Books about legends usually retell those stories that target a limited audience: children aged six to ten, the age of innocence, wonderment, and discovery. This fact can convey the wrong idea—that adults are not interested in legends or the medium does not appeal to them. But legends are often more than simple stories: they can be enchanting, bizarre, or instructive in nature. They may shed light into the soul of a nation and the aspiration of its people.

Legends are also the awakened dreams of a nation and at times serve to inflame people's minds. Vietnamese legends include stories of ancient heroes like the Trưng sisters, Lady Triệu, and the Genie of Phù Đổng to name just a few. The Trưng sisters are revered in Vietnam as nation liberators and freedom fighters. And in spite of their defeat, they instill in people the desire to fight back and to recover their national independence. Shrines have been built to commemorate their fighting spirit. Soldiers and leaders have often visited them to pray and ask for advice in times of need. People have reenacted parts of their stories to shed light on their deeds for younger generations to see.

Legends sometimes reflect the thought process and morality of its people. They imply that good people should be rewarded and bad ones punished, a notion often at odds with reality. They also express the deep wishes of the nation for peace, love, friendship, justice, riches, and stability.

Preface

My search for a good book about Vietnamese legends began years ago at local university libraries. Because the Vietnamese are newcomers to the States (most of them came after 1975), books in English about Vietnamese legends are a rare breed, except for some children's literature, such as *Toad Is the Uncle of Heaven: A Vietnamese Folktale* (1989) by Jeanne Lee; *The Brocaded Slipper and Other Vietnamese Tales* (1992) by Lynette Dyer Vuong and Vo Dinh Mai; *Children of the Dragon: Selected Tales from Vietnam* (2001) by Sherry Garland; *How Tiger Got His Stripes* (2006) by Rob Cleveland, and so on. Somehow lost in the shuffle was the intriguing *Beyond the East Wind: Legends and Folktales of Vietnam* by Dương Văn Quyền and Jewel Coburn, which I have just recently discovered. The book was first published in 1976 (one year after the first wave of Vietnamese arrived in the U.S.) then reprinted in 1981. This late discovery makes me wonder about the number of legend books that are lying out there waiting to be discovered. The book was most likely written for and targeted at the new immigrants who were at that time too busy remaking their lives to read books.

These disappointing searches for a good book on Vietnamese legends led me to write this one. Disappointing indeed, because in the early 1960s in Vietnam I read many books about legends from various regions of France and countries of Europe—and that was a long time ago. I figured then that if France (I borrowed these books from the library of the French Cultural Mission in Saigon) has books about legends, so does the U.S.

As I began collecting some legends, I realized that some of them deal with ancient heroes and the history of ancient Vietnam. A more in-depth search led me to discover ancient manuscripts like the *Việt Điền U Linh Tập* (1321) and the *Lĩnh Nam Chích Quái* (1492) and books written by Frenchmen Landes (1880) and Chivas-Baron (1920). I was stunned by these findings, which add a new and extraordinary dimension to the world of Vietnamese legends, now extending from the fourteenth to the twenty-first century. I am delighted to share these legends with you in this book.

This work is organized into three parts.

Part One deals with the Vietnamese cosmos, explaining the mores, thought processes, and religions of Vietnam, a country whose long history has been shaped by a number of religious thoughts and ideologies that have survived the test of time (chapter II). Understanding them allows for a deeper knowledge of Vietnamese culture. The fact that Vietnam had been divided politically and militarily into two different countries for more than three centuries may explain the regional differences between northern and southern legends (chapter III). This is followed by a discussion about leg-

Preface

ends in general throughout the world and in Vietnam in particular (chapter IV). Next, the analysis of three personalities who became legendary institutions that have attracted a lot of followers may help us to understand the mechanics of legends, at least in Vietnam (chapter V). And finally, the differences and commonalities between the legends of four Asian countries (Japan, China, India, and Vietnam) are analyzed (chapter VI). What do legends in neighboring countries look or sound like and did they migrate across frontiers? What are their particularities and differences?

Part Two deals with northern legends. We begin with the *Việt Điền U Linh Tập* (Compilation of the Potent Spirits in the Việt Realm, VDULT), which, written in 1321, was the first recorded Vietnamese legend book (chapter VIII). Few readers are aware of this 70-page book, although it was there all along. *Lĩnh Nam Chích Quái* (Wonderful Stories of Lĩnh Nam), written in 1492, has also been ignored by the public (chapter IX). These two ancient manuscripts form the basis of Vietnamese legends, and therefore its belief, culture, and history. Neglecting them seems like leaving a big chunk out of Vietnamese history and culture.

The French have left us two good books on Vietnamese legends. Written in 1880 and 1920 respectively, they give us an insight on the culture of the time through the eyes of foreigners (chapter X). Nguyễn Đổng Chi's book is too big to summarize. The other books written in the first part of the twenty-first century contain various legends that are not widely known throughout the country until recently. They are addressed in (chapter VII).

Part Three deals with southern legends. Following an introduction (chapter XI) that explains the differences between northern and southern legends, I present a new collection of southern legends based on recollections of stories I have personally heard from parents or relatives over the years or on writings by other authors (chapter XII). A new section about war and postwar legends has been added (chapter XIII). Huỳnh Sanh Thông was the first to spearhead this topic in his 1988 book *To Be Made Over: Tales of Socialist Reeducation in Vietnam*. I am glad to continue his work and contribute my own. This section concludes with "A Tale of Deception and Failure," dealing with the way some leaders have deceived their people throughout the millennia (chapter XIV).

Overall, a large collection of legends has not been methodically analyzed in the past. The field of legends has all along been neglected by serious intellectual minds, who to this day have considered it to belong to the children's realm. This work is probably the first detailed analysis of the legends of one country. It is also the first longitudinal study of legends of any country in the world. Readers may realize how legends, used as a medium for propaganda by the government in the fourteenth century, have evolved over time to become a form of news, entertainment, culture, and thought for common people and readers alike.

Legends are the mirror or means through which we can see and learn about a country—Vietnam in this case—its society, religion, history, and traditions. Its world is indeed complex, fascinating, and sometimes enchanting. I hope you enjoy this book as I have enjoyed writing it.

Part One
The Vietnamese Cosmos

I. Introduction

To talk about legends is to talk about spirits, ghosts, animism, and religions, especially for the Vietnamese peasantry, which makes up more than 80 percent of the population. Besides ornate and well-attended temples, especially during the festival days, the Vietnamese man lives a private "spiritual" life limited to an in-house and outside altar. The ritual he follows conveys his respect to the spirits as well as his attempt to appease them. He knows that the world is populated by spirits, which he has to ask for protection—a relic of thousands of years of practice and tradition weighing down on his psyche.

The Lý kings in the eleventh century were the first to use spirits and deities to their advantage. They "establish[ed] a personal relationship of trust and loyalty with the different local spirits,"[1] brought them to the "center," gave them titles, and made them protectors of the royal authority being developed at the court. "Responsive" spirits—those who answered prayers—were enshrined and bestowed more titles, while nonresponsive ones were replaced. Details about the titles can be found in chapter VIII.

Although Buddhism and Confucianism were introduced into Vietnam in the second century CE, and Buddhism peaked in the thirteenth and fourteenth centuries before being supplanted by Confucianism, these religious thoughts have never completely soaked into the Vietnamese psyche, which remains attached to animism colored by some Buddhist and Confucian traits.

This attitude may explain the appeal and the rise of modern goddesses like Princess Liễu Hạnh and Bà Chúa Kho (the Lady of the Storehouse) in the North and Bà Chúa Xứ (Lady of the Realm) in the South (chapter V). In fact, these goddesses have a huge female following in Vietnam, which in a sense serves to counterbalance the mostly male power holders. The power in the country has always been divided along gender lines: while males are dominant or hold major positions in society (outer generals), females supported by goddesses run the household and commerce (inner generals).

II. Spirits and Religions

If one asks the Vietnamese about their religion, 80 percent of them would claim they are Buddhist.[1] In reality, their belief is a mixture of animism, ancestor worship, Taoism, and Buddhism. One example is Cô Tuyết, who in 1997 as a devout Buddhist went twice monthly to pagodas to make offerings; went on pilgrimages; and attended lectures and special events at Chùa Quán Sứ, the largest pagoda in Hanoi. While reciting sutras, she also sought advice from fortune tellers and gave offerings to gods, goddesses, ancestors, spirits and ghosts for family protection and protection from bad fortune.[2]

Today, the most visited religious site in Vietnam is that of Bà Chúa Xứ—a nondenominational goddess of uncertain origin.[3] In 1984, when đổi mới (renovation) had not even been approved and religious practice was under communist state control, 75 goddesses were venerated in Vietnam.[4] Goddess worship, thus, is an indigenous belief, a remnant of Vietnam's religious and cultural prehistorical past that has outlasted foreign and elite cultural accretion, including Confucianism.[5]

A. Animism

Kwon recounted in his book[6] his 2008 encounter with a retired local army lieutenant during a field trip in Cam Ré, central Vietnam. In 2007, when the lieutenant was still the commanding officer of the local military camp, one of his soldiers told him about a ghostly apparition of an American officer who had died in Cam Ré during the war. As reports of apparitions became more frequent and caused a lot of concerns among his soldiers, he decided to teach them a lesson. He took them to the site, and after scolding them, dropped his pants and urinated on the spot. The apparitions immediately stopped and the frightened soldiers returned to their routine. A few months later, without warning, the lieutenant was struck by a severe headache and began stuttering to the point of being unable to do his work. When he did not get better, friends and family suggested he seek hospitalization. However, on the advice of a relative, he consulted a medium instead.

The medium told the lieutenant that the foreign ghost was outraged by his behavior and demanded to be removed from that inconvenient spot. Based on the advice of the medium he decided to excavate the area. The bullet-ridden skull and remains of a U.S. officer were found and exhumed. After lengthy negotiations between the Vietnamese and U.S. authorities, the remains of the officer missing in action (MIA) were repatriated.

The lieutenant's medical condition dramatically improved, and after working for a few more months, he retired and set up a repair shop nearby. He told Kwon that the U.S. officer had "nearly defeated him, a soldier of the Vietnamese Army, many decades after the end of the war." As an epilogue to the story, his business prospered because of rumors about his dealing with the foreign ghost. Local people commented that the ghost was first upset at the lieutenant, but to thank him for returning the remains to his homeland, had decided to go for a joint Vietnamese-American venture with the Vietnamese and did everything he could to help him out.

This story reinforces the idea that the other world—the spirit world—remains real, especially in today's Vietnam. The Vietnamese actually live in two worlds. Besides the real and present one that constitutes their daily lives, they also navigate through the world of invisible spirits that surrounds them. They realize they have bumped into a spirit when they face some setback. They then consult a medium or sorcerer who tells them that the setback indeed was the result of an encounter with a spirit. Although the scenario was more frequent five or six decades earlier, it is still happening in today's Vietnam. In the case mentioned earlier, the lieutenant, despite not believing in spirits, went to see his medium instead of going to the hospital to have his head checked. Although not every case of severe headache and stuttering can be traced back to an encounter with a ghost, this one was pretty obvious because of the lieutenant's previous challenge to the ghost.

In the 1960s, across from my grandparents' house in the village of Vũng Tàu lived a healthy, somewhat florid Chinese store owner in her late forties. She was stronger and healthier than her frail and diminutive mother, who was then in her seventies. The daughter suddenly passed away one day, and the family attributed the sudden death to *trúng gió* (bad wind).

II. Spirits and Religions

They presumed that a force of nature (the wind and the spirit that inhabited it) had caused a detrimental and harmful effect on the daughter. But, had she been brought to the hospital, she might have been diagnosed with a heart attack or disabling stroke, as her plethoric constitution suggested.

The world of spirits is complex and hierarchical because men have structured the spirits' realm according to human society.[7] Some spirits are promoted, others demoted by government officials or by the people themselves; some are thought to be powerful, others feeble. Some are bad, others good. Spirits, however, might not live according to design, because as spirits, they are free and beyond human control. And, there are many types of spirits.

First, local spirits are not known beyond their village or region and have limited power. There are plenty of them, but overall they exert minimal damage; they, therefore, are rarely mentioned, except by the local people. Then come the patron saints or guardian spirits particular to villages, especially in the north. In the south, one rarely sees these cults. Spirits are venerated by entire villages and were once sanctioned by the emperor. They could be founders of dynasties, national heroes, great literary heroes, living persons of exceptional achievement, or sometimes bandits, or strongmen who appeared to have protected the village. They are prayed to at the local temple right at the village gate, if it is a small village, or at the *đình* (communal hall) if the village is larger. Villagers are often ambivalent about using bandits or bad people as guardians, but sometimes they have no choice. They have to either side with or be harmed by them. Then come the higher spirits of the mountains, rivers, and earth. They dwell over large territories and wield greater power. The damage they could cause is greater than that of the lesser spirits. That is why each year in the past, the emperor or king, on behalf of the people, prayed to the spirit of the god of agriculture to keep drought and tornadoes away. And above all is the *Ông Trời*, the ruler of the earth. Other people also call him *Ngọc Hoàng Thượng Đế* or Jade Emperor.

In the beginning of time, gods and spirits lived among humans, as recorded in the legends. They then assumed human features and even married humans. Some of these marriages worked out well, while others did not. Then, the spirits pulled back and cloistered themselves—that is what people thought—in a world separate from that of humans. One of the first legends presented in part three deals with the spirits of the mountain and the sea. They were friends before fighting with each other over who would marry the king's daughter (related in southern tale # 2). The kitchen even has its own god (described in southern tale # 21). He makes his report on the household to the Jade Emperor at the end of the year on the 23rd of each lunar calendar year, about one week before the Tết festival.

Besides these helpful spirits are the evil ones that are capricious, hypersensitive, petty, and vengeful. They are plentiful and always ready to cause harm.[8] While the educated minds of westerners look for the physical cause of a problem, the Vietnamese mind looks for a spiritual resolution to the problem. That tradition has been so engrained into the minds of the Vietnamese that, consciously or unconsciously, they basically follow a ritual that has been passed down to them from generation to generation. Therefore, prior to building a house, opening a business, or working on a major project, they pray to the spirits with a medium's help or advice. They even talk to geomancers to look for the right orientation of the house or the most auspicious opening date for a business.

The following story shows how spirits are still chosen in today's North Vietnam. In the village of Giáp Tự south of Hanoi, the *đình* (communal house), which was damaged by the revolution in 1947, sat undisturbed for 40 years. Since the atheist communist government "endeavored to desacralize communal houses,"[9] no one dared to repair it until the late 1980s following relaxation of rules on religions. Since the guardian spirit—a former herbal doctor—was unable to protect the village from war ravages, some villagers felt he had become ineffective. Old men—former communist soldiers—decided to put up a bust of Hồ Chí Minh as the new guardian spirit. Women who were using the *đình* for religious practices argued that it was a sacred place of worship, not a government office. After lengthy debates, a deal was struck; the bust was removed and replaced by a lacquer portrait of Hồ that sat in a newly built lacquer cabinet with folding doors on the main altar in 1992. When women conducted Buddhist prayers, they closed the cabinet doors, pretending not to see Hồ; when men celebrated rites dedicated to guardian spirits, they opened the cabinet doors for everyone to see whom they were honoring.

By default, Hồ thus became the new village's guardian spirit, although women still worshipped the herbal doctor. When women performed rites, they propitiated the herbal doctor first, then Hồ and former village mandarins, and finished with chants and prayers to Buddha.[10] The order of propitiation shows that spirits have taken precedent over Buddha, who was further pushed to the periphery.

Some women were still unhappy with the presence of Hồ's portrait on the main altar. In December 1995, the government disbanded a Hồ cult in the village of Vĩnh Phú, northwest of Hanoi, where the worship of Hồ as the 18th king in the mythical Hùng Dynasty had begun.[11] Concerned about the proliferation of such unorthodox rites, the government ordered the removal of Hồ's portrait from the main altar and its hanging in another room of the *đình* complex. The old herbal doctor has retaken his place on the main altar at Giáp Tự village.

B. *Taoism*

Taoism and Confucianism came to Vietnam at about the same time, within the first two centuries after 111 BCE, the date of Chinese conquest of Vietnam. While Confucianism had clear, uncompromising philosophy, Taoism remained as vague and elusive as its founder, Laotzu. The solution the latter offered ran opposite to that his contemporary, Confucius. He suggested to let the people realize themselves so they can follow the *Tao* (or the way of nature), which was left undefined. In other words, the more the master or sage stayed in the background and did not interfere with his students, the better, for they will discover their own Tao. Taoism is thus a doctrine of individual salvation and the search for happiness in this and the other world. Salvation in the end lies in the renunciation of power and the return to nature.[12]

Laotzu apparently was fleeing the unrest of the world to retire in isolation in the woods when royal guards at the border asked him to write down his thoughts. After writing his essays, he disappeared and was never seen again. He probably did not mean to write a theological opus, let alone found a new religion or an army of followers. His thoughts, however, became the basis of the *Tao Te Ching*, although he did not write every chapter of the book.

> The sage says little
> and does not tie people down.[13]
>
> If you try to possess it, you will destroy it;
> If you try to control it, you will lose it.[14]

Laotzu's philosophy of nothingness and harmony with nature did not appeal too much to his followers, who in the third century BCE not only copied the sutras (the Buddhist scripture), but also adopted the concepts of rebirth, and the judges of hell and salvation. So when Taoism came to Vietnam, it was loaded with deities like the Jade Emperor and the kitchen god or *Ông Táo*, which attracted the Vietnamese. The male Buddha became the female goddess of mercy Quan Âm. Other goddesses included Liễu Hạnh, which will be discussed later.[15]

Taoism, therefore, covers a broad spectrum of practices, from Laotzu's high philosophy to a pantheon of deities: emperors, officials, thunder gods, wealth gods, or terrifying demons. Worshipers could today attend services at temples or hire a monk or nun to help them solve their problems: illness, death, business matters, school exams. They pray to a deity while the monk summons heaven's assistance. They also engage in physical cultivation aimed at wellness and contemplation.[16]

The Vietnamese while adopting Taoism kept the deities without getting deeply involved in the religion itself. Therefore, they do not build any exclusively Taoist pagodas, except for the famous Ngọc Hoàng pagoda in Saigon. Although Taoism is not a major religion per se in Vietnam today, it accounts for much of the mysticism, magic, and sorcery that is popular in Vietnam.[17]

C. Confucianism

Confucius (551–479 BCE), brought up during a period of social unrest and civil war under the Chinese Zhou Dynasty, suggested that people's fate, from the lowly peasants to the king, had been preordained as part of a cosmic order. Stability and order in the country could only be realized if everyone followed a strict code of moral conduct. Far from wanting to destroy the feudal system—it was there for a reason—he only wanted to consolidate it.

To achieve harmony in the system, peasants had to obey state officials; officials, the king; and the king, the higher moral authority, of Heaven. Within the family, children had to obey their parents, and the wife her husband. The king, through ritual offerings, should secure the favor of cosmic forces or "heaven's mandate." If that harmony were destroyed, the country would be ravaged by instability, wars, epidemics, or drought. The doctrine asked each person, from the lowliest to the highest, to continuously perfect himself and to help others perfect themselves.

After offering his service and advice to court officials without much success, Confucius set up a school to train young men for public service according to his ideals. When he died, he was an embittered and lonely man. It was only three centuries after his death that the new Han dynasty sanctioned and put into practice his teachings, assuring that they became the norm in China. His influence would continue until today, more than two millennia later.

All this teachings implied that the ruler should not be greedy for

II. Spirits and Religions

power, the bureaucrats not abusive of the system, and the individuals not selfish. Although this was too much to ask from human nature, the system somehow took hold in Vietnam when the Chinese annexed it in 111 BCE. The Vietnamese, who adhered to a matriarchal system at that time, slowly switched to a patriarchal one and incorporated Confucian ideas in their religious life. Ancestor and spirit worship took form along with official religious ceremonies to worship earthly and heavenly powers.

Once Vietnam regained its independence in 939 CE, it continued to observe the Confucian tradition. In 1070, King Lý Thánh Tông (r. 1054–1072) set up the *Văn Miếu* (Temple of Literature) in Thăng Long (Hanoi) to train mandarins—state officials—who would administer state and provinces on the king's behalf.[18] Alas, the teaching, based on the Chinese model, was designed to preserve tradition and the privileges of the aristocracy. Candidates were not required to think for themselves or better themselves and those they served. They only learned the Confucian political and moral philosophy in Chinese script in order to pass the test, which guaranteed them an official position in the government and security for life. They failed to observe Confucius' idea that access to the elite should be open to anyone regardless of origins or rank.[19] That failure, by allowing the concentration of power in the hands of a few, ended up oppressing the masses and led to revolts and social instability. A system that was initially designed to foster social order and stability eventually led to inequality and instability. Under this system, the country was unable to modernize and face the foreign invasion that eventually toppled the monarchy.

Unger notices that Confucianism was stronger after the socialist revolution and argues that Hồ Chí Minh was trained in a Confucian tradition and people saw him as a reformer—an executor of the heavenly mandate.[20] In fact, communism and Confucianism are as different as day and night. Communism has always wanted to topple the Confucian system, which it called corrupt and feudal. While Confucianism has altruistic goals, communism is a "criminal totalitarianism" that has killed 85 to 100 million people worldwide[21] and one million people in Vietnam.[22] Brigham also concludes that "Hồ was not a Confucian ... Hồ never promoted himself as a Confucian."[23] Marr writes, "It would be wrong to characterize Hồ Chí Minh or any major Vietnamese communist leader as a nationalist."[24] As early as 1922, Hồ considered nationalism to be a dangerous siren that can lure people away from communism.[25]

Ancestor worship is based on the belief that the human soul survives after death and becomes the natural protector of the family line. To have him restless or angry is not only shameful, but also dangerous. Therefore, he needs to be venerated and honored regularly, especially at the anniversary of the death of the ancestor (*ngày giỗ tổ*).²⁶

Ancestors play an important part in the family even if they have passed away. They remain part of the family because they—as spirits—can protect the family from bad spirits.

Therefore, people make offerings to them through worship. They invite them to eat first or have special portions reserved for them. There was even an invocation for them to eat first at every major dinner. People talk and pray to them. They guide the family through difficulties, usually by means of flashes of insight or sudden clarity of thought.

Family altars can be large, although most of them are small in size. No more than one by one foot in size, they serve as a place of acknowledgement and offering to the spirits. The *bàn thờ gia tiên* (family altar) sits in the middle of the house and is used to worship the spirits of the ancestors of a family. The *bàn thờ tổ tiên* (household altar) is used for the ancestors of an extended family.²⁷ They are large enough to contain a small incense holder and a bowl or a plate. The household head or usually his wife would place some rice or a fruit in the bowl, light incense, hold it between his or her fingers, and say a short prayer to the spirit before bowing a couple of times in front of the altar.

D. Buddhism

Prince Siddhartha Gautama grew up confined in a castle because his father did not want him to face the harsh realities of life. He was destined to a life of privilege, power and wealth until he sneaked out of the palace one day with the help of his servant and saw in succession a sick man doubled up with pain, a funeral procession, and a beggar who did not have enough to eat. Troubled by what he saw, he left his pampered life, his wife and child to look for the truth. He found enlightenment after six years of soul searching.

He taught that life is suffering, which results from men's attachment to their instincts, greed and sensual desires. To get rid of the cycle of suffering, men have to renounce all wrong behavior and vice.

After his death in 483 BCE of old age, his message was spread from India throughout Asia: by land through China into Vietnam (Mahayana or Greater Vehicle) and by sea through Thailand, Cambodia, Vietnam (Theravada or Lesser Vehicle). The conservative Theravada Buddhism closely follows Buddha's teaching and suggests that everyone is responsible for his enlightenment, which is not possible for everyone. Mahayana Buddhism, which broke away from the Buddha's teaching, proposes that everyone could achieve that state by a willingness to demonstrate religious faith, virtuousness, and service to others. The original Buddha, who had refused deification for himself, now shares the stage with countless other buddhas and bodhisattvas.[28]

Mahayana pagodas, limited to northern and central Vietnam, are fabulously decorated with phoenixes, dragons, unicorns, tigers, and tortoises, symbolizing longevity and wisdom, along with many buddhas and bodhisattvas. Theravada pagodas, limited to South Vietnam, displayed mainly buddhas and bodhisattvas but often brightly painted and enlarged to a gigantic size.[29] This is another difference between North and South.

Although Buddhism came to Vietnam around 194–195 CE, it circulated mainly among immigrants, diplomats, and merchants. It was not until the tenth century that Đinh Tiên Hoàng (968–979) instituted a system of royal support of the religion. Buddhism did not spread to the masses until the eleventh century, where it coexisted with Taoism and Confucianism. It saw its peak in the thirteenth and fourteenth centuries when it competed against Confucianism. The religion continued its slow decline and became mixed with mysticism, animism, and polytheism. It began to slowly revive toward 1920.[30] After 1955, Buddhism in the North came under communist state control, while in the South it remained independent but became deeply involved in politics until 1975, when it too came under communist state control.

Following *đổi mới*, northern Buddhism slowly, under southern influence, moved toward the Zen (Thiền) doctrine, directing their followers to spend more time with meditation than simply chanting sutras. Followers also wore the southern grey robes during ceremonies in place of their northern brown robes.[31]

Leopold Cadière compared the Vietnamese mind to an impenetrable forest, with "gigantic tree trunks sinking their roots into unknown depths, the impenetrable canopy of leaves form dark shadowy vaults; ... climbing plants twine from tree to tree—you can see no beginning and no end...."[32]

Decades or even centuries of war, turmoil, poverty, misery, cruelty, killing, and trauma have shattered people's natural faith in the government, state, and religions and caused them to turn to cultic veneration of spirits and goddesses. By embracing goddesses, they openly express their insecurity toward and distrust in state institutions.

III. A Tale of Division

When April 30, 1975, came, northern communist tanks broke through the gates of Independence Palace and took over the country. The first wave of 130,000 Vietnamese fled the country to look for freedom somewhere else.[1] The consequences—psychological, social, political, economic, and moral—were often tragic and painful.

To fully understand these consequences and their impact on the South Vietnamese, one has to discuss the loss, the little Saigons, and the two Vietnams.

A. Loss

With the fall of Saigon, the world as the South Vietnamese knew it ended abruptly. Changes included the following:

Incarceration Trương Như Tảng acknowledged that "in the first year of liberation, some three hundred thousand people were arrested."[2] Overall more than a million government officials and military personnel were hauled to reeducation camps, where they were starved and forced to do hard labor.[3] This was a wholesale enslavement of the country not heard of in human history, except under communist regimes. Prisoners were treated harshly without any rights "We were less than animals and not really human."[4] Even the communist Bùi Tín wondered after visiting various re-education camps in the South as well as in the North "why pursue a policy of such harshness towards hundreds of thousands of people?"[5]

Suppression of Basic Freedoms[6] One could not even visit one's friend a few miles away without approval of government officials. Basic freedoms were abolished and replaced by communist rules—those of the invaders. "In the eyes of our communist leaders, an enemy 'puppet' whether alive

III. A Tale of Division

or dead, was always a puppet—a second class citizen who had no citizen's rights at all.[7] Even today, Father Lý, who fought for human rights in Vietnam for decades, was hand-gagged in court by a *Công An* (secret police) to prevent him from speaking up. This was a far cry from the so-called *liberation* of the South.

Impoverishment Private properties, bank accounts, houses and businesses were confiscated and turned over to communist officials. The latter "fought each other over houses, cars, prostitutes, and bribes. Soldiers and officials... were suddenly confronted with what seemed to them an almost fairy tale richness, theirs for the taking."[8]

Escape and Readjustment Unable to tolerate an illegitimate and cruel regime, more than two million people braved the seas, storms and pirates to look for freedom.[9] This was a massive exodus by sea and land.

Nightmares Many Vietnamese have been followed by nightmares over the past three and a half decades, especially those went gone through reeducation camps. The inhumane treatment[10] of the prisoners by sadistic jailers—"They did not kill you outright in the camp by shooting you. Instead they slowly tortured and terrified you"[11]—left an indelible and painful mark on many. And today, a scratching at the door will wake up a former camp inmate inducing a sweat.[12]

San Juan wrote about a refugee who had relocated to the U.S.

> It is hard to say that the war was over...
> The past like a nightmare endlessly haunts...
> It is like a dream he cannot forget...[13]

Memories have become a prominent feature of those who escaped from Vietnam—the overseas Vietnamese. They led to community building and place making.

Periodically these festering wounds bleed again...resulting in vigorous protests. What the Vietnamese-American community wants to do with these protests is to remind themselves, and other Americans too, not to forget the old South Vietnam that they know and love.[14]

A loss can be categorized into three levels: First, there is the casual loss—loss of money, wallet, keys—that could be momentarily replaced. The second type of loss is that of a friendship. One day, she left us: that person who has been so dear to us in many ways is no longer around. We become heartbroken. And until we recover, we feel that something in us is missing. We are no longer wholesome. Our mind wanders around, making it difficult for us to concentrate or work. The third type is the loss of a country: the biggest of all losses.

"There is no greater loss than that of losing one's country," claimed Phan Bội Châu, one of the Vietnamese revolutionaries in 1906.[15] What he meant was losing independence to the French was akin to losing one's country, although the country was still there.

But in 1975, the South Vietnamese lost everything—country, houses, businesses, belongings, jobs, bank accounts, and so on—without any chance of regaining it. It left them disoriented in space and time. It left them hanging between two worlds—"Vietnam and Vietnamese America—and to neither, and of responsibility for the communities to which [they] are not always sure they belong."[16]

B. *The Little Saigons*

With time, Vietnamese immigrants become Vietnamese-Americans, people who walk around with hyphens between their names. They may no longer be Vietnamese but are not yet or never Americans. They are in limbo between the two worlds: one that has rejected them and one they have not become familiar with.

This is not a new phenomenon; the sociologist Georg Simmel once confronted it in the 1900s. He wrote about the immigrant, "The stranger intends to stay, although he cannot ever become native." Born of Jewish parents in Berlin, Germany—his father later became a Roman Catholic and his mother a Lutheran—he never felt accepted by German academia, despite his talents. He was turned down from many vacant chairmanship positions before being elevated to full professor without chair in 1901.[17] He, therefore, knew what it meant to be a "stranger" in a new land.

Along the same vein, a successful Vietnamese business woman despite having married an American military lawyer and having children with him, declared

> As for me and the Vietnamese of my generation, there will always be memories of another time and place, another life. I will forever remain an immigrant here. And even when I am happiest, I will remember my beloved Vietnam and the fate of my people.
> I am the child of war, I am a Vietnamese.[18]

The Vietnamese-Americans, therefore, have to define themselves and their identity before being able to sell it to the American public. They have

III. A Tale of Division

to submerge into or feel confident about their native culture before feeling comfortable with the American culture.

Vietnam for them is an "era, an epoch, and of course the war, but not a people or a nation. Vietnamese-Americans put forth their own social memories as a way to assert their presence in this country."[19] In order to preserve their identity, their wholeness, to validate themselves, and to some degree to boost up or restore their pride, they congregate in ethnic enclaves that are called "Little Saigons," where they can express their Vietnameseness within the boundaries of the American society.

This may apply to the older generation, those who were officials of the Saigon government, who wielded power in the past, were sent to reeducation camps for a long time, and lost everything, including their prestige. This may not apply to Vietnamese who came here later to make a new life or to second generation Vietnamese Americans.

The latter, born and raised in the U.S., feel at ease within American society. At home, however, they might feel pressure from parents who force them to follow Vietnamese traditions and remain Vietnamese instead of Vietnamese-Americans. Those who do not want to disrespect their parents, therefore, can be torn apart by the different Vietnamese and American traditions.

The Vietnam War was a war of conquest—an invasion of superior northern military forces against the Southern Republic of Vietnam. By April 1975, Hanoi had sent all of its military divisions—minus one left to protect North Vietnam—racing down National Route One toward Saigon. The arrival of northern communist tanks through the gates of the Independence Palace in Saigon was a flagrant violation of the 1972 Paris Accords, one of a long series of violations of human rights against the South Vietnamese. Hanoi had finally thrown down its mask and proved to the world it had waged a war of conquest against South Vietnam.

When the South Vietnamese Trương Như Tảng, a National Liberation Front (NLF) official and minister of justice of the Provisional Revolutionary Government (PRG), returned from the jungle to Saigon on the bandwagon of the northern communists, his mother told him:

> *My son. You have abandoned everything...to follow the communists. They will never return to you a particle of the things you have left. You will see. They will betray you, and you will suffer your entire life.*[20]

On May 15, 1975, in Saigon, Tảng witnessed with northern officials a parade in celebration of the conquest. One organization after another paraded in front of the officials, followed by representatives of all the northern military units. At last came a few unkempt NLF troops under

Hanoi's flag. Befuddled, Tang turned to General Văn Tiến Dũng and enquired about the NLF divisions one, three, five, seven and nine. Dũng told him "the army has been reunified."[21] Tang soon realized that the PRG was subordinate to the Hanoi government and all the orders then came from Hanoi. Realizing that he had been betrayed by Hanoi, Tảng retired from the PRG and escaped from Vietnam as a refugee in 1976.

Hanoi has thus committed a crime against humanity by invading South Vietnam, waging a 21-year war, killing millions of people, incarcerating hundreds of thousands of people and shoving millions of others to the seas. By reaction, it has caused tens of thousands of vocal overseas Vietnamese to become more vocal and anticommunist than before. Anticommunism has become the rallying point against the new rulers and the Vietnamese-Americans' new identity. The old divide between expatriates and present Vietnamese rulers—capitalism and communism—has become more visible than in the past as the former affirm their identity.[22]

C. The Two Vietnams

The Two Vietnams was the title of a book published by Bernard Fall in 1963 in which he compared the two Vietnamese states—northern communist and southern democratic—following the partition of the country in 1954. What people did not realize was that the country has been psychologically, socially, geographically, and politically divided into two or more entities on various occasions since its formation some 4,000 years ago.

According to mythology, the Vietnamese are the offspring of King Lạc Long Quân (Dragon King) and the Fairy Âu Cơ. The latter gave birth to a sac containing 100 eggs that developed into 100 children. The idyllic dragon-fairy union, however, did not last long because Lạc Long Quân one day asked for a divorce. The couple split up, with Âu Cơ taking 50 children to the mountains and Lạc Long Quân guiding the remaining 50 others to the seaside.[23] It is worth mentioning that this probably was the first recorded divorce by any country in the world. The legend has been so engrained into the Vietnamese psyche that it has almost become a reality. Descendants of the highlanders (Thượng or Mường) and lowlanders (Kinh) presently account for 15 and 85 percent of Vietnam's population respectively. That ancient division between Thượng and Kinh gave way to a northern-southern rivalry by the end of the sixteenth century. Either by design or fate, the Vietnamese originally were divided into two different entities. That design eventually became a "curse" for the Vietnamese people.

III. A Tale of Division

Between 1600 and 1802, for more than 200 years, Vietnam was geographically and politically divided into two states: đàng ngoài (north) and đàng trong (south), the boundaries of which roughly corresponded to the 1960's North and South Vietnam. The north was ruled by the Lê kings with the support of the Trinh lords while the south was controlled by the Nguyễn lords. Without connection between the two states during these two centuries, northerners and southerners had evolved apart. The short period of reunification (1802–1859) could not erase the two-century cultural and economic differences between North and South.

When the French moved into and controlled Vietnam (1859–1940), they separated central Vietnam from the south and re-attached it to the north to reshape the country according to administrative and political realms of the times. Since the Vietnamese king ruled from Hue, central Vietnam, the French could not leave it connected to the South without destroying the unity of his kingdom. Cochinchina (south), which was first occupied in 1859, became a French colony that was directly ruled from Paris. The bloc Annam (center) and Tonkin (north) in 1884 became a protectorate that was nominally administered by a Nguyễn king, but again controlled by the French. Cochinchinese subjects, as a result, enjoyed rare political perks unknown to those living in Annam or Tonkin: they could become French citizens and had the rights to own a newspaper (freedom of press).

During the Vietnam War (1954–1975), Vietnam was again divided into two regions as described earlier by Bernard Fall: a communist North Vietnam and a western-style democratic–leaning South Vietnam.

Therefore, throughout its almost 400-year history, from 1600 to 1975, North and South have evolved separately for more than 300 years or 80 percent of the time.[24] That separation no doubt has left deep marks in both sides of the country, marks that manifested by major cultural, social, economic, and political differences that will not be erased by a short reunification period and lingering suspicions between northerners and southerners.

Table 1. Differences Between Northern and Southern Vietnamese Governments Since 1600

Years	North	South
1600–1802	đàng ngoài	đàng trong
	Lê-Trinh	Nguyễn
1859–1944	Annam, Tonkin	Cochinchina
1954–1975	North Vietnam	South Vietnam
	Communist	Nationalist Democratic
1975–present	Socialist State	Little Saigons
	Dictatorship	Democracy

The history of the fall of Saigon is that of a country, divided by two ideologies, totalitarian communism against democratic capitalism,[25] one party state against democracy, repression, enslavement against freedom,[26] red flag against yellow flag.

The history of the fall of Saigon is that of the "Little Saigons," of Vietnamese-America, of Vietnamese who walk around with hyphenated names.

It is the history of injustice against justice.

And as long as there are injustice, corruption, a one-party state, and communism in Vietnam, there will always be TWO VIETNAMS.

IV. Legends and Folk Stories

After Vietnam recovered its independence from China in 939 CE, the first known legends recognized as uniquely Vietnamese were written in the twelfth or thirteenth centuries. As the identity of the Vietnamese state solidified, tales and legends slowly emerged from the common popular psyche. There must have been many legends circulating at that time, which could have been written down somewhere, but were "lost" again, especially in the early 1400s.

In 1408, China invaded Vietnam once again, carted away all the Vietnamese culture[1] and replaced them with Chinese literature (Four Classics and Five Canons, Buddhist and Taoist texts) in an attempt to sinicize the Vietnamese. The essence of Vietnamese culture from 939 to 1408 had thus completely disappeared. What was left from that period was the *Việt Điện U Linh Tập* (VDULT).

We know that the VDULT was written sometime before the fourteenth century CE, because Lý Tế Xuyên told us he was not the main author but was only updating it in 1329. Through his labor, the VDULT remains one of the rare manuscripts from that period. It is, above all, a legendary history of heroes, heroines, and spirits of the times. One is amazed that someone had been ordered to redact these notes with the only goal of uplifting the spirit of the people against the mighty Chinese. From that time onward, the Vietnamese were constantly reminded of the Chinese who were breathing over their shoulders.

The goal of the VDULT was to remind people to be brave and to defend the country against the invaders. The message was that the Vietnamese may be small in numbers, but they were always protected and supported by a legion of spirits. The kings, whether they knew it or not, were using psychological warfare to convey knowledge and the idea of nationalism. They taught their people that they were different from the Chinese, their oppressors. They reminded them that the Chinese, although close neighbors, harbored suspicious and sometimes dangerous motives.

Stories give form to a people's hopes and dreams; they transmit values, they instruct, entertain, and unify the group they belong to.[2] Storytelling is one way of transmitting traditions to other generations, defining and reaffirming the identity of the group. These stories entertain debate about belief. They can be long or short, complete or rudimentary, local or global, horrible, mysterious or grotesque.[3] They went through the usual phases: elaboration, variation, decline, revitalization.

Although Vietnam has its legends, they have not been thoroughly evaluated and studied. Back in the fourteenth century, Lý Tế Xuyên had collected 27 tales, compared to Japan's more than 200 during the same period.[4] One explanation was that Xuyên did not write simple tales: he wrote tales about spirits. Beside the fact that there may not be enough good spirits to list, expanding that list may unnecessarily diminish the importance of the spirits.

Europe has universities whose role was to gather and study legends as a field in the realm of science. In the early 1960s, I remember going through the books at the French cultural mission's library in Saigon, close to the private French Grall Hospital, and being surprised to find many books about France's legends. One publisher had come up with one book of legends for each of the French departments (provinces). There were legends of Bretagne, Alsace, Provence, and so on. All these legends, which had minimal overlap among them, gave the reader the impression that each department was a separate state. This speaks of the breadth of the field of legends in France and Europe many decades ago.

Legends are everywhere, and if one takes the time to document, categorize, and study them, one could probably find as many legends as there are people. The staff of the Volkskunde of the University of Freiburg in Breisgau, Germany, in the heart of the Black Forest was busy inventorying and classifying German legends. Two bookstores in town displayed books about occult sciences, cults, folk medical practices, witchcraft, magic, shamanism, and the teaching of famous gurus. At the University of Indiana in Bloomington, Degh asked her students to do some field work on "real" haunted houses. The result was the documentation of a large number of such houses in Indiana. Many of the students' stories were published in the journal *Indiana Folklore* (1968–1986) with professional annotations from the editorial staff.[5] Vietnam so far has not been able to elevate the field of folklore study to the level of science.

IV. Legends and Folk Stories

Legends are about unusual personalities: spirits, witches, monsters, criminals, extraterrestrials, or people with abilities to foresee the future, recognize evil forces, and protect us from their destructive powers.[6] All these stories are centuries old—maybe older—from when primitive people had the tendency to blame any unexplained phenomenon on spirits or ghosts.

While every country has its stories about witches, ghosts, and demons, their depiction and composition seem to be different depending on the culture and society. Western countries have their witches—depicted as the ugliest women one could describe: unkempt hair; curved nose; long, curved fingernails; wicked eyes; and ragged clothing. The tall, one-eyed Frankenstein is the male version of the witch. There are also ghosts, although there seem to be more stories about witches than ghosts in the west until recently. This probably has to do with physical representation: one can describe, draw, or paint a witch more easily than a ghost. In a commercialized society, the more versions of witches one could draw, print, or write about, the more sales one could make.

Vietnamese also distinguish between *bà chằn, bà phù thủy* (witch) and *ma* (ghost), although there are more stories about ghosts than witches. A witch is always a female; hence the name *bà chằn* (lady) witch. One has never heard of *ông chằn* (male witch). Despite their ugliness, moral and physical, witches are rarely depicted in Vietnamese literature; not because they are rare, but because of the respect society reserved for elderly people. Witches, no matter how ugly or wicked, could be someone's grandmother, mother, or aunt. That topic, therefore, has been avoided as much as possible. Stories about ghosts abounded because they have been handed down from generation to generation since the beginning of time. Anything that could not be explained was attributed to the work of *ma* (ghost), although a *ma* has never been described in detail or pictured by an Asian before.

On the other hand, the Vietnamese needed benevolent spirits to protect them from evil ones. Legends tend to evolve with time. In ancient times, they deal mostly with spirits, and ghosts, but these stories are less prevalent in modern days. It seems like the more primitive the culture, the more stories with spirits, monsters, and witches we hear. Such is the case of the highland minorities in Vietnam. Most of their legends deal with spirits. However, this is not always the case because stories about ghosts are also present in modern Vietnam and in the U.S., particularly in Indiana.[7]

Legends are "empty formulas" or vehicles that can be used and abused for both creative or destructive purposes. They play a leading role in the development and maintenance of a "culture of fear."⁸ The danger about the legend is that, although not founded in reality, it can create reality. The European witch-hunt crazes of the sixteenth and seventeenth centuries made way for the butchering of innocent people in Europe, Africa, and Asia in the twentieth century. Legends, like religions, have the power to mobilize and motivate people into doing good or not so good things. In modern times, mass media has helped legends reach a larger audience and power never imagined before.

The legend of *Ông Giỏi* ("The Genie of Phù Đổng," southern tale # 4) paints a picture of an infant who grew up into a giant within days by eating just rice. His mother's neighbors took turns to cook for him, for his appetite knew no bounds. He basically grew a few inches every hour and became so tall that he had to have special armor plate and a horse that could fly him away. He used a huge sword with which he slew hundreds of enemies with each stroke. In no time, the Chinese were driven back home and the young hero flew away on his horse. He promised to come back to help his people in case of need. The hero Lê Lợi used many stratagems to overpower his enemies. He once wrote his name on leaves with honey. Ants would come, attracted by the honey, and eat it, creating holes and thus carving his name on the leaves. He then let the latter drift down the river to the enemies' camps. Enemies were stricken by fear when they imagined Lê Lợi as having supernatural power. Better not fight against spirits, they thought, and they fled home. The same thing happened in South Vietnam in 1913. Followers of Mekong delta sects believed they were invulnerable against firearms when they wore amulets to battles against the French. A few hundred of them showed up in Saigon on March 28, 1913, only to be slaughtered; the rest were taken prisoner.⁹

For the last two centuries, researchers have attempted to define "legend," only to end up with a vague definition: "a story, a narrative, a communicative act...." The latter has been characterized as a reaction to threatening conditions¹⁰ and as a psychological need.

The fairy tale is poetic and situated in a world of fiction and fantasy not tied to time or location; it has a happy ending; it lives, grows and can be transplanted anywhere; (the well-known example is that of Cinderella, with more than 300 versions worldwide). It was only when I started looking into legends that I became aware that each country has its own version of Cinderella. The legend is more historical; it is tied to a certain culture, a certain place, and certain people.

Folktales are brief, with linear plots; they reflect the society and belief

IV. Legends and Folk Stories

systems of the audience. They often deal with familiar aspects of the human condition: greed, jealousy, poverty, life hardship, and difficulties of being married. They usually do not have happy endings.[11] They paint the society as it is, with all its ugliness and reality: life is hard and although the good person does not always win, he has to remain decent and fair. The cast of characters includes husbands, wives, mothers-in-law, peasants, merchants, mandarins, and an occasional monk. Mothers-in-law are a common fixture of Vietnamese tales because brides went on to live with their husbands' family. Antagonism between the difficult mother-in-law and the poor bride is frequently exploited.

"The Two Tea Boxes" (southern tale # 45) is an example of folktale. A merchant wanting to thank a mandarin offered him two bags of tea. Not wanting to compromise his integrity, the latter reluctantly accepted. Realizing that the bags contained gold instead of tea, he returned them to the merchant.

This straightforward folktale is designed to remind government officials (mandarins in the case of medieval Vietnam) about the need to remain honest and decent. Although any official (from top to bottom) has the chance to use his position to demand "gifts" from merchants or underlings, a decent official would not do that.

V. The Making of Vietnamese Legends

In this chapter, we will discuss three spirits: Princess Liễu Hạnh, Bà Chúa Xứ, and General Lê Văn Duyệt. Since they are more modern than the other spirits, analyses of their lives or tales of their lives may allow us to understand their progression from simple spirits to renowned deities.

Folk legends represent and embody the beliefs of the common people: peasants, itinerant workers, traders, artisans, low wage-earners in the cities, housewives, and uncultured people in general. Legends relate their joys, pains, struggles, miseries, hopes, failures, aspirations, dreams, and fears in the face of natural disasters or changing social, economical, political, and military environments.

Often powerless before these changes, they put their trust in the spirits who they hope will pull them through. This explains the plethora of spirits they worshiped or asked for help since antiquity. Any hero, man or woman of extraordinary strength or power, or even a criminal, a tiger, or a natural force (e.g., river, mountain) would do it. As society got organized, the state screened all these spirits, chose 27, and listed them in the *Việt Điện U Linh Tập* for the people to commemorate and remember. The common folk had no choice but to obey. They could also choose to venerate a spirit of their own liking.

Why spirits? Maybe because they did not have any other choice. Buddhism, although introduced into Vietnam in the second century CE, never really inflamed people's fervor, despite being sanctioned as the state religion in the fourteenth and eighteenth centuries. Neither did Hinduism or Islam, which are prevalent in other Asian countries. Catholicism, which was introduced in the seventeenth century, was banned outright by the nineteenth century kings who chose Confucianism over all other religions. But Confucianism was not a religion, only a code of conduct or behavior. Without alternatives, the common folk have recourse to their long-standing relationship with spirits.

In modern times, new spirits, Liễu Hạnh, Bà Chúa Xứ, and Lê Văn Duyệt emerged. They were chosen by the common folk and this time no longer had to be sanctioned by the state for approval. They were found to be more responsive to and reflected people's newer needs and aspirations: material gains, riches, and freedom. With improving economies and relaxing state control in the 1990s, these spirits were in turn showered with offerings, gifts, and recognition by the people who felt they owed their luck and material riches to the spirits. This explains the rise and increasing popularity of these new deities.

Folk culture represents the cultural core of the Vietnamese identity, which is completely different from the culture of the court, Chinese or French colonial rule, Confucianism, or Hanoi's communism. It is the symbol of freedom from which peasants, outcasts, and oppressed people draw their strength, vigor, and originality. It is also consistent with the original matriarchal values of Southeast Asian societies. This explains the resurgent popularity of modern spirits, especially the goddesses.[1]

1. Liễu Hạnh Công Chúa (Princess Liễu Hạnh)

The Four Immortals (*Tứ Bất Tử*) was an outgrown of the original 27 spirits included in the *Việt Điện U Linh Tập* in the fourteenth century. Three of them were part of these original spirits: Đức Thần Tản Viên (the Spirit of Mount Tản Viên), Đức Thần Gióng (the Spirit of Phù Đổng Village) and Chử Đồng Tử (the Consort of Hùng Princess Tiên Dung). The newest addition was Princess Liễu Hạnh, whose story began in the sixteenth century at the village of Vân Cát in Nam Định province, North Vietnam.

The pantheon of the Four Immortals was assembled sometime in the eighteenth and nineteenth centuries. An early twentieth-century French report cites, "There exists in the province of Annam four temples that are particularly venerated; they are designated under the name Tứ Bất Tử, that is the four temples of immortals."[2]

It was Landes who reported two stories about Liễu Hạnh and dated her presence at Đèo Ngang under the reign of King Lê Thái Tổ (1428–1433). She was the daughter of the Jade Emperor who, after breaking a jade cup while presenting it to the emperor, was exiled to earth. She emerged as the proprietress of an inn. Guests who behaved well and just came in for a drink were fine. Those who tried to court her either became insane or subsequently died. King Lê Thái Tổ's son was not even spared. He was only saved through the help of eight Buddhas. She was pictured as a rebellious and vengeful spirit who not only did tricks, but also harmed people.[3]

Đoàn Thị Điểm, an eighteenth-century poetess, wrote the novel *Vân Cát Thần Nữ Truyện* (Story of Vân Cát Goddess) about the princess. She also confirmed that Liễu Hạnh was the daughter of the Jade Emperor and dated her birth to 1557. In her story, she tried to portray the princess as a liberated and strong-willed lady who not only challenged men intellectually, but also dominated them. This was a revolutionary idea for people during this Confucian period: women were confined to kitchens and given no opportunity for schooling. Đoàn Thị Điểm, in fact, was portraying herself in the novel; she was also an emancipated feminist, one of the first in Vietnam. She excelled in poetry and did not want to get married just for the sake of getting married—a novel idea at that time—although she had many admirers. One male writer and colleague viewed Điểm's literary skill as a kind of monstrosity, something remarkable but abnormal. When she finally got married at age 37, her husband was sent to China as a diplomat for three years. On his return, he was sent to serve in Nghệ An where she finally joined him, six years after their marriage. She suddenly died one week after joining him.[4]

These stories immediately raise the question whether Liễu Hạnh really existed or was just an invention of the human mind, and in the former case, whether she had helped sentient beings or not. Everything taken under consideration, although the goddess was not a model of perfection, she had alleviated the hardships of women's lives during the fifteenth-century crisis era. The cult arose from the need for a mother-figure deity as well as a potent spirit-protector.[5] The goddess seems to be very responsive to her followers and her cult, despite the state's various attempts to control it, continues to expand and attract followers.

Although her cult is localized to North Vietnam, it has slowly spread to the central region of the country. She also has some followers among the overseas Vietnamese. The fact that Liễu Hạnh's cult is even bigger and better attended than that of the Trưng sisters and that she was elevated to the rank of Immortal indicates of her notoriety and rapid rise to stardom. Between the classic Confucian lady (Trưng sisters) and the nonconformist Liễu Hạnh, the latter has displaced the former and become a "representative [northern] Vietnamese deity."[6]

As Vietnam is a country of two states—North and South—very few Southerners know of Liễu Hạnh, whose opposite in the South is Bà Chúa

Xứ. Conversely, few northerners know of the southern Bà Chúa Xứ. The two goddesses, however, share some similarities: irreverent attitude, uncertain background, and recent notoriety. Their popularity is associated with the rise of a large number of followers, mostly female, who come to pray and ask for favors—mainly material gains in origin. They represent the modern "Mothers of Vietnam," just as the Trưng sisters were the original "Mothers of Vietnam."

2. Bà Chúa Xứ (The Lady of the Realm)

Since the early 1990s, Bà Chúa Xứ's shrine in Châu Đốc, South Vietnam, close to the Cambodian border, has become the most visited religious site in Vietnam: it welcomes about one million visitors annually. Her festival lasts not one or two days, but several weeks. Although the lady is a prestigious spiritual protector,[7] her origin is murky and widely disputed. Her cultural makeup bears Cham, Khmer, and Chinese influences, and the majority of her followers are Vietnamese.

French archeologist Malleret believed in 1943, that the lady had been painted over a stone statue of the god Shiva.[8] Within the shrine, on her right, is a large stone lingam covered in cloth. Other stone lingams are scattered on Sam Mountain in Châu Đốc where the shrine is located. The Mekong Delta was once a part of the Khmer empire whose people are known to venerate Shiva on top of mountains. Other people believe the lady was actually Thiên Y A Na—a Cham goddess that was appropriated by the Vietnamese during their southern expansion in the seventeenth and eighteenth centuries.[9] Still the Chinese, who came to the Mekong Delta in the seventeenth century, argue that they too worship the Lady of the Realm but call her Holy Mother Tiên Hậu. The latter is regarded as a patron of commerce and a goddess of fertility and travel. The Châu Đốc shrine, small in the early 1970s, was entirely rebuilt in 1972 with Chinese money.[10]

After the communist takeover of South Vietnam in 1975, all churches, pagodas, and shrines were closed; priests, and monks were sent to reeducation camps.[11] Some were later reopened under strict state control. After more than a decade of poverty, food restriction, and misery under the harsh communist system, and as the economy began to pick up, people turned to goddesses, *Bà Chúa Kho* (the Lady of the Storehouse) in the North and *Bà Chúa Xứ* in the South, to ask for help or fulfillment of their material needs. A set of blessed gifts or *lộc* from the goddess would cover their basic material needs for a year. They could come back anytime if further need arose. Once the requests were granted, recipients would come back to thank and give offerings to the goddess. These transactions keep people coming back and swell the crowd of people visiting the shrine. The majority are low wage workers, farmers, mobile vendors, hostesses, and those involved in petty trade, although there are also wealthy business people and members of the diaspora.[12] In the late 1970s and 1980s, people who planned to escape from Vietnam came to ask for the goddess's help. Once out of the country, they sent money back home to upgrade the shrine or came back to visit her.

In South Vietnam, the frontier land is a place where culture is less formal and hierarchical, and people tend to be more individualistic, egalitarian, and spontaneous than their northern counterparts. People, therefore, use less intermediaries like mediums to communicate with the spirits than northerners. They tend to interact directly with goddesses and spirits, muttering their wishes, presenting their own gifts, collecting their own benefits (*hái lộc*) or stroking the spirit to tap her power.[13] Since most of these visitors are females, they interact rather easily with the goddess.

For centuries, petty commerce in the South has been directed and managed by women: they bargain, trade, exchange, and sell all the basic needs. They are not wholesalers, just small- and middle-sized-volume merchants. Barrow, back in 1806, had seen these open markets in Saigon where sellers and buyers were all women.[14] It was these merchants who kept the postwar economy going by providing informal credit and being liaison points for smuggling.[15]

The upsurge of religious practice in Vietnam has been regarded as the result of renewed societal freedom and a proof of the decline in relevance of Marxism-Leninism. The ideological vacuum has been replaced by the emergence of the goddesses who stood for women and freedom. The goddesses are creations of women and symbolize predominantly feminine concerns.[16]

3. *General Lê Văn Duyệt*

Born in the Mekong Delta in 1763 (some say 1764), General Lê Văn Duyệt was the man who helped Gia Long regain his throne in the late 1700s. When Gia Long became king (1802–1820), Duyệt followed him to Huế and served as his trusted adviser before returning to the South to become the vice roy and governor general. He was a fearsome military commander, a colorful personality, and a regional kingmaker.

V. The Making of Vietnamese Legends

He was so stern that ordinary officials and soldiers did not dare to speak to him directly. After Tây Sơn forces killed his friend Tống Viết Phúc in 1801, Duyệt became so enraged that he killed any Tây Sơn soldiers he encountered, until he was admonished by Gia Long for his ferocity.[17] Other people, however, had a more moderate view. Chaigneau stated, "He [Duyệt] has great talent both in battle and administration. People fear him, but he is heartily loved by people here because he is fair."[18] He loved cockfighting and *hát bội* (southern folk drama), like many southerners. He even delivered a long speech in front of the emperor about the merits of this recreation. Above all, he dressed plainly and behaved like a down-to-earth person.[19]

His tomb, built in 1832, was small in the beginning: Minh Mạng had it razed the following year because he saw Duyệt as his nemesis.[20] There were not many more strongly contrasting personalities than Duyệt and Minh Mạng. The latter despised the general, although he could not do anything against him as long as he was alive. Duyệt was once his mentor and his father's trusted servant. Duyệt also had opposed Minh Mạng's ascension to the throne. As soon as Duyệt passed away, Minh Mạng unleashed his wrath and took revenge on him. Rehabilitated by Thiệu Trị, Minh Mạng's successor, the general's shrine was rebuilt, then enlarged in 1937, and is known as *Lăng Ông* (his Lordship's Mausoleum). It was refurbished in the late 1950s with funds provided by the Republic of Vietnam. A pair of vertical hardwood panels inscribed with contrasting couplets describes the General:

> Spotless fame spread over the Southern kingdom, single pillar supporting frontier peace and lofty sky,
> Noble spirit kept forever in the Northern territory, shining star divinely protecting the country for thousands of autumns.[21]

After the communist takeover, the mausoleum was ordered to shut down from 1975 to 1989 because it was considered a place of "superstitious activities" (*mê tín dị đoan*). The Hanoi government even barred any maintenance and encouraged thieves and addicts to stay around to create an unsafe environment, with the goal of discouraging any cult to the general. But even drug addicts were scared of the general and did not cause any damage to his mausoleum. He is, therefore, propitiated for maintaining order and chasing away criminals and ghosts. The structure, however, fell into disrepair because of lack of maintenance. Attempts were also taken by the government to raze the mausoleum to make place for a park. Somehow, all these attempts mysteriously failed. People said his Lordship had warded off a frontal attack on his mausoleum.[22]

Monetary support from local people and the diaspora helped to restore the shrine of this warrior-scholar-official. The shrine sits close to the Bà Chiểu Market in Saigon and is considered the most auspicious site in the city today. It attracts men and women from the city and its surrounding urban districts. This shrine attracts fewer petitioners than do the shrines of the main goddesses because as a historical personality, the general is not worshipped (*thờ*) like the goddesses, but only paid respect to (*kính trọng*) like one honors ancestors.[23]

Besieged by natural disasters, wars, famine, poverty, lack of freedom, and frustrated by the inability and impotence of the state, the various religions, and the orthodoxy of various political regimes to help solve their daily problems and aspirations, the Vietnamese people turn in droves to their roots and identity, to meet with the spirits that since antiquity have been helping their ancestors and themselves in their moments of despair. They should not be blamed for being ignorant, misguided or treated as superstitious; instead the state and political regimes and religions should take the blame and responsibility for having failed to treat and solve their problems and to enlighten them.

VI. Asian Legends

Although each Asian country has its own tales, overlap can occur, especially between nearby countries or among those that share similar cultural mores. One can thus take a look at the legends and tales in nearby Asian countries to assess their differences, similarities, influences and effects on each other.

Back in 1995, Faurot published a series of Asian Pacific tales and legends. She classified them under the following six headings: How Things Came to Be, Animal Tales, Myths and Legends, Magic Gifts, Ghosts, Dreams and the Supernatural, Cleverness and Foolishness. She classified them arbitrarily and for "the convenience of grouping this particular set of stories."[1] Each culture, therefore, may have tales under each of these headings, although each country stresses one or more topics over the others. Each topic is treated differently by different countries according to their cultural backgrounds. Chinese culture has influenced Japan, Korea, and Vietnam, while Hindu-Indic culture pervades Thailand and part of Indonesia and Malaysia; on the other hand, Islamic culture has left its mark in Indonesia and part of the Philippines. Although China, Korea, Japan, Vietnam, the Philippines, Indonesia, and Malaysia have tales dealing with similar topics, a closer look reveals major differences between these countries' tales.

In this chapter, tales published in China, Japan, and India will be reviewed and compared against those of Vietnam. This is just a short overview of the similarities and differences of tales, because an in-depth review would probably require a book by itself.

A. Chinese Tales

Being a huge country, China has a large collection of tales that deal with the everyday life of mortals, the fascinating kingdom of birds and animals, and the supernatural world of gods and ghosts. The *Record of Things Strange in a Makeshift Studio*, written by P' u Sung-lin in the 17th century, but published in 1760 long after his death, encompasses more than 400 tales—one of the largest collections in the world.[2] Its cast of characters includes peasants, philosophers, officials, kings, tigers, and birds; the stories mainly illustrate the structured relationships within that society: emperor and subject, father and son, husband and wife (or wives), official and peasant, human and beast.

The Chinese society, modeled after the teachings of Confucius, is not an egalitarian system. It is conceived as a balance of obligations between superiors (emperor, husband, and father) and inferiors (people, wives, and children). Children obeyed parents, peasants obeyed officials, and wives obeyed husbands. Projected to result in obedient relationships and a harmonious balance between the two castes, it turned out to not always be the case. The tales show us that superiors always tend to take advantage of their inferiors, something that the famous and sage Confucius failed to appreciate or take into account.

Confucius, by trusting the good in human nature, erred in believing that masters will always behave fairly and justly and inferiors will always follow the rules. Human nature, however, is complex and multidimensional rather than linear, as he thought. That error was perpetuated for the last 2.5 millennia for various reasons. Emperors and masters entrenched in their superior—or inborn—rights did not want to desist from these rights. The people suffered passively until they one day became upset and caused major societal upheavals.

Within the Confucian society, the king or emperor sat at the center of the country and society. He ran the country, he thought, with a mandate from heaven and, therefore, should receive the allegiance of people and other creatures. As the Son of Heaven, he was the intermediary between heaven and the people; a semidivine figure, he could not be wrong. He ruled through an imperial bureaucracy where officials (mandarins) were chosen through three successive levels of examinations: the county, the provincial, and the metropolitan. These learned men were supposed to rule with fairness and judgment, but that was not always the case.

The bureaucracy was often a cumbersome and corrupt structure where patronage, bribery, and scholarship reigned. In "Social Connections," a hard-working and wealthy farmer met and helped a mandarin who happened to pass by his village on a stormy day. From then on, the farmer sent the mandarin one gift after another from his farm. Unable to reciprocate, the mandarin, through his subordinates, staged a crime and framed

VI. Asian Legends

the farmer, who was jailed. The farmer's son, unaware of the scheme, asked the mandarin to help his father get released. He was then told to bribe various people. Bribe after bribe, the son became short of cash and had to sell the farm and other possessions in order to free his father. The father, finally realizing that he had been set up by the mandarin, vented his anger at his daughter-in-law, who had brought the mandarin home in the first place. She hanged herself in despair. Furious at his father, the son also hanged himself. The farmer, upset at having no children left, hanged himself last.[3]

There were, however, outstanding and fair officials who strictly followed the rules. They remained poor all their lives for having upheld law and justice. This was described in "A Wise Judge" and "A Clever Judge."[4]

Within that society, the family was a political and social unit where freedom of love and marriage was not tolerated. Marriages were arranged to strengthen bonds between families and to satisfy parents' requests and needs at the expense of personal preference and appetite. The wife was supposed to obey her husband, and care for him and the children. Often she would have to agree to look for concubines for him. The quest for freedom to love and to marry against the norms of the society has yielded quite a few tales. There are tales of girls eloping with their lovers, and a young concubine loving a scholar.

This Confucian world was threatened by Taoism, a philosophy that suggested that all beings were created equal and no one was above the other. There was no mandate to rule and no transfer of property and influence beyond its ordained time. Animals existed on the same level as humans and each existed for a lifetime only, free of obligations to ancestors or descendants. Towering above all, was heaven or the benevolent Jade Emperor. The Taoists, in one stroke, shattered the fundamental premise of the Confucian order, which suggested that social hierarchy was founded on hereditary right.[5]

While Confucianism stresses obedience, harmony, orthodoxy, and social structure and has been the ideology of the ruling Chinese elite for the last two millennia, Taoism is a softer philosophy that offers refuge from the ills of society and the trap of material success.

Because legends reflect life in China in general and the society is dominated by Confucianism and Taoism, Chinese legends depict both Confucian and Taoist aspirations and concepts. While adopting Taoism as part of its belief (since the country was under Chinese domination for a thousand years), Vietnam does not have a strong hierarchical Taoist church to follow; Taoism, therefore, was not as strong in Vietnam as in China.

In the field of folklore, Chinese society is well balanced between Confucian and Taoist themes, one challenging or neutralizing the other. One could read tales of young people fighting to become mandarins through examinations only to want to return to simple ways (nature or Tao) when they grew old. Since Vietnam did not have a strong Taoist clergy, Vietnamese folklore ended up with more stories with Confucian rather than Taoist themes.

The legend of the "Herdsboy and the Weaving Maid" depicts a herdsman who stole a maid's robe while she was bathing in a river during an outing with her friends to the mortal world. By returning her robe, he earned the chance to marry her. They lived happily for a while until her mother turned both of them into stars of the Milky Way.[6] The tale is well known in Japan, China, Korea, and Vietnam. The country of origin of the tale is unknown, although there is a clear sign of cross-cultural pollination.

In Vietnam, the legend is known as "Tiên Dung and the Marsh Boy" or "Nhật Da Trạch" (southern tale # 7). Princess Tiên Dung was a tomboy who set out to explore the waterways of Vietnam until she met the marsh boy while taking a bath in the river. By custom, she was forced to marry him and they lived happily together. Each time her father's soldiers came to look for her, the area became foggy, causing them to finally cancel their search in frustration. Over the years, in a Confucian culture that valued boys, Princess Tiên Dung the tomboy was relegated to the back burner while the ignorant marsh boy, who wed a princess, was elevated to the rank of folk hero and later became the god of North Vietnamese agriculture.

The world-renown "Cinderella" began as the Greco-Egyptian "Rhodopsis" or "rosy cheeked," described by the Greek historian Strabo in the first century BCE. The tale spread to all over the world and in 860 CE. "Cinderella" became the Chinese "*Ye Xian*." Each country now has its own "Cinderella." By 1893, Marian Cox documented 345 variants of the *Cinderella* theme.[7] The Vietnamese version is the tale of "Tấm and Cám" (southern tale # 33).

B. Japanese Tales

In Royal Tyler's book of Japanese medieval tales (comparable to *Việt Điền U Linh Tập* and *Lĩnh Nam Chích Quái*), there are many tales related to Buddhist temple building with the assistance of spirits: "Kobo Daishi,"[8]

"Japan's First Gold,"[9] "The Emperor's Finger,"[10] "The Old Mackerel Peddler."[11] This reflects the imprint of Buddhism that was in full bloom in Japan in the twelfth through the thirteenth centuries, when all these stories took place. The religion had pervaded all levels of Japanese society and was stronger than spirit cults, while the reverse was true in Vietnam at that time. All 27 tales of the *Việt Điền U Linh Tập* dealt with spirits. On the other hand, the modern book of Japanese tales contains only a few medieval tales.

But there are also tales of monks having affairs with officials' wives: "Home in a Chest,"[12] "Not Quite the Right Robe."[13] There were also stories about one official having affairs with married women and monks courting married women. In "The Loving Fox"[14] and "Touched in the Head,"[15] a man met a beautiful woman in Kyoto, struck up a conversation with her, and took her to bed the same night. Tales about sexually explicit encounters abounded in Japan, but not in prudish China and Vietnam. In *"Elimination,"* Heichu was noted to have "courted every wife, every daughter, and above all, every lady-in-waiting within reach."[16] The text went on to describe his attempt to court one lady-in-waiting and how she responded to him. In *"Red Heat,"*[17] a widow became love struck with a young monk who, on his way to a monastery, spent a night at her house. At night, she stole to his bed and lay beside him. When he ran away from her, she died, turned into a snake and chased him down.

As Tyler indicates, courtship most of the time happened in the dark. Heichu had never seen the lady he was so desperate to love and when he joined her in her room, it was pitch dark. Having never touched or seen her, he did not know whether she was tall or short, slim or fat, ugly or beautiful. What counted were the tone of her voice and the first impression she made on him through a screen. It was like an encounter between two blind people.

Although written between the twelfth and fourteenth centuries in medieval Japan, these tales suggest that Japanese society was quite open in terms of sexual orientation.[18] The prudish China and Vietnam, on the other hand, were nowhere close in that department. This also suggests that Japan was not a true Confucian society, which has always shied away from nudity and sexual topics. Even displaying nude paintings in a Confucian world was carefully avoided. Although Confucian men were allowed to have many wives (concubines), open sexuality was shunned.

In any society, rivalry among officials — one minister playing tricks on another — was common. These stories are plentiful in Japan while they were absent in Chinese or Vietnamese tales. It is not that the latter countries did not have these types of infighting; they did, but they were considered too "indecent" to be recounted. In "Man's Best Friend,"[19] Lord Akimitsu commissioned a monk to cast a spell on Lord Michinaga by burying an object in Michinaga's path. The latter's dog saved his life by preventing him from crossing over it.

Histories of ghosts or spirits in the form of foxes are frequently described. There were instances in which people sometimes did not seem to be frightened by spirits. In "The Eviction,"[20] Kiyoyuki bought an old and haunted mansion and calmly moved into it on an inauspicious day. On the first night, spirits came out to disturb the peace. Kiyoyuki let them act and went back to sleep. The next morning, an old man showed up at the door and tried to scare him away. He simply explained to the man that since he had bought the house, it belonged to him and the spirits could move away if they liked. From that time onward, they left him alone.

C. Indian Tales

In his book *Folktales from India*, Ramanujan reminds us that he is retelling the tales that have been handed down to him. Each narrative thus ends up slightly different than the original version, and these differences magnify over time. He divides his tales into seven different topics.

The male-centered tales feature a male who moves out of the family home, conquers the world or his society, returns home victorious, and wins the hand of a princess. Women are just pawns, prizes, or helpers in his life's game.

In the women-centered tales, men are considered to be wimps dominated by their mothers, wives, or girlfriends. Women have to help men out, and solve the riddles the latter cannot answer.

Families represent a country in miniature with their endless infightings between parents, brothers, sisters, relatives, and those who marry into these families. Mothers, like in any other country, are split into good mothers and wicked stepmothers. Fathers could be good or authoritarian.

In tales about gods, ghosts, and fate, gods are depicted with human bodies; they smell, urinate and defecate. Goddesses menstruate like humans. Different views of fate are shown.

Other categories include humorous tales, animal tales, and stories about stories.[21]

In "The Clever Daughter-in-Law," a meek son and his mother mistreat the daughter-in-law by having her do all the chores and feeding her only with leftovers. The angry daughter-in-law takes her revenge by tricking her mother-in-law into leaving the house so that she could gorge herself with food for a day. The mother gets rid of her by dumping her into a pit and setting her on fire. She escapes unharmed, manages to steal thieves' loot, and frightens her mother-in-law by returning home. From that time onward, the mother and her son follow her orders.[22]

The tale "Killed by a Tiger" argues that no one can escape his fate, which is inexorable. A man overhears that his nephew will be killed by a tiger on his wedding day. Despite being forewarned, the nephew took a walk to the forest on that fatidic day, and a tiger jumped on him. Luckily, his uncle shot the tiger dead with his arrow. The nephew then kicked the dead animal, the fangs of which struck his feet and caused him to bleed to death.[23]

In the "Serpent Mother," the youngest daughter-in-law was mistreated because she was an orphan. As her pregnancy came to term, she had no relatives to care for her. When she complained about her fate, a snake touched by her despair decided to help her. When the time came, the snake and its family transformed into human beings and brought presents and food to her. They brought the girl home and nursed her through the delivery period.

In "Adventures of a Disobedient Son," a king one day asked his four sons what they would like to do when they grew up. The youngest answered that he would marry four celestial women and rule over a larger empire than his father's. Upset, the king disowned him and sent him in to exile. The son managed to marry one celestial woman after another and with their help was able to conquer a huge empire.[24]

In "The Prince Who Married His Own Left Half," a prince decided to marry only his own half because he thought women were uncontrollable. He had himself cut in half and buried the left part, which later became a woman he married. But when he left her alone in his castle, she took a lover who transformed himself into a snake to get into the castle. The father one day caught the snake and killed it. The woman became distraught when she heard of her lover's death. As her husband tried to console her, she gave him a riddle to decipher—whoever lost would kill himself. He agreed and lost at the game. After his death, she married another person.[25]

These Indian tales are interesting and unique in their own way. Although they address the common themes of family life, fate, and animals, these themes are treated differently according to Indian customs. They are, therefore, different from Chinese, Japanese, or Vietnamese tales.

Themes about daughters-in-law are common around the world. Although daughters-in-law are not well treated in Vietnam, they are treated worse in Indian tales than in Vietnamese or Chinese tales, especially if they come from poor families and do not bring a good dowry. In the case of the "Clever Daughter-in-Law," a mother and her son decided to kill the daughter-in-law by burning her. This method of disposing of the person does not fit into other Asian cultures. Just as each culture is different, each tale has a unique local flavor.

PART TWO

Northern Legends

VII. Introduction

The legends in this section are considered northern because they were written or published in the North. Such were the cases of the classic *Việt Điện U Linh Tập* (1321) and *Lĩnh Nam Chích Quái* (1492), which will be analyzed in chapters VIII and IX respectively. It should be noted that North and South have been clearly defined as two different parts of Vietnam only from the year 1600 onward (see chapter III) and that they both share a common ancestry and literature; this explains why many tales are common to both sides of the country.

Two other books were written by Frenchmen: one in 1880 by Landes and the other in 1920 by Chivas-Baron. Landes relied on northern informants to complete his repertoire of tales, and Chivas-Baron used a servant from the Huế area (central Vietnam), which at that time formed with North Vietnam a French protectorate.

Although Landes and Chivas-Baron were both French citizens, their writings were different: Landes' wording is simple, succinct, and modern while Chivas-Baron's text is poetic, flowery, and medieval. The Landes manuscript can easily pass for a twentieth-century book while the Chivas-Baron text reads like a relic of the Elizabethan era. Landes' book contains a whopping 127 tales, many of which are one page long, while Chivas-Baron collected only 31 tales. The latter book, first written in French, was translated into English in 1920. We will discuss in detail these first four books, which form the essence of northern tales.

Nguyễn Đổng Chi wrote the first volume of *Kho Tàng Truyện Cổ Tích Việt Nam* (The Treasure of Vietnamese Legends) in 1957. Over the years, one volume was added to another and by the time he died (1984), the book had grown to five volumes and 2,700 pages with an impressive collection of 201 tales. Strangely, the last edition (1993) was published by the Viện Văn Học (Literature Institute), a governmental institution, and not by his family or heirs.

VII. Introduction

According to Chi, northern Vietnamese legends have four characteristics:

1. They are pragmatic and based on people's daily life. He subdivided them into four groups[1]:
   - historical legends: 18 percent
   - fairy tales: 10 percent
   - folklore (*thế sự*): 30 percent
   - combination of folklore with a touch of fairy tale: 42 percent.

Chi concludes that folklore makes up the majority (72 percent) of Vietnamese tales and that relative to other countries, *Vietnamese fairy tales are a rare breed* (italics in the original text). Others can argue that the fourth group of legends does contain some elements of fairy tales and if one is not too strict with one's selection, a large chunk of this group could be moved to the fairy tale column, thereby changing the overall breakdown of legends. One also wonders whether Chi's beliefs—a Communist Party member since 1947[2] and an atheist who does not believe in fairy tales—have anything to do with his strict assessment.

2. The legends imply that the Vietnamese are compassionate and gentle.[3]

3. However, the legends' characters often try to change the usual social order because they are not happy with it.[4]

4. Women who play a crucial role in these tales wish to be loved and be free to marry whomever they like.[5]

According to Chi, of his 201 *selected* tales, only 75 are purely local (37 percent). The rest either share distant (China, India) or nearby origins (Laos, highlanders, Cham).[6] "The Lady of Stone" or Hòn Vọng Phu (southern tale #37) probably originated from the highlanders of North Vietnam where Mount Vọng Phu is located.[7] "The Genie of Phù Đổng" (southern tale #4) has its origin in the highland Tai, Bahnar, and Djarai people.[8]

Maurice Durand, commenting on Chi's work, noted that Vietnamese legends have changed over the years.[9] In protohistory, legends were populated with magnificent stories and deeds of heroes and gods. Then under the Lê (fifteenth through eighteenth centuries), the heroes were kings, mandarins, and learned men. Under the Nguyễn (nineteenth through twentieth centuries), with the influence of revolts and modernization, the tales turned satirical and sarcastic and were eventually replaced by novels. He also made the observation that Chi's legends were not always original, but a mixture of many versions. It would have been better had Chi written down the original versions without modifying them.

In the twenty-first century, Nguyễn Cầm's book contains only ten tales, and eight of them are part of the common core of Vietnamese legends, North and South. Seven of these eight tales ("The Anger of the Waters," "General Phù Đổng," "Three Drops of Blood," "The Toad is the Uncle of the King of Heaven," "Two Cakes Fit for a King," "The Watermelon Island, Thạch Sanh") are classic tales that are known in both parts of the country.

Trần Tú's and Hà Nguyên's books, published in Hanoi, are modern collections of one or two page tales targeted at children. Many of them are tales that have never been heard before in the South and are completely different from the classic tales of yesteryear. They are also different from Nguyễn Cầm's classic stories.

Of the eight books mentioned here, five are written in Vietnamese, one in English and two in French; one of the latter two was translated into English in 1920. Although there could be a few more books that have not been accessed, the 486 tales reviewed (there were some overlaps: the same tales may be been retold by different authors in their books) are representative of the northern legend repertoire.

Table 2 presents the breakdown of the consulted books.

Table 2. Books Dealing with Northern Tales

Book/Author	Year	Number of Tales	Language
1. VDULT	1321	27	Vietnamese
2. LNCQ	1492	23	Vietnamese
3. Landes	1880	127	French
4. Chivas-Baron	1920	31	English (transl.)
5. Nguyễn Đổng Chi	1955	201	Vietnamese
6. Nguyễn Nguyệt Cầm	2003	10	English
7. Trần Tù, Mai Thi	2006	23	Vietnamese
8. Hà Nguyễn	2007	44	Vietnamese
Total		**486**	

VIII. *Việt Điền U Linh Tập*

Việt Điền U Linh Tập (Compilation of Potent Spirits in the Việt Realm), a 70-page manuscript written by Lý Tế Xuyên in 1329, is one of the earliest documented Vietnamese literary works. In that work, Xuyên mentions that spirits are worthy of being worshipped with temples and sacrifices because of their great achievements. Since they are not equal in their merit, their deeds had to be documented and "authentically recorded." That was the reason behind the compilation of the *Việt Điền U Linh Tập.* To achieve that goal, Xuyên relied on oral transmission and documents that are no longer available. For having tried to scientifically document, record, and compile the stories of these spirits, Xuyên has been acclaimed as Vietnam's first great "historian." Although it was not based on science as we know it today, it was one of Vietnam's earliest scholarly, historical, and educational works.

By acknowledging the presence and actions of these spirits, the Vietnamese recognized a supernatural world different from and mightier than theirs. Each day they battled against the mighty Chinese as well as wild natural forces: rough winds, violent storms, raging floods, severe drought, frightening thunders, wild animals, and unexplained phenomena; they badly needed protection. And they prayed to the mighty spirits who hopefully would be there to help them out. The *Việt Điền U Linh Tập* thus gives an insight to the people's mind at the time.

The *Việt Điền U Linh Tập* contains 27 tales arranged under three headings: "sovereigns," "ministers," and "superhuman powers." The first seven tales under the first two headings include actual people who had achieved great deeds for the country.

Each tale successively records the actual life of the individual or spirit, gives information about the development of the spirit cult after the person's death, and official titles conferred to the spirit in 1285, 1288, and 1312.[1] Although some tales cite dates and locations, others do not. The document does not cite references but only reports what was orally available at that time. Therefore, *Việt Điện U Linh Tập* does not claim to be an accurate document, although by the standard of the time, it was a great work.

Each tale is one to two pages long at most, some a few paragraphs long. The tales are succinct to the bare bones and not very descriptive. They were the work of a government official, not that of a novelist. Over the centuries, one story was added to another, one title to another, making the one-page tale ten or twenty times longer.

The tales celebrate moral virtue, loyalty to the sovereign, and heroism in defending the country. Xuyên selected tales of those who were worthy of praise and worship and discarded the unworthy ones. "Intelligence and upright conduct are necessary to be called a divine being" and a worthy spirit should be able to "perform great achievements that are a mystery to the living."[2] He then cited the example of Lý Thường Kiệt, a military leader and provincial governor in the eleventh century who chased away professional mediums who deceived people by promoting ghosts and demons. From then on, shrines to evil spirits became places to worship benevolent spirits.[3]

The titles were conferred to the spirits during and after the Mongol invasions. Although the Mongols invaded Vietnam in 1257, 1284–1285, and 1287, their attacks had always been repelled.[4] Only spirits thought to be the most powerful and attached to the fortunes of Thăng Long, modern Hanoi, were qualified for the honor. Since the cruelty and viciousness of the Mongols had preceded their attacks, many ruling-class Vietnamese had gone over to the enemy because they considered resistance to be hopeless. Many more, however, believed in the spirits of the land and the power of these spirits to pull them through the battles. In the end, they resisted and succeeded in their endeavor.[5]

The Vietnamese at that time lived in a land they believed was filled with spirits. Each tree, rock, river, mountain, and forest had its designated or attributed spirit(s) and each village its own protecting spirit, some good and some bad. The selection was purely local and sometimes regional. All these spirits vied for recognition. Actually, people who were supporting for these spirits fought for recognition for themselves because if their spirits were recognized, so were they. It was the perennial fight between "my guardian spirit versus yours." As word spread to the authorities, the king ultimately took action and chose the spirits he liked or deemed responsive or worthy before bestowing them titles. Through that rite, the king thought he put himself one level above the spirits. But not all the spirits were responsive.

Of the hundreds or thousands of spirits, only 27 were selected and

VIII. Việt Điện U Linh Tập

enshrined. The king's goal reflected a "pedagogical and politicized agenda"[6] because in the end, despite their supernatural might, these spirits were sanctioned by the ruling power. In a sense, the king appropriated all these untamed forces and spirits to make them his. If these spirits supported his agenda, they were praised and given honorific titles, especially in 1285, 1288, and 1313. Temples were erected to honor them and people encouraged to pray to them and give them offerings.

These selections seemed to be random, although most of the spirits had once manifested or were presumed to have manifested their supernatural forces. Presumption is the word here because these simplistic people often randomly associated an unexplained phenomenon to a certain spirit, which happened to be standing by at that time. It turned out that they were often wrong, because over the years or centuries many of these spirits were no longer responsive to people's prayers and simply fell out of favor. In another word, the spirits were always there; it was the human perception of their responsiveness or unresponsiveness that made or broke the spirits.

What was unusual in the selection was that three of the spirits were Chinese. This suggests that the ruling monarchy must have been pro–Chinese or at least receptive to Chinese ideas. Although these spirits later fell out of favor, for a certain period of time they were venerated by the people and leadership. The first one was Sĩ Nhiếp (137–226), a Chinese Han governor. Why would the Vietnamese choose a Chinese as their spirit unless Sĩ Nhiếp was very accommodating and helpful to them during his rule? The story recounts that he was a supernatural being because his well-preserved corpse was found by grave robbers centuries later. Tô Lịch, a magistrate, was also a Chinese. Hậu Thổ, the Goddess of the Earth—whose cult came from China—apparently had helped a Viet king during an expedition against the Chams.

The story of A Man is about a 12-year-old girl who was impregnated by a Buddhist priest, Khẩu Đà La. She later brought her newborn child to Khẩu Đà La, who gave it to a tree. The latter, uprooted during a storm, was carved into four Buddhas dedicated to rain, thunder, lightning, and clouds. The infant turned into a rock and was later worshipped as Mother Buddha.

The story of the Trưng Sisters reveals how their cult changed over the years from divine ladies to national heroines. Vietnam being under Chinese control, the two sisters rose and chased the Chinese out of the country in 39 CE. They ruled over Vietnam for the next two years before being defeated by a Chinese general in 42 CE. The country then reverted to Chinese control. Xuyên in the *Việt Điện U Linh Tập* (VDULT) documented the death of these two sisters in battle. "The local people pitied them and built a temple to worship them. They [spirits] repeatedly demonstrated their divine power."[7] Based on these words, Dror recently argued that it was *pity,* not admiration for their bravery, that led to their deification.[8]

What Xuyên wrote in the VDULT was his own interpretation of the facts, because by the time the account was written, the event had happened some twelve centuries earlier and no recorded document had been left. In reality, the Trưng queens having ruled over the country for over two years, led the army to battles, and commanded 65 forts, must have inspired awe and respect among the people. It must have been a very unusual sight to spot the two sisters leading men to battles, despite the matriarchal system in vogue at the time. This could also be the reason—if not the prime one— why people decided to build temples in their honor. By paying respect to these fallen heroines, they in fact challenged the Chinese authorities, who by that time had reestablished control over Vietnam. The fact that the Vietnamese continued over the next nine centuries (42–939 CE) to openly pay their respect to the queens right under the nose of the Chinese suggested a defiant attitude toward the Chinese and a sign of deep respect for the queens' bravery and sacrifice.

It was, however, only in the twelfth century that Lý Ánh Tông (1135–1175) recognized the Trưng spirits for their power in making rain during a drought, but not for their martial prowess or bravery.[9] As rain came down after he prayed for it, Lý Ánh Tông saw in his dream the two sisters advising him that they brought the rain on order of heaven. He gave the title of "Chaste Divine Ladies" to the sisters in 1285, and to the elder sister "Victorious Lady Strategist" in 1288, and "Sincerely Chaste" in 1313. In modern days, one could characterize the king's move as chauvinistic since he not only failed to recognize the queens' bravery and idealism, but also demeaned their work by calling them "chaste ladies."

Over the years, the sisters have been recognized more for their bravery and resistance to invaders than their chastity, as officials and military leaders began to appreciate their bravery and went to their temple to pray for victory before a major battle.[10] As we can see, if the cult started from the people or bottom up, the branding of these ladies as symbols of resistance and war heroines came from the top down (the ruling administration). Year in and year out, the repetition of this cult through worship and offering kept it alive in people's memories from antiquity until today. Dror calls the process "a continuous tradition of cultic forms rather than of historical context."[11] That cult persists today in North Vietnam, as we have seen in chapter II.

VIII. Việt Điền U Linh Tập

In the same vein, the historicity of the spirits was not the primary concern of the followers who judged them through a different lens: by responsiveness to their prayers, and not by what they had done while they were alive. As we will see in part three, another version of the Trưng story mentioned that the sisters ran away and killed themselves by jumping off a cliff. One version stated that the killing of the elder Trưng's husband caused her to take revenge and to start the insurrection. Another version simply quoted that her husband was alive and served as a high ranking officer in her army.[12]

The Vietnamese spirit world, in a sense, was "a protective screen attached to the Vietnamese landscape and rooted in Vietnamese history." For the Vietnamese who just recovered their independence from the Chinese and still feared them, the spirit world formed a shelter from alien threats and domestic disorder. It was a spiritual world dominated by powerful patrons in the supernatural realm identified as guardians of the kingdom.[13]

These are summaries of seven of *Việt Điền U Linh Tập*'s 27 tales, which are still of interest to modern readers. The other spirits have been deselected by people over the ages because they were no longer found to be "responsive."

1. Sĩ Nhiếp

Sĩ Nhiếp (137–226) was born in the southern province of Guangxi from parents who had emigrated from northeastern China. He was a keen administrator and successful governor who knew how to play politics with shifting dynastic powers, maintaining peace and prosperity within his jurisdiction. The fact that he was able to remain in power for more than 40 years was seen as a sign of moral rectitude.[14] He died at the age of 90 and lived in the province for 48 years.

When grave robbers dug him up, they found a well-preserved body that had not decayed in the 160 years since his death.[15] They were terrified and reburied him. The local people made him a deity, built a temple in his honor, and called him King Sĩ the Immortal.[16] In the ninth century, general Cao Biền, a Taoist practitioner, while traveling in the area, met an extraordinary figure dressed in the colorful robes of a mountain immortal. He chatted with the person, who suddenly vanished. Villagers suggested it was Sĩ Nhiếp.

He is highly responsive to villagers' wishes. He was appointed "Excellently Responsive Great King," "Virtuously Compassionate," and "Divinely Militant" in 1285, 1288, and 1312 respectively.[17]

2. Phùng Hưng (d. 789)

Phùng Hưng was the head of a ruling clan on the Hồng River plain (present day North Vietnam). He was courageous and strong, and so was his brother Hãi. When the Chinese control waned between 766 and 780, the two brothers patrolled the region and made everyone submit to them.[18]

He changed his name and title to Cự Lão and Metropolitan Lord respectively. The Chinese tried to attack him, but could not beat him. He ran the region for seven years before dying. His son, An, succeeded him and named him Bố Cái Đại Vương or Great King Bố Cái.

An ruled the country for two years until the Chinese retook control of the region. By submitting to them, An put an end to a newly emerging free society.

Hưng's abilities were manifested after his death by the processions of a thousand chariots and ten thousand horses that flew over the region amidst flags and drum sounds. A shrine was built to worship Hưng, who always responded to prayers for sun or rain.

At the Battle of Bạch Đằng (939), Ngô Quyền easily dispersed the Chinese and regained freedom for Vietnam. In a dream before the battle, Ngô Quyền saw Hưng, who told him he would assist him in the battle. In a show of gratitude, Ngô ordered a huge temple built for Phùng Hưng.

Comments 1. Although he was only a warlord and in deference to him, people bestowed him the title of king.

2. Since life at that time revolved around war and agriculture, when they no longer needed him for support during war, they prayed to him for rain and sunshine.

3. Triệu Quang Phục and Lý Phật Tử

After chasing the Chinese out of the country, Lý Bôn took the title of Việt King and named the country Văn Xuân. He remained king for eight years (541–548) before losing to the Chinese and was succeeded by his two generals, Triệu Quang Phục and Lý Phật Tử.[19]

Triệu Quang Phục, a Chu Điền native, was Bôn's general from the left. After Bôn's death, he gathered 20,000 troops and attacked Chinese

VIII. Việt Điền U Linh Tập

military camps at night while hiding in Chu Điền marshes during daytime. Troops could not do anything about him and people praised him as the Night Marsh King.

One night, Phục dreamt about a golden-colored dragon removing one of his talons and giving it to him. The talon, once fastened on top of the helmet, would help him win battles. Bá Tiên, in the meantime, was ordered to return to China to deal with another problem. He left behind general Dương San who quickly lost the battle to Phục, who took the title of King of Nam Việt or Việt King.

Phật Tử was Bôn's younger cousin. When Bôn died, Phật Tử followed Bôn's elder brother, Thiên Bảo. After the latter died, people proclaimed Phật Tử as king. He called himself Southern Emperor and went into war against Phục, the Việt King.

Knowing the Việt King had supernatural powers, the Southern Emperor requested a truce. He pushed his son Nhã Lang to request a marriage from the Việt King. The latter gave his daughter Cảo Nương in marriage to Nhã Lang.

Nhã Lang tricked his wife into telling him the source of the Việt King's power. He then switched the dragon talon for a fake and made an excuse to see his father and gave him the talon. The Southern Emperor gathered his troops and attacked the Việt King, who lost and ran away with his daughter. At the seaside, Phuc asked for help; the golden dragon spirit told him the culprit was his own daughter. He turned around, killed her, and escaped with the Dragon's help. He reigned from 551 to 569.

The Southern Emperor, after defeating the Việt King, moved his capital to Lộc Loa. He reigned from 571 to 602.

Comments 1. This tale is similar to southern tale #3, "The Magic Crossbow," in which Triệu Đà's son tricked King An Dương's daughter, his wife, into revealing the reason behind An Duong's invincibility. In this case, it was a magic turtle's nail that was used as a trigger for the crossbow. With the nail present, the bow could kill a hundred soldiers per shot. Triệu Đà's son removed the nail from the bow, rendering it harmless. Treachery worked and An Duong lost his empire to Triệu Đà.

2. Triệu Quang Phục and Lý Phật Tử were two of the many warlords who tried to rebel against the Chinese; they were successful for only a very short period of time.

4. The Trưng Sisters

Trắc and her younger sister Nhị were daughters of Lạc generals in Giao Chỉ province.[20]

The elder wed Thi Sách, a courageous and heroic man. The governor To Định managed to have him killed. Trưng Trắc was furious, raised an army, and chased Định out of the country. She then subdued 65 other towns.

The Han king was furious on hearing the news. He banished Định to Đạm Nhĩ and sent Mã Viện to replace him. Mã Viện's troops defeated Trưng's army at Lang Bạc. The ladies retreated to Cẩm Khê, where they died in battle.

A temple was built to them in An Hạt subprefecture. Their divine responsiveness has been manifested on various occasions. Lý Ánh Tông (1138–1175) asked monks to pray for rain during a drought period. He was delighted to see the result. In his dream, he saw the two sisters, who revealed that they made rain on order of heaven. The king had their temple restored and offerings brought to them. Later, they appeared again to the king, asking for another temple to be built at Cổ Lai. He appointed them "Chaste Divine Ladies."

Comments 1. It is interesting to note that this classic half-page biography would in modern times be expanded into a three to four page length or even a full book. By the time the VDULT was written, a legend had formed around the Trưng sisters. But for the ruling dynasty, they were only good at rainmaking, not as warriors.

2. The text was adamant that the death of her husband caused Trưng to revolt against the Chinese and that the sisters died in battle.

5. Lý Ông Trọng[21]

He was an impressive twenty-three foot tall giant whom the Vietnamese gave to the Chinese Tần Thủy Hoàng (Qin Shi Huang) who made him Commander of Chinese troops against Lâm Thao. After a successful career and not wanting to wage war any longer, he returned to Vietnam. When Tần Thủy Hoàng requested him, the Vietnamese explained that Trọng had died. Suspecting foul play, the Chinese asked for his skeleton. Unable to hide any longer, Trọng committed suicide. A copper cast statue of him, placed outside the Tư Mã gate of the Hàm palace, still frightened the Hung

Nô when the latter visited the palace. They admonished one another not to violate the Viet borders.

When Triệu Xương served as governor general of Giao Chỉ, he visited Ông Trọng's old house, which he found dilapidated. He built another temple on a high and level spot with a multistoried tower. Ceremonial offerings were presented.

When Cao Biên destroyed the Nam Chiếu (866), Ông Trọng regularly manifested his divine assistance. Biên then ordered the temple repaired and expanded. New statues were carved and painted and offerings brought for sacrifice.

Comments This is the tale of a gentle giant who, because of his sheer size, inspired fear in his enemies. Although he was a good warrior, he did not want to wage war and returned to Vietnam to hide. When he was once again requested by the Chinese, he had to commit suicide because he could no longer hide from them. Even in death, he continued to inspire fear in his enemies.

6. Lý Thường Kiệt[22]

The duke was named Lý Thường Kiệt. He was from a family of government officials.

Under the reign of Lý Thái Tông (1028–1054), he was promoted to office inspector manager. Lý Thánh Tông (1054–1072) made him commandant grand guardian. He carefully did his duty. He was named general and led battles against the Cham. He captured the Cham lord, Chế Củ (1061–1074). Lý Nhân Tông (1072–1128) promoted him to defender-in-chief bulwark of the State, employing him as a high official.

When the Chinese Tống (Song) wanted to invade Vietnam, the duke petitioned the emperor to strike first. He led a great army and destroyed Ung, Khâm, and Liêm, subduing four forts and capturing innumerable riches.

The Tống retaliated by plundering Lục, Lược, and other provinces. The duke constructed a wall along the Như Nguyệt River and retook Vũ Bình Nguyên. Upon his death, his family was given rice land with ten thousand households.

When people were fond of demons, spirits, witches and wizards, he reprimanded them and sternly did away with vile customs. Wherever there were obscene temples, they were changed into places for offering incense to benevolent deities. People received great favor from him and petitioned to build a temple for his worship. He always responded to their prayers.

Comments 1. Born as Ngô Tuấn in Thăng Long (present-day Hanoi), he was bestowed the royal name of Lý Thường Kiệt because of his bravery, loyalty, and service to the State. He was a national hero who fought against the Chinese and beat them twice in 1075 and 1076. He devised the strategy of putting spikes in the Như Nguyệt riverbed to lure the Song navy into a deadly trap. The defeat forced the Song army to withdraw. He also defeated the Chams twice.

2. He was the first to declare Vietnam's independence by proudly proclaiming it through the *Nam Quốc Sơn Hà*, which is considered to be the first Declaration of Independence in Vietnam.

> Over the southern mountains and rivers, rules the Southern Emperor,
> As it stands written in the Book of Heaven.
> How dare you barbarians to invade our land?
> Your armies without pity will be annihilated.[23]

7. Tô Lịch[24]

Tô Lịch once served as a magistrate at Lông Đỗ (present-day Hanoi), where his forefathers had resided for many generations. Following a royal edict in the third century CE, the village's name was changed to Tô Lịch.

In 823, Protector General Lý Nguyên Gia built his headquarters in the area and made Tô Lịch its guardian deity. The town flourished and a temple was built to honor the deity.

When Cao Biên built the town of Đại La to replace the town of Tô Lịch, which had been destroyed by war, he again made Tô Lịch the protector of the village.

When King Lý Thái Tổ moved the capital to Đại La (1010),[25] he saw an old man appearing before him and wishing him well. "Long live the king," said the old man. The sovereign woke up from his dream, renamed the city Thăng Long, and made the spirit the deity of the city.

Comments The tale explains the story of how a Chinese magistrate, over the centuries, became the spirit guardian of the city of Thăng Long (present-day Hanoi).

IX. Lĩnh Nam Chích Quái

Although the *Lĩnh Nam Chích Quái* (Wonderful Stories of Lĩnh Nam)—a collection of 23 stories—was written by an anonymous person at the fourteenth-century Trần court (most likely between 1370 and 1400), it was not resurrected until the fifteenth century. Vũ Quỳnh wrote the preface to the work in 1492. The manuscript then was edited, expunged, and augmented many times, especially by Kiều Phú in 1493 and by others in the sixteenth and eighteenth centuries; therefore, it is difficult to know which of the nine remaining manuscripts is the original one.[1]

The late fourteenth century was a time of crisis and self-doubt among officials because the government was powerless in the face of repeated attacks by the Hinduized Chams from the South who marched north, sacked the capital and plundered the countryside.[2] They were followed by the Chinese Ming who came down from the north to occupy the country for two decades.[3]

The text was thus written to promote a sense of moral authority within the Vietnamese heritage and to make the Vietnamese aware of their identity. To achieve that purpose, the fifteenth-century Confucian literati produced a historical narrative using mythological material. It is a history of Vietnamese "prehistorical" times.[4] Fifteen of the twenty-three stories in the *Lĩnh Nam Chích Quái* deal with the origins of Vietnam, from Dragon Lord Lạc through the Hùng Dynasty to King An Dương. What the court did was to lay down the claim for an independent and free Vietnam, which is separate and different from China.

The first tale even traces the genealogy of the Vietnamese Hùng kings all the way back to the Chinese agricultural deity Thần Nông, from whom both Chinese and Vietnamese claimed to descend. The Chinese branch is illustrated on the left-hand side of the genealogy chart, where all the leaders were called *Đế* or emperors. The right-hand side of the chart corresponds to the Vietnamese branch: all the leaders were known as *Vương* or kings. The designation implies that the emperors are one step higher than the kings.

However, the chart was designed to prove that the Vietnamese branch was superior to the Chinese branch based on three factors: morality, natural resources and the mandate of heaven. First, despite the fact that his father, Đế Minh, relinquished his throne to him, Kinh Dương Vương (Lộc Tục) refused the honor and suggested his elder half-brother Đế Nghi as successor. Đế Minh was so touched by the gesture that he in turn appointed Kinh Dương to reign over the southern part of the empire. Second, the South was so rich in natural resources that Đế Nghi, who took vacation there, felt so happy that he forgot to return to his northern country. Third, the Chinese branch ended when Đế Du was defeated by a foreigner, the Yellow Emperor. The Vietnamese branch, however, continued to expand and proliferate as a result of Au Co delivering one hundred offspring.[5]

The *Việt Điển U Linh Tập* and *Lĩnh Nam Chích Quái* are much more than folktales; they are historical writings that should be viewed at the same level as official court annals. They are, however, different in terms of composition and goals. The Buddhist stronghold of the fourteenth century court, through the *Việt Điển U Linh Tập*, draws divinity from the peripheries to include it in its entourage. In the *Lĩnh Nam Chích Quái*, the Confucian center tends to swallow the peripheral divinity to justify itself as the sole divine power.[6]

Below are summaries of 13 of the 22 tales published in the *Lĩnh Nam Chích Quái*.

1. Legend of Hồng Bàng[7]

The great-grandson of Đế Thần Nông, Đế Minh had a son named Đế Nghi.[8] During a trip to Ngũ Linh, he met the beautiful Vũ Tiên Nữ, whom he married; they had a son named Lộc Tục.[9] Noting that Lộc Tục looked smart and intelligent, he turned his throne over to him. Not wanting to indispose his half-brother Đế Nghi, Lộc Tục suggested that Đế Nghi rule the northern part of the country while Lộc Tục succeeded their father. Đế Minh decided that Lộc Tục should be named Kinh Dương Vương, the ruler of the South or the kingdom of Xích Qũy.[10]

Kinh Dương Vương went to Thủy Phủ, married Thần Long Nữ (Lady Dragon Spirit) and had a son named Lạc Long Quân. Lạc Long Quân, replacing his father, ran the country; Kinh Dương Vương was often nowhere to be found. Lạc Long Quân taught people how to dress and to follow rules and customs. Although he sometimes returned to his maternal state, Thủy Phủ, people remained peaceful. When they needed him, they just had to call, "Father, where are you? Please help us." Very receptive, he would come back right away.

Đế Nghi abdicated in favor of his son, Đế Lai. Ruling over the North where people were at peace, Đế Lai one day remembered that his grandfather, Đế Minh, once journeyed to the South to find his wife Tiên Nữ. Đế Lai thus traveled to the kingdom of Xích Quĩ where he noticed that Lạc Long Quân was gone to Thủy Phủ.[11] He settled there and courted the beautiful Âu Cơ, whom he married.[12] He found the country bountiful from fruit to minerals and forgot his way home.

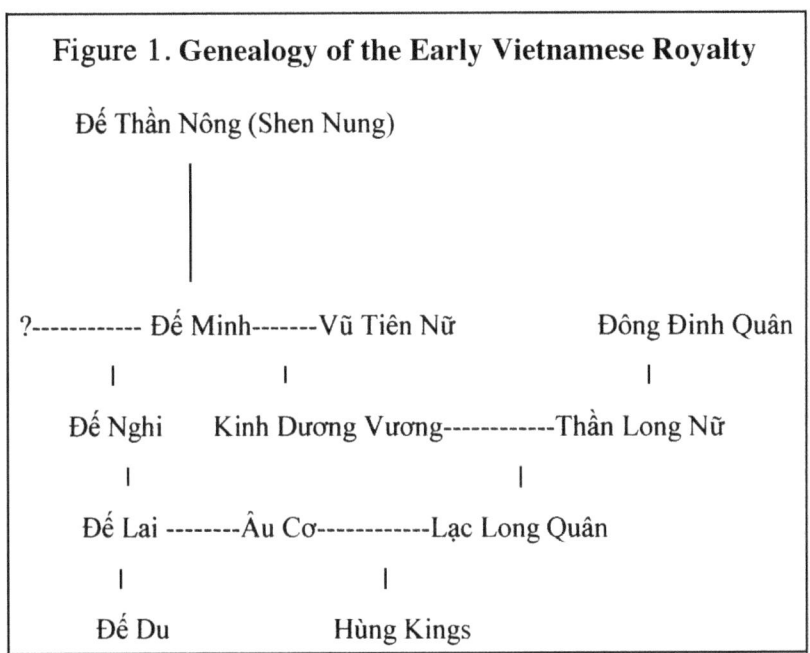

The people, however, unsettled by the presence of Đế Lai, dreamed daily about Long Quân's return. They then cried out, "Father, where are you? Come back and save us."

Hearing the calling of his people, Lạc Long Quân returned home and noticed the charming Âu Cơ, who was alone. In love, he transformed himself into a handsome young prince who began courting her with songs and music. Deeply touched, Âu Cơ followed Lạc Long Quân, who took her to Long Tràng Mountains. Đế Lai, on his return, realized that Âu Cơ was missing and looked for her everywhere. Lạc Long Quân transformed himself into one spirit after another, scaring away his pursuers. Đế Lai returned to his country and abdicated in favor of Đế Du.[13]

Âu Cơ lived with Lạc Long Quân for a year and delivered a sac that, being deemed not a good omen, was left outside. One week later, out of the sac hatched one hundred eggs that yielded one hundred sons. She nurtured them, although she did not feed them. They grew into nice and healthy boys.

Long Quân remained at Thủy Phủ a long time, leaving Âu Cơ and the children alone. Longing to return to the North, they moved close to the frontier and called, "Where are you, Dad? We miss you." Lạc Long Quân reappeared and met them at Tương Da. Âu Cơ said, "I'm from the North. Having lived with you and raised your one hundred children, we need to be together so that I would not be seen as someone without husband." Lạc Long Quân answered, "I am from the race of dragons, living in the sea realm. You are from the race of fairies whose realm is on land. We are different from one another. Although we could mate and have children, we are so different that we could not be together for a long time. We need to separate: I will take fifty children to Thủy Phủ to spread them over the villages. The other fifty will stay with you on land. Whether in the mountains or at sea, if needed, they will listen to one another and will not abandon one another."

The children listened and bid farewell. Âu Cơ with her fifty children stayed at Phông Châu (now the province of Bạch Hạc). They elected the eldest as king, with Hùng Vương as the dynasty and the country as Văn Lang. He ruled over ten provinces, named the second child as general, and Lạc Hậu as minister.

In the beginning, since people did not have enough clothes to wear, they used the shells of trees to protect themselves and tall grass as a mat to lie on. They used rice to make wine, shrimp and fish to make salted fish, bamboo as a pipe to blow on the fire, cut their hair short to move easily in the forest, and used banana leaves to lay a newborn baby on. They pounded in the mortar with a pestle to call neighbors for help if someone was having difficulty at home. They used salt to announce an engagement and killed a buffalo for the marriage. They did not have betel and areca at that time.

Comments There are two stories in this tale: the genealogy concerning the Vietnamese and the story about Lạc Long Quân and Âu Cơ. The LNCQ suggests that the Chinese and Vietnamese descend from the same Shen Nung, putting both on the same level and in a sense telling the Vietnamese that they do not have to be afraid of or feel inferior to the Chinese.

The Vietnamese, however, consider Lạc Long Quân as their direct ancestor and the progenitor of the Hùng Dynasty, the first royal dynasty in Vietnam. He was the main character with Âu Cơ (above) and in a fight against the sea spirit (below).

2. The Sea Spirit[14]

The sea spirit lived in the Eastern Sea (Đông Hãi). He was longer than 50 *trượng*[15] and had many legs, like centipedes. He changed forms very often, which made it difficult to detect him. When he moved, he trailed rains and storms behind, causing people to fear him.

In ancient times, there were fish with human faces. They traveled along the Đông Hãi coastline, transformed into human beings and gave birth to boys and girls who ate fish and shellfish.

The sea spirit dwelled in a cavern at the base of a mountain. Fishermen who passed by were often harmed; they did not have any choice. If they wanted to avoid that route, they would have to dig their way through sand or rocks, which was impossible.

One night, a group of fairies flew down to dig up a passageway for humans. When the work was almost completed, the sea spirit transformed itself into a white rooster that crowed on the mountain. As dawn approached, the fairies flew away: that channel was called the Buddha's way.

Lạc Long Quân, wanting to protect his people, built a large vessel and ordered Thủy Dạ Xoa to warn the sea not to make waves. He guided his vessel toward the sea spirit mountain, pretending to bring a human sacrifice to the spirit. As the latter opened its mouth, Lạc Long Quân threw in a mass of molten iron. The spirit jumped toward the boat. Lạc Long Quân chopped off the fish tail, peeled its skin and hung it on the mountain: that place was called Bạch Long Vỹ. The spirit's head became a dog that swam away. Long Quân chopped off the head and the body flushed back to the shore at Man Cầu; that place is now called Cầu Man Cầu.

Comments This is a fascinating tale of Lạc Long Quân fighting against the sea spirit among a background of sea monsters and fairies.

3. The Betel and the Areca Tree[16]

In ancient times, there was a man named Quang Lang who was of large stature. The king, therefore, named him Cao.[17] He had two sons named Tân and Lang. The boys' parents suddenly died, leaving them orphans. Luckily, a nearby teacher, Lưu Huyền, took them in and decided to raise them.

Lưu Huyền's daughter, a pretty girl of about 17 or 18, was looking for a husband. Since she did not know who was the most senior of the two, she served them a meal but brought out only one bowl and one pair of chopsticks. The younger one, in deference, let his brother eat first. Taking notice, she let her parents know which brother ate first. Marriage was arranged between the elder brother and the girl, and the two loved each other more every day.

As time passed by, the younger brother felt neglected, since his sibling did not spend a lot of time with him. He became upset and left the house. He walked and walked until he encountered a large river. Having no means to cross over, he sat down and cried until he died and turned into a tree.

The elder one, realizing the absence of his sibling, went to look for him. He found him dead against a tree. He too cried and turned into a rock close to the tree.

Since her husband did not come home, the wife went out to look for him. Finding that her husband had turned into a rock, she cried, died, and turned into a climbing tree that wound around the rock.

The parents, looking for their children, stopped by the rock, crying and complaining. They erected a temple at that place: passersby stopped there to pray, praising the loving brotherhood of the sons and the fidelity of the couple.

King Hùng Vương, on his summer rounds, frequently stopped by this temple to rest from the heat. Realizing the luxuriant vegetation and coolness of the area, he climbed on top of the rock to watch the surrounding landscape. He then inquired about the story of the temple. He ordered a nut and a leaf picked from the tree and the climbing plant respectively. He chewed them for a while and spat on the rock, giving it a bright reddish color. He told people to heat the rock to make lime and to chew betel leaf and areca nut. The compound would give a fragrant aroma, sweet taste, and make both lips bright red. He ordered people to use this tradition at weddings and meetings, large or small. The Vietnamese began chewing betel and areca from that moment onward.

4. *The Marsh Boy*[18]

Hùng Vương IV had a daughter named Tiên Dung Mỹ Nương. She was a beautiful 18 year-old who refused to take any husband. She loved sailing and each February or March set her boat to sail up and down the river, sometimes forgetting to return home. Her father listened to her and let her be.

At that time, in the village of Chử Xá lived a man named Chử Vy Vân and his son Chử Đồng Tử. Both were nice, but poor. Their house burned down one day, leaving them with only one piece of cloth which they both shared: one stayed at home while the other went out dressed with the cloth. Being old, the father told his son, "You can bury me naked, so you could use the loin cloth."

When his father passed away, the son did not dare do what his father asked and buried him with the cloth. Chử Đồng Tử, naked and hungry, took his fishing pole to the river. He saw junks passing by and asked for food. Then, Tiên Dung's boat appeared with its music, drum sounds and flying flags. Scared, Chử Đồng Tử did not know where to hide until he saw a small bay with reeds nearby. Hiding himself among the reeds, he covered his head and shoulders with sand.

Sometime later, Tiên Dung's boat stopped at the bay. After strolling along the river edge, she had a small area around the reeds covered with cloth so she could take a bath.

Tiên Dung took off her shirt before pouring some water on herself. The water drove away the sand, exposing Chử Đồng Tử's body and revealing a boy. Tiên Dung screamed, "Although I did not want to take a husband, I have encountered today another naked body like mine in this corner of the bay. Maybe it is heaven's will? You better get out and wash yourself."

She gave him some clothing and took him to the boat to eat. The people on the boat thought that the meeting was auspicious and noted that it had never happened before.

Đồng Tử told her his story. Tiên Dung could only sympathize and offered to marry him. Đồng Tử refused.

Tiên Dung said, "This is heaven's will. Why do you want to back out?"

Some of her aides returned home and reported to King Hùng Vương who became mad.

"Tiên Dung did not appreciate her name, nor my prestige. She ran around and depreciated herself by taking a poor fellow. From now on, she is banished from this place."

After hearing these words, Tiên Dung was afraid to return home. She decided to open a market, to build a village and with the help of locals engaged in trade. The area became a big market (known as Hà Loa Market today).

One successful merchant told Tiên Dung, "You are born in the age of gold. Go out to the sea with merchants and buy merchandises. They will bring in a lot of profits next year."

Tiên Dung reported to Đồng Tử: "Heaven has provided us with cover and shelter. It is time for us to buy and trade so that we could plan for the future."

Chử Đồng Tử went out to sea with the merchant; they stopped at an island where a Buddhist monk lived on a hill in a small pagoda. Đồng Tử gave his money to the merchant and told him to buy merchandise and pick him up on his return. In the meantime, he received religious instructions from the monk, who gave him a cane and a hat, explaining that they had special power.

Returning from a trip one day, Chử Đồng Tử and Tiên Dung could not find their way home and had to stop and rest in the middle of nowhere. They set the cane down with the hat on top to protect themselves. In the middle of the night, a whole town with surrounding walls appeared in front of them. There were temples, houses with gold, diamonds, beds, and guards.

When they woke up in the morning, people bought them presents and soldiers were available to serve them.

The king heard about Tiên Dung's new town and riches and thought she wanted to make war on him. He sent an army to the town to quell the rebellion.

Tiên Dung said, "This is heaven's will. I did not want to oppose my father. I just accept what comes ahead."

Villagers, realizing war had come to them, ran away, leaving Tiên Dung, her husband and a few other people in the village. The king's army finally arrived and camped on the other side of the river, waiting for the next day to attack. In the middle of the night, a fierce wind blew through, uprooting trees. Tiên Dung's town also uprooted itself and flew to the sky, leaving a huge hole on the ground. The next morning, there was nothing left of the town, and the people, realizing something supernatural had happened, put up a temple to pray to the spirits. The large gap was known as Nhật Da Trạch.

Comments The marsh boy is one of the Four Immortals venerated in North Vietnam, although he is less well known in the South.

5. Phù Đổng Thiên Vương[19]

Under King Hùng Vương III, people were prosperous and at peace. King An blamed Hùng Vương for not sending him the required presents, so he planned to attack the country. Hearing the news, Hùng Vương gathered his cabinet to hear the advice of its members. Someone suggested they should pray to Long Quân.

Listening to his ministers, the king had an altar set up and for three days prayed to the spirit. The weather turned dark and cloudy and people saw a large old man with a fat belly and long beard sitting at one intersection of the town. They suspected he was a spirit and guided him to the king.

"King An is planning to attack our country. Can you foresee the outcome?" Hùng Vương asked.

The old man pulled out a stack of papers, looked at them and said, "He will attack in three years."

When the king asked how he could fight back, the old man answered, "You have to prepare your soldiers and armaments. Then look for someone who could take care of the business and promote him. Once you have him, the war is won." The old man did not walk out, but flew away. By this, people knew they had dealt with Long Quân.

An envoy arrived at the village of Phù Đổng, province of Vũ Ninh, where a rich 60 year-old man lived with his 3 year old-son who could not speak or move around.

The mother kiddingly said, "My boy just knows how to eat; he does not know anything about fighting a war to receive award from the court."

The boy listened and suddenly said, "Mom. Please call the envoy so I can ask him a question."

"My son knows how to speak," yelled the happy woman.

The surprised neighbors invited the envoy to the house.

"You, who just learn to speak, what do you call me for?" asked the envoy.

"Please tell the king to give me an 18 meter-high steel horse, a 7-meter-long steel sword, and a steel helmet. This boy will ride the horse, and wear the helmet to fight the enemy. The king does not have to worry about anything."

The envoy reported to the king, who happily said,"I therefore no longer have to worry."

"How could one person fight a war?" a minister asked.

"That is what Long Quân proclaimed. His word is not to be challenged."

The king asked his men to look for steel to make the horse, helmet and sword. Everything was then brought to the child, whose mother became fearful about the fate of her son.

"Mom, make a lot of rice for me to eat so I can go fight the enemy. Do not be fearful," the child said.

The child ate fast; faster than his mother could cook. Although neighbors brought extra rice, buffalo meat, fruit and cookies, all that food did not fill his hunger. Since there was not enough fabric material to cover his growing body, leaves and flowers were used.

When An's soldiers came to Trâu Sơn, the child just began to stand up. He was ten *truong* high. He sneezed ten times then pulled out the sword and said, "I'm the spirit general."

He put his helmet on, jumped on his horse, and flew in the air, followed by King Hùng Vương's troops. They arrived at Trâu Sơn and jumped on the enemy, which disbanded. King An died at the battle. The rest of the army surrendered.

The spirit general flew to Việt Sóc Mountain, removed his helmet, then flew to the sky, leaving behind an imprint of his footstep on the mountain.

Hùng Vương did not know how to reward the spirit except to name him as Phù Đổng Thiên Vương (the king of Phù Đổng), have a temple built for him, and give him a parcel of land, the profits of which would be used to buy offerings to him.

The An Dynasty, throughout its 640 years, never brought its troops back to Vietnam.

Comments The king of Phù Đổng is one of the Four Immortals venerated in North Vietnam. The marsh boy, the spirit of Mount Tản Viên, and Princess *Liễu Hạnh* are the other three.

6. Bánh Dầy Bánh Chưng[20]

After defeating the An and seeing peace settle over the land, Hùng Vương thought about choosing an heir to his reign. He gathered his 20 sons and told them, "I will turn over my throne to the one who will bring the best food to honor our forefathers at the end of the year."

The princes set out to look for the best food available, whether through hunting, fishing, or at the market. They were able to gather various types of rare and delicious food. But prince number nine, Lang Liễu, because of his mother's severe illness and the lack of relatives, had not been able to gather anything and had become restless.

One night, in his dream, he saw a spirit who told him, "There is nothing more precious on earth than rice, which is the food staple of the people. They are never tired of it. If you take glutinous rice, shape it into a round form to remind people of the sky, or into a square to remind them of the earth, and insert meat filling to imitate the sky and earth that surround people and animals—in homage of the sky and earth that protect men and animals—your father would certainly be happy and give you his throne."

Frightened, Lang Liễu woke up and mumbled, "The spirit has helped me; I had better do what he mentioned."

Lang Liễu chose the whitest and best-shaped rice grains and wrapped them with green leaves into a square shape after inserting bean and meat fillings. After cooking, they were known as *bánh chưng*. He crushed the rice grains, added filling, and shaped them into a round form; after cooking, they were called *bánh dầy*.[21]

At the right time, the king convened all his sons, who brought in the most diverse types of food, except for Lang Liễu with his round and square cakes. Surprised, the king asked for an explanation. Lang Liễu explained what the spirit had told him. The king, after tasting them, found the cakes delicious; the other types of food could not beat them. The king made Lang Liễu the winner.

At the end of the year, the king brought *bánh chưng* and *bánh dầy* to the altar to pay homage to his forefathers. He later abdicated in favor of Lang Liễu.

Comments *Bánh chưng* and *bánh tét* are the two bean-and meat-filled cakes consumed during the Tết festival (Vietnamese lunar New Year) in North and South Vietnam respectively. *Bánh chưng* is square in shape while *bánh tét* is round, in the form of a log.

7. *The Watermelon*[22]

Under Hùng Vương, there was a foreign seven-year-old boy named Mai An Tiên that traders had brought to the country. The king bought him to use as a servant. He grew up into a nice man.

The king named him Yên or An Tiêm. He gave him a wife who gave Tiêm a baby boy. Tiêm served the king faithfully and through his diligence became a rich and esteemed man. He received a lot of presents, which made him say once, "I made all these things, without the help of the king."

Hearing these words, the king became mad.

"As a subject, he did not realize the favors he got from his master, but kept mentioning that he made all these things. I will deport him to a barren land to see if he can make everything himself."

The king sent him to Nga Sơn, where no soul had lived before, and gave him enough provisions to last him four or five months at most. His sister-in-law cried for fear of not being able to last long. An Tiêm said, "Don't be afraid. Heaven brought us to life, heaven will provide us everything."

He was not there long before a heron, which came from the west, stopped on a high hill and emitted a few sounds, then dropped six or seven seeds that grew rapidly into watermelons.

An Tiêm happily claimed, "Is that what heaven wanted to give to us?"

When the melon was split open, it emitted a sweet odor. A bite of it would give unusual strength. The melons kept growing every year. They were traded for rice.

Fishermen stopped by to trade their products for watermelons. People from near and far came to buy the seeds and tried to plant the melons.

The king, remembering An Tiêm, sent his soldiers to look for him. They reported to him that he was alive and well.

The king thought for a long time and uttered, "If he said he did it by himself, he was correct."

The king had An Tiêm brought back, returned his title and gave him another wife. He named him An Tiêm Sa Châu; the village was called Mai An and still remembers An Tiêm as one of its ancestors.

Comments The legend stresses independence and self-sufficiency as the two qualities required in adults. This teaching is new and contrary to the Confucian teaching that asks citizens to be obedient and subservient to rules and laws. Alas, the suggestion was never followed; Vietnam has remained a Confucian state for more than two millennia.

8. Lý Ông Trọng Story[23]

Toward the end of Hùng Vương's reign, in the subprefecture of Từ Liêm, province of Giao Chỉ, there was a giant named Lý Thân. He was 2 *trượng* 3 *thước* and bad. He killed people and deserved to be killed, but Hùng Vương did not want to kill him.

Under An Dương Vương, Tần Thủy Hoàng wanted to invade Vietnam. An Dương Vương appeased him by giving him Lý Thân as a present. Thủy Hoàng was happy and made him prince Ty Lệ Hiệu Uy. When Thủy Hoàng tried to unify the country, he ordered Thân to control Lâm Thao to prevent the Hung barbarians from invading the area. Thân succeeded at this task and was named Vạn Tín Hầu and allowed to return to his country.

When the Hùng barbarians began to reinvade China, Thũy Hoàng remembered about Lý Thân and sent people to look for him. Not wanting to fight another war, Thân hid in the forest. When Thũy Hoàng asked about the whereabouts of Thân, An Dương Vương told him Thân had died. When Thũy Hoàng asked about the cause of Thân's death, An Dương Vương retorted, "He died of dysentery." When Thũy Hoàng sent soldiers to ensure that Thân had died, An Dương asked his people to dump rice gruel into a small lake to make it appear like his remains. When Thũy Hoàng asked for his skeleton, Thân had no choice but to kill himself. They used mercury to preserve his body and sent it to Thũy Hoàng.

Thũy Hoàng expressed his sorrow about Thân's death and ordered a silver casting of his body, which he named Lý Ông Trọng. The belly of the cast could hold more than twenty people. When the barbarians' envoy visited the country, Thũy Hoàng ordered a few people to stay in the giant's belly to rock it. Thinking Lý Ông Trọng was still alive, the envoy did not want to come close to him.

9. *Kim Quy*[24]

An Dương Vương from Âu Lạc state was known as Thục Phán. Having been rejected when asking the hand of Mỵ Nương, Hùng Vương's daughter, for his son, he resented Hùng Vương. Taking his troops, he defeated Hùng Vương's Văn Lang, and renamed it Âu Lạc. He built a castle at Việt Thương; as soon as he completed it, it collapsed.

On the seventh day of the third month, he saw an old man from the west heading toward the castle gate.

"When will you complete this castle?" the man asked.

The king invited him in and explained, "I have completed it, but it crumbled. Why did it happen?"

"When the envoy Thanh Giang is with you, you will complete it," retorted the man, who then left.

In the morning, standing at the eastern gate, the king saw a golden turtle coming from the east; it stood on the surface of the water, claiming to be the envoy Thanh Giang, who knew the rules of heaven and earth.

The king invited him in, explained that the old man had told him about the envoy. He then asked him about the cause of the collapsed building.

Kim Quy said, "There are many spirits living around; besides Tiên Vương that helps to take revenge for the country, there is a white rooster that has been living for a thousand years on Thất Diệu Mountain. There is also a devil—a musician who was buried here and became a devil. Nearby is a hostel open to travelers; the owner is Ngô Không, who has a daughter and a white-rooster, both of them are incarnations of the devil. Travelers who stop by the hostel are bothered by the spirits who often kill them. Once the girl and the white rooster are killed, there will be fewer spirits left. But they will transform themselves into an owl that will fly to heaven with a request in its beak to destroy the castle. I will bite the foot of the owl, which will cause the bird to drop the letter. Catch the letter and no one will be able to destroy the castle."

Kim Quy asked the king to pretend to be a traveler who desired to sleep at the hostel. The king left Kim Quy close to the door.

Ngô Không, the owner said, "This hostel has many spirits that kill guests. You should not stay back and since it is dark already, you should go somewhere else to avoid trouble."

The king smiled and answered, "Each person has a fate. Personally, I am not afraid of spirits."

At night, spirits and ghosts came at the door and shouted, "Open the door now!"

Kim Quy retorted, "Since the door is locked, what would you want to do?"

The ghosts transformed themselves into various forms in an attempt to harass the guests, but could not get in.

When the rooster began crowing, the ghosts disappeared. Kim Quy asked the king to chase them all the way to Thất Diệu Mountain where they hid. The king then returned to the hostel.

In the morning the owner brought an acolyte to help him bury the guests killed during the night. Seeing the king still alive, he smiled, although he did not say a word. As he approached the king, he said, "Sir, you must be a saint, please help the lowly people."

"Kill the white rooster and use it as offering to heaven, and all the ghosts will disappear," the king answered.

When Ngô Không killed the rooster, his daughter fell ill and died. The king asked people to dig in Thất Diệu Mountain to look for an ancient musical instrument and a skeleton, to burn them and to throw their ashes into the river.

It was almost evening when the king and Kim Quy went to Việt Thương Mountain. The ghost had transformed into an owl that flew to a tree holding a letter in its beak.

Kim Quy transformed itself into a mouse that bit the bird's foot. The letter fell down and when picked up by the king, had been eaten in half by worms.

IX. Lĩnh Nam Chích Quái

From then on, the ghosts never disturbed the building of the castle again.

Kim Quy stayed with the king for three years before taking leave.

"Thanks to you, the castle is sturdy; if any external problem occurred, how should I handle it?" the king asked.

"Since you asked, I would not regret it." Kim Quy removed one of his nails and gave it to the king. "If you have any problem, use it and you will encounter no problem." He then left.

The king asked Cao Lỗ to make a bow using the nail as a trigger. When Triệu Đà brought his army to take over the country, the king used the magic bow to shoot at them. Triệu Đà's army disbanded and set camp at Trâu Sơn Mountain. Knowing the king had a magic bow, he asked for peace. Pleased, the king divided the country and gave Triệu Đà the upper half from Tiêu Giang River upward while the king controlled the lower half.

A little later, Triệu Đà told his son Trọng Thủy to ask for the hands of Mỵ Châu, the king's daughter. The king did not know about Triệu Đà's dishonesty. Trọng Thủy told Mỵ Châu to show him the magic bow; he made an imitation and stole the nail. He then went north to see his parents.

"Although I miss you, I also miss my parents dearly. Let me go and see them; when I return, how do I know you would be there?" Trọng Thủy asked.

"I am a woman who, facing a separation, cannot control her feelings. I often carry with me a pillow stuffed with goose feathers, which I will spread at each intersection. You will know where to find me," Mỵ Châu answered.

Trọng Thủy bid farewell and brought the bow to Triệu Đà. Pleased, Đà immediately raised his army to fight the king. The latter asked himself, "Is he not afraid of my magic bow?"

It was not until Triệu Đà's army came close that he took out his bow and realized that the magic nail was gone. His soldiers panicked and ran away.

The king took Mỵ Châu on his horse and rode south toward the seaside. When he arrived there, there was no boat to take him away.

"Is heaven forgetting me? Will my helper show up?" the king asked.

Kim Quy showed up and yelled, "The one behind you is your real enemy. Kill her and I will save you."

The king took his sword and beheaded Mỵ Châu.

She looked up and prayed, "I'm a woman. If I betrayed my father, may I become ashes when I die. But if I have been faithful but led into error by someone else, may I turn into a diamond that will rinse my honor."

Mỵ Châu died at the seaside. Her blood was consumed by clams that eventually bore diamonds.

Riding on Kim Quy's shell, the king was taken to Mộ Dạ Mountain for safety.

Triệu Đà's soldiers arrived at the seaside, and found only Mỵ Châu's body. Trọng Thủy buried her at Loa Thành. He became remorseful when he visited places where Mỵ Châu dressed herself and took her bath; in despair, he jumped into a well in a suicidal move. A long time later, it was found that diamonds collected at Đông Hải seaside, when washed with the well's water, gave the shiniest, brightest color.

Comments There are two tales in this legend. The first tale relates to the building of the Cổ Loa castle with the help of Kim Quy, the turtle. The second one deals with Mỵ Châu, whose betrayal caused her father's empire to collapse.

10. The Tale of Man Nương (A Man)[25]

Under the Han dynasty, in the Phúc Nham pagoda was a bonze named Gia La Đồ Lê who came from the west. He preached standing on one leg, and followers came by in droves to listen to him. They called him Master.

There was also a girl named Man Nương, an orphan from a poor family; a fervent practitioner, she was relegated to the kitchen because of her stuttering and inability to follow others during prayer times. She cleaned vegetables, and cooked for the bonzes and guests who visited the pagoda.

It was May and nights were shorter. Man Nương was busy cooking for the bonzes who were still praying. While waiting, she fell asleep at the doorstep. When the bonzes completed their prayers, they returned to their rooms. Bonze Đồ Lê stepped across her; she woke up and became pregnant. Ashamed of herself, she left the pagoda when she was three months pregnant. Đồ Lê also left for another pagoda.

After giving birth to a daughter, she looked for the bonze to turn the infant over to him. At night, he came to a huge banyan tree at the bifurcation of a river, set his daughter there, and said, "Take care of this infant and you will become a Buddha."

Bonze Đồ Lê and Man Nương parted ways. He gave her a baton and told her, "Take this baton. Whenever there is drought, wave it on the ground and water will spring out and save people."

Man Nương returned to the pagoda like before. When drought came, she waved her baton and water came out, benefiting people a lot.

When Man Nương was 80 years of age, the banyan tree fell into the water, drifted toward the pagoda and remained there. When people in the surrounding area used their axes to chop up the tree, all the axes broke down. Three hundred people tried to move it, but to no avail.

When Man Nương washed her hands in the water, she also tried to move the tree; as it moved easily toward the river edge, people became surprised and told her to haul it to the ground for woodworkers to carve four Buddha sculptures. When they hit the middle-part of the trunk where the infant was located, they noticed that the area had become calcified. On impact, their tools broke. They decided to throw the calcified section of the tree into the river; it gave off sparks and took a long time to sink. All the workers immediately died. The villagers asked Man Nương to pray for them, and fishermen went down the water to retrieve the calcified log. They took it to the pagoda, smeared a layer of gold on it and set it on the altar.

Bonze Đồ Lê named the four sculptures (goddesses): Pháp Vân (Dharma Cloud), Pháp Vũ (Dharma Rain), Pháp Lôi (Dharma Thunder), and Pháp Điện (Dharma Lightning). People came by to venerate these Buddha sculptures.

Comments 1. This is one of the first reported tales related to Vietnamese Buddhism, about the union of Man Nương (the mysterious female power of earth symbolizing the indigenous agricultural culture) with the Buddhist monk Đồ Lê (or Khâu Đà La, representing the new power, Buddhism).[26] This led to the building of the four temples dedicated to the four goddesses. The Pháp Vân Buddha who resides in the Pháp Vân temple is the most important of the four, since the Buddha was escorted to the National Temple where ritual prayers for rain took place whenever there was drought.

2. The tale also explains how Man Nương, after her death, became the "Mother Buddha," a unique characteristic of Vietnamese Buddhism. The union between the virgin young girl and the monk is symbolically described as "he stepped across her and she became pregnant."

11. Tản Viên Mountain[27]

Tản Viên Mountain—a chain of three mountains with dome-shaped tops—lay on the west side of Thăng Long City and was home to the extremely responsive mountain god. People prayed to it when drought or floods occurred, and the god responded immediately.

Hùng Vương XVIII had a beautiful daughter named Mỵ Nương. King Thục Phán asked for her hand in marriage, but King Hùng Vương turned him down.

A few days later, the spirit of the mountain and the sea spirit came to ask for her hand. Hùng Vương talked to them. The mountain spirit showed the mountain that opened and closed easily: one would not have problems getting in and out. The sea spirit blew air in the sky, producing clouds and rain. The king said, "You both have divine powers, but I have only one daughter. Therefore, whoever brings wedding gifts first will get Mỵ Nương's hand."

The next morning, the mountain spirit brought diamonds, gold, silver, and other gifts to the king.

The sea spirit came later. Not seeing Mỵ Nương, he gathered all the sea animals to get ready to fight back. The mountain spirit blocked the Từ Liêm River. The sea spirit opened a series of rivers from Lý Nhân to Hát Giang into Đà Giang River to get to the backside of Tản Viên Mountain. It opened Tiêu Tích Giang to move in front of the mountain. Winds and rain fell, obscuring the view, and water levels rose to fight against the mountain spirit. People living in the mountain set up a fence to fight back, beating on drums and yelling for help.

Each year, the fight recurred in July and September. People living at the base of the mountain suffered from rains, winds, and flooding and lost their harvests. People said that the mountain and sea were fighting each other.

Comments The spirit of Tản Viên is one of the Four Immortals venerated in North Vietnam. The South only recognizes the spirit of Phù Đổng. As a newly conquered land, it does not acknowledge the same cults as the ancient north.

12. The Trưng Sisters[28]

According to historic record, the Trưng sisters were from the Hùng lineage and the Lạc lineage. The elder sister was named Trắc, the younger one Nhị. They were from the subprefecture of Mê Linh, prefecture of Phong Châu, province of Giao Châu. Trắc married Thi Sách, from the subprefecture of Châu Điên. She was a faithful, courageous, and intelligent person.

At that time, Governor Tô Định was a vicious and greedy person who caused people to suffer a lot. To avenge her husband's death at the hands of Định, she and her sister raised an army to fight Định and surround Giao Châu. The Cửu Chân, Nhật Nam, and Hợp Phố provinces supported them. The two sisters pacified 65 forts in Lĩnh Ngoại and established themselves as queens with their capital at Ô Diên.

Tô Định ran away to Nam Hải. The Han king ordered Mã Viện and Lưu Long to replace Định. When the Chinese army arrived to Lang Bạc, Trưng Trắc fought back. The following year, seeing that the Chinese were stronger than her army, she retreated to Cấm Khê. The Chinese chased and defeated her army. The sisters died in battle. Some records mentioned that they escaped to Hy Sơn Mountain and disappeared.

People built a temple in their honor at the mouth of the Hạt Giang River. They were responsive to those who prayed to them. Under King Lý Anh Tông, there was a great drought. He asked Cảm Thỉnh to pray for rain. One day, rain poured down, cooling the countryside. The king went out to see the rain and fell asleep. He saw in his dream two ladies wearing green outfits with red belts and riding steel horses. He asked and they answered, "We are the Trưng sisters, making rain at the request of heaven." He wanted to ask more but the ladies held their hands out to tell him to stop asking. Once awakened, he told people to upgrade the ladies' temple and to bring offerings. Later, the ladies appeared again in the king's dream, asking him to build another temple at Đồng Nhân. He obeyed and promoted them as Chaste and Responsive Ladies.

Comments This LNCQ tale contains more details about the Trưng sisters than the VDULT. It, however, ranks the Trưng sisters very low on the scale, well beneath the marsh boy.

13. Tô Lịch River[29]

The Chinese Tang king sent Cao Biền as military commander of Giao Châu to fight the Nam Chiếu army. On his return, he was named governor of the province of Tĩnh Hải in Lĩnh Nam. Biền, knowing geomancy, chose the right place to build the town of Đại La, on the west side of Lô Giang.

A branch of the Lô Giang came down from the northwest, moved south, and coursed around Đại La before draining into the main river.

It was June, and since the river level was high, Biền sailed over the branch of the Lô Giang. About a mile downstream, he saw a smiling and laughing old man of unusual appearance and long hair bathing in the middle of the river. When Biền enquired about his identity, the man said, "I'm Tô Lịch."

"Where do you live?" Biền asked.

"Right in this river," the man answered.

After finishing these words, he hit the water with his hands, causing it to spring up everywhere. There was no trace of the man. Biền knew he dealt with a spirit and called the river Tô Lịch River.

One morning, as Biền stood on the edge of the Lô Giang river on the west side of Đại La, he saw the wind suddenly blowing, causing strong ripples on the water, clouds to move rapidly, and the sky to become dark. He saw an unusual person standing above the water, with a yellow outfit and a purple hat, holding in his hand a gold bar that lit up part of the sky. Upset, Biền wanted to put a curse on the spirit. At night, in his dream he saw the spirit telling him, "Do not try to put a curse on me. I'm the spirit at Long Đỗ, the elder of all the spirits. Since you have built a fortress here, I'm here to see it. I'm not afraid of curses."

Biền was scared.

The following morning, Biền did some incantations and prepared his curse. That night, thunder struck, winds blew and rain fell, the ground shook. In an instant, the silver wires used for the curse broke open and turned into ashes. Scared, Biền said, "This country has strong spirits. It is not healthy to stay here a long time."

Later, the king recalled Biền, who was killed. Cao Tàm was sent to replace him.

X. Other Northern Legends

These legends were recorded in the nineteenth century by Antony Landes, a French official who was working in the Huế area (present-day central Vietnam). His book was published in Paris in 1886, only 27 years after the French landed in South Vietnam.[1] This was a remarkable feat for a foreigner who did not even speak Vietnamese. Landes' goal at that time was to collect these legends in order to understand the socio-economic habits, traditions, and ideas of the Vietnamese.

The majority of the legends came from the North (Tonquin) and center (Annam) of Vietnam because his informers lived in these regions.[2] These legends, therefore, could be labeled as nineteenth-century legends (date of collection) or northern legends to indicate their origin. One could note the differences between these northern legends and those described later as southern legends.[3]

Landes did have difficulty in having the legends explained to him. When he asked questions to try to better understand the language, the informer would stop and say nothing else; when pressed further, he would repeat the legends from the beginning instead of explaining the facts involved.[4]

Compared to earlier legends, the nineteen-century legends deal with ghosts, spirits, mandarins, and Buddhist monks who were representative of the society at that time. Because the country had stabilized politically and learned its identity, there seemed to be no need for heroes to show the way: this explains the low number of stories about heroes and gods fighting for the independence of Vietnam and more stories about mandarins, ghosts, and Buddhist monks. Particularly, there were no further stories about kings bestowing privileges or titles to spirits or heroes and no new temples erected to spirits. That era was long gone.

Nine of the 127 tales are translated and reviewed by the author. This sample of tales reveals the breadth of northern legends.

1. The Two Exam Laureates[5]

Under the Lê dynasty, two brothers lived in Nghệ An. Their parents were poor and gathered wood from the forests to sell for a living. Villagers treated them harshly and did not like them because of their poverty. When the brothers grew up, they both took the national exam and succeeded. The king congratulated them and sent them home escorted by soldiers with horses and elephants. Along the way, local authorities went out to meet and greet them. When they arrived home, villagers had to throw celebrations and parties for them for three consecutive days. Even those who disliked them in the past had to welcome them with pomp.[6]

When the celebrations ended, the mother of the laureates said, "When we were poor, no one acknowledged us. We had to work all day long in the forests and at night officials made us stand watch at the village's gate.[7] If we missed it, they beat us. We were miserable. But when our sons passed the exam, they all celebrated. We have to tell our sons to be nice to those who cared for us in the past. But they need to take revenge on those who had made our lives difficult. If they could kill them, I would be satisfied."

It turns out that the two boys were spirits who were sent to that family because of their virtue. As soon as the mother uttered these words, all her merits disappeared. A spirit who was passing by reported to the Jade Emperor what he had heard. The emperor called back the laureates and they died on the spot. Before their death, a spirit appeared to the mother in her dream and told her the reason why she was punished.[8]

A temple has been erected to honor the two laureates, who have manifested their power on various occasions.

Comments One could not blame a person for talking about taking revenge on those who had caused harm in the past. But once the lady had spoken these words, all the merits she had accumulated over the years suddenly vanished. This is a typical Buddhist thought. For the common people who have been mistreated either by the government or their employers and not been able to fight back, the thought of divine justice around the corner ready to hand down reward or punishment must be soothing. This lady, in her rage, however, did not recognize that she had already been rewarded by divine powers with two smart boys who should have soothed her pains and rage.

X. Other Northern Legends

2. Under the Protection of Quan Đệ[9]

In the province of Hanoi lived a young girl who had lost her parents and worked as a seamstress. In the market one day, she saw pictures of Quan Đệ on sale.[10] Although she did not know who he was, she thought of him as a god who deserved to be venerated. She bought one of his pictures and brought it home. She gave him daily rice offerings and if she had something good, she would offer it to him too.

One day, she traveled to the village of Nhơn Lý, province of Hải Dương. That village venerated a pig spirit. On the last day of each year, villagers would bring a young girl to the *đình* as offering to the spirit.[11] In the middle of the night, the spirit would appear and the girl would die. Without offering, the village was severely punished.

The young seamstress happened to be in the village that fatal day. The village leaders deceived her into working in the *đình*. They left her there during the night. The young girl put the image of Quan Đệ up and gave her daily offering. When night came, the spirit showed up ready to molest her. Quan Đệ jumped on him and cut him into three pieces. Blood filled the whole floor of the *đình*. Quan Đệ appeared to the girl in her dream and said, "I like you for the devotion you have in me; that is why I have saved you tonight." Having said these words, he disappeared.

In the morning, when villagers brought a casket to bury the girl as was the routine, they were surprised to see her alive with blood on the floor. She told them how Quan Đệ had saved her and they accepted Quan Đệ as their savior. They destroyed the spirit's temple and erected another one to Quan Đệ.

Comments This village venerated a pig as guardian. Once it was toppled down, the village picked the winner as the new guardian. There was just no methodical selection, no thorough screening.

3. The Three Men-Snakes[12]

Under the Lý (1010–1225), in the village of Chi Châu, province of Hà Tĩnh, lived a man named Trần Thế Vinh and his wife Nguyễn Thị Thoại. They were over 40 years of age and had lived together for 15 years without having a child.

One fall day, during a heavy storm, the wife went out to collect water coming down from her roof. She saw a star falling into her vase. Astonished, she called her husband and told him the story. They decided to keep mum and drink the water. She subsequently became pregnant; but three years later, she had not delivered her baby, despite taking one remedy after another.

She finally delivered three blue eggs. Surprised, her husband decided to keep quiet. Ten months later, three snakes hatched out: one with a red head and blue body, the second with a blue head and spotted body, and the third with a black head and white body. They were about two feet long and grew rapidly. They followed their father everywhere. One day, as he cutting grass in the field, he accidentally cut the tail of one of the snakes. Blood came out and the snake turned into a 12-foot tall man. He said, "My brothers and I are celestial spirits. We have committed a mistake and were sent down here to protect your country. My brothers will stay here while I will return to heaven with the help of a storm."

The other snakes stayed back. Sometimes they transformed into young men to help fight the Chinese, whose attacks were always turned back. The king, therefore, conferred on them the title of Generals of the Army. Later, a temple was been erected in their honor and they always manifested their power.

Comments This is the story of three snake-spirits who were sent to earth to redeem their own mistakes.

4. The Fisherman of the Celestial Lake[13]

In the province of Quảng Bình is a lake named Celestial Lake. One could go around it in one day. In the village of Đông Hải lived a poor fisherman who only knew sea fishing. One day, he decided to go fishing in a lake to see if he could catch anything.

He arrived early and for a few hours tried but could not catch a single fish. Tired, he went into the shade to rest. Then, he saw two giants dressed in red with turbans on their heads coming out of the water. Each one held a sword. After looking around, they reentered into the water. Ten other giants came out and made the tour of the lake. Scared, the fisherman made himself small while continuing to watch. Then, 30 boats with dragons sculpted on the prows and colorful flags emerged from the lake, along with a golden boat. Amidst the singing and rowing, the boats reached shore. Soldiers held three palanquins to pick up the lords.

The curious fisherman stood up to look at the cortege. Seeing him, the lords sent soldiers to catch him.

"What are you doing here?" they asked.

"I was fishing here this morning. Being tired, I went to rest in the shade and I saw these two giants coming out of the lake. I was so afraid that I did not move. Since I have seen this unusual spectacle, I just came out to look at it."

"I'll forgive you and let you go. But you must not tell anyone about what has happened here. For security reasons, you must swallow this sword. You'll live 100 years if you do not say anything. Otherwise, the sword will come out of your mouth and you'll die. On the side, I'll give you a copper pan; three times a day, all you have to do is pour water and the rice will be there. You do not have to go fishing any longer."

The lord then had the soldiers who made the rounds decapitated for their negligence.

The fisherman returned home. From that time onward, he had enough food to eat and his life became better. He lived until he was 90 years of age without telling anyone about his encounter. One day during a family reunion, he thought to himself that he had lived a good and long life, was rich and had a large family. That was more than any person could expect, and he did not need to live any longer. He then decided to tell his story to his family and should he die, so be it. As soon as he completed his storytelling, the sword came out and he died on the spot.

From that time onward, the Celestial Lake was taken into veneration and no one dared to fish there.

5. *Legend Of Princess Liễu*[14]

Under Lê Thái Tổ's reign,[15] princess Liễu, daughter of the Celestial Emperor, was sent into exile for bad behavior. She transformed herself into a beautiful girl who opened a tavern at the foot of the Đèo Ngang Pass in central Vietnam. Travelers often stopped by the tavern to have a drink or to tease her. A few would have liked to go farther, but when they returned home, they either died or became crazy. Lê Thái Tổ's son and crown prince was a womanizer. Having heard of the beautiful girl at the Đèo Ngang Pass, he decided to try his luck.

The princess knew everything. When the prince arrived, he met and talked to her. He found her beautiful and lively. At night, he told her he would like to sleep close to her, being far away from home. She agreed.

She retired into her room while he stayed in the tavern room. He came close to the partition and began flirting with her. She cheerfully responded to him.

Finding himself alone, he went into her room, but found it empty. The princess had made herself invisible. He did not know where she was and began complaining.

She told herself, "Although this man is the king's son, he is not wise. He cannot distinguish a divine person from a vulgar lady. I have to punish him." She took a monkey from the wood, transformed it into a beautiful girl and sent her to see the prince. The latter, happy to see the beautiful girl, took her hands and asked, "Who are you?"

"My big sister sends me to take care of the tavern."

The prince lifted her up to take her into the room, but the girl transformed herself into a large snake that was throwing flames. The prince got scared and left. He wept on his way home. At home, he fell sick and began laughing like a mad person. No remedy could cure him.

The mother said to her husband, "No remedy has cured our son. I believe he has been under someone's charm. Let's look for the eight Kim Căng's amulets,[16] which hopefully will help him out."

They made him drink the amulets of the "eight Kim Căng" and he was cured in three days.

"There was a beautiful girl at the Đèo Ngang Pass. I flirted with her and she made me sick. I believe she is an evil spirit," the prince explained to his father.

The king asked his ministers for advice. They told him he would need the help of "the eight Kim Căng" to fight the devil spirit. The eight Buddha statues were transported to the capital, where the king asked for their support. They created a heavy thunderstorm during which they fought against the princess. For three days, the sky and ground shook at Đèo Ngang Pass. Finally, the eight Buddhas brought Liễu to the king, who asked who she was.

"I am the Celestial Emperor's daughter, who has been punished to this earth. Having seen men behaving badly, I have decided to punish them."

"Take these three gold chaplets and stop tormenting men. Enter a pagoda and follow the Buddhist law," said the king.

The king also elevated the eight Buddhas to Supreme Spirits.

Comments This is the first legend dealing with Princess *Liễu Hạnh*, who later became one of the Four Immortals venerated in North Vietnam. It is specified that she was the daughter of the Celestial Emperor.

X. Other Northern Legends

6. The Crocodile and the Old Monkey[17]

A crocodile befriended an old monkey. The latter lived in the trees while the former lurked in the river. The crocodile wanted to eat the monkey. It said, "Someone has invited me to a feast on the other side of the river. Do you want to come?"

"How could I if I cannot swim?" answered the monkey.

"Stay on my back and I will take you to the other side," the crocodile responded.

The monkey jumped on the back of the crocodile and the two went away. In the middle of the river, the crocodile said, "I have heard that eating a monkey's entrails allows one to live up to 100 years. That is why I have misled you and brought you here so I can eat you."

"Why did you not tell me beforehand? Since you have told me we are going to a feast, I have left everything over there so that I could have an empty stomach and eat better. Let's go back and I'll give you everything you need," answered the monkey.

The crocodile agreed to turn around and took the monkey to the river edge. The monkey quickly jumped into a tree and said, "They say you are dumb and you lie. Do I have the heart to let you eat me?"

Comments This is a nice legend about the monkey and the crocodile. Crocodiles were prevalent in the southern swamps centuries ago. Still present when the French arrived in Saigon in 1859, they are now almost extinct, except in crocodile farms where they are raised for their skins and meat.

7. A Bonze Transformed into a Chalk Pot[18]

A poor thief decided to join a pagoda to make penitence. The superior, finding him ignorant, put him in charge of keeping the fire alive. Because the pagoda was isolated, getting a new fire burning would be difficult.

The novice bonze did such an excellent job that the pagoda was never out of light. One night, a bad bonze decided to harm him by extinguishing the fire. When the novice bonze woke up, he realized the fire was gone. He ran to the next village to look for fire. Halfway out, he met a tiger that blocked his path.

He told the tiger, "You can eat me if you want. But let me take care of the pagoda's fire first and I'll come back and you can eat me."

The tiger agreed and let him go. After taking care of the fire, the bonze told the superior he had to meet a tiger.

The Tiger then told him, "I'm old and do not have any teeth left. Your bones will be very hard for me. Climb up this tree and let yourself fall down in order to cause your bones to break." The novice bonze climbed up the tree. Heaven and Buddha had pity on the brave bonze, caught him in the middle of the fall, and made him a Buddha.

The bad bonze, seeing how easily his colleague had achieved nirvana, asked the superior to let him take care of the fire at the pagoda. One night, after letting the fire extinguish itself, he then ran to look for more fire. He met the tiger, to whom he made the same request as the first bonze, and came back to be eaten by the tiger. He too jumped out of the tree, but no one stopped him midway. He broke his bones and was transformed into a chalk pot.

It has been said that because he had a bad heart (literally belly), he was transformed into a chalk pot so that people could always check his belly.[19]

Comments This is one of the legends about Buddhist monks in Vietnam. A good monk was rewarded and a bad one punished.

8. *The Pig King*[20]

There was an orphan whose family name was Pig. From the forest, he came down to a village where he was hired by a mandarin. One day, the boy was told to wash the mandarin's legs, but not to injure three red spots that were located there.[21] Otherwise, he would kill all the orphan's family.

The boy told him, "If you have three spots, I have nine. I'm worth more than you."

"If he has nine spots, he is destined to be king," thought the mandarin.

He asked the maid to prepare a poison to get rid of the boy. She, however, had pity for the boy and uttered as if she were talking to the pigs, "Pig. O pig. If you eat, you'll die. If you don't, you won't die."

The boy understood and asked her for the meaning. She refused, but told him, "If you promise to marry me when you become king, I'll tell you."

"When I become king, come to me with your hair falling down to your shoulders, and I'll recognize you and take you as wife," Pig answered and left the house.

Afraid, he went to a pagoda where he was told to wash the Buddha statue. While washing it, he asked the statue to raise its arm, and it did; to raise its leg, and it did. One day, he forgot to ask it to drop the arm down and returned the statue to the altar with the arm raised. The monk came by and asked him why the Buddha's arm was in an upright position. He told him he forgot to ask the statue to drop it down.

The monk realized that the boy must be a king because the statue listened to him. He went to the authorities to have him arrested. But the boy escaped in time.

He was then hired as a gardener whose job was to water the trees. Noting that the areca trees were similar in size, he told the trees, "This one is the father; this one the son." And the trees changed in size, one taller than the other. The owner came by and asked him why the trees were of different sizes. The boy retorted, "I ordered one to be tall, the other short." When the owner asked him to return the trees to their usual sizes, the boy said, "The sage has only one word. I will not retract my order."

The owner wanted to beat him, but he ran away. Tired, he did not know where to go and just slipped into a house. Unable to find any sleeping area, he pulled a statue off a table, placed it on the ground, and made himself comfortable on the table. He got out of the house early. When the owner woke up and saw the statue of a spirit on the floor, he attempted to put it back in its place, and it refused. Through a medium, it declared, "The king put me on the ground, I'll stay there." People in the house understood that the predestined king had spent the night on the table.

Pig revolted against the authorities and was made king. A woman came by with her hair down. He recognized her as his wife.

9. The Celestial Emperor and the Poor Man[22]

There was a poor man whose family had been poor for three generations. A Vietnamese saying goes, "No one is rich or destitute for more than three generations." But this man wondered whether his case was the exception to the rule. He sought to raise the question to the Celestial Emperor who lived on an island.

On his way to see the emperor and running out of food, he knocked on the door of a rich man, who asked him the reason for his travel. The rich man said, "I'll give you money, if you would ask the emperor a question for me. I'm rich and have done good deeds. And yet, I do not have a boy, only a girl who has been mute since birth. Ask him the reason for this misfortune."

The man gave him food and money and the poor man set back on the road. Running out of food again, he entered the house of another rich man to ask for help. The latter had beautiful trees planted in his garden for the last 30 years; however they did not bear any fruit. He gave the poor man food and told him to ask the emperor for an answer.

The poor man arrived at the seaside and found no means of getting to the island. A turtle would give him a ride if he asked the emperor why, after having been penitent for a thousand years, he was still a turtle. The poor man agreed and the turtle took him to the island.

The poor man bowed in front of the emperor and told him, "I have arrived on this island thanks to the help of a turtle. He has requested me to ask why he is still condemned to be a turtle after a thousand years of penitence."

"This turtle has a jewel with him. As long as he doesn't give it to another person, he will remain a turtle," the emperor responded.

"A rich man who despite doing innumerable good deeds wonders why he does not have a son, but only a mute daughter," the poor man asked.

"The destiny of that girl is to marry a mandarin. As soon as she sees her future husband, she will start talking," the emperor said.

The poor man then asked why a certain gardener has only sterile trees. The emperor retorted that the man had great wealth buried in his garden. Once it was removed, the trees would bear fruit.

The poor man would have liked to enquire about what was bothering him, but the emperor got mad and said, "I come here to this deserted area to rest and people still bother me." He left for heaven and our poor man was left with answers to every question but his own.

The turtle gave the poor man a ride and the latter gave him his answer. The turtle thought that since no one knew about the jewel, the poor man must have told the truth. He regurgitated the jewel and gave it to the poor man. The turtle was immediately transformed into a man. And the two departed.

The poor man arrived at the gardener's house and gave an account of his mission. A lot of wealth was dug out of the garden and the gardener gave it all to the poor man. The latter accepted only half. Now richer, he settled down and began to study. A few years later, he passed the exam and was promoted to mandarin. On his way home, he stopped by the house of the rich man to give him an account of his mission. As soon as he finished

X. Other Northern Legends 87

his report, the daughter recovered her speech. Thankful of the deed, the rich man gave the mandarin his daughter in marriage.

Comments This is the tale of a poor man who decided to find out from the Celestial Emperor the reason behind his poverty. Along the way, he found other people who had more problems than he did. By helping them out of their miseries, he was rewarded for his deeds and became rich. This Asian legend carries the same universal message as any other legend: help people and you will help yourself.

Part Three
Southern Legends

XI. Introduction

Any country with a history stretching for more than one millennium will have a wide range of folktales that can easily be subdivided into medieval and modern. Since contemporary authors prefer to write about modern rather than medieval tales, because the latter do not fit into the rapidly moving and changing modern culture, comparison between the two types of tales is not possible.

Royall Tyler tries to bridge that gap by writing about medieval folktales in his *Japanese Tales* and briefly comparing his work with Fanny Hagin Mayer's. The latter, *Ancient Tales in Modern Japan*, despite its title, details mainly modern tales with a few medieval tales. This suggests that there are very few books that deal only with medieval tales. According to Tyler, medieval collections are not "folk literature,"[1] because they catered to a very select group of highly literate writers and readers. Many stories can thus be accurately dated because their authors were interested in accuracy.

In this book, tales are collected from the fourteenth, fifteenth, nineteenth, twentieth, and twenty-first centuries, along with the more recent and often poorly known war and post-war tales. Throughout this book, readers will see how Vietnamese tales have evolved and changed with time, how new tales are made and reworked, and how unknown figures became new deities and acquired new followers. They will be able to compare Vietnamese tales to those of surrounding countries—China, Japan, and India—and see the different ranges of topics described in these countries. Overall, this work is probably one of the few longitudinal works on folktales in the world.

In the beginning, legends blend themselves into historical accounts. Everything defied the norm of reality because that was the way that legends worked. Gods and goddesses abounded: they belonged to a special realm where humans were too small to be included. As gods, they did things that were magical, grandiose, and unheard of or thought of within the human world.

It was the same in Vietnam at the beginning of times. The fairy Âu Cơ was described as having given birth to a sac containing 100 eggs that eventually hatched into 100 children (southern tale # 1). The genie of Phù Đổng was a giant who rode a gigantic steel horse and slayed one thousand soldiers at a time with one swing of his sword (southern tale # 4). Although the gods of the mountains and the seas lived among humans, they secluded themselves inside their vast kingdoms, which no human was allowed or dared to enter (southern tale #2). They had great powers and spoke human language too. With time, they retreated back into their realms and left the world to humans. Then began the slow road into history, where everything was brought back to reality: it was the beginning of the realm of human beings, these Lilliputian individuals who dared to take center stage and displace the giant gods.

Historical legends bear a strong resemblance to history because they stand at the borders between history and legend. In ancient Vietnam, since writing was neither codified nor well known by many people, only a few lettered men knew the language and writing and kept their secret for themselves. They behaved like witches who brew special recipes or recite strange incantations known only to themselves. Oral stories were therefore prevalent, which made it easier for people to embellish or distort facts for whatever reason. They are part of the ancient culture. Ly Tế Xuyên in 1329 wrote some of these tales down for the first time in his *Việt Điển U Linh Tập*—an important source of the early history of Vietnam, which is discussed in chapter VIII. These medieval stories were used to educate people, give them some background about their culture, stimulate their heroism, urge them to sacrifice for the good of the nation, and teach them civic duties. They were the media of the times, crude certainly, but nonetheless a unique way to educate and inform people, the majority of whom were illiterate.

Heroes were placed on a pedestal and rapidly enshrined and venerated. With time, new attributes or heroic deeds were embroidered into the overall story, which gave these heroes a grandiose new look. From men or women with earthly deeds, they acquired new powers that propelled them into the realm of genies, then gods. Their shrines became bigger: crowds that visited them, and asked for favors. Chú Đồng Tử or the Marsh Boy was one example (southern tale # 7). He was a poor, insignificant fisherman who could barely feed and clothe himself. His only achievement was to put himself in the path of a princess who married him. Over the centuries, he displaced her and was given one godly attribute after another. He became, through the adulation and veneration of his followers, the genie of North Viet-

XI. Introduction

namese agriculture and one of the Four Immortals, although he was never as heroic or fearless than the Trưng sisters (southern tale # 5).

Modern tales, on the other hand, vary in scope and topics. They deal with the broad range of down-to-earth issues that face human beings and can be categorized under five headings: historical, traditional, social legends, animal-related tales, and legends pertinent to the highlanders who are culturally different from the lowland Vietnamese. Gods and heroes no longer play an important role in human behavior and are set aside.

Historical legends are used to reinforce and/or document the historical deeds of important personalities (Lạc Long Quân, Trưng sisters, Lady Triệu). Since legends are not historical records, they do not pretend to provide accurate historical details. Generals, heroes, and men and women of courage were elevated to the rank of spirits and bestowed titles and temples where they were honored. People pray to and call on them for help in case of need. The spirits in return protect the people from their enemies and forces of nature. Should the spirits respond in kind, they were called *linh thiên* (responsive) and could be elevated to the rank of god or goddess.

Animals play an important role in Vietnamese legends. Besides being funny, they think and act like humans. They voice their opinions, and even argue with the Jade Emperor (*"The Toad Is Heaven's Uncle,"* southern tale # 11). By making them in the image of men, they could stand in for them and teach a lesson here and there without antagonizing anyone.

Readers may want to know why mosquitoes—these annoying little insects—buzz around humans all the time. They just dive on their skin or irritate them with their strident sounds. Readers might like to know why frogs croak all the time, especially when rain is scarce. Why is the buffalo a resilient animal and why do tigers have stripes? Why do sand crabs—tiny crabs readers could see on the beach—spend their time digging tunnels? They are all part of Vietnamese legends.

Vietnam is traditionally the land of fairies. Its history began with the union of a fairy and the Dragon Lord. From then on, encounters and unions between fairies and men were not infrequent: they are described in "The Land of Bliss" and "The Fairy's Portrait" (southern tales # 27 and # 28). Fairies—idyllic creatures who appeared out of the blue—attracted men like bees. But unlike western romances where couples met and got married right away, Vietnamese fairies are reserved people: they are shy and would disappear before coming back another time to meet the person they love. Although fairies and humans could love each other at first sight, it did not seem right for them to be together right away. Encounters between princesses and commoners do occur, although they are not frequent: "Tiên Dung and the Marsh Boy" is one of the rare examples.

Although Vietnamese society is deeply influenced by Confucian, Buddhist, and Taoist concepts—which have been discussed earlier—peasants' thinking is rather simple. The legend "A Devoted Daughter-in-Law" explains the deep Confucian roots that direct these people's lives (southern tale # 48). But they also believe in Buddhist karma, reincarnation, and the law of action-reaction, stressing that a good deed leads to good results, while a bad deed often ends in disaster.

Peasants are practical and pragmatic people: they just want to survive. Oftentimes, they are so poor they cannot afford more than one set of clothing per person. Worse, sometimes husband and wife or father and son share the same pair of pants. If one needs to go outdoors, the other has to stay home. The marsh boy similarly shares one pair of pants with his father. Within this poor economic environment, it is difficult for anyone to entertain complex theological or religious thoughts.

The Vietnamese, some more than others, believe that the world is populated by spirits—some benevolent and some bad. Spirits that represent the supernatural forces of the realm are much stronger and more powerful than human beings. People, therefore, feel the need to be protected by good spirits to counteract the effects of the bad ones. Veneration of spirits remains an important part of Vietnamese culture.

There are wandering spirits of those who have passed away but have not been appeased or received appropriate burial rites, or whose lives have been suddenly cut short by wars, accidents. The two-decade Vietnam War, with more than three million civilian and military deaths, has generated a multitude of spirits that need to be propitiated or guided back to their relatives.[2]

Spirits fought against each other; they also conspired against human beings for some reason or another. The thousand-year-old white chicken that prevented the building of Cổ Loa citadel is an example of a bad spirit: although it did not harm people, it caused a jinx on a major building project: the construction of a citadel (southern tale # 3). The golden turtle is, on the other hand, a good spirit: it neutralized the work of the chicken and allowed the construction to move forward. Evil spirits, although low-ranking, are more common than good ones. They cause most of the daily problems in the lives of people. They are hypersensitive, vengeful and capricious.[3]

Then there are goddesses, who are the new phenomenon in today's Vietnam after years of religious repression by Hanoi. In the Mekong Delta,

XI. Introduction

three goddesses are being venerated: the *Bà Đen* or Black Lady of Tây Ninh, the *Dinh Cô* in Long Hải close to Vũng Tàu, and the *Bà Chúa Xứ* or the Lady of the Realm in Châu Đốc. To see their impact on people's minds, one just has to look at the size of the *Bà Chúa Xứ*'s festival, which attracts more than a million pilgrims annually, a bigger attendance than at the largest urban temples and Buddhist pagodas.[4]

The first documented southern tales were written in the early twentieth century by Trương Vĩnh Ký: *Chuyện Đời Xưa* (1909). Unfortunately, many of them have either been lost or out of print, therefore impossible to access, except the most recent ones.

George Schultz was the executive director of the Vietnamese-American Association in Saigon from 1956 to 1958. He learned the language, culture, and history of Vietnam and soon became an expert. In 1965, he released a nice small book in which he penned 32 legends. Even without any additional explanations or comments, his clear, simple, and succinct writing remains a standard against which other books should be compared.

Dương Văn Quyền and Jewell Coburn penned the first legend book written in English by a Vietnamese-American. It is a work of art which contains ten classic Vietnamese legends; nine of them are among the southern legends described in this section (tales 1, 2, 3, 5, 20, 22, 26, 36, and 38). It was a good introduction to Vietnamese legends, which was not only targeted at the new refugees arriving from 1975 onwards, but also at the American public in general. I found this out-of-print book only recently.

Thích Nhật Hạnh wrote 12 legends, which were subdivided into four sections: 1) beginnings; 2) food and customs; 3) conflict; and 4) changes. His language is more flowery than others.

Alice Terada penned 27 legends, which are grouped into four sections: 1) foibles of man and quirks of animals; 2) tales from the lowlands and the highlands; 3) spirit world; and 4) food, love and laughter. Her book contains many ethnic tales and tales about spirits.

Nguyễn Gia Cư wrote four small legend books containing from 17 to 29 tales each and targeted at school children. They are published in Vietnam.

Table 3. Books Dealing with Southern Tales

Book/Author	Year	Number of Tales	Language
1. Schultz	1965	32	English
2. Dương Văn Quyền	1976	10	English
3. Thích Nhật Hạnh	1993	12	English
4. Terada	1989	27	English

Book/Author	Year	Number of Tales	Language
5. Vo	2012	50	English
6. Nguyễn Gia Cư			
• Thạch Sanh	2004	17	Vietnamese
• Sử Tích Con Dã Tràng	2005	25	Vietnamese
• Cá Hoa Long	2005	29	Vietnamese
• Chim Chèo Beo	2005	29	Vietnamese
Total		**231**	

The 50 tales in this section were collected in South Vietnam during the war. I have heard many of them from my parents or relatives or read them in books dealing with the South. Sources of the tales are listed in the bibliography and in table 3.

Some tales are well known by a large number of people, while others are rarely heard of. The latter are confined to books, although many of these are interesting and enriching. The purpose of this project is to reveal the breadth and depth of southern legends, as exemplified in the 231 tales cited in table 3 (many are duplicates, others are waiting to be discovered).

Why these tales are less well known than others remains a mystery. It is like asking why the bumbling marsh boy is an Immortal while the heroic Trưng sisters are not. Other differences are noted between the two stories. The Marsh Boy story is well known in the North Vietnam while it is less popular in the South. The Trưng sisters, on the other hand, are well-known in both the North and South. They are real historical personalities while the Marsh Boy lacks historical anchors.

Ramanujan notes that in India each teller's repertoire consists "of twenty or thirty tales, not much more."[5] The number seems to be the same for other countries, unless the person is a professional storyteller. This explains the large number of books on legends, many of them containing fewer than 30 tales each.

The scope of southern legends is different from that of northern legends, both in historical contents and in the variety of the topics. Southern tales deal with day-to-day life topics, peasants' stories, and war tales, while northern tales pay note to historical legends, mandarins, and ancient stories. Some stories are uniquely regional: legends about Princess Liễu Hạnh, which are commonly heard in the North, are almost unknown in the South. Legends about Bà Chúa Xứ and Lê Văn Duyệt are uniquely southern.

Vietnam, by virtue of history or fate, is one of three countries in the

XI. Introduction

world that have been divided into two states by political ideologies (communism versus capitalism) for a certain period in modern time. The others are Korea and Germany. Vietnam also had a two-century division in the seventeenth and eighteenth centuries, which caused people and tales to evolve differently with a particular regional flavor (chapter III). This, in part, explains the differences between northern and southern tales.

XII. Southern Legends

A. Historical Legends

Each author has his or her own way to subdivide legends, and this imperfect approach remains true with authors writing about Vietnamese legends. In this book, we will group legends into historical, animal, traditional, social and ethnic sections.

The tales in this group either carry some historical meanings or are directly or indirectly linked to Vietnamese history.

1. Lạc Long Quân
2. The Gods of the Mountains and the Seas
3. The Magic Crossbow
4. The Genie of Phù Đổng
5. The Trưng Sisters
6. Lady Triệu
7. Tiên Dung and the Marsh Boy
8. The Lake of the Sword
9. The Marble Mountains
10. Côn Sơn Island

1. Lạc Long Quân

Lạc Long Quân (Dragon Lord of Lạc), according to Vietnamese mythology, was the father of the Vietnamese people and the first true king. His father was King Kinh Dương (Kinh Dương Vương) who reigned over Xích Quỷ (the Bountiful Land) and his mother was Thần Long Nữ.

Lạc Long Quân, the dragon king, one day was hunting in the mountains when he met Âu Cơ, a beautiful fairy who lived in the mountains. She traveled around to provide support to those who were ill or sick because she had a good heart and knew some medicine. She fell in love with Lạc Long Quân, who brought her back to his palace by the sea.

This was a magical union between a fairy and a mortal—one of those blessed unions—from which derived 100 offspring, all males according to some. To others, there were 50 boys and 50 girls. How Âu Cơ could have 100 children was unknown to mortals; only the fairy herself knew. She had plenty of help to care for the babies, who needed one hundred nannies and a lot of helpers. The quiet palace turned into a zoo with 100 crying babies, cribs, clothes and so on. So much activity was going on that confusion was the norm. The queen, recovering from a major delivery, tried to restore some semblance of order. But she too was swamped by a deluge of requests for help.

Feeding 100 mouths at the same time turned out to be a nightmare. Washing and cleaning them up became a big headache. One hundred pans were needed at the same time. Food had to be prepared for 100 mouths. The babies would be asleep at the same time until one of them started to cry and wake up the rest. One hundred nannies had to get up to care for the babies, soothe them and feed them.

If the king was happy in the beginning about having a lot of offspring to populate his kingdom, he soon felt the pressure of having to deal with 100 crying or hungry children. He became irritable, if not upset about the care and needs of a large household.

As the children grew older, their sheer numbers caused a logistical jam that stressed family relationships. To keep pace with a few children was already difficult, let alone caring for 100 youngsters. Fighting had to be broken up. Disagreements had to be ironed out, arguments and questions solved, and discipline administered. The king and the queen had their share of normal disagreements that were amplified by those related to their numerous offspring. Stress tore the family apart and the two gradually kept their distance.

One day, Lạc Long Quân took his wife aside and told her, "Beloved Queen, although I love you a lot, I do not think we can go on like this forever."

"I agree with you, dear Lord. Could you tell me what is on your mind?"

"I thank you for giving me all these children, although I did not expect that many in such a short time."

"We haven't had a minute together since they were born, have we?"

"They are strong and healthy, thanks to you."

"They are the replica of their father."

"Of their mother too. I do not know whether it is a good thing or a curse to have that many children. We are now drowned in our own problems."

"You could be right."

"We need to split up and go our own way."

"Are you sure? This makes me feel sad."

"The world does not want you, an immortal, to marry a mortal man. We want to change the rules and must pay for it."

"Do you really think so?"

"I descend from the dragons, you from fairies. We are like fire and water. It is difficult for us to live in harmony."

"I understand, my Lord, although I would rather stay with you."

"We each need to pursue our own life."

Any breakup is difficult and painful. This was also the case for the king and the fairy. The couple divided their children in half. Fifty accompanied their mother to the highlands while the rest followed their father to the coastal area. The scene of the separation was sad and tragic: fifty children looked at the other fifty heading in a column toward another direction. In their minds, they did not understand anything. They used to be together, play, eat, and sleep together, but from that time onward, half of them would not see the other half.

They cried, screamed, and stamped their feet but did not know what else to do. Some wanted to follow their mother, others their father, but they were not allowed to choose. Lost and confused, they could only cry. They did not understand why they had to split up and follow either their father or mother, but not both. They did not know why they could not go with such and such brother or whether they would ever see each other again.

The royal breakup also made local people sad. Their reactions were subdued. They thought that if marital breakup could happen to a royal family, it could happen to any of them. In the end, it was a marriage made in heaven and torn apart in the land of humans.

Lạc Long Quân was succeeded by his eldest son, Hùng Vương. The latter ruled over the kingdom of Văn Lang and the land of the tattooed people. He founded the Hồng Bàng dynasty, which lasted until 258 BCE and was comprised of eighteen kings.

The people were mostly fishermen and farmers. Since they were fre-

XII. Southern Legends: Historical

quently attacked by various sea animals—poisonous sea snakes they often called crocodiles—king Hùng Vương told them to tattoo their bodies to ward off the crocodiles. Therefore, they were named tattooed people. Their boats were also painted with various designs, including two eyes in the front of the boats to scare away any sea monster.

They fished in the present Gulf of Tonkin but also ventured far out to the South China Sea. Their main fishing site was the Hà Long Bay. Hà Long means "where the dragon descended into the sea." Legend has it that one day a group of dragons fell from the mountains into the sea and while trying to hang on to the cliffs, their tails wildly hit the shores, creating big crevasses that later filled with salt water. The resulting landscape was a beautiful bay filled with thousands of small islands that emerged from the clear, emerald waters of the bay. Seashells, crabs, fish, and lobsters are found in abundance in the bay.

Comments 1. The legend of Lạc Long Quân has been recorded in the *Lĩnh Nam Chích Quái* (LNCQ) and the *Đại Việt Sử Ký Toàn Thư* (Complete Book of the Historical Records of Great Viet by Ngô Sĩ Liên, TT, fifteenth century). According to the LNCQ, 100 sons were born from a single egg-like sac. From the 50 sons who followed Âu Cơ to Mount Tản Viên, one was chosen to be the first Hùng king. According to the TT, the first king was one who followed Lạc Long Quân, thus stressing patriarchal values.

However, according to the *Mường*, the highland descendents of Âu Cơ, 50 sons and 50 daughters were born instead of 100 sons. Fifty of those who followed Âu Cơ became the Mường ancestors while the remaining 50 went with Lạc Long Quân to become the Vietnamese ancestors.

According to historical genealogy, Lạc Long Quân came from the northern and southern branches. The function of these branches is to claim a more ancient lineage for the Hùng kings than that of China's first emperor, Huang Ti. The latter defeated Đế Du, the last emperor of the northern branch. Đế Du's uncle was Lạc Long Quân.

2. Books recorded that Lạc Long Quân came from the realm of the sea. He kidnapped Âu Cơ, the wife of a northern intruder, and took her to Mount Tản Viên, which overlooks the Hồng River. Unable to retrieve his wife, the intruder departed in despair. Âu Cơ gave birth to the first of the Hùng kings. Lạc Long Quân and Âu Cơ are considered the progenitors of the Vietnamese or the Lạc people.[1]

For the Vietnamese to conceive that the aquatic spirit was the source of political power and legitimacy gave away the hint that they were a distinctive and self-conscious people. The Lạc settled around Mê Linh in the northwest corner of the plain where the Hồng River emerges from the mountains and is joined by its tributaries, the Chầy and Đa rivers. Mê Linh, 100 miles from the sea, is dominated by Mount Tản Viên in the southwest and the Mount Tam Đạo in the northeast.

3. The Lạc civilization dated from the third millennium BCE (Phùng Nguyên culture, early Bronze Age) and culminated with the Đồng Sơn civilization (seventh century BCE to the first century BCE, Bronze Age). They worked in paddy fields; *Lạc* came from *lạch,* or *rạch* (canal, ditch, or waterway). The society at the time was matriarchal in nature: leaders were women.[2]

The breakup between Âu Cơ and Lạc Long Quân was the first divorce recorded in Vietnamese history. Both sides were agreeable and divided properties and children equitably. Since women were allowed to become household heads, Âu Cơ took 50 children to live with her to the highlands.

4. The breakup could also reflect the loose and bilateral nature of the Vietnamese family of the time. Men and women "joined at random and there was no concept of husband and wife, parent and child." People tended to follow their individualistic tastes. It was only in the first century BCE that the Chinese introduced the patriarchal system based on monogamous marriage. In reality, only women were monogamous, for men could have many concubines besides their primary wives. The goal of the patriarchal system was mainly economic, for if a couple got married and settled down, they would develop an agrarian economy and pay taxes to the Chinese. The Lạc people tattooed their bodies, stained their teeth black and wore their hair in a chignon behind their head. Women wore jewelry and earrings. They squatted and chewed betel (see southern tale # 20). Their country was once called *Giao Chỉ* for "intertwined feet," based on the fact that people slept in groups with each person's head extending outward while their feet came together at the center. They were either farmers or fishermen. They painted all kinds of animals on the outside of their boats with two eyes in front to scare away sea creatures.[3] All these characteristics suggest that the Lạc people were culturally different from the Chinese.

2. The Gods of the Mountains and the Seas

Under Hùng Vương XVIII—the last emperor of the first Vietnamese royal dynasty—the gods lived on earth among humans. The best known were Sơn Tinh, the god of the mountains and Thủy Tinh, the god of the seas.[4]

Sơn Tinh was an affable and good-natured god who liked all living creatures. While he was strolling on the beach one day, he witnessed a loud discussion among a group of fishermen. They apparently had hauled in a big catch: a large fish with glistening scales and beautiful sad eyes. Some wanted to make a big meal out of it while others desired to sell it on the market.

Since they could not make any decision, Sơn Tinh suggested they sell the fish to him. Once the price had been negotiated, he took the fish and returned it to the sea. The fish expressed his thanks by making numerous flips above the seawater.

Late that night, a nice young man came to visit Sơn Tinh. He introduced himself as Thủy Tinh and thanked Sơn Tinh for having saved his life earlier that day. He told him that he had taken the form of a fish in order to swim around the seas until he was caught by the fishermen. Having lost his magical power once he had assumed the fish form, he was vulnerable like any other fish.

To express his gratitude, Thủy Tinh took Sơn Tinh for a tour of his kingdom, which was as magnificent as everyone would expect. There were islands, the sea with its multiple treasures, and many varieties of fish. There was also the kingdom of the deep sea where exotic animals lived among castles, sea canyons and shipwrecks. Thủy Thinh wanted to offer a gift to Sơn Tinh, but the latter refused. In the end, he gave his benefactor a book of wishes that allowed him to fulfill any wish he wanted to make.

The Hồng Bàng king had a beautiful and charming daughter whose name was Mỵ Nương. She had many suitors who had lined up to catch a glimpse of her. One of the king's neighbors, the King of Thục, had asked for the daughter's hand. The Hồng Bàng king, fearing his neighbor's territorial ambitions, turned him down. The King of Thục, feeling slighted, would later invade the Hồng Bàng kingdom. Other suitors were also eliminated one by one.

The two remaining suitors, Sơn Tinh and Thủy Tinh, were both strong and powerful, and the king did not know which one to choose as his son-in-law. If he chose one over the other, he would make an enemy of the loser. After thinking for a long time, he told them: "Dear spirits, you are both talented and valiant. Either of you would make me a happy father-in-law. The choice is indeed difficult."

"Your Highness, I would like to be your son-in-law. I could give your daughter tall and magnificent mountains from where she could rule the earth, reach the skies, and look at the horizon as far as her eyes could see. The soaring eagles and the mighty dragons will be her friends. She could refresh herself among the multitudes of waterfalls. There is plenty of wild game in the forests. She will be well protected amidst my mountains," said Sơn Tinh.

"Your Highness, I would give her a large domain: the world of the oceans. She will have plenty of food to eat and would never be afraid of starvation. She will make friends of dolphins and whales and could ride on them around the world. She could visit many foreign lands and all the people she had never seen before. She will be lulled to sleep by the soothing noise of the rolling waves. She will be very happy with me," said Thủy Tinh.

"Again, the choice is most difficult. Therefore, I have decided that whoever brings me the best ritual gifts tomorrow morning will wed my daughter," said the king.

All night long, the suitors were busy scouring their lands in search of the required presents. They had to think of and then look for the best present for the bride. Sơn Tinh then remembered about the book of wishes that Thủy Tinh had given to him. He opened the Book, read some incantations and the gifts miraculously showed up in front of him. He brought the magnificent presents to the king, who marveled at their variety and quality. He was given Mỵ Nương to wed and immediately took her to Mount Tản Viên.

Hearing the news, Thủy Tinh got angry for having lost the bride. He gathered the winds and waves and thrashed the mountains without mercy. The country was battered day and night by heavy storms and strong winds. There had not been such violent storms in eons.

The local people, caught in the middle, worried for their lives. They were scared of being washed away and holed up in their straw and mud houses; they also prayed for the end of the storms. They knew that nothing good would come out of a fight between the two gods.

But Sơn Tinh was ready and waiting. He threw thunder and lightning down into the sea, causing Thủy Tinh to be hurt. The skies lit up with fiery thunders and fierce winds. Having lost this round, Thủy Tinh pulled back the killing waves and the weather returned to normal.

Since those legendary times, every year during the sixth or seventh lunar month (between July and September), Thủy Tinh wakes up angry and acts up again, throwing wave after wave of seawater against the mountains before slowly relenting.

This is the legend behind the continuing fight between the two gods, which resulted in the summer monsoon rains that batter Vietnam each year.

Comments 1. According to Vietnamese mythology, Sơn Tinh is the son of Lạc Long Quân and Âu Cơ; he followed his father to the sea and returned to dwell at Mount Tân Vien, 30 miles west of Hanoi. In Vietnamese mythology, like in the Greek world, the country was populated by gods and spirits. The above story relates the fight between two gods, which explains the annual monsoons rains that thrash the country. The Vietnamese still worship Sơn Tinh's Mount Tản Viên (present day Mount Ba Vi located 30 miles west of Hanoi) as the ancestor mountain.

Vietnamese culture has always tried to express the duality of nature: land and water, sun and rain, good or evil. Life results from the balance of or the competition between two opposing forces. Even the creation of the Vietnamese nation begins with the union of Lạc Long Quân, the father dragon who comes from the realm of the water, and Âu Cơ, the Fairy or Bird, who originates from the sky.

2. Mỵ Nương or Mỵ Châu is a title name—similar to Princess—reserved for the king's daughter.

3. The Magic Crossbow

The Hùng kings reigned over the kingdom of Văn Lang for many generations. Having been successful during all this time, the last and eighteenth Hùng king relaxed his vigilance over state security and lived in idleness. His enemy, Thục Phan from the Thục kingdom—one of Thục Phan's forbears had been refused a Hùng princess's hand—gathered an army, invaded Văn Lang and easily defeated the Hùng king more than 2,400 years ago. The new country that emerged was named Âu Lạc and Thục Phan took the name of An Dương Vương or King An Dương.[5]

An Dương Vương was a Chinese king who loved and followed Vietnamese traditions; the Vietnamese reciprocated by accepting him as a Vietnamese king. Wanting to protect his kingdom from the Chinese hordes, he decided to build a huge wall the keep them out. He almost completed the first one when it collapsed on him during a heavy storm.

He had it rebuilt two more times. However, for unknown reasons, what had been accomplished in the morning was destroyed at night. He had his soldiers stand watch to try to catch the culprit: although they saw nothing, the work was again destroyed. An Dương Vương decided to watch the place himself. He too saw nothing, but the work lay in ruins the following morning.

One of his ministers suggested the gods might not like him. An altar was erected and sacrifices were offered. King An Dương then prayed to the gods and fasted for three days, as tradition called for. He also prayed to the genie Turtle, Kim Quy, whom he had met in the past. Years ago while fishing in the Eastern Sea, he saw a large turtle being caught in his net. He had the turtle released: the latter turned out to be a genie turtle which promised to help him whenever he needed it.

When consulted, the genie turtle told King An Dương that many genies led by a thousand-year-old chicken had conspired to tear down the wall. He, therefore, suggested that the king built a conch-type citadel (*Cổ Loa Thành*) with many concentric layers. When the work began, Kim Quy himself stood watch. He warned the chicken-spirit not to interfere with the work and the latter agreed.[6] The Cổ Loa citadel was finally completed and stood firm against natural elements. Remains of the citadel are still visible today in North Vietnam. King An Dương happily settled in his citadel.

Since the king had powerful enemies, he decided to ask Kim Quy for a warranty. The genie turtle gave him one of his own claws.

"Take one of my claws and incorporate it into a crossbow. It has magical powers: killing enemies and driving away evil spirits. But never forget that the ultimate safety of your realm depends on your vigilance."

The king commissioned a man named Cao Lo to make a crossbow with the magic claw incorporated. He christened it "Saintly Crossbow of the Supernaturally Luminous Golden Claw." He finally believed that he would enjoy peace and prosperity for years to come.

The powerful Chinese emperor Shih Huang of the Ch'in dynasty decided one day to conquer the kingdom of Âu Lac to increase the size of his territory. This time, the Chinese army was rendered harmless by the magic crossbow even before it approached the Cổ Loa citadel.

Three years later, Shih Huang sent under the direction of General Triệu Đà a larger army, which converged by land and sea on the Cổ Loa citadel. The Chinese came with flags floating in the air, weapons clashing together, and a multitude of soldiers marching elbow to elbow. King An Dương let the Chinese army approach. He then took his magic crossbow and whack... The arrow hit the formation right in the middle and ten thousand soldiers died. Whack, another ten thousand were laid to rest. Whack, another ten thousand fell. Triệu Đà called for a retreat and left the field.

Defeated, Triệu Đà did not want to return to China. Since he could not win on the battlefield, he decided to take King An Dương down deceitfully. He proposed a peace treaty between the two countries, which would

XII. Southern Legends: Historical

be sealed by uniting the two families. King An Dương had a beautiful daughter, Mỵ Châu, while Triệu Đà had a good son, Trọng Thủy. King An Dương, tired of the long and costly campaign against the Chinese, thought that peace would be good for the country and his people. After much mulling, he agreed to the marriage. During the ceremony, King An Dương, under the mild effect of liquor, revealed his secret weapon: the magic crossbow that killed ten thousand soldiers per shot. Triệu Đà immediately whispered to his son to get his hands on the bow.

Although it was not love at first sight, Trọng Thủy and Mỵ Châu gradually warmed to each other. Trọng Thủy took time to win his wife's confidence. He was extremely nice to her and took her to the mountains and lakes. He did everything to charm her. They spent many lovely evenings at a nearby lake where she loved to swim. Yet, he never forgot that his main goal was to get hold of the crossbow.

He then pressed her to show him the bow. With a lot of reluctance, Mỵ Châu showed him the secret weapon. She had to wait until her father slept before she could sneak into his room and get it. He borrowed it, studied it, took out the magic claw and replaced it with a fake one.

Sometime later, he requested King An Dương's permission to go home and visit his parents. Since the king did not see any problem, Trọng Thủy told his wife, "Dear Mỵ Châu, it has been a long time since I have seen my parents. I have some duty toward them and need to see them. I would like to take you along with me, but the road is long and dangerous."

"In that case, do you really need to go? How long will you be absent?"

"Just a few weeks. It will not be long."

"My lord, I do not know why, but I am afraid. I will be alone for a long time. Who knows what will happen? You are not around to protect me. Is the road safe? Will I see you again? It may not be anything, but I will miss you so much." And the princess wept bitterly.

"I will be fine, I promise you. I will be back in a few weeks and we will live happily again."

She continued to cry and he had to reassure her repeatedly.

"Do you remember the winter coat lined with goose down you gave me? If something happens to me, I will leave a trail of white goose down and you will know the direction I have taken."

The separation was very emotional. It was filled with tears and vows of love and devotion. He was mad at himself for having to betray his wife for the sake of his father and country. He got on his horse and headed out of the citadel without turning back. After having gone through the gate, he went straight to Triệu Đà's camp.

"Mission accomplished, father. This is the magic claw. Without it, they will no longer be invincible," he told Triệu Đà.

"Very good, my son. I will get the army ready."

"That soon?" questioned Trọng Thủy, who again felt the angst of having betrayed his wife and was worried about her life as his father contemplated war.

Triệu Đà's army, like a big snake, converged toward the Cổ Loa citadel. The war drums were beating, the soldiers' armaments were glittering in the sun and the multicolored flags were flying in the winds. The soldiers notified King An Dương about the enemy's presence. Having defeated the Chinese twice, he simply laughed at them.

"Let them come. I know how to meet them. If they have not learned their lesson before, they will this time."

Cocksure, he did not even order his army to get ready for battle. When the enemy came in view of the citadel, he said, "Let them come closer."

He sent someone to get his crossbow and loaded it with one arrow. He aimed and shot. The arrow fell harmlessly twenty feet away while the enemy came closer. He took another arrow and again shot it. It fell harmlessly on the ground like the first one. He realized it was not the same crossbow he had before. On inspection, he noted that the magic claw was gone. In its place was only a cheap imitation. He threw it on the ground with such force that it broke in half.

"Who on earth has taken my magic claw? Who?" he yelled madly.

As the enemy came, he realized that the end had come. He was devastated. All his confidence was gone. For a moment, he stood there shaking. He regained enough poise to ask for his horse. He then grabbed his daughter and galloped away. He did not even have time to request a retinue. He crossed the fields, climbed mountains, and descended slopes. Behind him, Mỵ Châu left a trail of white goose down so that Trọng Thủy might follow it.

Trọng Thủy, who had entered the citadel, looked in vain for his wife. He ran from one room to another and finally noticed the trail, which he followed.

King An Dương drove his horse hard. He knew he had to reach the sea, where he could get help from his friend, the genie turtle. Each time he slowed down, he heard the gallop of his pursuer's horse. He finally reached the shore. No boat could be seen anywhere, no fisherman was around. Desperate, he called the genie turtle.

"Mighty Genie, where are you when I need you?"

"What can I do for you," the genie asked as he rose out of the sea.

XII. Southern Legends: Historical

"Could you help me out of this mess?"

"Beware of the person who is sitting behind you."

An Dương looked back and saw a trail of white goose down on the ground. Mỵ Châu was shivering out of fear, with tears rolling down her cheeks.

"What are you doing? Betraying me?"

He got mad, pulled his sword out, stabbed her in the chest and decapitated her. Filled with horror at his violent deed, he followed the golden tortoise and disappeared in the water.

Trọng Thủy, arriving at the scene, found the decapitated body of Mỵ Châu. He became inconsolable: he knew he was responsible for her death. He took her body and brought it back to the capital to give it a decent burial.

His grief knew no bounds. Desperate, he threw himself into the nearby lake where Mỵ Châu had loved to bathe. He hoped his soul would meet the one he had loved.

Mỵ Châu's blood, washed away by the sea, was absorbed by the oysters along the shore. The latter have produced some of the best pearls in the area. These pearls became more brilliant when washed in the pond water where Trọng Thủy drowned himself.

Comments 1. Although the 18—or many more—kings of the Hồng Bàng dynasty formed the first Vietnamese royal dynasty, minimal documentation is available from that period. An Dương Vương—their successor—became the first historically documented Vietnamese king.

The cause of the delayed construction of the Cổ Loa citadel was a thousand-year-old chicken that each night led local spirits to tear down whatever was built during the daytime. Eventually Kim Quy, the genie turtle, came by and overcame the chicken, thereby allowing the construction to continue. This tale explains the defeat of An Dương Vuong in 207 BCE by Chinese General Triệu Đà. The date marked the beginning of a thousand-year Chinese domination.

Although the story displayed two flawed people; Mỵ Châu (betraying her father because of love) and Trọng Thủy (betraying his wife because of loyalty to his father), it was love that transcended the story in the end. The crossbow, the genie Kim Quy, the Cổ Loa citadel were all relegated into the background.

The Vietnamese poet Ánh Ngọc wrote: "about lore and betrayal."[7] It was the love of two people who sacrificed their lives for love. If Mỵ Châu died for love, Trọng Thủy committed suicide when he realized his mistake. The blood of Mỵ Châu was reincarnated into glistening pearls that brighten significantly when dipped into the pond water where Trọng Thủy killed himself.

2. The chicken is an ancient indigenous symbol while the turtle is a symbol of the Chinese god of war. The theme behind the Cổ Loa legend is the test of strength between the white chicken and the golden turtle: it is about the suppression of forces bent on preventing Chinese construction.

Chinese sources do not mention the turtle claw but state that the son-in-law "rendered it useless" by sawing the crossbow in half. The Vietnamese version emphasizes that he made another trigger and exchanged it with the magic turtle claw. It stresses a transfer of power from An Dương Vương to Triệu Đà. Although they were both Chinese, they defended the independence of Nan Yuệ (Vietnam) against the Chinese Han and behaved as if they were *Lạc* or Vietnamese. They would be the last two Chinese to find a place in Vietnamese mythology.

Triệu Đà divided Âu Lạc into two prefectures: Giao Chỉ and Cửu Chân. He sent two legates to oversee the prefectures. The Lạc lords continued to rule the land as vassals. For the first time, Nan Yuệ became part of a kingdom encompassing southern China.

4. *The Genie of Phù Đổng*

King Hùng Vương one night awoke from his sleep. He was sweating heavily. He remembered vividly having talked to Lord Dragon who had appeared in his dream. Lord Dragon looked worried and told him in no uncertain terms, "The enemy will invade in three years. If you can find a hero to chase the enemy away, you will be all right. Otherwise, you will lose your throne."

In the small village of Phù Đổng lived a nice couple. Both were hard working farmers: he labored all day in the field while she tried to help him as much as she could. They were happy except for the fact that they had been childless for a long time. They returned home each night to an empty house without having a child to greet and no one to scold or teach.

They often sat in a corner of their hut wondering whether they could ever have a child. They prayed to heaven to let them have a son. The wife even consulted fortune tellers who adamantly predicted that she would have a child. She did not know what to think about them because fortune tellers tended to predict whatever their clients wanted to hear.

As she walked in the field one day, she saw a giant footprint. It was bigger than any footprint she had ever seen. Surprised, she stepped on it and immediately got sick with stomach pain. A few months later, she was stunned to find herself pregnant. Elated, she told everyone about the news and people were happy for her.

Nine months, ten months, then eleven months passed by without any sign of imminent delivery. Villagers started to worry about her pregnancy. She finally delivered a nice boy on the twelfth month. But the child was not like any other child in the village. He never cried or talked. He was quiet all the time and did not even walk by the time he was one. The mother, however, never lost hope. Everything was slow with her child, but she was sure she had a good one because heaven had blessed her. She named him Gióng.

The country was peaceful until northern neighbors invaded it, as Lord Dragon had predicted. The Hùng king's army fought back but the invaders overpowered it by their numbers. They were as numerous as ants marching on their prey. The king had sent emissaries to villages around the country for the last three years to look for a hero, but found none.

When the emissary arriving at the Phù Đổng village explained the critical situation of the nation, three-year-old Gióng, who had not spoken since birth, told his mother, "Mother, tell the emissary that I can help."

"How can you help, Gióng, when you are that small and when even soldiers so far have failed?" asked his mother.

"Mother, just tell the emissary that I will be able to help. And I will need a lot of rice so I can grow up."

Although she was elated to hear his voice, she was more impressed by his demeanor and forceful language. She ran out and shouted; "My Gióng can talk. He can talk."

She looked for the emissary, told him about her child's suggestion and invited him to see Gióng. Bewildered, the emissary did not know how to react. However, realizing the dire condition of the country, he decided to see the child.

"Child, what do you want from the king's emissary?" he asked.

"Sir, I will be able to help defend the country. Just give me a lot of rice and some armament."

"How do you think you could help, child?"

"Just trust me. Give me a lot of rice, a sword, a shield, and a horse, and I will do the rest."

"I will relay your message to the king and let him make the decision," answered the startled emissary. In his mind, he was not sure how to react to this child, although he found him convincing. How could a three-year-old talk in such a way unless he could do something, he thought to himself.

He reported the encounter to the king, who asked him to repeat the story quite a few times. The king then said, "He must be our hero. Have someone make him the biggest horse, shield and sword. Lord Dragon will guide him."

Meanwhile at the Phù Đổng village, Gióng's mother cooked some rice for him. He just swallowed it as soon as it was ready and there was nothing left a few minutes later. For the first time, she was amazed at his appetite. She stood there not knowing what to do.

"Are you still hungry?" she asked.

"Mother, cook for me a lot of rice," Gióng answered.

"As you wish," she said.

She rushed to cook another meal for him. When it was ready, he kept his nose down and swallowed it in no time.

"At this rate, I will run out of rice in the morning," she said in a surprised and somewhat excited voice.

She went back to the kitchen and started cooking again. And Gióng ate and never seemed to have enough. As he ate, he also grew in size. His clothes stretched and came apart at the seams. His mother ran to her neighbors and told them about her fast growing son. She looked tired and worried. She had never seen anyone consuming that much food in such a short time. But she knew she was not dealing with a real person but a genie the country needed to drive away the invaders.

"He will be a giant soon," she said.

All her neighbors rushed to see her. Realizing her problem, they brought their own supply of rice. They also assisted her with the cooking and sewed new clothes for him. However, he was growing so fast that clothes became useless in a very short time.

Days went by and Gióng continued to eat and take breaks in between meals. He soon grew taller than his house. The king was also notified of Gióng's rapid growth and gargantuan appetite. Although he was not sure in the beginning about the story of the boy, he reasoned that Gióng must be a good genie that was sent to help him and his people. As for the sword, shield, and iron horse, he asked his blacksmiths to make the largest sword and shield they could make. He knew that the genie could transform the armaments to suit him.

When everything was ready, the king ordered his soldiers to bring the armaments to the genie. The latter had become a giant who was taller than the tallest tree in the village. He was ready to fight.

He stretched himself out and shouted; "I am the genie sent by heaven to help you. I thank you for your help and warm hospitality. I will chase your enemies away."

He slid into the iron armor, wielded his sword and lightly touched his horse, which became as big as he was. He bid farewell to his parents and the villagers, got on his horse, and rode to war. The enemy did not see him coming until he slashed to death 100 of them with one single swing of his word. His mighty roar caught everyone by surprise. He swung his sword a second time. And a third time. Blood flew all over the camp. Frightened, the Chinese soldiers ran away without stopping. They had never seen such a fierce, giant fighter in their whole life. They ran and ran. Their generals and leaders could no longer hold them back. The Chinese finally surrendered to the Hùng king.[8]

Genie Gióng's horse ran all the way to Mount Tản Viên. He dropped his armament and the horse and the genie flew up to the sky.

The Hùng king thanked the Phù Đổng villagers for their help and generosity. Genie Gióng became a hero to all the Vietnamese. In recognition of his valiant deeds, the king named him *Phù Đổng Thiên Vương* or the Heavenly Genie from the village of Phù Đổng. He had a temple built in his honor, which also served as a worship place in the village.[9]

Comments Phù Đổng Thiên Vương represents the national hero who sets an example for his countrymen. At the young age of three, he responded to the call to defend the nation, ate to become a giant, and went to war to repel the enemy. He was unselfish and did not make any personal demand. Once his job was completed, he rose to the sky and disappeared.

This is one of the legends that originated from the Tây Vu mountainous regions of present day North Vietnam. Tây Vu lies between the Câu and Hồng rivers at the foot of Mount Tam Đạo. The valleys of Tây Vu connect with China through low passes, making the region susceptible to Chinese invasion. The first legends from this region are about defending the country against foreign invasions.

Ông Gióng has been interpreted as an incarnation of Lạc Long Quân, who came back to help his people in need. There is an Indonesian story similar to that of Ông Gióng.

5. The Trưng Sisters

By 39 CE, the province of Giao Chỉ with its capital Mê Linh had been under Chinese control for more than 100 years. The greedy and inept Chinese Governor Tô Định (Su Ting) oppressed the people (the Lạc) with heavy taxes and other burdens. He "opened his eyes to money but closed them when it came to punishing rebels; he feared to go out and attack them."[10]

The Mê Linh's district chief had two daughters, Trưng Trắc and Trưng Nhị, who were brought up in a family that was well versed in martial arts. The elder, Trưng Trắc, was brave, fearless, and a fast learner. She was reported to be involved in "various acts of bravery such as slaying a ferocious people-eating tiger."[11]

Trắc married the fierce Thi Sách, the son of the Chu Điền district chief. Tô Định, in his eagerness to collect more revenues, pressured the Lạc lords to raise taxes. Because the latter resisted, he decided to restrain Thi Sách with legal procedures.

Thi Sách was killed, according to the Vietnamese, by order of Tô Định. Trưng Trắc, on hearing the bad news, was devastated. She was divided between her loss and a desire for revenge. Soon from Mê Linh, a deeply hurt Trưng Trắc rose, rebelled against the Chinese and chased Tô Định out of the country in the spring of 40 CE. The rebellion spread to other districts: Nam Hải, Cửu Chân, Nhật Nam, and Hợp Phó. Seeing Tô Định running away, Chinese soldiers either fled or surrendered.

With the Chinese administration suddenly collapsing, Trưng Trắc proclaimed herself queen and took her sister as deputy. The people rejoiced and partied. There had never been two female leaders in Giao Chỉ since who knows when. She proceeded immediately to cut the "taxes" enacted by the Chinese on the Lạc people and reverted to the system of gift exchange based on hereditary rights and mutual benefit—a former practice that was widely preferred by the Lạc lords.

Trưng Trắc continued to attack the remaining Chinese commanderies to expand her territorial control. She liberated one town after another and in the end captured 65 cities. In 40 CE, the Chinese emperor ordered General Mã Yuan to crush the Trưng revolt. The Trưngs realized that waging war at the same time as running a country was tricky. Political infrastructure and the reorganization of the army could not be established in a short time. The Lạc, however, were enjoying a period of true independence, although the concept of freedom was still new for them.

In 41 CE, Mã Yuan's army began its march in China, followed the

XII. Southern Legends: Historical

coastline and settled on the hills of Lang Bạc (present-day North Vietnam). Soldiers were tired after the long march (three to six months) and were besieged by rainy and damp weather. The Chinese army, however, was well organized under a unified leadership. Supplies came up the Cầu River to the Lang Bạc natural lake.

The Trưng army was not a disciplined one. It was a loose association of the local lords' militias, each looking out for his own best interests. They had never fought together, especially not for such a vague and new concept as independence. Many of them just focused on their own survival free of interference from the central government—be it Chinese or Vietnamese. They were ready to go over to the Chinese or stay with the Trưngs, whoever gave them the best deal. Besides, they had doubts in their minds. Trưng Trắc—a new and young leader who was not battle hardy—feared that she could not succeed. Her followers feared she could not stand up to the enemy. Facing the strong and disciplined Chinese army, the Trưng's army wavered amidst command disunity. Strategically, it failed to interrupt the riverine supply routes of the Chinese army. Without access to these supplies, the morale of the Chinese soldiers would have been greatly affected.

The Trưng army gathered in the valley while the Chinese took the high grounds.[12] Realizing inaction would further encourage disaffection, she gave the order to attack. Despite isolated instances of bravery, her army was badly defeated. Several thousand of her soldiers were captured and beheaded and more than ten thousand surrendered to the Chinese. Phùng Thị Chính, a noble pregnant lady, gave birth on the front line. Then with her baby in her arm, she continued to fight the battle before killing herself in the end.

Trưng Trắc retreated to Mê Linh at the foot of Mount Tản Viên, her ancestral lands, hotly pursued by the Chinese. The Trưng drowned themselves in the Hạt River, ending Giao Chỉ's three-year independence. Mã Yuan reestablished Chinese control over the country, which lasted until 939 CE.

Had it not been for the courageous actions of the Trưng, there might not be a Vietnamese nation today. What the Trưng did was to crystallize the idea of independence in the mind of the Lạc people, to show them that it could be achieved and to remind them that the Vietnamese are different from the Chinese.

In the fifteenth century the Hồng Đức anthology recorded a tribute to the queens.[13] Shrines to the Trưng have been erected in present-day North Vietnam.

The uprising of 40 CE effectively froze the Đồng Sơn heritage in a moment of heroic courage, insuring that it would not degenerate and invite the scorn of later generations.[14]

The Trưng sisters are recognized as national heroines. Legends and lore about the Trưngs increased as centuries passed by. The thirteenth-century historian Lê Văn Hữu marveled at the fact that the Trưng sisters were fighting while men "bowed their heads and folded their arms." In the seventeenth century, their story was romanticized: a combined ideal of romantic love and revenge for the death of her husband were the motives for the rebellion. Later, the Trưng sisters became symbolic guardians of the cultural heritage of the society. They rose to the level of national spirits able to give supernatural aid in time of need.

The Trưng festivals were organized throughout the country from north to south each year. In Mê Linh, the festival took place on the sixth day of the first month of the lunar calendar. In Saigon, a monument to the Trưng sisters was dedicated in the early sixties by Mme Ngô Đình Nhu, President Diệm's sister-in-law. The monument was torn down by the mob after the fall of the Diệm regime in 1963 because the statues bore a striking resemblance to Mme Nhu and her daughter.

Comments 1. If the fifteenth century historian Ngô Sĩ Liên maintained that Thi Sách was killed on the order of the governor Tô Định, the Chinese argued that he was alive at the time of the rebellion and served as one of Trưng's generals. This discrepancy exists because the fifteenth century patriarchal society could not accept that a woman was not only a revolutionary leader, but also had her husband serving under her. The names and biographies of over 50 leaders of Trưng's uprising are recorded in temples dedicated to her cult; a large percentage of them are women.

If Thi Sách was indeed alive and fighting under her during the rebellion, Trưng Trắc was a truly masterful leader. What she did was unique in history. She made herself queen, promoted her sister as her deputy, and had her husband serve under her command. A weaker woman would have simply named her husband as her deputy. She, on the other hand, felt secure enough to lead by herself; she made sure to separate affairs of state from those of the heart.

2. Legend recorded that the Trưng sisters avoided capture by riding their horses off the cliffs into a river, where they drowned. This was a heroic way of dying, for this simple act endeared them to the Vietnamese for generations to come. According to Chinese annals, however, they captured and killed the Trưngs and sent their heads to the Han court at Lo-

yang by the first month of the New Year: an infamous treatment reserved to the defeated.

The upside of the story was that they were brave in life as in death and therefore rightly belonged to the pantheon of the Vietnamese heroes, the only two women in an otherwise all-male cast. It is remarkable to think that when opportunity came to her to lead the revolt, Trưng Trắc just snatched it and went to war. And for more than two years, she led the Lạc lords from one battle to another until her defeat.

History might have been different had she had more time to organize her army, to win the hearts and minds of the Lạc lords, and to attack the Chinese supply ships on the Cầu River. Without those supplies, the Chinese army would have been demoralized and easier to beat.

6. Lady Triệu

Lady Triệu (225–248 CE) was born Triệu Thị Minh in Sơn Trung village of Thanh Hóa province (North Vietnam). The region was under the Wu Kingdom at a time when China was ruled by three different kingdoms. Orphaned at a young age, she lived with her brother and sister-in-law more as a slave than a sibling.

She killed her sister-in-law—for unknown reasons—and escaped to the mountains where she gathered around her about 1,000 men and women. She led a rebellion against the Wu king, who sent Inspector Lục Dân (Lu Yin) to control the insurgency. She attacked the commanderies, won 30 battles, and controlled the region for many months before finally losing a battle.[15] She did not have the support of the local lords, which was the primary force behind the Trưngs' rebellion.

She was known to be a very clean person. Realizing this fact, the Chinese came out of their encampment naked, yelling, swearing, and kicking dirt during the last battle. Triệu Âu, unable to stand this rude behavior, ran away. Her demoralized army just followed her.

She was depicted with large breasts, which she tied behind her neck, and she often rode to battles on her elephant. Her size—more than six feet tall—may have forced her to opt for an elephant as carrier instead of a horse.

She killed herself instead of surrendering to the enemy. One story stated that she drowned herself in a river; in the other she was trampled to death by elephants.

She was not mentioned in the Chinese annals until the late Ming dynasty although was widely revered by the Vietnamese.[16] She was known as the Vietnamese Joan of Arc, although she might have been only a minor historical figure. She was remembered for the following words:

"My wish is to ride the tempest, tame the waves, kill the sharks. I want to drive the enemy away to save our people. I will not resign myself to the usual lot of women who bow their heads and become concubines."[17]

Comments Lady Triệu Ẩu is not as well known as the Trưng in history books as in life. This probably has to do with the fact that she did not belong to the ruling class and had to rebel against the Chinese by herself without the support and participation of the Lạc lords. The political, social, and military impacts of her rebellion were therefore limited and short-lived. While the Trưng caused a countrywide rebellion that forced the Chinese to send a whole army to control it, Lady Triệu Ẩu's actions probably had affected only one or two provinces. The revolts were suppressed by regional forces.

The Chinese did not even record her actions until a few centuries later. Our knowledge of her came from the fact that people in North Vietnam worshipped her. This does not make her a lesser hero, because she had proved herself to be a leader who could challenge the Chinese. She was brave and fearless and was willing to sacrifice her life for a larger ideal. One could only wish that many more people like her had stood up, so the Chinese would have been sent back to China earlier.

7. Tiên Dung and the Marsh Boy

The third Hùng king had a beautiful, although contrary, daughter whose name was Tiên Dung (Fairy-like Beauty). When she was young, she tried to compete with boys rather than girls. During her teenage years, she explored all the surroundings of the city she lived in; she also traveled from one province to another like young males of her age. She liked open spaces and loved nature as well as animals. She was a very independent person and her father just shook his head when he learned about another of her multiple escapades. When it was time to get married, she refused, arguing that she wanted to learn more about the world rather than remaining confined to her father's castle.

One day, she set out to travel along the waterways to see where they really ended. She took off with a small retinue. The guard thought she would be gone for a few hours as usual; when she did not come back after this period, he reported the escapade to the king.

From the river, she could see the landscape that stretched all the way to the horizon: huts here and there among rice fields. Farmers worked with their spouses and helpers in the fields along with their buffaloes. There were hills, mountains, trees and flowers. And her boat seemed to glide smoothly on the river.

In the village of Chú Xã (present day Hanoi) lived Chủ Văn Cư and his son Chủ Đồng Tử (the marsh boy). They were poor fishermen, so poor that they had to share the same loincloth year round. When one was working outdoors, the other remained indoors. The father, sensing he was about to die, told his son to keep the loincloth for himself. But Chủ Đồng Tử felt that he could not bury his father without a shroud. Following the funeral, he found himself without clothes. He therefore fished at night and sold his catches during the daytime, immersed in water up to his waist.

Tiên Dung came to the marshland area, which was close to the ocean. She could smell the fresh and salty air of the ocean. There was no mistake about it. She longed to see the ocean and its beaches, but decided to stop there for the night. At the sight of the boat, Chủ Đồng Tử hid behind the reeds.

The air was calm, as well as the water, which was very inviting in this summer weather. Tiên Dung looked around and saw no one. She entered the water, disrobed and dipped herself in the water that was warm and refreshing. It was at that time that she saw a head popping out among the reeds.

"Who are you?" she asked.

"Chủ Đồng Tử, your servant," he answered without daring to raise his eyes. "Would you please pardon me? I am a poor fisherman who was forced to hide at the approach of the royal barge."

Tiên Dung rushed to put her clothes on and threw a piece of cloth to Chủ Đồng Tử. She then questioned him lengthily and began to like him.

"I am exploring the ocean and the beaches," she said.

"I shall be glad to show you these marshlands and the sea."

"That would be great. I have never seen the sea and beaches before."

He led her to a forested area close to the river where he lived. The hut was small but nicely built, with a small garden in the back. Being surrounded by trees, it was not visible from the river. It was no wonder that Tiên Dung did not see anything from the river. He served her fish for dinner. It was not the elaborate meal she used to having at her father's castle, but it was better than the dry food she had been consuming for the last few days.

She returned to her barge for the night and the following day decided to marry him. Although she had not intended to marry before, she thought that after this fateful meeting, they were predestined to live together.

She knew she would be disinherited if she returned to the palace after marrying against the advice of her parents. Therefore, she sold her boat and jewelry, settled down, and opened a trading post that soon thrived.

In the meantime, the king sent search teams all over the country to look for Tiên Dung. One team followed the river while the others searched on land. The search ended up in the marshland area called *Nhật Dạ Trạch* where the Hồng River (Red River) meandered in the delta before reaching the Eastern Sea. They had heard of a princess living in the area.

The king, notified about the findings, sent troops to take the princess home. However, when they arrived at the marsh a thick fog descended on the area. It spread out right and left and engulfed the land. Troops could not understand how the weather could change that rapidly. They had a hard time seeing their way around, lost their track and ended up falling in the marshes. The light of the hut that flickered in the darkness would disappear and reappear in another place. It was like a game of hide and seek. Strange noises rose from the marshland. There were the croaking of toads, the hissing of snakes, and other strange and weird noises they could only hear in the marsh. Frightened, they huddled together in an attempt to rebuild their confidence through their numbers. The more they walked, the farther away the light would become. Despite back tracking, they had a hard time finding their way out. After a lot of struggle, they returned to their camps.

They tried again the next day. The same fog again descended on the area. Not wanting to get lost in the marsh, they soon backed out. Other attempts were later made but also resulted in failure. The king, believing the fog came down by divine intervention, made the decision to abort the search.

Tiên Dung was happy to see troops leaving one day. She knew they had decided to leave her alone. She had built herself a new life in a new environment and was happy with the choice. She and her husband became successful, built themselves a palace and lived happily together for a long time. This legend is also known as *Nhật Dạ Trạch* or "One Night Marsh."[18]

Comments It is in the historical legends of ancient times that we see all these strong women like Âu Cơ, the Trung sisters, Lady Triệu, Tiên Dung in "The Marsh Boy," and Mỵ Châu in "The Crossbow." They of course lived in a matriarchal society that allowed them to express themselves freely, voice their opinions, and behave as men's equals. They were leaders who went to war or decided the future of the nation; they were independent and charted their own course in life.

The legends of *Nhật Dạ Trạch* and the Crossbow describe two strong-willed women who disobeyed their fathers and followed their husbands. This could only happen during the time when matriarchal society was in vogue. In a patriarchal Confucian society, these women would have to obey to their fathers, then their husbands, by order of merit.

It does not mean that women did not exhibit courage during the Confucian period. Their voices, however, were drowned out by male voices. Despite these prohibitions, some women—like the iconoclastic nineteenth-century-poetess Hồ Xuân Hương—have left indelible marks on the Vietnamese society.

By recording the nature of the society, these legends recorded the identity of the country and how it changed over time. Without them we would not have known that Vietnam was once a matriarchal society.

The legend of *Nhật Dạ Trạch* focuses on two ideas: first, the building of a new village and country, and second, the freedom of children—a concept that is anathema in a Confucian world.

Princess Tiên Dung is the Vietnamese tomboy par excellence—at a time when the Wild West did not even exist. She did whatever she wanted. She explored the countryside, traveled down the river, married a lad, and did not want to return to her father's castle. She was the free spirit, the one child who escaped from home to build a new life from scratch. She wanted to build her own happiness and home with a stranger rather than through a prearranged marriage.

The legend of *Nhật Dạ Trạch* is similar to that of "The Watermelon Island." In the first case, the princess made up her mind to find the solution to her life by herself. Mai An Tiêm in "The Watermelon Island," who was banished to an island, found salvation for himself by building a new community. The two legends stress self-sufficiency and independence instead of reliance on the power, wealth, and authority of parents or forebears.

Strangely enough, the patriarchal society was not as kind to Princess Tiên Dung as to Chử Đồng Tử. Although she was the person who found the naked man, provided him with seed money to start his business, and made up her mind to stay with him, she remained a secondary figure in real life.

Chử Đồng Tử, on the other hand, has over the centuries been elevated to the status of a folk hero. He later became the god of North Vietnamese agriculture for having conquered the marsh and developed agriculture and trade. This deification process explains the multitude of gods, genies and shrines in North Vietnam. There is no equivalent god of agriculture in South Vietnam, although the South produces the bulk of rice in Vietnam.

He even has his Chủ Đồng Tử festival, which is celebrated on the 10th–12th days of the third lunar month at the Chủ Đồng Tử temple in Du Hòa village of the Hưng Yên province, about 12 miles east of Hanoi.

8. The Lake of the Sword

The Chinese Ming invaded Vietnam in 1407 and tore the Vietnamese system apart. New taxes and rules went into effect, causing people to suffer as a result. The latter formed militia groups to take action against the invaders. One of these groups was led by Lê Lợi, a wealthy landowner from Thanh Hóa province.

In the same province lived a fisherman named Lê Thân. He went fishing one day and pulled up something heavy, which he thought was a big fish. It turned out to be a piece of metal, which he threw back in the water. He threw his net into the water again and pulled up the same piece of metal, which he again dumped into the water. He moved to another place on the river and threw his net a third time. He again retrieved the same piece of metal. Exasperated, he brought it home, cleaned it and worked on it. It turned out to be a nice sword.

Lê Lợi, along with a few friends, visited Lê Thân—his militiaman— one night. In the dark hut, he saw the reflection of the light on the sword. He picked it up and read on the blade the words "*Thuận Thiên*" or "Heaven's Will."

"How did you get this sword, Lê Thân?" he asked.

"I got it out of the river a few weeks ago."

"Out of the river? You must be kidding?"

"I was fishing on a nearby river when I retrieved this blade three times. I therefore decided to keep it."

"It must come from a noble man because of the words engraved on the blade."

No one, however, knew the significance of the sword at the time.

The resistance movement suffered multiple setbacks in the beginning. It was not well organized and the militiamen were too few compared to the Chinese soldiers. Lê Lợi had to retreat to his secret headquarters. When he saw something sparkling on top of a tree, he climbed up it and pulled down a metallic sheath, which looked like a sword cover.

He then remembered Lê Thân's sword. The next day, he went to Lê Thân's house and got his sword. Since it fitted well inside the sheath, Lê Lợi exclaimed, "It is god's will. He wants us to accomplish an important work. Let us gather our men to flush out the Chinese."

From that time onward, Lê Lợi always carried the sword with him. With it, he defeated many of the invaders. Ten long years of resistance (1418–1427) had weakened the Chinese and allowed Lê Lợi to win one battle after another. He finally got rid of the Chinese in 1427. He ascended to the throne under the name of Lê Thái Tổ and became the founder of the new Lê dynasty. Peace finally settled on the land.

A year later, King Lê Thái Tổ rode on a boat on Lake Lục Thủy (green water, named for the color of its water). When he reached the middle of the lake, a giant turtle (Kim Quy) popped out of the water.

"Sire, please return the sword to Lord Dragon," said the turtle.

Astonished, the king took a few minutes to realize what the turtle was talking about. He pulled out his sword, lifted above his head. From there, it flew directly into the mouth of the turtle, which grabbed it. The turtle slowly submerged into the water and disappeared.

The king told his people: "Lord Dragon had lent me his magic sword so that I could fight against the Chinese. Now that peace has been achieved, he wanted me to return his sword."

From then on, the Lục Thủy Lake was known as *Hồ Gươm* (The Lake of the Sword) or *Hồ Hoàn Kiếm* (the Lake of the returned Sword).[19]

Comments Hoàng Kiếm Lake is located in the historical district of Hanoi, North Vietnam. Once a part of the Hồng River, it is now located several kilometers east of the river. On a small island at its center was built the Tháp Rùa or Tortoise Tower to commemorate the place where King Lê Thái Tổ returned his sword (Heaven's Will) to the genie turtle Kim Quy. Several turtles are known to live in the lake, although their numbers are unknown. Endangered, they are of the species *Rafetus swinhoei* or *Rafetus leloii*, in honor of the emperor. A huge turtle was sighted there in 2008.

On the northern shore of the lake lies Jade Island, on which the Ngọc Sơn (Jade Mountain) Temple stands. It honors the thirteenth-century Trần Hưng Đạo who fought against the Chinese Yuan dynasty. A red-painted Húc bridge connects the shore to the island.

9. The Marble Mountains

An old man lived all his life close to the sea in central Vietnam. His hut was small, although decent for a single man. He loved the clear days where he could see far away into the horizon and the soft breeze that soothed the hot summer months. He was also used to the monsoon rains that beat down on the beaches.

One day, a violent storm struck the coastal area. Trees and his hut bent under the force of the winds. The sky was filled with black clouds and rains came in a downpour. A huge dragon with scintillating scales descended on the beach from the sky, lay down, and deposited a huge egg. It then flew, away taking with it clouds and winds. The sky became bright and clear again.

Our old man came out to check out his hut, which although not in great shape, still stood up. When he looked at the beach, he saw a monstrous egg, which measured about three to four feet in length. He had never seen such a big egg in his life. As he was inspecting it, a huge golden turtle slowly made its way from the sea toward the egg and said, "I am Kim Quy, the golden turtle who works for Lord Dragon. Please take special care of Lord Dragon's egg."

"How could an old man like me take care of this egg?" inquired the man.

"Take this claw. If you have any problem, just put it into your ear and I will come to your aid."

The turtle pulled out one of his claws and gave it to the old man. It went back to the sea and disappeared.

The old man was thrilled to be of help to Lord Dragon. He dug around the egg and tried to cover it with sand, although it took him some time. He watched it grow bigger and bigger every day. One day, a couple of troublemakers riding on an ox cart moved directly toward the egg. Noticing the danger, the old man pulled out the claw and placed it into his ear. He heard Kim Quy tell him, "Stay down. Stay down."

He was just lying down when he found himself transformed into a huge tiger. Seeing the tiger, the troublemakers turned the cart around and moved away.

As the egg grew in size, the old man set his hut over it to protect it from the sun and winds. Every day, he came out and threw sand or leaves over it to try to cover it. The egg, however, continued to grow in height and width and soon became a small hill. The more he worked, the more useless it became because of the speed of the growth.

XII. Southern Legends: Historical

His hut one day tilted, toppled off the hill, and broke in half. When he called Kim Quy for help, a voice told him help was on the way. He heard a sharp noise and a crack developed in the shell. It soon became a cave where he found a small bed. He lay down and fell asleep.

In his dream, he saw a little girl emerging out of the egg and sitting down close to his bed. Milk that dripped out of the wall of the hill had nourished her throughout childhood. She played with groups of monkeys that came to bring her fruits. Everything happened like in a fairy tale.

The old man did not realize he had taken a long and peaceful sleep. He was quite surprised when he woke up to see a young girl sitting by his bed.

"Dad, for the last fifteen years, I have been watching you breathing regularly. I am pleased to see you finally awake," said the overjoyed teenager.

The old man remembered his dream. He also recognized the little girl who came out of the egg. Things had changed quite a bit since he took his nap. A year in real life appeared like a few hours in his dream. What was strange was that the egg had become a huge mountain by the sea covered with lush trees. Birds were singing nearby. As he was about to get up, he felt a small object on his bed. It was his claw, which he tucked into his ear. He heard Kim Quy giving him new instructions: get out of the cave and instruct the young girl about society and the rules that bind humans together.

Surprised to see a mountain suddenly appear in their district, villagers believed that heaven had come down to earth to help them. They came to visit the old man and the young girl and to ask them for remedies to their medical problems.

The young girl took different pebbles of varied colors and threw them in all four directions. A special type of tree grew up with a five-petal flower that was designed to cure malaria. Rumors about their power grew and even reached the walls of the palace. Having heard of a beautiful and gentle girl living in the mountains, the king sent an emissary to ask her hand for his son. Since the old man did not know how to respond to the request, he placed the claw into his ear and was told, "Let the marriage proceed forward."

Serving as the girl's stepfather, the old man agreed with the king's request, and soon the maiden and the prince got married. She later went to the capital to live with her husband. She asked whether the old man would join her at the imperial palace. He told her that he needed to talk to

Kim Quy. Sometime later, people could see the old man smiling and riding on top of Kim Quy toward the sea.[20]

The Marble Mountains are still visible today. They form the most beautiful mountain range in Quảng Nam, central Vietnam. The range is also called Ngũ Hành Sơn or the Five-element Mountains.[21]

Comments Ngũ Hành Sơn is a cluster of marble and limestone hills located south of Danang in central Vietnam. It is named after the five elements: Kim (metal), Thủy (water), Mộc (wood), Hóa (fire), and Thọ (earth). The mountain limestone has been used in the construction of many buildings in North as well as South Vietnam.

The mountains have numerous caves and tunnel entrances. The famous Huyền Không Buddhist temple is located in one of its caves. Daylight reaches the Buddhist altar only during midday through an opening in the cave roof. Ngũ Hành Sơn Mountains have become a tourist area. During the war, some of these caves served as hiding places for the Viet Cong.

Mountains have always been places of veneration for the Vietnamese, who considered them holy places. In the Mekong Delta, the Seven Sacred Mountains, close to the border with Cambodia are a well known retreat, holy place, and training center for Buddhist priests.

About one million people each year come to visit the shrine of *Bà Chúa Xứ*, the Lady of the Realm at Sam Mountain—one of the Seven Sacred Mountains—close to Châu Đốc, about 100 miles west of Saigon. For them, the Lady is viewed as a mother, provider for children, benevolent creditor, healer, and relationship advisor. The rise in popularity of these gods is symptomatic of the ideological unmooring of contemporary Vietnamese society, a sign of post-revolutionary demoralization.

10. Côn Sơn Island

Gió đưa cây cải về trời,
Rau răm ở lại chịu đời đắng cay
The wind blows the flower toward the sky,
The plant stays behind to suffer from a bitter life.[22]

It has been said that these two verses describe the tumultuous life of Hoàng Phi Yến, born Le Thi Răm, a secondary wife of Nguyễn Ánh.[23]

In 1782 Lord Nguyễn Ánh, scion of the Nguyễn dynasty, was fighting against the Tây Sơn rebels to regain his throne. Chased out of Saigon,

Ánh and his retinue one day landed on the Island of Côn Sơn, about 80 miles south of Saigon. Underarmed and overpowered by his enemy, he decided to send his son, the four-year-old prince Cải, to Paris with Bishop de Behaine in an attempt to secure military help from the King of France.

Răm advised him that the Tây Sơn are "an internal problem. To ask for outside help may not result in a good outcome." In a fit of rage, Ánh accused Răm of siding with the enemy and condemned her to death. Counseled by his advisers, he commuted her sentence to banishment to one of the islands.[24] As for prince Cải, he refused to go to France without his mother. Ánh threw him overboard into the sea. Eventually prince Cảnh was sent to Paris with the bishop.

As for Răm, she died on the island—now called Lady's Island—and local people built a small temple in her honor.

Comments 1. *Cải* is the name of a flower in central Vietnam. *Cải* also means to argue. It has been said that the prince liked to argue and therefore was given that name. Răm is coincidentally the name of a bitter but edible oriental plant.

2. Nguyễn Ánh regained his throne in 1802 after a 20-year struggle against the Tây Sơn. He was enthroned under the name of Gia Long (1802–1820). Whether the story is a true one or just a legend is not known.

Although Bishop de Behaine was not successful in getting any help from the King of France, he brought back a few boats and armaments that were financed by private donors. He assisted Ánh in the reconquest of his throne.

3. Côn Sơn Island is the largest island of the Côn Đảo archipelago, where the French built a prison for political prisoners.

B. ANIMAL LEGENDS

Vietnam has many legends about animals. This is in keeping with the 12-year Chinese cycle in which a different animal represents each year. Therefore, even the most insignificant animal or insect, even the fly, has a tale attached to it. Who would ever think that the lowly toad could be heaven's uncle? This is one of the stories that would make anyone laugh. In this case, the toad turns out to be a witty leader in spite of itself. The crab is depicted in two stories. Even the dumb duck has a tale for itself. The tiger is smart, but not as smart as man.

11. The Toad Is Heaven's Uncle
12. How the Tiger Got Its Stripes
13. The Crab
14. The House Gecko
15. The Flies
16. The Mosquito
17. The Silkworm
18. Dã Tràng Crabs
19. Why Ducks Sleep Standing on One Leg

11. The Toad Is Heaven's Uncle

A long time ago when heaven was closer to earth and animals could talk and communicate with each other, a long drought had settled on earth. In the beginning, no one paid attention to it because everyone thought the drought would be short-lived. As it got worse and no rain was forthcoming, fields became parched, harvests were lost and rivers and ponds shrank in size. Animals died in great numbers.

An ugly alpha male toad decided he could not stand it any longer. He wanted something done about it. If conditions remained the same, his pond would run out of water and he would surely die.

He decided to go and see the King of Heaven to request a direct action from him. He set out on a long journey with only one goal: relief from the drought. He leapt and leapt and a few hundred yards down the road met a swarm of bees.

"Where are you going, Mr. Toad?" one bee asked.

"To see if the King of Heaven could fix that drought for me," the toad answered.

"You are correct. This condition cannot last. The fields are parched, the flowers dead. We cannot find any honey anywhere. We will gladly follow you," the bees said.

And the bees buzzed along. A short distance away, the group met a rooster, who asked what they were doing. The toad explained the reason why they were heading to heaven. The rooster decided to go along because the drought had caused a shortage of grain and insects. Soon, he said, there would be nothing left to eat.

The enlarged group moved along until it met a fox. Upon hearing the explanation, the fox too joined the group. Because of the drought, game was getting scarcer and he could not find enough food in the forest. The group thus became larger with time and headed straight to heaven. The road was long and bumpy. Many animals died during the trip. The rest went on and even jumped from star to star.

When they arrived at the gate of heaven, the toad told them to wait for him while he discussed the matter with the king. He jumped over the gate, went inside and found himself in the Hall of Mirrors, where mirrors covered all the walls. A loud laughter greeted him. Surprised, he headed straight to the main room from whence the noise came. He found the King of Heaven playing a chess game with the angels.

Furious to see them engaging in a pastime while animals were dying, he made a big leap and landed in the middle of the table.

"How dare you, insolent animal, to disturb my game?" the king said.

"Your Majesty," the toad answered, but could not finish the sentence. Facing the king for the first time in his life, his jaws just locked up.

"What? How dare you to speak in my august presence? Guards, take him away."

The guards rushed in to take care of the toad. The latter, realizing the imminent danger, gathered all his courage and leapt off the table. He called the bees in for help. The hungry bees buzzed in and stung the guards, who just ran away. The king called the chief of the hounds to take care of the insolent toad. The toad called tigers and bears to the rescue. The tigers drove the hounds away. All the other animals rushed in to the rescue.

The king facing, a crowd of angry animals, calmed down and asked the toad what he wanted.

"Sire, it has not rained on earth for more than a year. Everything has dried up, the rivers and the ponds are empty, the fields parched. Animals are dying. There will not be any life left if you do not let the rain fall."

"Very well, uncle," the king said stressing on the latter word. "I will see that it be done. Next time, you do not need to make such a long trip to see me. Just croak and rain will come down."

He ordered the skies to open up and the downpour fell on earth. It filled up the rivers and ponds, and life came back, although two-thirds of the animals had already died. New growth and new animals were seen and nature normalized again.

The animals were happy and multiplied fast. When the toad died, the animals built a temple to him to commemorate the glorious day when he led them to Heaven. That was the reason why the toad earned the title of "Uncle of Heaven."[25]

Generations of toads have been watching at the supply of water and they never fail to croak when it becomes low. When you hear the toad croak, you know the rain will come down soon.

Comments 1. This is a nice short story that surely will delight all children. The main theme is unity. A toad by itself cannot do much. However, with the help of bees, lions, tigers, and other animals, it could even force the King of Heaven to send rain down to the earth. The secondary theme is that oppression—whether its cause is political or a natural disaster—could lead to revolt. Vietnam, like any country, has its share of oppression and revolts. In this legend, the animals finally revolted because the drought not only decreased food sources but decimated many of their populations.

2. Another corollary has to do with the messenger. Anyone who is brave enough can become a messenger in difficult times. One does not need to be a genius to lead others. Leadership is just loudership: big mouths take charge.

A recent study published in the *Journal of Personality and Social Psychology* showed that those who spoke up were rated as having high intelligence. Those who did not were labeled as "conventional" and "uncreative." However, the highest scorers were not the ones who gave the most correct answers nor were the most competent. They just "behaved as if they were."[26]

3. Vietnam has a saying that stresses unity:

> Một cây làm chẳng nên non,
> Ba cây chụm lại nên hòn núi sông.
>
> One tree cannot make a hill,
> Three trees put together will create mountain and river.

Three trees, of course, would not create a mountain. But by uniting themselves, people could gain much more than from going alone. Mountains and rivers could be created out of the union of people. Vietnam has not always been a united country. On the contrary, it has been more divided than any other country in the world. However, when they became united they could do miracles.[27]

Therefore, this lesson particularly does apply to the Vietnamese themselves. Someone once compared them to diamonds. Each of them shines brightly, is articulate and brilliant on his own, but they do not stick together as a group to make their influence felt. A better analogy would be to compare them to crabs, which could easily crawl out of a trap once they got caught. But each one grabs, and holds on to another so tightly that no one is able to escape. As a result, they all remain trapped. The same thing occurs to the Vietnamese who do not want anyone to outshine them. In the end, there is only a uniform crowd with no superstar or leader. This has been the biggest drawback of the Vietnamese.

The success of the Việt Kiều or overseas Vietnamese in political and economic fields remains individual in nature. They are small-business owners, private entrepreneurs, professionals, and scientists who owe their successes to themselves and their families. There are no Vietnamese-American corporations employing thousands of employees yet. Things could change. The ultimate challenge would be to prove their maturity by gaining political and economic leverage through mutual trust and solidarity.

12. How the Tiger Got Its Stripes

A long time ago when animals were still talking, the tigers did not have any stripes at all. Their yellowish fur let them stand out among the tree trunks. They stayed away from human beings because they saw them as opponents. They got stripes only recently, when they began to deal with humans.

A no-stripe tiger was watching from afar as a farmer worked with his buffalo. Every day, the farmer came with his buffalo, attached him to his plow, and the two of them worked all day long without fighting. Occasionally, if the animal slowed down the farmer would whip him with his cane. The tiger was curious as to how the buffalo could cooperate with humans.

When the farmer took his nap under a palm tree, the tiger approached the buffalo and asked, "You have been working hard for the farmer every day. How can you tolerate him?"

"I do not have any choice."

"What do you mean? You are strong and muscular. Yet, he rules you and puts you in bondage."

"He has some kind of power that he calls wisdom. That is why I have to listen to him."

"How do I get this wisdom? If I had this power, I would not have to hunt any longer. I could tell the animals to come to me and I would have dinner right away."

"You have to ask the farmer about that."

A while later, the tiger approached the farmer and enquired, "Your buffalo told me you have a strange power over the animals. Could you share your secret with me?"

"Certainly, but it will cost you a lot."

"How can I acquire this power?"

"I will show you. I have it at home."

"May I follow you?"

"No, you better stay here. People would shoot you if they see you around the village."

The farmer told him he would get the magic formula for him. However, he was afraid to leave his buffalo alone with the tiger because the latter could harm it.

"I do not feel safe with you around my buffalo. Therefore, I will have to tie you to a tree while I get your formula."

"Fine," the tiger responded, knowing he had no choice. He was so eager to lay his paws on wisdom that he would have agreed to almost anything.

He stood up; and the farmer took a rope and tied him against the tree. The farmer went home and stayed there for a long time. When he came back, he brought with him straw and firewood and placed them under the tiger's feet. He lit the fire up, which slowly burned the tiger. The latter roared so loudly that it awakened the whole community. He was singed and burned. He pleaded with the farmer to release him, but to no avail. When the ropes finally burned, he freed himself and rapidly ran away with his tail under his legs, vowing never to deal with humans again.

He was never able to get rid of the black stripes of the ropes where the flames had left marks in his flesh. Therefore, he is running around with stripes on.[28]

Comments Although the peasant is not always educated, he is very pragmatic and down to earth. He knows what is good for him. He knows that if he owns a piece of land and works hard, he will have enough to eat. He does not think beyond that. His thinking is never esoteric because his life depends on something concrete.

Faced with a wild tiger that could kill his buffalo or livestock, he simply thought he needed to tie him down. Once the animal was immobilized, he could do anything he wanted to him. He went home, took a long nap and let the animal worry about his fate. He brought firewood to burn him and scare him away. There was nothing grandiose about his thought: just simple and basic thinking.

Because of his "wit," he is set forward to represent humanity, to rule over the world and the animals, and to domesticate buffaloes, horses, sheep, and chickens for his own needs.

During the war, many peasants in the Mekong Delta remained neutral. They just wanted to be left alone. Although the majority believed in the GVN (Government of Vietnam), they were under heavy pressure from the Viet Cong, who used terrorist tactics to force peasants to follow them.

13. The Crab

Huệ was a nice and cute girl who lived with her widowed father in a small village. The latter remarried. When she was ten, Huệ's father died unexpectedly, leaving her by herself.

The stepmother had a daughter of her own, Hồng, who was vain and did not do anything good all day long. She stood in front of the mirror to comb her hair and get dressed up. Since her mother complimented her all the time, Hồng had become selfish and arrogant.

Huệ had to do all the work, from washing clothes to cleaning and cooking. Knowing her situation, she bent her head and kept working. She listened, obeyed, and accepted criticisms, yells, and screams that rained down on her. Everyone loved her and pitied her, although no one could do anything.

One day, Huệ put on a beautiful red shirt. She was a pretty girl to begin with and the shirt just accentuated her beauty much more. Hồng, on the other hand, could have worn any fancy shirt without looking any better. The boys in the neighborhood just wanted to befriend Huệ, while they shunned Hồng all along.

The stepmother, seeing Huệ in that outfit, could not contain her rage.

"How could she dare to be more beautiful than my Hồng?" she thought to herself. She then screamed at the top of her lungs: "Where did you get that shirt, lousy girl? Did you steal it?"

"No, dear mother."

"Did any guy in the neighborhood give it to you?"

"No, mother. An old lady gave it to me."

"Which lady? You better tell me the truth, otherwise I will beat you."

"I really do not know who she is. I was pulling water out of the well the other day when she approached me. Her clothes were dirty and ragged. She told me she was thirsty and asked if she could have a drink. I poured some water in a bowl and gave it to her. She later gave me a small gift, which turned out to be this shirt."

The stepmother thought for a moment and told herself, "This girl may be right. She does not lie. Villagers have told me about a fairy who has come around recently. I need to send Hồng out there to see if the fairy might help her look prettier."

From then onward, Huệ did not have to fetch water. Hồng had replaced her for that job. Although Hồng did not like it, the thought of getting prettier had enticed her to work. Therefore, she went to the well every day, trying to meet the fairy.

One beautiful morning, as the sun was high in the sky, an old woman in ragged clothing came by. Seeing Hồng, she said, "Young girl, my shirt is all dirty. Do you mind washing it for me?"

"Dirty old woman," Hồng yelled. "Who do you think I am to do that dirty job for you? You are not even worthy of holding my shoes."

"What an insolent girl. She is definitely not like her sister."

"How do you know my sister?" Hồng immediately realized that she had made a big mistake. She had ruined weeks of hard work trying to meet the fairy and at that moment had insulted the person who could have made her prettier.

"A bad girl like you does not deserve to be pretty," the fairy said. "You will be punished."

The old woman left. Hồng also disappeared, and was replaced by a small, ugly animal that has eight legs and two claws. It looks like no other animal on earth. It runs sideways and down the river as soon as it encounters a human being. It is the crab.[29]

Comments This is a nice and interesting story about the crab. Actually, the crab has not done anything wrong, except being ugly, with its thick shell, dark black or blue hues, multiple legs and two formidable claws. Its grip is painful and powerful. Otherwise, it is a benign crustacean that people love to eat.

Like in *Tấm Cám* (Vietnamese Cinderella), the legend is about a naughty daughter and an abusive stepmother. Stepmothers have been depicted to abuse their stepchildren, especially stepdaughters, while protecting their own daughters. This is the danger that faces men who get remarried—a frequent occurrence in today's society. Luckily, there are fairies who wander around and help abused stepdaughters. In most legends, good people are rewarded while bad ones are punished. They serve as teaching tools that stress the consequences of each deed.

14. The House Gecko

In a small village by the sea lived a poor couple. They worked hard but could barely make ends meet. The man did odd jobs but suffered from one setback after another. Their straw hut, which was the smallest in the village, had only a table and two mismatched chairs. They used second-hand broken dinnerware their neighbors gave them.

The man, Thạch Sùng, was good at locating water. When villagers decided to dig a well, they asked him to pinpoint the right spot for them. His success rate was high and the extra fee he earned from these predictions went to pay the interest usurers charged him.

There was a drought at that time during which his service was frequently requested. He of course made a lot of money, which he spent on gambling. Because of the drought, his reputation went to the king. The latter enrolled him in his service. His job was to help find water for the villagers. He was handsomely rewarded for his work and soon was able to buy new furniture and dinnerware. He bought himself a new house because the old one could not hold all his furniture. He continued to gamble, although now he was very lucky. His winning streak was unbroken. With the extra income, he bought himself fancy lamps, furniture, dinnerware, and clothing. While before he was dining with broken silverware, now he only used the most expensive dinnerware that came from China.

His neighbors of course envied him. A poor lad who suddenly became rich always excited jealousy and admiration. He befriended the king's brother Tâm, who was also a gambler. The two were seen together a lot because their common interest—gambling—united them.

As he grew richer, he became more arrogant. Considering himself the center of the world, he made fun of his "poor" neighbors. He looked down on them because they were not as cultured as he was and did not own China wares.

The king's brother was also mad at Thạch Sùng, who won on every occasion. He wanted to get back some of the belongings he had lost to Thạch Sùng. The odds were low because Thạch Sùng was always lucky. One day he asked his brother's opinion:

"How could I win against him? He has everything in the world: dinnerware, furniture, lamps. Many of the princes do not have half of his belongings."

"You are correct, brother," answered the king.

"What can I do?"

"Let me think for a minute. Since all his belongings are new, I bet that he does not have anything old or broken. Just ask him whether he has an old broken teapot."

"Are you sure?"

"Definitely. The lad has disposed of his old stuff now that he is rich. If you ask him for a broken teapot, he surely would not have it."

Tâm went to see Thạch Sùng and proposed to him another round of wagers. Whoever wins this time will win the other person's possessions. Thạch Sùng's eyes lit up with greed. The chance of owning Tâm's belongings gave him a big thrill. He would win for sure, for he believed in his luck. He would then be the richest person in the country, except for the king.

The two friends set up an appointment for the following day. They also invited the local mandarin as a witness, since the bet was so high. The two contestants showed up as scheduled. Each one would draw a piece of straw. The one with the shortest straw would ask first.

Thạch Sùng went first because he had picked up the shortest straw.

"Are you ready?"

"Yes, go ahead," said Tâm.

"Do you have a very special Chinese vase made during the Song dynasty?"

The vase was very rare, and Thạch Sùng knew Tâm did not have it the last time he went to his house.

"As a matter of fact, I just bought one last week. I did not have time to show it to you. It was in my living room."

The group went to Tâm's house to check it out. The vase was right there. Thạch Sùng thus lost the first round. The group returned to Thạch Sùng's house and Tâm asked:

"I am going to ask you a simple thing, knowing you have everything in the world. Do you have an old broken teapot?"

Thạch Sùng thought for a moment, then answered:

"Well. I have many teapots, but an old broken teapot, I do not have it. I discarded all my broken dinnerware a long time ago."

With that, he became silent. He smacked his tongue a couple of times to express his regret and went back to his home with his shoulders slumped down. He realized that with one answer, he lost all the possessions that had taken him two decades to collect. From this time onward, he always smacked his tongue in regret for the loss of his personal fortune.

He moved out to a small hut that was lacking any furniture. Deeply consumed by the loss, he soon passed away. His spirit turned into a house gecko that crawled up the walls and on the ceiling and continuously produced a smacking sound similar to what Thạch Sùng did. People said the gecko—his spirit—missed his possessions so much that it smacked its tongue all the time.[30]

Comments Financial failure has been present since immemorial times as suggested by the above legend, although probably less than today. It could be caused by harvest failure, drought, war, politics, gambling, illnesses and so on. Harvests are frequently affected by natural causes like drought, flooding, plant diseases, and locust invasions. People at the time had a single-crop culture; that crop could be easily wiped out by natural causes. They did not have insecticides and diversification was unknown. Today's farmers know how to diversify their investments, plant multiple crops, and so on, although they are still at the mercy of nature.

In a sense, this is another story about greed. Gambling is not only an addiction, but also another face of greed. The gambler is a person who wants to win at all costs—win everything that other people own. He does not care whether the other person would go bankrupt or not, he only cares about his own success. The end result could be financial ruin. Thạch Sùng thought that he would always win but had not prepared himself for a setback. Success rendered him arrogant and contemptuous. When he lost the biggest gamble of his life, he could not withstand the loss and died soon after. A Vietnamese saying suggests that fortune fluctuated in cycles:

> *Khong ai giàu ba họ, khổ ba đời.*
> *No one is rich or destitute for more than three generations.*

Based on observations recorded over many generations, elders have predicted that fortune could be made or lost within a three-generation span. Rich and arrogant investors would gamble their fortunes away thinking they could beat the odds. In the end, they faltered like Thạch Sùng. Fortunes could, however, be kept longer if people carefully managed their portfolio. In the same vein, no one would be destitute for a long time if they tried hard to get out of their economic woes. The saying suggests a healthy attitude about money.

15. *The Flies*

There once was a handsome and well-educated gentleman who lived in a village by the sea. He was good to people as well as to flies. When dinner was served, he always asked that a portion of the meal be served to them. The flies enjoyed the daily treat, for no human being had cared for them before. In return, they protected his house and kept insects away.

The country was at the time ruled by a good king who was looking for a well-intentioned and good husband for his daughter. She was a beautiful maiden who was also smart and wise. The king devised his own strategy to look for a son-in-law. He had a palace built in the woods with nine identical rooms. He then placed his daughter in one of the rooms; whoever could guess her location would marry her.

Many princes and warlords who thought they were smart and ingenious volunteered for the trial. They had one out of nine chances to succeed. They all walked around the house, stopping in front of each room to try to locate her. They all failed and each received 20 lashes as part of the deal. No one dared to volunteer any longer because of the punishment and the ridicule that came with failure.

Our gentleman of the flies—so named because of his association with the flies—decided to try his luck. He went to the palace and looked at all the rooms carefully, but like the others had no clue. The flies, however, flew around and noticed the room where the princess was hidden. They advised the gentleman, who then nonchalantly announced the answer to the king. The king could not understand how he could have solved the puzzle.

Upset, the king designed another puzzle for the man to solve. He had nine meals prepared and displayed on nine similar tables. Underneath one of the platters, he had someone place a piece of paper indicating the suitor's name. The gentleman of the flies had to guess which table was the correct one. The flies once again helped him out and showed him the right table. The king could only shake his head and give his daughter in marriage.

This was how a man's association with flies turned to his favor.[31]

Comments This is a simple and straightforward legend. Life was unsophisticated at that time and revolved around simple guesses. There was no magic or trick to be played. The king was giving away his daughter in marriage not to the most educated or richest man, but to the most skilled person available. Skill is based on the ability to solve puzzles, not on experience or education. The gentleman of the flies had one advantage over all his competitors: he was a good and kind man who could secure the help of flies. Others could have titles, riches, or education but did not possess street smarts to solve the puzzle. This is similar to the peasant's wisdom discussed in "The Tiger's Stripes." Other people call it *emotional intelligence*, as opposed to *book intelligence* that comes from studying or reading books.

In the contest about winning the hand of the princess, anyone could try out; but the price of failure was 20 lashes. The legend tells us that there is a price to pay for everything. Nothing is free in this world. The king certainly did not want any lad to come in and try to get his daughter in an irresponsible manner.

16. The Mosquito

Mosquitoes are the most dreaded insects in tropical regions of the world, especially in Vietnam. They irritate people by buzzing constantly into their ears, by refusing to go away, and by disrupting their sleep. The more one wants to chase them away, the faster they come back. They transmit viral and bacterial diseases like malaria and dengue fever—diseases that could lead to death.

Ngọc Nhân was a poor but responsible farmer. He worked all day long in his field, happy to make ends meet. He got acquainted with Lan Điệp, a farmer's daughter from across the river where he lived. She was talkative and had an engaging smile. He would sit down, listen to her talk and feel happy. Thinking she was a good woman, he married her. She, however, hid her feelings so well that our farmer thought she was in deep love with him. She was a coquettish woman who liked clothes and material riches, which our simple farmer had a hard time providing for her. He worked harder all the time to support her needs, but always came up short.

One day, she felt sick and passed away. He was inconsolable because he was very fond of her. Although he did not say much, he craved her babbling and listened endlessly to her talks. He was so attached to her that he refused to have her buried. He sold his land and hut, loaded her coffin aboard his sampan and sailed away.

He just paddled from place to place like a man who had lost his mind. How long had he paddled and to where, he did not even know. He eventually landed on a strange and idyllic place sometime later. There were nice fruit trees, beautiful flowers, and fragrant hillside trees. Everything was peaceful and quiet. When he put his feet down for the first time during the trip, he met an old man with whitish hair flowing down his shoulders and a whitish beard. His eyes sparkled like those of a young person. He walked with the help of a twisted and spiraled cane that looked as old as he was. He greeted Ngọc Nhân.

"Welcome to the land of peace, Ngọc Nhân. I am aware of your virtues and will be glad to take you as my student."

As Ngọc Nhân recognized him as the genie of medicine, *Thiên Thai*, he kowtowed before the old man and responded, "Respectable genie, I do not know how I got here. But you are the person I am looking for. Although I am deeply touched by your offer, I am not eager to learn anything new. I would only like to ask you for one single favor, Sire."

"What can I do for you?"

"Please bring my wife back to life. I miss her so much that I cannot live without her."

"Do you realize what you are asking for?" the genie asked with a mixture of kindness and pity. "Why would you want to hang on to a fragile and inconstant creature instead of learning about the truth of life? Why are you so attached to a world of change and bitterness?"

"Sire, I miss her a lot. My life is not the same without her."

"Very well, my dear. I hope you will not regret your wish later on. Just give me three drops of your blood."

Ngọc Nhân opened the coffin as the genie had suggested, made a cut on his finger and let three drops of blood fall on his wife's body. The latter soon woke up, stretched herself and wondered where she was.

"Where am I? What am I doing in this small and tight bed?" asked Lan Điệp.

"Welcome back to the world, honey. You have slept a long time," said her husband with joy.

"I did not realize that I slept that long. Let's go home."

After thanking the genie profusely, he and his wife headed home on their sampan. He rowed and rowed, eager to return home and enjoy a new family life. They stopped at a local harbor to get some food. While he was shopping in the store, a boat captain, seeing the beautiful Lan Điệp by herself, invited her to his boat. Having never seen a large boat before, she was flattered to be invited aboard. While showing her the deck, he had the anchor lifted and sailed down the river.

Once Ngọc Nhân got out of the store, he looked for his wife and found no trace of her. He waited and waited and soon realized that she had been kidnapped. He asked for directions, followed the trail and caught up with the boat one month later. He challenged the boat captain and asked him to let his wife go. Lan Điệp showed up and told her husband she was used to her new life and wanted to stay with the captain.

Deeply hurt, Ngọc Nhân realized the true nature of his wife. Although the genie had warned him before, he had not paid attention to it. Distraught, he just asked for one thing.

"Give me back my three drops of blood," Ngọc Nhân asked. "I do not want to leave any trace of myself in you."

Glad to get away with only losing three drops of blood, Lan Điệp cut the tip of her small finger. As blood dripped from the wound, she fainted and passed away.

Her spirit came back as a mosquito, which continuously hunted for a human victim in search of the three drops of blood that could bring her back to life. She relentlessly buzzed around her husband, protested her innocence, and asked for his pardon. Since that time, she has generated many more mosquitoes that kept going after people.[32]

Comments One has to recognize that Ngọc Nhân was a very fortunate person. First, he was allowed to paddle all the way to the land of bliss for no one could get there unless invited. Then he encountered the genie of medicine, who offered to teach him the truth of life. Not too many people would get the same chance. The Vietnamese would say that he had to "purify himself through seven lives," or *tu luyện bảy đời*, to obtain these privileges.

Ngọc Nhân personifies many of us. We all tend to run after trivial things like physical beauty and riches that are ephemeral in nature and neglect to learn wisdom. Despite receiving blessings from the genie, and being warned about possible consequences, he only wanted to have his wife revived and to spend the rest of his life with her. In his denial, he sounds like many of us. After realizing the true nature of his wife, he was brave and reasonable enough to let her go. He was also smart enough to ask for his three drops of blood, without which Lan Điệp could not survive.

17. *The Silkworm*

A beautiful young woman named Hoa once lived in a small village with her old babysitter. The latter had cared for Hoa since childhood. With years flying by, she had become an old woman who could barely move around. Hoa, therefore, had no one to talk to and was often bored. She knitted all the time and when bored, looked out through the window at the river, which was meandering in front of the house.

Her father was on business trips all the time. He would come back to visit his daughter only during fall or spring. No one knew his whereabouts, but he was out of town most of the time. This made Hoa quite frustrated at times.

One day, she went outside and saw her father's beautiful horse grazing in front of the house. The strong and vigorous animal had in the past carried the merchant to various places, near or far. She approached the horse and told him, "I do not know where my father is. Just go and look for him. If you bring him back, I will be your wife."

Whether she was serious or just kidding with the horse, no one knew. The horse, on the other hand, felt very happy. The chance to live with the young woman was uplifting.

As soon as he heard these words, the horse leapt over the fence and ran across valleys and mountains. He ran from one county to another until he found a beer shop at the base of a mountain. He neighed three times. The merchant was inside the tavern sipping on his wine after a long day's work. He immediately recognized his horse. He thought that something must be wrong at home for the horse to seek him.

He came out, caressed his horse and jumped on his back. The horse literally flew back home. He was so happy to find his master and to be able to bring him home that distance and fatigue were no matter to him. He arrived home in no time.

Hoa was so happy to see her father that she forgot everything else. She hugged her father, hung around and talked to him.

The horse sat idle in his barn, morose and sad. He lay still on the ground, too depressed to move. Each time he heard Hoa sing or talk, he woke up and came to the barn door to look at her. Each time Hoa walked by, he tried to get up to catch a glimpse of her. Then he lay down too tired to move. He did not eat anything for days and days. He just hoped for a few words from her but got nothing.

The merchant asked his daughter about what was going on with the horse. She told him about her promise and how the horse ran to get him back. He became afraid the horse might hurt his daughter while he was away. He took his arrow out to get rid of the animal. It took it three days to die.

He had someone skin the horse, then placed the hide up on the fence to dry. He then went away on his trip again. He told Hoa to care for the hide so that he could make a saddle for the next horse.

One day, the wind blew hard and the hide fell on the ground. Hoa had to go out and bring it back home. She said, "You are just causing me too many problems. I might as well throw you away."

As soon as she said these words, the hide straightened out, wrapped around her body and flew all the way to the sea where mulberries grew. The hide became a cocoon and Hoa a silkworm.

From then onward, for the next thousand years, the silkworm would braid silk, protected on the outside by the cocoon. This is indeed the fate of life.[33]

Comments This is a rather sad legend that reminds us about keeping our promise. Sometimes we are unwise to make promises we can not keep. They eventually come back to haunt us later on. Sometimes we do not pay attention to what we say or promise until we face the consequences. In the present legend, Hoa, without thinking, promised to marry the horse if it could find her father. She did not expect the horse to have feelings and to understand what she said. Once the horse brought Hoa's father home, she quickly "forgot" her promise. The end result was a tragedy. The horse became sick and Hoa's father had to kill it so it could not harm his daughter.

18. Dã Tràng Crabs

Being a hunter is not always rewarding or fulfilling. Some days, Dã Tràng could catch plenty of game; on others, he would simply go home with an empty stomach. The joy of a hunter, therefore, lies in the adventure itself, the freedom to roam around, to see the countryside and to enjoy fresh air.

Back from his hunting trip one day, he noticed two snakes with white dots on their heads rolling side by side in the sun in front of the local shrine, which was dedicated to the god of agriculture. Villagers came by to give offerings, to pray for a good harvest or to thank the god for their bountiful harvest.

Surprised by the sight, he stepped back. But since they did not threaten him, he continued on his way home. From then onward, each time he passed by the shrine, he noticed the two nonchalant snakes taking a sunbath. How they got there was not known. Villagers, however, did not seem to mind their presence and continued to bring their offerings to the shrine.

One day, he saw a large black snake attacking the two smaller local snakes. He took his bow out and shot the larger one. Wounded, it ran away, chased by a small snake. The second one lay dead on the ground. He cleaned the blood around the shrine and took time to bury the snake with care. He went home satisfied after the work was completed.

At night, the spirit of the small snake appeared.

"Thank you for saving me today and for having been kind to my wife. You have been a good person. For all your good deeds I will give you this pearl, which when placed in your mouth will give you the power to understand and talk to the animals. Make good use of this new power."

With that, the spirit changed into a snake that opened its mouth and let drop a small white pearl. Shaken and sweating, the hunter woke up. He thought it was a bad dream. He had neither thought about having helped a spirit nor known animals that could talk or spit out pearls. He lit up his oil lamp and there on the table he noticed the small pearl he had seen in his dream. He put it aside and went back to bed, knowing he needed some rest before the long hunting day in the morning.

As he went out to hunt with the pearl in his mouth, the usually quiet forest suddenly came alive. Instead of the chirping of the birds, he heard them talking to each other, sharing the location of prey, and the presence of dangerous birds in the vicinity. The bees were talking instead of humming. He was fascinated by his new power and took some time to recover from that surprise. As he listened, he learned new things every single minute. He knew then that animals behave like human beings and do have human-type feelings. They do feel pain, joy, and anger like people. He thought to himself that he should shoot animals only when needed. The thought caught him by surprise.

The voice of a crow at his back brought him to reality.

"A deer at 200 feet on the left. Did you see it?"

The hunter strained his eyes to try to locate the game. He moved slowly and carefully, trying not to make any noise. He soon found the animal, positioned himself and shot it down. It ran away but soon staggered to the ground. Elated, he looked at the beautiful game he had just shot. Then he heard the crow telling him, "Remember my reward."

"Fine. I will give it to you. What do you want?"

"The entrails, just the entrails."

The hunter took the game's entrails and left them near a tree for the crow. He was happy to have the bird locate the game for him. He sure could use some help occasionally. From then on, he became very successful at hunting whenever the crow was around. There was no need for him to look for games, for the crow would take care of it. He would then share his game with the crow; the silent deal worked out fine for both of them.

XII. Southern Legends: Animal

Not for long, though, because nothing lasts forever on this earth. One day, the crow flew by and was visibly angry. It shouted at the hunter.

"Where was my share yesterday?"

"What do you mean?" retorted the hunter. "I left your share at the base of the tree. Did you not see it?"

"It was not there. I was hungry and mad yesterday because I did not receive my share. I will no longer work with you."

"But it was at the base of the tree."

"Thief. You did not leave anything."

Anger boiled in the hunter's blood. He could not be responsible if someone had taken the crow's share. Angry and excited, his face turned red. He was mad at being called a thief. In a moment of rage, he took out an arrow and shot the bird. The latter avoided the arrow and yelled back, "Revenge. Revenge."

The bird flew away with the arrow in his beak. Things seem to quiet down for some time. The hunter took it easy. He did not shoot as many game as when the crow was around. However, he felt happier to spend more time listening to the animals talking to each other.

One day, the mandarin summoned him to his office and confronted him with the death of a villager's buffalo. The villager apparently found his dead animal a week earlier. An arrow with the initials of the hunter was found close by. The hunter argued that it was a setup. He explained to the mandarin about his deal with the crow and how the two became estranged. The mandarin found the story unbelievable and sent him to jail.

The jailhouse was an old thatched hut where Dã Tràng had to fight against ants and mosquitoes. The guard overheard him arguing with the mosquitoes, telling them to leave him alone and not to bite him. The guard thought he was a disturbed person because of the way he conversed with ants and mosquitoes. A few days later, Dã Tràng overheard two sparrows talking to each other about how they found a way to loot the royal granary by coming from an opening between the roof and the wall. No one had noticed that opening and the birds had the time of their lives. Upon hearing the talk, Dã Tràng told the guard to report the message to the king's official. They checked the granary and indeed found the opening where Dã Tràng had described it. By sealing the opening, they cut down on the grain loss.

On another occasion, Dã Tràng noticed that ants had been relocating their eggs and provisions to higher grounds. He asked the ants about their move and was told an imminent flood had forced them to relocate. He immediately reported the news to the guard, who again related it to the king. The latter did not want his people to suffer in vain and warned them about the imminent flood. Everyone relocated their belongings to higher ground and when the flood came, the loss turned out to be minimal.

Having heard Dã Tràng's story, the king, who was an inquisitive leader, had him brought in for questioning. Dã Tràng told the king about the snake's generous gift, the crow's revenge, and his many discussions with other animals. Since the king wanted to know more about animals' lives, he kept Dã Tràng close to him. He believed that animals could teach many things to humans.

One day the king took Dã Tràng to the sea to check whether fish could talk. It was a beautiful day, the sea was calm, and the water warm. Dã Tràng, having never been to the sea, marveled at the fish frolicking around the boat. He only paid attention to what happened underneath the water. Two large fish came by and chatted about their day, how they caught their prey, the forthcoming wedding of their neighbors, the birth of their new cousins, and so on. The story was so interesting that Dã Tràng leaned overboard in order to catch all the words exchanged between the parties. In the process, he opened his mouth and the magic pearl fell into the sea.

Surprised, he stood up and almost tilted the boat over. The king caught him and told him to remain seated. Dã Tràng was distraught and cried. Having lost his precious pearl, he could no longer hear anything. There were no noises at all: no songs, no talk. The undersea world became quiet, although the fish were still frolicking around the boat. It was as if someone had shut off the music, resulting in a deafening silence. The magic life of the animal world came to a sudden end.

Realizing the loss, the king ordered the boatman to return to shore. He told Dã Tràng he would send out his best divers to try to recover the pearl. The king's divers went to work the next morning. They systematically explored one area after another but were unsuccessful in recovering the pearl. Dã Tràng, however, would not quit. He dug holes in the sand to try to locate the lost pearl, thinking that by going underneath he could retrieve his pearl. He soon lost his appetite, wasted away and died.[34]

His spirit came back as tiny crabs (*con cồng* or *con dã tràng*) that relentlessly dug holes in sandy beaches in search of the magic pearl. They worked all day long and never seemed to run out of energy. They rolled the sand into tiny balls and dragged them out of the tunnels. Soon clumps of sand balls could be noted around the openings of the tunnels. When they saw people, they ran back into their holes. Otherwise, they would

XII. Southern Legends: Animal   145

continue their work until waves collapsed their tunnels. Since that time, the name of *dã tràng* has been linked to these sand crabs.

A Vietnamese proverb goes like this:

> *Dã Tràng xe cát biển Đông*
> *Nhọc lòng mà chẳng nên công gì cán gì.*
>
> *Dã Tràng works in the Eastern Sea*
> *Although he struggles hard, he achieves nothing.*

Comments There are at least four stories in this legend: the snake and the pearl, the crow's revenge, the beauty of nature, and the lost pearl that leads to a futile search. First, the moral of the story is that a good deed is always rewarded. The hunter who thought he was just helping a few snakes ended up with the biggest surprise of all: he would receive a pearl that would allow him to understand and talk to animals. The best reward, however, is doing a good deed for itself instead of waiting for a tangible reward. Second, life is full of misunderstandings. The hunter, who left entrails for the crow—although he did not hand them over directly—was blamed for not having delivered them. Most likely, another animal intercepted those goodies prior to the arrival of the crow. The misunderstanding led to a war between the crow and the hunter, who finally landed in jail. Third, the reason we do not realize the beauty of nature is that we do not understand the language of animals. The hunter became fascinated with the animals (crow, ants, mosquitoes, fish, and so on) once he had acquired the power to understand them. They had a life of their own as well as rules and regulations. The story of Mowgli from Kipling's *Jungle Book*—the fictional Indian child who was adopted by wolves and knew how to talk to them and other animals—is another example.

When the Vietnamese talk about *công dã tràng*, they imply a "futile work, one that does not accomplish any meaningful purpose." Everyone knows how hard these small sand crabs are working: digging one tunnel after another only to see it collapse under the next wave. The legend conveys an image of futility toward much work done by humans. In a land of Buddhists, humans looking for worldly riches or highly placed positions instead of tending to their souls are considered to lead a futile life.

That pessimistic thought, however, may have its drawbacks. It has led many Vietnamese, especially southerners, to take it easy instead of trying harder. The resulting benevolent or *laissez-faire* attitude has been termed as Asian "passivity" by westerners. Asian passivity is often used as an excuse not to do anything. It thus may have contributed to economic underdevelopment or even poverty. Struggling to find a balance between aggressiveness and passivity has been difficult for some Vietnamese. As Buddhists, they were taught to be passive, but knew they had to be aggressive to be successful economically.

19. Why Ducks Sleep Standing on One Leg

There was a time when animals could talk and voice their complaints. At that time, four ducks were born with only one leg each. They could hardly move around and would fall down constantly. They could not do anything the other fowls could on their two legs. They were also less successful in hunting for food. Irritated, they debated among themselves about how best to solve the problem.

After quacking and arguing a long time, they decided to send a message to heaven. Ignorant of the protocol, they decided to ask for the help of the rooster, which was good at writing letters. One duck, however, argued that his writing was illegible and heaven would not understand what the ducks were asking. Another stated he was inconsiderate. After much arguing, they decided to settle on the rooster because no one was more knowledgeable about drafting a letter than the rooster.

They went and talked to the rooster, who asked them what they wanted.

"We would like to ask heaven to grant us another leg so we could move around like other fowls."

The rooster wrote a letter for them and showed them the way to heaven. Our four ducks set out for the trip. They walked for a while, then tripped and fell. They realized that with one leg, they could not go very far, let alone go to heaven. They argued among themselves again and after a lot of quacking and fighting decided to ask the rooster if there was any way they could send the letter without having to make the journey.

The rooster told them to go to the temple and the priest there might be able to communicate with heaven for them.

They hopped on their unique legs and after a lot of struggle arrived at the temple. On arrival, they heard the god screaming.

"Why does this incense burner have eight legs? I want four of them removed right now."

The ducks rejoiced on hearing the news. Although they knew nothing about an incense burner, the fact that four legs were available brightened their hope. They decided to go in and talk to the god.

XII. Southern Legends: Animal

"What do you want?" asked the god on seeing these four ducks.

"Sire, this is our request, which has been written by the rooster. We would like to know if you could give each of us one extra leg."

"No. What I have created is final. I will not change anything from what I have created."

Caught off guard by the forceful explanation, the four ducks fell silent.

"But Sire," ventured one duck, "we have just heard that you want to get rid of four legs."

The god laughed out loudly.

"You would not want these legs, would you? They would not fit with the other ones. You can have them if you want them. Just do not lose them because they are golden legs."

The god granted them the four legs they requested, and they thanked him profusely. And each of them attached the new leg to their bodies. They were overjoyed to be able to walk normally like other fowls. They were so happy that they practically danced in the streets.

At night, however, since they were afraid of losing their leg, they would pull it up during their sleep. The other fowls, seeing that the ducks were sleeping only on one leg, decided this was the norm and began sleeping the same way.[35]

Comments In this legend, the one-legged ducks were exasperated by their lingering disability. Since they could not move around, they fared less well than their peers. After getting four new legs, they noticed the world had changed completely for them. The moral of the story is that one has to fight for one's rights. The same message can be found in "The Toad Is Heaven's Uncle." This is an unusual message that we do not often hear about in a Confucian land. Confucians follow a patriarchal rule where seniority, not rights, is the rule. In that society, the king—the representative of god—is above everyone else; therefore, one should obey him whether he is right or not. Within the family, the father rules over the rest of the household: he decides everything and all the children have to obey him.[36]

Confucian rules have been in existence for over two millennia and worked well in Asia, especially in China, Japan, Korea and Vietnam. They have stabilized and brought prosperity and peace to these countries. Since no rule is perfect for every condition, rules should be amended, corrected or changed to accommodate social changes. Failure to amend and modernize them has led to conservatism and economic and political backwardness and later the demise of these Confucian states.

C. Traditional Legends

Traditional or classic legends are representative of Vietnamese culture, and, therefore, are recognized and used by both northern and southern authors.

20. The Betel and the Areca Tree
21. The Kitchen Gods
22. The Story of Bánh Chưng
23. The Flying Banyan Tree
24. The Tailor and the Mandarin
25. The Watermelon Island
26. The Fisherman and His Flute
27. The Land of Bliss
28. The Fairy's Portrait
29. Nguyễn Kỳ and the Songstress
30. The Little Statesman Lý
31. A Scholar's Dream
32. The Stone Dog

20. The Betel and the Areca Tree

Under King Hùng Vương III lived a mandarin with two twins, Tân and Lang, who looked so similar that oftentimes their mother could not tell them apart. One day, a fire burned down the family home and caused the death of both parents. Tân and Lang, newly orphaned were raised by a friend of their father, mandarin Lưu. The latter had only a daughter, a lovely girl by the name of Hương.

When the boys grew up, Lưu decided to offer Hương in marriage to the eldest one. However, he did not know who the eldest one was since they looked like two drops of water. The two boys were similarly attracted to the graceful Hương. They both loved her in silence and vied to marry her. Although Hương was attracted to the boys, she could not distinguish between the two. For her, any of the two would be fine.

The mandarin, therefore, devised a stratagem to pick out the eldest one. He had a dinner prepared for the brothers but asked that only one pair of chopsticks be displayed. When they began their meal, Lang, in deference to his elder brother, picked up the chopsticks and gave them to Tân. The latter was recognized as the eldest and given Hương in marriage. He was elated to marry the beautiful Hương and become the son-in-law of a well-known mandarin.

The marriage was an elaborate affair for the mandarin who could boast of having one of the brightest sons-in-law in the district. Tân and Hương were thus happily married. While Tân spent a lot of time with his brother in the past—they were their only blood relations within the mandarin's family—after the marriage, he dedicated his time exclusively to his newlywed wife. He was around her all the time and Lang felt neglected. The emotional disconnection tore him apart.

"Alas. My brother no longer loves me," he sighed to himself.

Lang's world had crumbled under his feet. Not only had he lost his brother's affection, he also lost Hương, whom he secretly loved. The double emotional loss affected Lang a lot. Confused, he did not know how to react. Although he loved his brother and wished him well, he also envied him. He was divided between his affection for his brother and his own pride, ego, and survival.

As time went by, Lang's isolation and depression became worse. He could not even see his brother and had no one to talk to. He felt that something had died in him. His strength came partly from his brother; without him, he was like a flower that no longer received its share of the soil's nutrients.

Lang felt that by staying around the happy couple, he might spoil their happiness. He, therefore, decided one day to take a long trip. Without being seen, he sneaked out of the house and walked along the countryside road. He walked and walked until he got tired. The landscape, although beautiful, no longer interested him. Everything took on a gloomy look. He finally reached the dark blue sea. Tired, he sat down and wept—the weeping of a deeply wounded heart. He wept until he died of exhaustion and was transformed into a block of white chalk.

His brother, who finally realized that Lang had left, went out to look for him. He blamed himself for being selfish and neglecting him. In his despair, he walked and traveled the same route through mountains and countryside until he reached the blue sea. Tired, he sat down with his back against a white chalky rock. He wept until he too died of exhaustion and was transformed into an areca tree.

His young wife, not seeing her husband coming back, became nervous. She set out to look for him. She followed the same road and ended up at the same place where the two brothers had arrived. Tired, she sat down and cried in despair until she died. She was transformed into a betel tree—a climbing tree—that wrapped around the areca tree.

A nearby villager saw in his dream the death of the three people. He told his fellow villagers about building a temple in commemoration of the fraternal and conjugal loves of the two brothers and the maiden.

King Hùng Vương came by and heard the story from the local people. The latter tried to chew betel leaves with areca nut along with some chalk. The mixture produced a bright red liquid, which became the symbol of fraternal and conjugal loves.

He suggested that brothers and sisters should chew betel to demonstrate fraternal love while newlyweds chew it to demonstrate conjugal love. From that time onward, the habit of chewing betel and areca nut with chalk spread all over the country and became the social hallmark of the Vietnamese.

Ever since, a bridegroom would include areca nut, betel leaves and limestone paste among the gifts sent to the bride.[37]

Comments This is one of the oldest and probably best-known Vietnamese legends. The Vietnamese have used betel and areca nut for more than two millennia. And each time they used it, they reminded their children or grandchildren about the legend, thereby keeping it alive.

Chewing betel, staining their teeth black, tattooing their bodies, wearing their hair in chignon in the back of the head and earrings, and adopting the matriarchal system are five characteristics that differentiate the Vietnamese (*Lạc Việt*) from the Chinese. For the last two millennia, they have fought to preserve their uniqueness and identity. This is good in a sense because these characteristics have allowed them to reclaim their independence and to form a nation. The bad thing is that nations are becoming more and more connected and integrated together. A nation cannot survive alone but with the help and assistance of others.

This legend celebrates brotherhood and fidelity, two important relationships in society. If brotherhood and sisterhood link siblings within a family, marital fidelity connects a man and a woman who are forming another family. Once new relationships have developed, they sometimes conflict with old ones. The advent of a new sibling within a family often causes emotional disruption, let alone a new stranger. Therefore, familial conflicts cannot be avoided.

Brotherhood and sisterhood and marital fidelity are valued at the same level because it is difficult to put one ahead of the other in real life. In the above legend, Tân, worrying about his brother, placed brotherhood ahead of marital fidelity and went in search of his brother. Had he forgotten about his brother, he would be chastised for having abandoned him. The wife in turn had to search for her husband. In the end, everyone had suffered in the story. That is why the king had the three elements bound together: betel, areca and chalk and brotherhood and sisterhood and conjugal love celebrated together.

21. The Kitchen Gods

A couple once lived in a small village at the edge of a huge forest that provided game to local people. They were poor but loved each other. He was a farmer and part time woodcutter while she was a homemaker. The two lived frugally off the land and rarely complained of anything.

A massive drought struck the area and villagers had to look for new jobs elsewhere. The couple struggled hard to get by, but finally the husband decided to leave home to look for work. The wife wanted to follow him but was told to stay home to take care of the house. He promised to be back within three years. If he was not, she could consider him dead. This was a moving farewell between two people who had never been separated before. They cried and promised to stay connected despite adversity.

Time flew by. The mango tree in front of the house had flowered three times but the wife still had no news of her husband. The drought was not improving and she survived as best as she could with whatever grew out of her tiny plot of land.

One night, she heard a knock at the door. Who else would knock at her door if not her husband, she thought. It was about time he came home, whether he was successful or not. She peeked through a small hole in the door and was elated to see the figure of a man. She opened the door and faced a stranger.

"Who are you? What can I do for you, sir?" she asked.

"Madam, I am a hunter. I have been following this game all day long and finally caught up with it. I tried to make my way home but it is too dark to go anywhere. Could I ask you a small favor of letting me stay on your porch until daytime. I would gladly share half of my game with you," the hunter said.

"I do not know what to say, sir. Please come in and enjoy my humble hospitality."

"Thank you, Madam. I will be out early in the morning."

"You must be hungry. Let me prepare for you something to eat."

She did not have much to offer, as the hunter could see, except for the best soup she could make. And also the best bed he could have: she offered him the only bed in the family, as tradition required. She then retired for the night to the kitchen.

The next morning, the hunter carved a big chunk of the game for his host. She could trade it at the market for something else she needed, he said. He thanked her for her hospitality and left.

From that moment onward, each time the hunter was in the area he stopped by to share with the woman part of his game. His visits became more and more frequent. The woman also benefited from the visits. She took the meat to the market to sell or traded it for rice and other goods. She prepared special dishes and sold them to the market, for the meat he gave her was rare and of special quality.

As her business flourished, her relationship with the hunter became closer. He stayed at her place many days in a row to hunt in the nearby forest. He was so successful that his game-meat was in constant demand: it was cheaper and tasted better than regular market-meat.

One night, someone knocked at her door. Thinking it was the hunter, she told him:

"Just come in. The door is open."

Not seeing anyone coming through the door, she opened it and was surprised to find another man.

"Madam, I got lost. Could I please stay here until tomorrow?" the man said.

She looked carefully at the stranger and did not fail to recognize her husband under his shabby clothes and unshaven face. She thought to herself that he must have struggled hard and apparently had not been very successful. She pitied him.

"Come in, old man. This is your home. Don't you recognize it any longer? I guess you have been away for so long that nothing looks the same as before."

She pulled him in, showed him the table and prepared a good meal for him. She brought him grilled deer and pheasant meat served with mushrooms. The husband had never tasted anything that good. It was a feast for a man who had not eaten for a while. He chewed it slowly because he was not used to eat that much. As he ate, his color came back and he started engaging in conversation with her. He told her he had been wandering from town to town in search of a job. There were temporary ones, but he was never lucky enough to get full employment. That was the reason why he did not dare to come home.

XII. Southern Legends: Traditional

While the husband was talking, she heard noises outdoors and the voice of the hunter.

"I am bringing you a new game," he said.

"Oh, dear," she mumbled. "What an unfortunate coincidence. The hunter was not supposed to come this night, but there he is."

She pulled her husband in a corner and told him to hide in the foyer under a bale of hay.

"Stay here," she said. "Do not make any noise. I will explain to you later on."

Although the husband did not understand what was going on, he followed the order. He was also too tired to argue or protest. It was the 23rd of December according to the lunar calendar, or about one week before the Tết festival, the Vietnamese New Year. The hunter thought he would make a big surprise by bringing her a big game. He pulled the deer inside the house to show it to her.

"I will prepare the fire and we will cook this deer in celebration of the festival," he said.

And he lit up the fire, not realizing that a man was hiding under the bale of hay. He then pulled the deer out to make it ready.

The woman was distraught and did not know what to do. She was too stunned to do anything. The hunter was "frying" her husband and she just stood there, her eyes fixed with horror at the fire. She could stand it no longer. It was her fault that her husband was burning in the foyer. She jumped into the fire asking for forgiveness. She and her husband thus burned and their souls went together to the other land.

The hunter did not realize anything until later on. He did not know why his friend decided to kill herself in the fire. He had not done anything wrong at all. Knowing he could not survive without her, he too jumped into the fire, hoping to join her in the other land.

Ngọc Hoàng Thượng Đế or the Jade God presiding over the other world saw these three human beings arriving at his court. The first husband told him the reason he came back was to be with his dear wife. The second man said he loved the woman, although he was not married to her yet. The woman in turn said she loved both of them and had trouble figuring out which one she loved the most.

The Jade God, seeing these three loving people, had trouble separating them. He promoted them as kitchen gods. Their job was to make the rounds of all households and to report to him each December 23rd (lunar calendar) about what was going on in each household.

The Vietnamese to this day celebrate the departure of the three kitchen gods each December 23rd by giving them offerings and praying for good luck for the following year. They hope that with a good report from the kitchen gods, the Jade God would grant them peace and prosperity for the new year.[38]

Comments The above legend, like the one about the betel and the areca tree earlier in this book, deals with fidelity and marital love. According to the 2,500-year-old Confucian *tam tòng* rule (The Three Submissions),[39] a woman has to submit by order of importance to her father when young or unmarried, to her husband when married and to her son when widowed. Within this patriarchal society, she is not thought to be an independent person. She would be deemed virtuous only if she strictly follows the guidelines. For a man, his first marriage is also prearranged. He could not choose the woman he loves. It is only afterward that he could select the concubine of his choice. Men, therefore, could have more than one wife.

These precepts teach women to be submissive and force them to make painful decisions about duty and love. Decisions often arise because marriages in Vietnamese society, until recently, were prearranged. Women did not have the choice of marrying the person they love. If they followed their heart, they would feel guilty about failing to obey their parents. If they accepted the prearranged marriage, they felt forced to live for the rest of their lives with someone they did not like.

Not only did they have to live with a "prearranged husband," they had to remain chaste throughout their lives: "In life as in death, there must be only one husband."[40]

The drawback of this rigid Confucian system is that individuality has to be suppressed for the good of the society (read men) and the individual is not allowed to fight back even in cases of disagreement with the system. The Confucian society—like the Islamic society—is tilted in favor of men who make the rules. The dislocation of the women's real personality has led to severe psychological damage. "They became bitter with time and discharged their bitterness on the newest member of the family. And the vicious cycle perpetuated itself."[41] The price of uniformity and maintenance of patriarchy fell on the weakest members of the society: the women.

It is interesting to note that in the above legend, the Jade God allowed the woman to keep her two husbands—an unusual combination under Confucian rule. He not only decided not to separate loving people, he also made them his representatives on earth. This exception does prove the rule.

XII. Southern Legends: Traditional

22. The Story of Bánh Chưng

The Vietnamese celebrate New Year—the first three days of the first month of the lunar calendar—by eating *bánh chưng or bánh tét*. Bánh chưng is a square rice cake wrapped in banana leaves. It contains a filling of bean paste, seasoned pork meat and fat surrounded by glutinous rice or *nếp*. The square shape expresses their gratitude for the abundance of the Earth. While bánh chưng has a northern origin, the bánh tét—round in shape with the same ingredients—is of southern origin.

King Hùng Vương VI, having fulfilled his ambition and accomplished a lot during his reign, decided to retire and enjoy his old age. His goal was to choose a successor among his 22 sons. This was a difficult task, for they were all able princes. He told them, "Dear sons. You are all able princes who could replace me any time. Go out in the world and gather all the ingredients this earth has produced. The person who can prepare the most tasteful dish with any of these ingredients will succeed me."

The sons were euphoric. They had the chance to prove themselves by preparing a meal. The winner would inherit the throne. There was no better reward than that. They spread out and went to all the corners of the kingdom, searching for the best recipes and foodstuffs the country had. Some went to the mountains looking for exotic mushrooms, nuts, and foods. Others went to the seaside to search for the best seafood recipes and the best oysters, shrimps, and fish the sea could provide. Others moved to the countryside to test rural recipes. The rest went abroad to try unique foreign foods.

Only prince Lang Liêu stayed home. He did not have the same connections his brothers had. He did not know where to go to find his recipe. Because his mother died while he was young, he was raised by a substitute mother. He was, however, very studious and respectful of the gods and genies. And the genies loved him. One night a genie appeared in his dream.

"Since rice is the basic ingredient in Vietnamese food, it should be included in your preparation. Meat also needs to be included. Use raw glutinous rice that has been soaked in water.

"Prepare seasoned pork meat and bean paste. Wrap the rice in the form of a square around a core of meat and bean paste using banana leaves. Tie the whole thing with strings so that the shape and contents are preserved. Cook it overnight and you will have the best meal right there," the genie said.

The prince woke up in the morning and wondered whether he had had a bad dream. He wrote down the recipe and decided to try it.

On New Year's Day, when apricot trees blossomed, the 22 princes brought their prepared meals out for the king to taste. This was probably the first and oldest culinary competition in the world. There were delicious foods from the most extravagant recipes from all corners of the country. The princes did not spare anything to prepare these meals.

The king went to each table to taste each recipe. Although each meal was good, he was not impressed by any of them. At prince Liễu's table, he saw the *bánh giầy* and *bánh chưng*. The bánh giầy is a whitish rice cake with fillings of pork meat. It was convex on top to represent the dome of the sky. The unwrapped bánh chưng was greenish-colored rice with a lemon-yellow bean filling and pork meat. The rice that had taken the green color of the banana leaf reminded people of the green rice stalks ready for harvest.

The king took the first bite. Hum ... not too salty, not too hot. He took a second bite ... good. He took a third bite and said, "This is the best food I have ever tasted. How did you prepare it?"

"A genie told me to wrap rice around a piece of seasoned meat and bean and to cook it overnight," answered the prince.

Lang Liễu was declared the winner and the food was named *bánh chưng*. The king told his minister to give the recipe to the people so they could make bánh chưng for the New Year. From then on, the Vietnamese have always celebrated Tết with either bánh chưng or bánh tét depending upon their personal preferences.[42]

Comments This legend describes how the two-millennia-old tradition of celebrating the Tết festival and consuming bánh chưng and bánh tét came about. It even codifies the recipe of the bánh chưng, which has stood the test of time. The cake is still prepared the way it was two millennia ago.

The Tết festival is celebrated during the first three days of the first lunar month, which usually comes between January and March. It is the equivalent of New Year, Thanksgiving, and a birthday combined together. It is the birthday of all the Vietnamese who are one year older—according to the lunar calendar—no matter which month they were born.

Stores close during these three days and people try to cut down on working and cooking. Each family cooks food in advance so they do not have to work during these three days—housewives get their three-day break of the year. They stock up on bánh chưng or bánh tét—which could be stored for weeks—and candies, and fruits. They eat watermelons—the redder the meat, the more auspicious they are. Among all trees and flowers, flowering apricot trees are de rigueur.

Although it is not a religious holiday, Buddhist temples are crowded with followers who come to pray, to burn incense, and to ask for longevity, happiness, and luck. They also pray for their ancestors' souls at either temples or cemeteries. Children receive *lì sì* money that they use to buy games or go to the movies.

23. The Flying Banyan Tree

Born of poor parents, Cuội's job was to care for his neighbor's buffaloes at a young age. He led them to the field to let them graze and to give them a bath. Buffaloes liked to swim and roll over in muddy puddles as a way to relax, to clean, and to protect themselves from the heat. In the hot tropical climate of Vietnam, mud rolling was one of the delights of animals, especially buffaloes. They may have thick skin, but thick-skinned animals may like water more than other animals. Cuội did what he could to help his parents out: he gathered wood in the forest and brought it home for his mother to prepare meals. He also prepared food for and fed the family's pigs.

While his buffaloes were frolicking in the mud one day, Cuội was playing with a tiger cub that had escaped from its mother's watch and was standing alone on the edge of the field. He played with it until he heard a roaring noise among the trees. Recognizing that the mother was looking for its cub, he threw it away and rapidly climbed up a tree to hide. The cub fell hard on the ground and lay still. The mother came out to inspect her cub. Seeing it lifeless, she loudly moaned her sadness and sorrow. She went to a banyan tree, picked up a few leaves, chewed and left them on the cub's forehead. After a few minutes, the cub moved its legs, then sprang up. It ran around as if nothing had happened. Both mother and child walked away.

Cuội was glad the tigress did not see or care about him. Although fearless like any youngster, he knew that an encounter with a tigress could result in a disaster. Aware of the tigress' size and power, he was afraid she would change her mind and come back to look for him. He quickly gathered his buffaloes and led them home.

On his way home, he noticed a dead dog lying on the side of the road. He remembered what the tigress had done earlier that day. He hoped he could save the dog. He ran back to the banyan tree, collected a few leaves, chewed and placed them on the dog's forehead. After a few minutes, the dog came back to life and happily walked away.

He realized the banyan tree indeed had magical properties and might be useful to him and his parents in the future. He uprooted the tree and carried it home with him. He dug a big hole, planted it in his backyard and told his mother jokingly, "Mom, do not throw any waste on the tree, otherwise it will die."

His mother was too busy to care for a tree, since she had many of them around the house. She threw discarded items and waste on its roots. With time, Cuội's joke became a reality. The tree slowly uprooted itself as it tried to get away from the dirty waste. Day by day, it pulled itself out of the ground and gradually exposed its roots.

When Cuội returned home, he saw the tree gradually flying off the ground. He grasped the lowest roots, trying to hold the tree back. Alas, it was much stronger than him and pulled him up in the air. For a moment, Cuội found himself suspended above ground: he climbed up and hung on to the tree trunk. After a few days' voyage, the tree landed on another world: the moon. Cuội secured it to the ground so that it would not fly away any longer. The tree had become his home in the new land.[43]

On clear days, people on earth could therefore see the shadows of Cuội and the banyan tree against the backdrop of the moon. He was always alone, looking at the stars in the sky and sometimes waving at the people on earth.

With time, Cuội was no longer the young and unwitting buffalo boy who happened to end up on the moon, but a respectable old man with flowing beard akin to the western Santa Claus. Children kindly remember his story. At the *Trung Thu* (Mid-Autumn or Harvest Moon) festival, carrying lit lanterns they paraded around neighborhoods chanting

> *Oh Cuội, I would like to tell you*
> *There was a big banyan tree*
> *There was an old Cuội*
> *Who borrowed a ladder...*

There is another version of Cuội. He apparently borrowed a ladder to climb on the banyan tree, which somehow miraculously kept growing, forcing him to climb even higher and higher until he reached the moon. The result was that he went to the moon and from there was watching the world.

Comments Vietnamese legends are about poor peasants, mandarins, or kings and princesses. These three groups of people form the basis of the agrarian society.

XII. Southern Legends: Traditional

Because peasants form the backbone of the society, stories about them abound in the legends: "The Flying Banyan Tree," "The Jar of Gold," "The Orphan and the Princess," "A Brother's Devotion." They are described as simple, hard-working, conscientious people who believe in their work ("The Jar of Gold"). Elder brothers tend to be greedy and to exploit their siblings ("A Brother's Devotion," "The Sister-in-law," "The Starfruit Tree," "The Narcissus"). They, however, tend to stick together. In general, they are not educated but have a lot of common sense ("The Tiger's Stripes").

The moon has been the subject of many writings around the world: it has been the muse of many Vietnamese poets. Lettered men used to drink wine and make poems to celebrate the moon or to discharge their dissatisfaction against society.

Vietnam can claim to have sent the first explorer to the Moon, although it was just a figment of the imagination. However, he was forever stuck up there because no satellite had been sent to retrieve him. He has aged beyond belief and become the old Cuội. He is revered by children who sing to him during the Mid-Fall festival—at a time when the moon is brightest and roundest.

24. The Tailor and the Mandarin

This story occurred at a time when mandarins were the high officials of the empire and wore their traditional robe—a sort of loosely fitted *áo dài* that hangs down to the ankles, splits at the waist and forms two lappets, one in front and one on the back. Mandarins, like all politicians, are very fussy individuals. In a land where face was important, the mandarin robe was the first thing his subjects stared at. Therefore, the robe should look nice and fit perfectly. The robe not only upheld the tradition, it was also the sign of authority and power. It was like the judge's robe. Without it, the judge appeared a diminished person.

A famous tailor once lived in the capital of the empire. He made beautifully fitted mandarin robes that rendered all his customers happy. His reputation, therefore, spread far beyond the city he lived in.

A high mandarin who had just arrived in town sent for the tailor. He wanted two sets of robes made. The tailor came and took all measurements: waist, chest, height, arm and leg lengths and so on. Specific requests and robe color were discussed. The mandarin was happy with the meeting thus far. Before leaving, the tailor turned to the mandarin and asked him about the length of his service.

"What kind of question is that? What does it have to do with the robe?" the irritated mandarin asked.

"Please excuse me, dear mandarin. But it has to do with the way I cut your robe."

"How?" the mandarin enquired.

"New mandarins tend to be proud of their new job. They hold their head slightly backward and thrust their chest forward. In this case, I would cut the front lappet longer than the back piece to compensate for the positional attitude of the mandarin.

"Having faced difficulties during his career, the mandarin toward the middle of his career tends to stay erect. I would then cut the two lengths evenly.

"At the end of his career, burdened by many problems and setbacks and besieged by arthritis, the mandarin tends to bend forward with slumped shoulders and head down. I would cut the front lappet shorter than the back one."

"Thus you see, sire. If I do not know the length of service, I cannot correctly fit my customers."[44]

Comments Face (social status, or more exactly the mask one projects to society) is important in any country. In 1665 Nicolas Fouquet, the French superintendent of finances, in trying to upstage the suspicious King Louis XIV by throwing a lavish party for him, was jailed a few days later and sentenced to life in prison.

Face is more important in Confucian countries like Vietnam than in a western country. Even at the village level, elders were revered and given the top spots at village meetings. They sat at the top of the table and had the honor of taking the first bite. Every guest would wait for him to eat first before beginning the meal. The head of the fish, chicken or pig—whatever was served at the meeting—would be given to the eldest member or the guest of honor of the community. The latter would wrap the head up and bring it home to demonstrate to family and neighbors his position within the community.

Within a family, the household head—usually a man—would decide what needs to be done in the outside world: he is "the foreign minister" (he deals with the professional and political aspects of life, meetings, jobs). The wife is the "interior minister" who supervises children's schooling, cooking, gardening, and housekeeping.

Both men and women wear áo dài—the traditional Vietnamese dress. Gradually, under French influence, the áo dài is now only worn by women while men picked up the western coat. The tailoring of mandarin robes, once thought to be simple, is more complicated than expected. It does not have to be always symmetrical because it is related to the length of the service. If the tailor does not pay attention to this factor, the robe would look uneven when the mandarin stood up.

25. The Watermelon Island

A trading ship sank during a heavy storm, sending a young boy ashore. Local people rescued him and brought him to the king, who adopted him as his own son. Mai An Tiêm thus grew up at the court and turned out to be an intelligent boy who excelled in school. As mandarins came to seek his advice, the king's natural sons were jealous of him.

The king gave him one assignment after another, which he completed successfully. The king used him as an example wherever he went, causing courtiers to resent Tiêm. As a reward, the king later gave to him his daughter Cô Ba in marriage, and the couple settled in one of the king's castles.

During a reception, Tiêm loosely mentioned that the key to his success was hard work and good behavior from his past life. Money, he said, was not necessary. Upon hearing this, resentful courtiers reported to the king that Tiêm was an ungrateful person who claimed to owe his success to himself. They also made up other things. Upset at Tiêm, the king exiled him to a far away island in the South with one month of food supplies.

Fortune thus changed rapidly for Tiêm and his family. From a well-respected member of the king's entourage, he became a disgraced and shunned person overnight. He, however, was a man of rectitude. Believing that the banishment was the result of bad deeds done in the past, he accepted it with calm and dignity. He knew he had not said anything wrong. He was only sorry to have made the king mad, but was grateful to him for his help. He should have clarified his statement instead of leaving others room to speculate.

The king wanted to teach him a lesson and expected him to beg for forgiveness. But Tiêm did not. Although people tried to dissuade Cô Ba from going along with her husband, she insisted on following him. When they advised her it would not be wise to make the trip, she said, "Heaven gives birth to elephants, heaven provides them with grass."

Soldiers dropped Tiêm, his wife, and two favorite servants on a deserted beach, which was home to flocks of seagulls. No one else lived on the island. The group began having second thoughts when they looked at the dense and untamed forest and the hills that lay in front of their eyes. They were not used to dealing with virgin forests. Tiêm, seeing their hesitancy, tried to reassure them.

"It is going to be difficult. But we will figure out a way to make this place hospitable. Heaven will help us. Let us look for a place to rest now."

They looked around but could not get very far the first day because of the unfamiliar landscape and the fatigue occasioned by the trip. For the next few days, they settled close to the beach and made themselves comfortable with the supplies given to them.

They explored the island to get used to its layout. They were happy to find a few fruit trees and a cave where they could protect themselves from the wind and storms. There was water from a mountain spring and a place that was convenient to set up a garden. Although work advanced slowly, they felt more comfortable as days passed by.

One day, Tiêm saw a flock of birds coming from the west, landing on the beach and then hopping around. As he approached them, they flew away. They dropped many black seeds, which he gathered and planted in the ground. Months later, he saw green vines creeping on the ground. Later they bore green fruits the size of a man's head. Since he had never seen these fruits before, he cautiously opened one of them and tasted it. The inside was red and juicy. He called it "Red melon" because of the hue of the fruit meat. Everyone tasted it and liked it. The fruit was refreshing and good: it quenched thirst and boosted energy. Therefore, he decided to plant all the seeds and soon had rows and rows of watermelons.

A few fishermen dropped by the island to look for food and drink. Some got lost during storms, while others were attracted by the new islanders. Tiêm offered them a few watermelons that quelled their thirst. They liked the fruit's sweet and juicy meat and began discussing an exchange or trade: watermelon for rice and other types of food. Little by little, the island became known as the island of watermelons. People dropped by to buy watermelons or trade other goods.

As trade flourished, people on the mainland came by and settled on the island. Population grew as a result: some worked full time as fishermen while others became settlers, traders, artisans, and so on.

The king one day wondered what had happened to Tiêm. The thought came to him after one mandarin messed up a vital project. He believed that had Tiêm been around, he would have solved the problem correctly. When the king asked around, no one knew what happened to Tiêm. He sent a

XII. Southern Legends: Traditional

trusted emissary to look for Tiêm. A few weeks later, the latter came back with a present from Tiêm.

"Sire, Tiêm sends you his wishes along with these red melons," the emissary said. "He is well established on the island and a large community has thrived on the once-deserted island. There are houses and businesses there."

The king decided to taste a piece of red melon. He liked it and realized that Tiêm may be correct in stating that heaven protected those who had done good deeds in the past. Besides, Tiêm was a self-made person who could survive and thrive by himself.

The king regretted having punished Tiêm harshly. He sent a team to bring him and his family back and gave him all his titles back. Tiêm returned to a hero's welcome.

Years later, the king even abdicated in his favor.[45]

Comments There is a strong Buddhist influence in this legend. Tiêm talks about how past deeds (good or bad) influence the present. He blames his downfall on the wrongs he had done in his past life. He relates his success to the good deeds he had done in the past. There is also some Taoist element in the legend, as exemplified by the belief in *Trời* or heaven. Everything is controlled by heaven and once heaven has created an elephant, it also provides grass to feed it.

The above legend is one of the rare few that stresses self-sufficiency, independence, courage, and initiative. These characteristics are rarely taught to Asian children, who tend to follow Confucian rules of pleasing their parents by obeying them, staying home, and taking the wife their parents have in mind. They lack initiative, shun adversity, and do not involve themselves in commerce or science. Without science and technology, Vietnamese and Asian societies have remained backward compared to western societies. In the late nineteenth century, a few thousand French soldiers armed with canons and guns blasted their way through Vietnam and conquered it easily. Without commerce, Vietnam could not expect to be a rich country. Society was divided between *sĩ, nông,* and *công, thương* or scholars, peasants, workers (soldiers) and merchants. Although learning was respected—scholars studied poetry, Confucian teachings, calligraphy, but not science—commerce was shunned. Artisans and merchants were relegated to the bottom of the society. King Lê Thánh Tông even wrote

> *They gain their ill-got wealth throughout the land—*
> *Their venal motives serve as butts of songs.*[46]

The Chinese—who also were Confucians—had no problem with doing commerce. As a matter of fact, they are master merchants. Arriving in Vietnam in the eighteenth century, they filled the business gap left by the Vietnamese and since then have controlled a large share of the country's commerce. It is interesting to note the divergent interpretation of Confucian rules between the Vietnamese and Chinese.

Our hero Tiêm accepted the banishment with humility and courage. He could have backed out and begged the king for forgiveness. But he did not. He went through a miserable life before succeeding. He was the prototype of a self-made man, a man who controlled his destiny. He was the antithesis of the recluse Confucian scholar. As Nguyễn Công Trứ has suggested, a man is supposed

> *To roam the universe in length and breadth!*
> *To pay a man's full dues and be a man!*[47]

This legend parallels the experience of Lord Nguyễn Hoàng—the founder of South Vietnam.[48] Hoàng competed against another lord, Trịnh—who was actually his brother-in-law—for control over the reigning Lê king. Controlling the young Lê king meant being the interim king of the country. Nguyễn Hoàng, knowing he could not compete against Trịnh, made up his mind to move south in 1558 and establish a new political entity there.

For many years, he organized and managed the lands he was placed in charge of. This region corresponded to present-day central Vietnam, which was taken away from the Chams. The "new South" was at that time an unglamorous land reserved for criminals, convicts, and settlers. Hoàng was a good administrator and dutifully paid his tribute to the Lê emperor as a vassal and died peacefully in 1613.

He and his sons transformed the South into a strong country that soon competed head-to-head with the north. From 1620 onward, the South waged a 50-year war against the North. North (*Đằng Ngoài*, the outer land) and South (*Đằng Trong*, the inner land) were separated for the next two centuries before being finally reunited in 1802.

26. *The Fisherman and His Flute*

Mỵ Nương was a beautiful princess whose father built a palace for her in the woods on the edge of a river. The marble palace had mahogany doors and spacious rooms. The furniture was made of fine sandalwood

XII. Southern Legends: Traditional

encrusted with ivory. She had a large suite on the second floor with a spectacular view of the river, which on the right side enlarged itself into a cul de sac before continuing its course eastward.

As the only child of the family, she was visibly spoiled. She had a delightful childhood and did not want for anything. All her wishes were fulfilled so fast that she had no idea about poverty and suffering. She spent her days walking along the river and in the forest with her maid when not studying or playing an instrument.

One day, a song coming out of a flute struck her—a soft and melodious song she had never heard before. She had always lived in that corner of the wood and had never heard anything that interesting. Where was it coming from? Who did it? How did this happen? She rushed to her window, which gave her a direct view of the river. She looked and looked and saw nothing except a fisherman on his boat.

The melodious music occurred on every day, five days a week around noontime each day. My Nương caught herself waiting for the time when music came out of the flute. It was a smooth sound, one that melted her heart away. It made her heart race faster and her blood boil. There was something soft, languorous, and exciting in this music, something that made her feel wholesome, strong, desired and desirable.

The music had captured her heart and mind. She could not stand it any longer. She wanted to know who made this beautiful and languorous music. She guessed that the musician must be a handsome young man, as gifted as he was. She requested to see him. In the gilded meeting room, My Nương, in her expensive outfit, anxiously waited for the man who had captured her heart the last few months. The door opened and the smell of fish pervaded the room. A young, dark, and embarrassed fisherman in tattered clothing showed up. He did not know what he was doing in this luxurious ambiance. The soldier just told him to see the princess in the castle, and he showed up without thinking.

What a shock. She turned her eyes away and quickly dismissed the man. What a deception. It must have been a big mistake. What was the link between the fine musician and this fisherman? There could be nothing in common. She cried in despair. Could that be it? Is reality that bad, that unfair?

Trương Chi, the fisherman, had a glimpse of the princess: a svelte body with distinctive features in a purple brocade gown. Long hair descended to her waist, pinned with a flower. Her voice was soft. She was a heavenly apparition for Trương Chi, who had never seen anyone like her.

He was a poor, and certainly not very good-looking person. Having lost his parents at a young age, he worked his way up and had remained self-sufficient by becoming a fisherman and farmer. He brought his catch and products to the market and exchanged them for food. He worked so hard outdoors that his skin was tanned and leathery in texture. The girls in the village shunned him because of his gruff manners. But he was a good person who enjoyed his free time playing his flute. Who taught him to play the instrument, no one knew for sure. He had not confided to anyone, for he had no friend.

Dismissed on the spot, Trương Chi slowly walked home. What had he done to make the lady unhappy? She probably did not like his look. He was only a fisherman; nature had given an unsightly human body. That was not his fault. Dispirited and hurt, he returned to his hut among the few belongings he had. He fell on his bed distraught. He lay there not knowing what to do next. He vowed never to play music again. He just wanted to die, to disappear in the void, and to get away from this place.

He lay alone in his bed; he did not know for how many days. He did not want to get up because the future was so frightening. He could not do anything. His mind stopped working. His lips stopped singing. He saw a large black hole in front of him. The future was nothing but a black hole.

Mỵ Nương, meanwhile, lay on her bed. She was fascinated by the music, but not by the musician. She longed for that music that soothed her spirit as well as her heart. She eagerly waited for its melody. One day passed by. Two, three, four ... a whole week flowed by slowly without that music. She gradually fell sick. It was as if the sap that nourished her was no longer there. Her parents became worried. She had not taken any food or drink for some time. Nothing would help her. The fanciest food, the close attention of her parents, and the wariness of relatives did not do her any good.

Her parents consulted one doctor after another. One proposed a mixture of roots, another some honey. None of these remedies worked. In despair, a medium was invited to make a diagnosis.

He looked at her, held up her arm, checked her pulses at various levels and declared, "Your Highness, this is not a disease that is curable with medications. Your daughter has a rare disease of the heart. Let the person who knows her cure her."

"What should I do?" asked the king.

"There is one person who can cure her."

"Who is he?"

"Have you noticed something unusual recently about her? Has she been interested in anyone?"

"She has spent a lot of time at her window listening to someone singing on the river."

"Would you get that person; he might be able to help her."

The king ordered his soldiers to look for Trương Chi and to have him play the flute again. They scoured the neighborhood and asked for the man with the flute. They finally found him in his hut—a depressed person. They told him the king would like him to play again and hopefully save the princess. Trương Chi sprang up from his bed on hearing the word "save the princess." He would do anything to save her even if he should lose his life. He told the soldiers to give him some time to get some strength back and he would play again.

There is nothing like love to put a person back in shape. Rejuvenated, Trương Chi paddled to the castle and right underneath the princess' window. Taking out his flute, he began to play his melodious songs. Somnolent in bed, she sprang back to life on hearing the music. She listened intensely to the songs and in no time was back on her feet. She wondered why she had been sick for that long and for what reason.

Trương Chi played for many days for the princess, who did not even acknowledge him. Distraught, he continued to play for a while and returned to his hut more depressed than ever. There would be no future for him. He soon realized that his wish might not be fulfilled on this earth but possibly in the next life. He slowly went downhill and died.

His spirit went into a sandalwood tree, which grew beautifully until the king had it cut down to make a few utensils for the princess, including four nice bowls.

The princess one day took one of the bowls and filled it with the soup of the day. As the water was closing on the rim, the picture of Trương Chi appeared at the surface. My Nương was taken aback by the picture. As she suddenly remembered that she had not been nice to him and did not even thank him for all his songs, a large tear rolled down her cheek and fell into the bowl, dissolving the picture at once.

It was said that My Nương's regret was a liberating force for Trương Chi, whose spirit was finally set free and raised to the sky.[49]

Comments This is a story about a poor fisherman and a princess under the Vietnamese monarchy of years past. Princesses are out of reach of commoners and these two social classes rarely mix, except under unusual circumstances like the one in the story.

Unlike the story of *Nhật Dạ Trạch* where a princess wed a fisherman (southern tale #7), or "The Land of Bliss" (tale #27) or "The Fairy's Portrait" where fairies wed commoners (tale #28), this relationship went nowhere because Mỵ Nương refused to accept it from the beginning. This was not a love story because Mỵ Nương had never liked Trương Chi to begin with. She was only attracted to his music. In fact, when she saw him for the first time, she was so disappointed that she turned around and never cared about him.

She fell sick because of the lack of the music and not because of the absence of the fisherman. In fact, she did not care when he fell sick and passed away. She did not even know he had passed away. She remained a princess imbued with her title and class, not a lady with feeling or compassion, and definitely not someone who would hang around with commoners. She was the archetype of the "imperial" princess, far different from the "people's princess" in *Nhật Da Trạch* or the "people's fairy" in "The Land of Bliss" or "The Fairy's Portrait."

However, in the end she did have a slight change of heart, which eventually set Trương Chi's spirit free. Without Mỵ Nương' approval, his spirit would have remained on this earth forever attached to her. What made her change her mind was probably the Buddhist mentality of the time, which sought to soften her image as well as to introduce the concepts of reincarnation and detachment from worldly possessions.

27. The Land of Bliss

Have you ever heard of the land of bliss where everything is beautiful and sorrow or suffering is unknown? No one who has ventured there has returned to tell us about that idyllic place, except maybe Từ Thức. This is his story.

A long time ago under the reign of King Trần Thuận Tông, there was a man named Từ Thức. He was a poet, a learned man, a mandarin and chief of the Tiên Du district. He had visited many interesting places in his country, which by itself was an unusual feat since people rarely traveled outside their district at that time. Part of it was due to lack of public transportation and accommodations.

Since childhood, Từ Thức had always wanted to visit the land of bliss, although no one could tell him its exact location. Only Emperor Đường Minh Hoàng was said to have visited by chance that land where peace, pleasure, and joy abounded. Having seen beautiful dancers execute an elaborate dance, on his return to earth he taught to the ladies of the imperial palace the dances he had witnessed. The newly minted dancers would then dance for him in the silver moonlight while he sipped wine.

One beautiful spring, as Từ Thức was passing by a local temple he saw a maiden—about 16 or 17 years of age—of radiant beauty who was admiring a flowering cherry tree. While pulling a branch downward to have a closer look at the flowers, she accidentally broke it. The local priests caught her in the act and forced her to pay a fine. Having no money, she was held against her will. Having witnessed the proceedings, Từ Thức decided to bail her out by leaving his brocade robe. The offer was accepted and the lady was released. She sped away after profusely thanking her savior.

Years later, tired of political infighting and life's struggles, Từ Thức decided to retire and spend time traveling around the country. Taking with him his gourd of wine and flute, he set forth to visit the famous Pink Mountain and Grottoes of Seven Clouds. One day while rowing on the river, he saw five clouds coalesce to form a beautiful lotus flower in the sky. On each side of the river, tall mountains abruptly descended on the river, creating an image of wilderness he had never seen before. Struck by the beauty of the landscape, he began singing.

As he finished his song, the sky seemed to open up and the mountains to recede, giving way to a small passage that was shrouded by whitish fog. Hidden behind tall trees, the passage could not be seen by anyone. Astounded, he climbed the rocks and reached it. A door closed behind his back and a new land opened up to his view. The sky was bright and clear, the weather balmy. The air was pure, calm, and laced with the scent of lilies and roses. A soft and melodious music was heard amidst the chirping of the birds. Rolling hills spread unto the horizon. The path, strewn with fallen golden leaves, led to a gorgeous garden full of starry flowers. He felt relaxed and at ease in this environment.

A group of maidens—the most beautiful peach-complexioned ladies he had ever seen—came to greet him as he set foot on land.

"Greetings to the handsome bridegroom."

Although they spoke without opening their mouths, the sounds emitted were so melodious that he thought he was in heaven. Unlike human beings, they glided away softly and without effort. They came back and invited him to enter a golden palace dotted with scintillating stars. They were not real stars but only reflections of soft lights on the walls. The halls were covered with brocaded walls and gilded doors. A majestic lady dressed in a snow-white dress was seated on a carved throne. She looked ageless; he wondered how old she was. She bore no wrinkle, scar, or imperfection. She looked stunning even without makeup, jewelry, or bracelets. She motioned him to sit on a sandalwood chair.

"Welcome to this place, learned scholar," said the lady.

"May I ask where is this country, most noble Lady? I have been to too many places, but this is one I do not recognize," answered Từ Thức.

"You are in the sixth of the thirty-six grottoes of the *Phi Lai* Mountains, which appears and vanishes according to the winds. No mortal has ever ventured here. I am the fairy queen of the *Nam Nhạc* summit. I know that you have a beautiful soul and a noble heart, and I invited you here."

"So this is the place I have always dreamed of. Can I ask how I got the honor of being invited here?"

"Let me present to you someone you have met before."

The maidens ushered in a beautiful maiden who looked like someone Từ Thức had seen before, although he did not remember where.

"This is my daughter, Giáng Hương. You saved her in the past when she wandered on earth. Without your help, she would have been stuck there. To express my gratitude, I have invited you over here. I also offer you her hand in marriage and invite you to stay in this land."

"I do not know how to thank you for the offer. I feel so privileged to be admitted to this land."

The wedding was much simpler than on earth, although with the same pomp and majesty. Từ Thức enjoyed much bliss during his marital life. He did not have to work and every day was a new day of bliss.

Like any human being, he soon got tired of this blissful life and asked his wife whether he could return to earth to see his relatives. She did not know what to say and worried about him not being able to come back.

"It would be just a few weeks, dear. I will be back as soon as I can," he said.

"Let me talk to my mother first," she answered.

When the fairy queen was told about the request, she retorted, "So be it. If he wants to return to the land of human beings, the land of misery and gall, let him go. He will regret having asked for it."

Từ Thức was asked to close his eyes, and when he opened them he was back on earth. Things, however, had changed a lot since his departure: he did not recognize the landscape or the village any longer. When he asked about the village, people told him he was already there. He only met people he never knew. He enquired about his old acquaintances, but no one knew them. He approached a very old man, hoping he could learn more from him than from the other villagers.

"Venerable grandfather, I am Từ Thức from the Tiên Du district. I am looking for my old village," he asked.

XII. Southern Legends: Traditional

"People mentioned Từ Thức, the mandarin of the Tiên Du district, when I was young. That was 100 years ago. Everyone has passed away. I am the only one left from that time. One day, he decided to retire and travel around the country. He left town and was never seen again. Whether he went to another country or died somewhere, we do not know. Let me show you where his hut used to be."

The old villager showed him a decrepit place where a hut once stood. The place looked horrible. It was no longer hospitable. The village too had changed. Time had gone by fast, he thought to himself. He did not realize he had been gone for more than 100 years now. One day in the land of bliss was equal to one year on earth. Disappointed and distraught, he left town. There was nothing there for him: no friend, no relative, and nothing in common. He longed to return to his wife and the land of bliss but did not know the way.

Whether he got back to the and of bliss again or not, no one knows for sure. He never returned to the village and no villager knew him anyway.[50]

Comments Although this legend began beautifully, it ended miserably for Từ Thức. For saving a fairy's life, he was "invited" to the land of bliss, where he was given the honor and privilege of marrying her. He could have stayed there forever, but because he was a human being with perfectly human feelings, he missed his country and the people he knew. He did not know that once he left the land of bliss, he would not be able to return. He did not know that he had in his hands the ultimate happiness.

Từ Thức is the Vietnamese archetype of a man who is bestowed happiness but can not handle it. In a sense, this is the dichotomy of human nature. As a human being, a person tends to be pulled back to earth by his "human" nature, instead of reaching for the stars.

This story could presently apply to the Việt Kiều—the overseas Vietnamese[51]—who "migrated" to the western world for political reason following the 1975 fall of Saigon. For a long time, they were not able to return home, which had been taken over by the communists. They now live scattered in more than 50 different countries worldwide and long to return home to visit their relatives, land of birth, and other familial markers that binds them to their native land. Like Từ Thức, although they are happy to live in their adopted country, they feel that twinge in their hearts or that appeal of the motherland that calls them back home. They are also curious to see what has happened to the homeland they hastily left more than three decades ago. Those who have gone back felt lost in a country they no longer recognized. Vietnam, which has evolved socially, culturally, and politically, is no longer the old country of their youth before 1975. They too have evolved: being Americanized for some time, they no longer fit in their old country. The lack of political freedom, the obvious poverty among islands of riches, the crowdedness of the cities, the smoke that pervades the air, the unruliness of the street traffic, the heat and smell, all contribute to despoil the beauty of the countryside.

28. *The Fairy's Portrait*

Years ago in the village of Bích Cầu, there was a young scholar by the name of Từ Uyên. He came from a distinguished family of scholars and was reared in the best literary tradition. He spent his time studying, in an attempt to follow the footsteps of his ancestors. He recited aloud with pleasure the famous poems required for the examination. Many young and rich maidens in the village would have been happy to marry him, although he did not like anyone.

One beautiful spring day, he decided to take a walk in the field to enjoy the balmy weather and the flowering trees. The air was fresh and perfumed with the scent of lilac. Flowers and new sprouts were emerging from the ground. Birds sang in unison to greet the return of spring. Roosters and hens were frolicking behind the farmers' huts. Even the buffaloes in their pens were eager to get out to work.

He walked past the Lông Đổ temple on his way to the Tiên Tích pagoda, taking his time to enjoy the natural beauty of the countryside. By the time he reached it, the sun had begun its descent behind the trees. He then saw a lady with a beautiful peach-blossom complexion and flowing black hair. She slowly but gracefully walked around the pagoda as if she were lost there. She stood out from the background of the grey pagoda, the nuns in their brown robes and the flowering trees and appeared like a nymph out of an old painting. Từ Uyên thought she looked like one of those ladies who were known to topple cities and empires because of their beauty. What she was doing there amidst the peaceful ground of the pagoda was not known, although her presence did bring a magic color to the scenery.

Từ Uyên took a quick glance at her gracefully shaped face. He would have liked to take a longer look, but social etiquette did not allow him to stare at unaccompanied women in general. As he approached, he heard himself speak.

XII. Southern Legends: Traditional

"Since it is dark, would you, gracious lady, allow your humble servant, the unworthy scholar of Bích Cầu, to accompany you to where you were going? The road may not be safe," Từ Uyên asked, trembling at his own courage.

After a short silence—which for Từ Uyên was almost an eternity—the lady acquiesced. The two set forth on the road. When he started reciting a few verses praising the beauty of spring, she responded with a few verses of her own. Surprised by the beauty of her composition, he became speechless for a moment. He quickly regained his composure and shot a few more verses, to which she responded right away.

Thus back and forth, they challenged themselves into making poetry. The exchange of thoughts was so exhilarating that Từ Uyên forgot about the time, and the walk in the countryside turned out to be short. When they reached the crossing of the Rapid River, the lady suddenly disappeared. It was then that he realized she must be a fairy. He returned home excited about the meeting but depressed about not knowing how to meet the fairy again.

For days and weeks, he never stopped thinking about her. She was on his mind all the time. He could not get rid of her picture. He figured she must be somewhere in the clouds or above the trees, somewhere he as a human could not go. He did not tell anyone about the encounter because he wanted to keep that magic moment for himself. He could not eat, work, or think logically. He was struck by love, this earthly languor for which there was no cure.

He prayed he could die soon so that he could rejoin her in the other world. A genie came to him in his dream one night and told him to go to the river of two gorges and he would be able to see her again. He woke up with the sweats and wondered whether this was just the product of his imagination.

The next day, he got dressed and went to the river but did not find anyone except for an artist. Looking through the paintings, he noticed a picture that resembled the fairy. He bought it and hung it in his room. He looked at it constantly and even talked to the picture. He kissed and caressed it as if it were a real person. At mealtime, he would place two bowls and two pairs of chopsticks on the table and pretended to have a meal with the fairy.

One day, the picture did smile at him. He rubbed his eyes, wondering whether he had been dreaming. But the picture grew larger and larger and became the fairy he had met before.

"Here I am, my lord. You have waited for me a long time," she said.

"Who are you, honorable lady?"

"I am Giáng Hương, a fairy. It seems like we are predestined to be together. That was the reason I met you at the pagoda. The fairy queen was so moved by your love and faithfulness that she has decided to send me here to be your wife."

Life had completely changed for Từ Uyên, for his wish had become a reality. The fairy had become his wife. He loved her so much he stayed around her all the time. He could not stop admiring her fair complexion and beautiful figure. As a result, he could barely focus on his studies. Giáng Hương took him to the side and told him to study.

"Dear Giáng Hương, you have changed my life. You do not know how happy I feel when I am around you. You are the realization of my dream," he answered.

"My lord, if you want to be successful, you must study. If you do not, I will leave you."

But he could not keep away from her. One day, she went back in the painting. Realizing it was his fault, he begged for forgiveness.

"Dear Giáng Hương, please come back. I will focus on my study."

"You have told me the same thing many times and you have not changed," she said.

"With your help, I will do it."

He begged and begged and finally she relented. As promised, he put all his energy into his studies and passed the mandarinate exam. He was given an important governmental position and became a good mandarin. They lived happily together and had a son. They even had a live-in maid to take care of her child.

One day she became serious.

"My time on earth is up. The fairy queen has recalled me back to the purple hills. But do not worry, you are also on the list of the Immortals. Therefore, you can come with me and we can live happily in the purple hills."

The two deeded their house to the maid and told her to care for their son. Giáng Hương then murmured some prayers, and two huge eagles came down. They sat on the eagles' backs and flew away. The villagers built a temple at Từ Uyên's house to worship the Immortal.[52]

Comment This is a story about a human being marrying a fairy, which ends happily for both of them. In this legend, Từ Uyên and his fairy live in the land of humans for many years before making the final decision to fly to the land of bliss. In the previous story, Từ Thức was "invited" to live in the land of bliss before having said farewell to friends and family. Therefore, after having lived in the land of bliss for a while, he missed them so much that he wanted to return to the human world to reassure them and to disconnect his human bonds. Of the two legends dealing with the land of bliss, the two lucky men share the same last name, Từ, although they are not related.

The legend also shows a separation between the various social groups. On one side are the king, princes, princesses; on the other, the learned men, mandarins and fairies who are associated with humans. The third group consists of common people, peasants, workers, artisans, and merchants. Although they lived in the world of humans, the man and fairy couple retired beyond the reach of common people.

Why do fairies wed learned men instead of princes or commoners? First, it has to do with education. Learned men are more educated and often more knowledgeable than princes. They have inquisitive minds: they want to know and understand the land of bliss. They know words and poetry, which allow them to communicate easily with fairies. Second, they are also closer to commoners than princes who live in their walled quarters. They live in the same village as commoners and deal with them almost on a daily basis. From the point of view of commoners, to whom these legends are told, they are easier to understand than princes.

29. *Nguyễn Kỳ and the Songstress*

Nguyễn Kỳ was noted to be bright and intelligent since he was a child. His parents sent him to be educated by the best teacher in the neighborhood and as a result, he made remarkable progress. When his mother passed away early, his father remarried. His stepmother took him out of school and sent him to work in the fields. He had to care for buffaloes, plow, spread fertilizers and suffer from hardships and insults. His father, who was a weak man, did not argue with his wife. By the age of 15, tired of the manual work, Nguyễn Kỳ left home searching for a better life.

He moved from one place to another looking for a shelter and a place to work. Not being successful in the beginning, he had to beg for a living. He finally presented himself to an old scholar who asked him if he could write. Asking for a pen and a piece of paper, he wrote down two quatrains. The teacher was impressed not only by his manly features, but also by the firmness of his script and depth of his knowledge. He accepted him as a student.

The teacher let him use his shed for lodging. Under the teacher's instructions, he made rapid progress and was able to catch up on lost time. Besides studying, he had to do odd jobs to get pocket money. As years passed by, he became a well-known scholar who was studying for his examination.

One day his friends took him to a village festival. Nguyễn Kỳ was ashamed of himself because the area was frequented by sons of mandarins and wealthy land owners. The group was well dressed for the occasion while only he wore poor clothing that had been stitched up in various places. He hid himself in a corner of the temple, observing the activities from a distance.

He did not have to worry because all eyes were focused on a beautiful songstress whose performance was simply amazing. Each time she opened her mouth, words came out like gems. Guests were delighted by her performance and frequently clapped their hands, visibly enjoying the spectacle. As she was leading during a dance performance, her eyes fell on Nguyễn Kỳ. No one knew what she saw in him, but she stopped singing at once. Was it the air of sadness in this physically strong-looking young man? Was it the brightness of his eyes that reflected his intelligence? Was it the modest clothes he had on him? No one knew.

The next morning, as Nguyễn Kỳ was sitting on the bench reading his book, she lightly touched his shoulder and said, "Why is fate so unfair to such a talented man?"

She begged him to accept some money and a few rolls of fabric. She then left before he could open his mouth to thank her. He did not think about accepting anything from an unknown person, especially a woman, although he really needed it.

She came a few days later for a visit and stopped by more frequently later on. On each occasion, she helped clean his shed, cook his meals, and mend his clothing, as if she were his wife. This was pure friendship on her part and he appreciated it. She felt like she had a duty to serve him; there was no physical attraction or romance. He felt more and more attracted to her, although he kept a safe distance.

One day, he felt so close to her that he put his hand on her waist. She pulled back and reacted violently.

"Who do you think I am? I could have named my price, if I were the person you thought me to be. The reason I take you as a friend is because I am looking for the future. I need someone who can help me later. In our profession, beauty and artistry will fade away and we will be left with ill health and destitution. If you want something immediate, I can leave you now."

Nguyễn Kỳ apologized for his behavior and from then on kept a respectful distance from the woman.

As the date of his examination approached, Nguyễn Kỳ decided to return home to get ready for it.

"I will have to go home to see my parents. I do not know how to express all my gratitude. You have brightened my poor life a lot. Without you, I probably would not have been able to get this far. Life in the city is quite difficult for a student without parental support and guidance. Would you give me your address so I can get in touch with you afterwards?" he asked.

"You do not have to worry if you still want me around. Once you have passed your examination, I will be the one who will look for you. If it is written that we are not to see each other again, what good is it for you to know my name and village? I do not ask you to make any promise. Just remember me."

Nguyễn Kỳ headed home with a lot of apprehension. He did not know whether his father would recognize and receive him after he had been away for so long. Luckily, he was warmly welcomed by his father. His stepmother was also nice to him because of his potential future. Sometime later, he passed the district and then the provincial examinations.

His father thought that it was time for him to get married. He had already selected a young woman from a good family for him. Nguyễn Kỳ tried to explain that he owed gratitude to a certain songstress who had helped him during this difficult period. However, he became entangled in his explanations. He felt uncomfortable for not being able to voice a strong opinion. To be convincing, he had to reveal all his intimate life. He had to explain how he basically had lived with this woman for many years. A future mandarin could not do that. Who would believe a district official who had followed his heart instead of his duty? Who would follow a weakling? The king would be leery to select an official who did not have the heart to do his duty.

His father thought that it was a banal adventure and his son would soon forget about the friendship. Besides, he knew what his son needed: a woman with good lineage. He would never accept a songstress in his house.

Nguyễn Kỳ rationalized that he had made no vows to the lady, although he felt strongly about her. He also had a duty to obey his father, which resonated stronger than the romantic links to the songstress. In the end, he obeyed his father and married the woman his father chose for him.

The following year, he went to the capital for the doctoral examination. The songstress came to see him.

"I knew you would come back. How have you been?" she said excitedly.

"Not too bad," he answered in a hesitant voice.

"How long will you be here?"

"I don't know. A week maybe."

"Can I bring you anything?"

"That will not be necessary."

"Do you think we could take a walk to the temple?"

"I do not think so. I am busy."

"What is going on? It seems like you are not happy to see me."

"Nothing," he murmured in exasperation. He wanted to say he still loved her. He did not want to hurt her. He simply did not know how to express all these feelings. He wanted to tell her he had married to make his father happy. But he felt his throat tightening...

Feeling the constraint in the voice of the young scholar, she knew the reason behind it.

"I understand. You have someone else already. There is no need to talk further. Each of us will have to go on a different road. Good-bye, I wish you good luck," she said before leaving.

He put his head between his two hands and wept.

That year, Nguyễn Kỳ passed the doctoral examination and was made mandarin. He received the mandarin robe from the king himself, who congratulated him for his knowledge. He was placed in charge of a province in the highlands. A few years later, he was sent to the South to put down a Cham rebellion and pacify a province. Following these successes, he was awarded the title of duke. He had reached the top of his career in a very short time.

Sometimes when his friends reminded him about his difficult years, he felt like choking from emotion and would reproach himself for not having done anything for the songstress. He did send his servants to look for her, but no one could locate her.

One evening at a banquet given at the home of a marquis, he noticed among the musicians someone who looked like her. On closer look, he recognized her familiar traits: a tall stature with a lean and beautiful face. Although her beauty had somewhat faded, her voice and acting remained strong and precise. She had not lost the freshness and the manners of years before.

When he inquired further about the lady, his friend told him that she

XII. Southern Legends: Traditional

had married a gentleman from Thanh Hóa, but he had passed away and she had not remarried. She was living and caring for her elderly mother with savings from the past. Unfortunately, a younger brother had squandered the rest of the savings, forcing her to go back to the singing business.

Moved by the drama of her life, he invited his friend and her mother to live in his home. After a lot of thinking, she accepted the invitation. The two women were allotted a special room and their wishes were fulfilled. When the old lady passed away, Nguyễn Kỳ gave her a decent burial.

When the funeral was over, his friend came to see him.

"My lord, I would like to thank you for all you have done for my mother and me. I cannot forget your generous heart. Allow me to take leave from you and continue my life," she said.

"Dear friend, my home is yours. Please stay here with my family and me."

"I appreciate your generosity, my lord, but I do not want to abuse it."

"You are not abusing anything."

"Thank you, my lord. I have a long way to go."

"In that case, please accept these banknotes."

"That will not be necessary, my lord. You have done enough for me. Our roads have intersected twice. That is more than enough, my lord. Thank you again and good bye."

When she left, he was overcome with a melancholy that lasted a long time.[53]

Comments Life was simple at that time, maybe because there were not too many people around. No identity card was needed, for one only had to ask for X from village Z and villagers would show you where that person lived. Commoners were poor: they lived day by day from the fruit of their labor. If they had spare money, they would send their children to a teacher to be educated. There was no state school, only private teachers providing the teaching. Schooling therefore was neither uniform nor standardized. Good teachers were expensive and could accept only a small number of students; poor students would go to the least expensive, therefore not the best teachers.

Examinations were held at the district, provincial and state levels. Those graduating at the first two levels would go on to become teachers or district leaders. Those who graduated at the state level would become mandarins and assume high-level positions at the court or provincial level.

During the imperial period, society was composed of four groups: *sĩ*, *nông, công,* and *thương* or lettered-men, peasants, artisans, and merchants. Lettered men, who were at the top of the society, were well respected and honored. Artists, musicians, and *ả đào* (songstresses) were considered the pariahs of society. They formed a group outside of the society and were not allowed to hold governmental positions. Their children were not allowed to sit for the examinations or hold governmental positions.

This legend reflects the nature of the Confucian society. Although his parents pulled him out of school and sent him to work in the fields, Nguyễn Kỳ, as a good son, returned home prior to taking his examination to let them know about his status and to seek their approval. Having heard he was a scholar ready to become a mandarin, his parents changed their attitude toward him and became proud of him. They right away wanted to look for a wife for him.

Although youngsters could be romantically involved with other people, they would eventually toe the line and obey their parents, who would choose their eventual partners. Parents who demanded conformity claimed that children needed to follow tradition and respect the family's interests. Children felt guilty if they resisted their parents' demands. Marriages were thus pre-arranged by parents to build up either power or status for the families involved. Nguyễn Kỳ's father stated he would not let a songstress live in his house, since she belonged to a classless society.

30. *The Little Statesman Lý*

Statesman Lý was so short that he barely came up to a man's waist. Despite his stature, he was a good statesman and was employed by the court. He was sent to China once to discuss important matters related to the two nations.

The emperor of China, from the top of his dragon throne, wondered out loud if the "Vietnamese are short people."

Lý answered, "Sire, in Vietnam we have short and tall people. Our ambassadors are chosen according to the size of the problem. Since this is a small matter, they send me to negotiate it. If the problem is big, we send a big man to deal with you."

The emperor thought for a while.

"If the Vietnamese think that this important problem is a small one, they must be a great and powerful people."

He therefore lessened his demands and the matter was settled right there.[54]

Comments Vietnam has been, for more than two millennia, a David compared to the colossal Chinese Goliath. One only has to look at the 1,000-year Chinese domination over Vietnam to understand the power of China.

Instead of lessening, the problem has grown worse under the Hanoi communist government. Three hundred thousand Chinese soldiers helped the communists during the war, and China supplied Hanoi with armaments and supplies. After the war, to repay its debt Vietnam had to cede territories at its border to the Chinese, as well as the Paracel and Spratley Islands in the Pacific Ocean.

The original Vietnamese (*Lạc Việt*) stained their teeth black, tattooed their bodies, wore their hair in chignon, chewed betel and their women wore earrings. Their society was matriarchal in nature while the Chinese embraced a Confucian patriarchal society. Vietnamese women were given a lot more freedom than Chinese women were allowed. Their native language, which at one time used Chinese script (*nôm*), was romanized and became the *quốc ngữ* or national language. It is one of the rare Asian languages that was not written in Chinese or Sanskrit scripts.

31. A Scholar's Dream

This was the third time Lưu Sinh took this road back home, from the capital to his humble village on the coastal plain. It traversed villages, rivers, fields, hills, and forests. The road was long, and arduous, and he had plenty of time to think about it.

The first time was six years earlier, when he failed the doctoral examination. He thought to himself that it was just a triennial examination and he would try again three years later. When he failed the second time, he was less upbeat and thought about all the sacrifices he had endured. He was just a lowly local teacher who had even put off his wedding because he simply could not afford to feed a family.

He put in three more years of studying, and when he began his trip to the capital, he had high hopes of succeeding this time. Alas, there would be no congratulations from the emperor, no mandarin robe, no imperial cortege to accompany him home, and no village celebration. This time, he was definitely morose and did not know what to think. Six long years had turned into a big disappointment. Some of his friends who were less knowledgeable than him had succeeded and gone to higher positions, such as district or provincial chiefs, or governors. He was still stuck at his lowly post. He blamed himself all the way home.

When he reached the mountains that night, a heavy downpour forced him to take refuge under the trees. He could not see very far while he looked for a cleft between the rocks to hide in during the night. He then noticed a cave and tried to explore it. It turned out to be the grotto of a hermit, who welcomed him in.

The hermit enquired about him and his plans. Lưu Sinh told him about his failed examinations and his frustration with life. Since the scholar looked tired, the hermit told him to lie down on his bed and rest while he prepared supper. The hermit's only possession was a homemade bed of wood and straw, which looked quite comfortable for a tired traveler.

Three years later, the scholar passed the doctoral examination and received the mandarin robe from the king himself. He returned in triumph in his village on a white horse with a small retinue of soldiers. One soldier carried a parasol to shield him from the sun. Because the villagers were proud of having produced a mandarin, they took turns throwing receptions for him. For a week he was dined and wined and was obviously happy. He was then made provincial chief in the highlands. Being a progressive leader, he was able to help many local people.

The king loved him and gave him his daughter in marriage. He received a cabinet post and worked closely with the king. There were big celebrations when he had two nice children in a row and his future was assured.

At the time the Chams from the southern land decided to invade the country. Following a few early defeats, the king dispatched Lưu Sinh as a general to fight the invaders. He managed to beat them back without problems. The enemy surrendered and gave him a princess as booty. He felt in love with the woman and switched sides. The king ordered him to return home but he refused, neglecting his family and country. In despair, the king sent a new general to fight against him. The Chams, seeing disaster coming, turned him over to the king. Despite the pleas of the princess, the king ordered him executed. The night before the execution, he saw his life parading in front of him: his scholastic struggles, his career success, his marital success, his passion for the Cham princess and then his downfall.

He became frightened and woke up. He saw the walls of the cave, the bed, and the old hermit stirring his pot.

"Young man, you have taken a long nap; but dinner is not ready yet. In a few moments, I shall share dinner with you," said the hermit.[55]

Comments This legend gives the reader an overview of the examination system under the imperial regime. Civil service examinations appeared in

Vietnam as early as the eleventh century. In the nineteenth century, winners of the regional examinations were called *cử nhân* ("recommended man or in Chinese, *chu-jen*). Scholars who went on to succeed at the triennial metropolitan or palace examinations were saluted as *tiến sĩ* (presented scholars or *chin-shih*). The titles carried a lot of prestige in the Vietnamese traditional society. The *tiến sĩ* holders and their families were entitled to (*vinh quy*) glorious return from the provincial capital to their native village. Villagers had to pay for these festivities.

Those who passed three of the four stages of the regional examinations were called *tú tài* (flowering talent or *hsiu-ts'ai*). Therefore, only one stage separated the *tú tài* from the *cử nhân*.[56] Candidates came from all around the country to sit for the doctoral examination, which was given triennially. Those who passed the first two days of examinations would be eligible to sit for the third day. Results were given at the end of the week and the names of successful candidates were proclaimed by a herald. They received the mandarin robe from the king and were given a horse and retinue to go from the capital to their hometown. They were then assigned administrative posts.

Examinations were grueling. The first stage of the examination took place on the first day of the month, the second stage on the sixth day, and the third stage on the twelfth day. Candidates have been compared to beggars (they carried their own luggage; they raised their own tents and bamboo beds); convicts (they had their bodies searched); bees (they crawled in and out of their cubicles); sick birds (they dizzily got out of their cubicles after writing their essays); dead flies (those who failed); and pigeons (they smashed the furnishings of their huts if they failed).[57]

For the Vietnamese candidate, the focus of the examination was acculturation to the Chinese style. He had to prove his qualifications in writing Chinese-style poetry and conforming to Chinese behavioral demands like bowing, and meditating. Once successful, the bureaucrat looked Chinese: he wrote in Chinese, wore a Chinese robe, lived in a Chinese house, rode in a Chinese-type sedan chair, and followed Chinese-type idiosyncrasies. He, like a foreigner, ruled over the native peasant. In the end, the process created a gulf between the elite and the ruled in Vietnam.

32. The Stone Dog

On his way to school, a student walked through the main street of the village. Houses were simple but nicely kept with trees adorning the street.

The village was quiet and peaceful. In the front yard of a house bordering a unique intersection of the village sat a white stone dog.

Each time the student passed through that intersection, the dog turned its head toward him, smiled and wagged its tail. It, however, stayed immobile and silent when it encountered other people. Having noticed these behaviors on many occasions, the student walked to the dog and asked, "Why do you smile at me each time I pass through here?"

"You are the only one who will pass the examination this year. That is written in the book of Heaven. I smile because I am happy for you," the dog answered.

"Thank you. It is good to hear that. I have been studying very hard lately. I will tell my parents this evening."

When evening came, the student told his parents about his encounter with the dog. The father was obviously proud of his son and thought about being the only mandarin's father in the province. Day by day, he became more assertive and arrogant, knowing that he would soon be an important person throughout the province. He was soon recognized as being a bully. He treated other people like dirt. When people argued with him, he would tell them, "Watch out. My son will be a mandarin." Villagers wondered among themselves what was going on with him. When they saw him coming, they avoided him as much as possible.

One day as the student crossed the intersection again, the dog remained immobile. It neither smiled nor wagged its tail any longer. After a few days, the surprised student walked up to the dog.

"What is the matter with you recently? You do not seem to be happy to see me at all."

"I am sad these days. The book of heaven mentions that you will fail at the examination."

"Did I do anything wrong?" the boy asked very surprised at the turn of events. "You told me that I would succeed and now that I would fail. How do you explain your statements?"

"It is not you. Because your father has been a bully, your name has been taken off the list. I therefore cannot be happy for you."

The student reported the news to his father. The latter thought for a while and began to see the light. He became humbler, kept his mouth shut, and stopped harassing people. When the student took the examination, he failed as predicted, although he had studied hard. Despite putting in more hours in his studies, he failed at the second trial. And he failed a third time.

The father finally came to his senses. He became nice to everyone and helped them as much as he could. Villagers came to talk to him and welcome him. No longer was he an insensitive or overbearing person. One day, as the student walked through the intersection, he saw the dog smile and wag its tail again.

"Your father has finally learned his lesson. You will pass the exam. I am happy for you," the dog said when the student approached him.

The student did indeed pass the exam, with honors too. And not a moment too soon, for he had become desperate. Having studied very hard, he did not understand why he could not pass the exam. When he returned to his village after the results were posted, the villagers who were proud of his success greeted him with affection. The stone dog, however, had disappeared.[58]

Comments Vietnamese and Asians in general believe in fate, which is written in the book of heaven. The concept has a strong Buddhist influence. Nguyễn Du—a nineteenth-century Vietnamese poet—summarized it well when he wrote

> All things are fixed by Heaven, first and last
> Heaven appoints each creature to a place.[59]

Fate is preordained: there is finality in it.[60] We cannot change it. We are either born white or colored, in a rich or poor family, in America or Asia. Karma is another Buddhist concept. Although it has been used interchangeably with fate, it is the process by which one cleans up one's life in order to reincarnate into a better life. One can change one's karma to lead a better life afterwards. One could become rich by working hard despite being born poor.

D. Social Legends

These tales depict events that occur in the daily life of common people; they describe how people react to or deal with others in normal or unusual circumstances (friendship, brotherhood, parents and children, greed, love, and so on). They paint the Vietnamese society as it is.

33. Tấm and Cám
34. Thạch Sanh
35. The Balance
36. A Perfect Friendship
37. The Lady of Stone
38. The Lady of Nam Xương

39. A Brother's Devotion
40. The Sister-in-Law
41. The Starfruit Tree
42. The Narcissus
43. Peacock Hash, Phoenix Pie, And Dragon Whiskers
44. The Grain of Rice
45. The Two Tea Boxes
46. The Jar of Gold
47. The Magic Gourd
48. A Devoted Daughter-in-Law

33. Tấm and Cám

In a small village lived a nice couple with their daughter Tấm. They had built themselves a comfortable straw hut and even planted a star fruit tree close by. The good wife passed away following a short illness. Several years later, the husband married a widow who had a daughter of her own, Cám.

The stepmother did not like Tấm at first sight, for very simple reasons. Tấm was more beautiful and of fairer complexion than Cám. She was also well liked by her father. Since the latter did not want to indispose his new wife, he agreed with whatever she said or wanted. After a long day of work, he just wanted to relax and sip his hot tea. Knowing his weakness, she ordered him around and assigned all the house chores to Tấm. While Tấm had to clean the house, sort out the rice grains and feed the chicken and the pigs, Cám did not have to do anything. Tấm also had to fetch wood in the forest and to draw water from the well and carry it home. Life had changed for the worse for her. She was the unpaid and unloved maid of the house: she was the earliest to rise and the latest to go to bed.

Tấm was a good-natured girl like her own mother and did not complain. To whom would she complain now? Not to her father, who was afraid of his wife. Certainly not to Cám, who despised her. Not to her wicked stepmother who, had told so many lies about her that her father no longer liked her. Therefore, Tấm talked to the animals she cared for and sometimes to her fairy. She just wished she had less work to do or a nice place to sleep. Cám had taken her bed, forcing her to sleep on the ground in the kitchen. She wished to have back her nice clothes that were given to Cám: she only wore worn-out rags.

The stepmother looked for ways to punish Tấm—the more the better. Each time Tấm messed up or failed to complete her assigned chore, she would receive ten whippings. Although she was used to the whippings, she still dreaded them.

One day, the mother told Tấm and Cám to go fishing at the local river.

"Don't come home with an empty basket," she told Tấm, "otherwise you will be punished."

Tấm knew what that meant: no supper and ten whippings.

At the river, she worked as hard as she could and soon caught enough fish for the day. Cám spent her time talking to friends, playing and resting. In the afternoon when they were ready to go home, Cám came by with an empty basket. Seeing her sister's basket full of fish, she conceived an idea.

"Sister, your hair is dirty," she said. "Go wash yourself in the river, otherwise mother will punish you."

When Tấm went to clean her hair, Cám dumped her sister's catch into her basket and ran home. When Tấm realized what her sister did, she could only cry.

The fairy of mercy appeared to her and consoled her.

"I am touched by your cries, my girl. What can I do for you?"

"Cám took all my fish. My stepmother will not believe the story I will tell her, and she will beat me."

"Do not cry, my girl," said the Fairy. "Look into your basket."

And there it was: her basket was again full of fish. She profusely thanked the fairy, who told her to keep the fish with red fins and golden eyes in her backyard pond and feed it three times a day.

She went home and dropped the golden-eyed fish in the pond before giving the rest of the catch to her stepmother.

"How did you do it? Cám told me your basket was empty a while ago," asked the surprised stepmother.

Realizing that Cám had already made her report, Tấm calmly answered, "I was lucky, mother."

From then on, she often went to the pond and called

> Baby fish, baby fish, come here.
> I have something I like to share it with you.

As the fish emerged on the surface of the water, Tấm fed and talked to it like to a person. She told it about her work, sorrow, and wishes. The stepmother, finding it strange that Tấm spent a lot of time at the pond, decided to spy on her. She listened to Tấm talking to the fish. When Tấm was away, she went to the pond again and called the fish the way Tấm did. The fish miraculously appeared. She quickly scooped it out of the water, fried it and ate it.

When Tấm came back, she called her fish as usual but found it nowhere. As she looked around, she noticed some evidence of struggle: footprints and trampled ground. She called her fairy who told her, "Your mother has caught and eaten it already. Find the fish's bones and bury them in the ground underneath your mat. They will help you get whatever you want."

A rooster walked by and said, "I will help you find the bones if you give me some grains."

The rooster dug the ground under the pile of garbage and showed her the fish bones. Tấm buried them under her mat as the fairy had advised her. And every day she confided her apprehensions, fears, and joys to the fish bones. If she had too much work to do, all she needed to do was to talk to the fish bones and somehow her work got lighter.

The spring festival was underway and villagers rushed to attend it. When Tấm expressed her desire to attend it, her stepmother frowned on her. Despite all the whippings and chores she imposed on Tấm, the girl had matured quite a bit and become more beautiful than Cám. Instead of getting calluses from her work, her skin remained soft. On the other hand, Cám, who did not have to struggle in life, remained somewhat childish.

The stepmother gave her a bag of grain, mixed with husks and told her to sort them out, after which she could go to the festival. She knew fairly well that the job would prevent her from going. Realizing the difficulty, Tấm talked to her fairy. A crow flew down from a tree and offered to help. Between the two, the work was done in no time. Tấm was so happy that she rewarded the crow with grain.

Since Tấm did not know how to proceed next, she again asked the fairy for help. In no time, the latter transformed her into a gorgeous young lady and Tấm proceeded to go to the festival. Her stepmother and Cám saw her coming and marveled at her look.

"Look, is this Tấm coming over here? Where did she get that beautiful outfit?" asked the stepmother.

"Impossible. It could not be her because she does not have any clothes at all," answered Cám.

Tấm breezed through the rows of merchants and quickly disappeared. She did not want to be seen by her stepmother. In her rush to get out, she lost one of her slippers. Frightened, she did not dare come back and pick it up.

The king happened to be at the festival that evening. He caught a glimpse of the beautiful maiden who walked through the crowd but was unable to catch her. One villager found the golden slipper and turned it over to him. Since the slipper was nicely made and exquisitely embroidered, the king reasoned it must have come from someone belonging to a noble family. The following morning, he announced he would marry the girl who could wear the beautiful slipper. Anyone could try on the slipper, which was left at the local temple.

All the girls attempted to put the shoe on, but no one succeeded. Their feet were either too large or too small. Tấm sneaked out of the house and tried it. It fit her just fine because it was hers to begin with. The soldier in charge of monitoring the shoe notified the king. Tấm was then brought to the court wearing the slippers and a beautiful *áo dài*. The two got married and had a happy and satisfying life.

Cám and her mother could not stand seeing Tấm happy. They thought that if Tấm could do it, Cám could too. They did not realize Tấm and Cám had two different personalities. When Tấm came home to visit her parents, the wicked stepmother thought out a murderous scheme. When Tấm arrived, the stepmother pretended to be very happy to see her. She then asked her to climb up the star fruit tree and pick the sweetest fruit for her. She had an ailment, she said, that could be improved by eating a sweet star fruit. The good-natured Tấm obeyed without any suspicion. Once Tấm got up the tree, the stepmother shook it in order to dislodge her. Having no success with that plan, she went inside, got an axe and cut the tree down. Tấm fell and was killed on the spot.

The king was saddened to learn the news about his wife. He dearly missed his gentle Tấm. The stepmother pushed him to take Cám as wife.

Tấm, in the meantime, was reborn as a nightingale. Each morning, the bird came to the palace and sang the same song Tấm used to sing in the past.

Puzzled, the king one day asked, "Dear bird, if you really are the spirit of my Tấm, please come and rest on my forearm."

The bird came down and rested on the kings's forearm. The king caressed it and gently put it in a golden cage. The bird sang most of the day for the king, who spent time caressing it and listening to its songs. He spent so much time with the bird that Cám became jealous.

On the advice of her mother, Cám killed the bird and buried it in the garden. The king realized the loss on his return. The door of the cage was wide open. Besides a few feathers on the window, there was no trace of it. The prince asked whether Cám had seen the bird.

"Maybe it was tired and has flown away," answered Cám.

The king was saddened by the loss. He could not do anything beyond accepting his fate.

Tấm's innocent spirit could not find any peace. She turned into a magnificent star fruit tree that bore only one single star fruit. The fruit was larger than usual, ripe-yellow, and good smelling with five spines like the fingers of a star. An elderly lady passing by said, "Golden fruit, golden fruit, drop into the bag of this old woman."

The fruit dropped into the woman's basket. She placed it on her table at home. In the morning, she did her errands. On her return, she found that her hut had been nicely cleaned and arranged. She wondered who could have done it in her absence. The next day, she went out again and found her hut cleaned and rearranged again.

Surprised, she decided to find the culprit. She went out the next morning but came back soon after. She found a lovely woman coming out of the star fruit and cleaning up the hut. She rushed in the room and tore the fruit apart. Tấm therefore could not hide anywhere and had to become the old lady's daughter.

The king went hunting one day. When it became late, he stopped by the old lady's hut and asked for shelter. When he woke up, he found betel leaves and nuts prepared the way Tấm used to at the palace. The king asked to see who was preparing the betel.

"It is my unworthy daughter, sire," answered the old woman.

"Could I see her?"

The king immediately recognized Tấm. They held each other for a long time, glad to be together again. He brought her back to the palace, made her queen again and relegated Cám to the rank of concubine. Cám one day asked her sister's advice.

"I know that if I were as fair-skinned as you are, I could win back the king's heart. How could I get as fair-skinned as you, sister?"

"Boil yourself a pot of hot water and get in there," answered Tấm.

Cám boiled a large pot of hot water and jumped in. She died right away. Her mother, hearing the news, cried for so long that she became blind and died soon after. Tấm who, had finally gotten rid of her enemies, lived happily with her king.[61]

Comment This is the Vietnamese version of the western Cinderella. However, the story was adapted from the Chinese version, *Ye Xian*, which was written in 860 CE. And the original Cinderella version may be older than that: it could have been told in the Middle East as the tale of the Greco-Egyptian girl Rhodopis around the first century BCE. The earliest European version of the tale—"The Hearth Cat"—appeared in 1635. There are today many hundred versions of the same story.

The story revolving around a naughty stepmother, a mistreated daughter-in-law, a prince in search of a wife, a golden shoe, and a fairy is the common thread to all the Cinderella stories. The Chinese-Vietnamese version is different from its western version in the fact that it is more convoluted. It does not stop when the king married his princess. This story stresses Confucian ethics—which rewards good deeds and punishes bad behavior—and the Buddhist beliefs in reincarnation and spirits. Tấm is reincarnated as a nightingale, a star fruit, and then a maid.

34. Thạch Sanh

A poor woodcutter once lived with his wife in the forests of the northern highlands. He worked hard climbing high in the mountains to take down trees, rafting them downstream, and selling them at the market. He and his wife were very generous with their time and money: they made themselves useful to their neighbors, who liked them a lot. They had been together a long time but had no children of their own. Because she prayed often, the Jade Emperor—the Ruler of Heaven—one day decided to bless the couple in reward for their virtues.

Although she had been pregnant for nine months, she still had not given birth. A year passed by, then two. Her husband passed away when she was on the third year of her pregnancy. A few months after his death, she gave birth to a healthy boy named Thạch Sanh. She raised him as best as she could. Several years later, she too passed away. Having no relatives, the boy survived on his own. He followed in his father's footsteps and became a woodcutter, exchanging the products of his work for food. If he could not find work, he would eat wild berries and moss. A genie once stopped by to teach him a few survival techniques.

A wandering merchant, Lý Thông, passing by and recognizing the teenager's innate talents and skills, decided to exploit him. He congratulated him for being smart, resourceful, and for having successfully taken care of himself. He told him:

"It is hard to live alone by yourself. You need someone to help you occasionally. Let's live like brothers so we can help each other," said Lý Thông.

The young man consented and they both went to meet Lý Thông's mother. The latter, seeing the profit she could gain from his labor, adopted him as her son.

In that part of the land lived a mighty and cruel monster that often terrorized and killed nearby villagers. Because of its unusual powers, no one had ever been able to get rid of it. The king, therefore, was required to send a human sacrifice every year in order to appease it. Feeling bad for the victims, he had a small temple built in their memory. That year, Lý Thông was the chosen sacrificial person. Once he heard the news, he became so frightened that he fainted. As he recovered his senses, he began plotting his strategy. A perfidious smile lit his face up. He would send the unsuspecting Thạch Sanh in his place.

When the latter brought home a load of wood at the end of a working day, the wily Lý Thông invited him to a sumptuous dinner, which he said was given to honor his father's death. Although surprised by the nice reception, the good-hearted Thạch Sanh did not suspect the motive behind it.

"Brother, I have to stand guard at the temple next week. I will be busy because I have to take care of mother. Would you like to go in my place?" Lý Thông asked.

"This should be no problem. I am pleased to be of service to you," said the gullible young man, eager to help.

On the scheduled date, Lý Thông led him close to the location high on the mountain and showed him the spot he would have to guard for the night. The site was beautiful, with tall mountains on either side of a meandering river. Cold water rushed downhill with force. Thạch Sanh, who had worked in the mountains before, felt secure in this setting. For others, the isolated environment with its gorges and cliffs could be frightening.

He waited at the temple as suggested, although no one came for him. Slowly darkness set over the area. Suddenly the monster appeared with fire spouting through its mouth. It emitted loud and strident noises and rushed toward its victim. Anyone besides Thạch Sanh would either be frozen in fear or run away immediately. Knowing his strength and magical powers, he valiantly stood up, and fought against the monster in a long and bloody battle. The latter was surprised and irritated to see someone resisting him. The more Thạch Sanh resisted, the more ferocious and powerful it became. In the end, it transformed itself into a long black snake with glistening scales and tried to strangle the young man. In a swift and rapid move, Thạch Sanh beheaded the serpent. Tired, he sat down to recover his breath and rested for a while before heading home.

On reaching Lý Thông's home, he called him. The latter thought that Thạch Sanh's spirit had come back to take revenge. His whole body shook in fear. He hid behind a piece of furniture and did not dare to show up. He asked his brother for forgiveness. It was only at that time that Thạch Sanh recognized his brother's perfidy. When his adopted mother opened the door, he showed her the monster's head. Lý Thông immediately conceived another evil scheme.

"Brother, the snake is a distant relative of the king. If he knew about its demise, he would put you to death," said Lý Thông.

Terrified, Thạch Sanh dropped on his knees and begged for pardon.

"Sorry, brother. I did not know about it. The snake was so ferocious that I had to kill it, otherwise I would have been dead."

"Leave now. Let me take care of this problem. I do not want you to get caught and suffer the consequence of this killing."

Thạch Sanh ran away as fast as he could. He returned to his old hut where he sought refuge. A simple-minded person, he could not figure out what had happened. He stood watch for Lý Thông, killed the monster, and now had to run for his life.

The next morning, Lý Thông brought the monster's head to the king, who was happy to see that someone had finally got rid of it. He was grateful to Lý Thông and named him commander-in-chief of the royal army.

From a wandering salesperson, he suddenly became a highly esteemed official. He was given a house and maids to serve him. He and his mother thus enjoyed a luxurious life while Thạch Sanh returned to his old job as a woodcutter. He, however, never complained and was happy to lead a simple life.

The king had only one daughter. She was beautiful and graceful and the king loved her a lot. Her skin was the color of peaches and her beautiful hair was flowing down her back. Since she was of marriageable age, he decided to invite princes from surrounding countries to a banquet. They all came expecting to be able to impress the princess, although the latter walked past them without any apparent interest.

The king was disappointed but understanding.

It was a beautiful spring day and the king's garden was in bloom. The princess loved to stroll in the garden to watch the blooming lotuses in the pond. She and her maid took a boat out and paddled among the lotuses. She slowed down to take time to feed koi fish that were swimming around. While she was bending down to talk to her fish, a huge eagle swooped down and snatched her with its claws. The maid screamed and fainted. All the guards could do was to watch with horror as the princess became airborne. They were afraid to shoot at the eagle for fear of hitting the princess.

Thạch Sanh was taking a break beneath his banyan tree. He suddenly saw the huge eagle flying by and holding a woman in its clutches. He pulled out his bow, placed an arrow and shot the bird, hitting it on the right side of the belly. The eagle, with its magic powers, was able to pull the arrow out and to continue its flight, leaving a trail of blood on the ground. Thạch Sanh followed the trail that led to a mountain cave.

The king was deeply saddened by the loss of his daughter. He immediately sent out search teams that came back without bringing any news. He promised to give her in marriage and big rewards to anyone who could bring her back. Lured by the rewards, Lý Thông sent out notices to anyone having any lead in the case. One day, villagers told Thạch Sanh about the rewards and made him aware of the search for the princess.

Thạch Sanh went to Lý Thông and told him about his battle with the eagle and the location of the cavern where the eagle had taken refuge. Since the area had not been explored before, he had not looked into the cavern because of lack of help. Lý Thông was happy to hear the news. He promised Thạch Sanh big rewards if he could help save the princess.

A whole search team was organized and headed to the cavern the following morning, led by Lý Thông in full mandarin regalia. The poor Thạch Sanh, walking on foot, guided the column. On arrival, he told Lý Thông, "This cavern is huge and unexplored. You need to lower me down with a rope. When I tug three times, pull it up and the princess will be at its end. Remember to drop the rope back down so I can get up."

"Agreed," Lý Thông answered.

Thạch Sanh used the rope to descend into the cavern. He brought a torch with him because of the darkness. At the bottom, the princess ran toward him.

"Help! Help me," said the princess. "The monster is holding me hostage in this cold and dark place."

"That is what I am here for, princess. Are you all right?"

"Get me out of here, my prince, and I will marry you."

"Thank you, princess. But let me help you out of here, first. Where is the monster?"

"He is wounded and is resting at the end of the cave."

"Dissolve this powder in some water and give it to the bird. It will make it sleepy and we will be able to escape."

The princess gave the medicine to the bird, which gladly took it. After a while, Thạch Sanh tied the princess to the end of the rope and signaled to the soldiers, who lifted her up. Lý Thông then conceived a diabolical plan. He told the soldiers to return home with the princess while he took care of the monster. The soldiers gladly obliged. Once they departed, Lý Thông rolled a big rock over the entrance of the cavern.

"Thạch Sanh will not be able to get out, and I will receive all the rewards," Lý Thông thought to himself. The job done, he returned to the palace.

Thạch Sanh was very unhappy when he realized that someone had shut off the cavern's entrance and removed the rope. At the same time, the eagle had recovered from the medication and was upset to see the princess gone and a stranger in his lair. He screamed so loud that the rocks shook like in an earthquake. Thạch Sanh knew he had to take care of the monster if he wanted to get out of the cavern alive. Using his axe, he delivered 100 strikes to the animal before the latter slumped down and died. The fight lasted a couple of hours. Tired, Thạch Sanh sat down and rested before looking for ways to get out of the cavern.

During the exploration, he found a youth imprisoned in a cage in one of the cavern recesses. Once released, the youth profusely thanked Thạch Sanh.

"Thank you, my savior," said the youth. "I am the son of the sea king. About a year ago, the monster swooped down on me while I was walking on the edge of a river. It brought me here and held me in this cage. If you help me out of here, I will forever be indebted to you."

"Let's go," said Thạch Sanh.

"There is another passage out of here. The monster once told me about it, although it is never used."

The two men found their way out of the cavern. The narrow and tortuous passageway through the rocks led to an opening high on the mountain.

Once out of the cavern, the prince proposed, "I would like to invite you to my father's palace of the waves. He will certainly want to meet and reward you with gems and diamonds. But do not take them. Ask for the magic flute that had once been given to him by the Jade Emperor. It will help you overcome any danger in the future."

The king of the sea was overjoyed upon seeing his lost son. He had lost hope of ever seeing him alive again. He had a big banquet prepared to celebrate his son's return and to thank his savior.

"Thank you, Thạch Sanh, for bringing back my son. I do not know how to express my thanks to you. I would like to give you something to remember us by."

"Dad, only the magic flute would be a worthy reward," said the sea prince.

The king of the sea reluctantly agreed. He had the magic flute brought in and gave it to Thạch Sanh.

"This flute was given to me by the Jade Emperor. However, I have never had the occasion to use it. But I hope it will be useful to you. You can stay here as long as you want to."

"Thank you, sire. But I would like to go home tomorrow if I could. I have been away for quite some time now," Thạch Sanh answered.

The following morning, he bid farewell to the king of the sea and his son. They promised to see each other once a year. The king had the genie of the sea accompany Thạch Sanh to the shore. After a long walk, Thạch Sanh finally reached home. His banyan tree had been waiting for him for so long that its leaves seemed to have withered away. Shortly after his return, the leaves turned green again. When a tree can show such fidelity, how can humans fail to express gratitude to their benefactors?

At the court, Lý Thông was waiting for his reward: the hand of the princess. He had told the king that he had saved the princess and was waiting for him to fulfill his promise. The king explained to him that although he had made the promise, he had to wait for his daughter's consent.

When the princess realized that Lý Thông had taken credit for her rescue in place of Thạch Sanh, she could not believe how a person could be so mean and unfaithful. She was so upset she fell into a speechless state.

The king was so distressed that he had prayers sung and offerings made to heaven in the hope of an early recovery. However, the month-long ceremony had no effect on the princess' health.

When the eagle died, its restless spirit began wandering around begging for alms. One night, it met the wandering spirit of the snake, which was also killed by Thạch Sanh. The two spirits became friends and plotted revenge.

"Thạch Sanh is very strong physically. We would have difficulty fighting him face to face. What we could do is steal the king's jewelry and bury them under the banyan tree. The king would punish him once they were recovered."

The two spirits broke into the king's treasury, stole his jewelry and buried them as planned. The search team one day found the lost jewelry under the banyan tree close to Thạch Sanh's hut. This could not be done without the help of the spirits. The soldiers accused Thạch Sanh of theft, tied his hands and placed a cangue around his neck, although he vehemently denied the accusation.

Instead of taking him to the palace, they put him in the local jail and tortured him. The warden ordered all his belongings, which were not much, seized. When the soldiers tried to take away his crossbow and axe, they were thrown to the ground. When they wanted to take away his flute, it felt so heavy they could not lift it up. Lý Thông remembered that Thạch Sanh possessed some magic powers. Fearing Thạch Sanh's revenge, he condemned him to death.

In his cell, Thạch Sanh realized the dangerous situation he was in, and decided to use his magic flute. As soon as he placed the flute to his mouth, a melodious but sad tone came out, relating the story of Lý Thông's perfidy and betrayal. The music rolled into the air and reached the palace. The princess immediately awoke to the sound of the music and recovered her speech. She ran to her father and asked him to invite the flutist to the palace. Although delighted, the king was surprised to see his daughter's rapid recovery. While one month of festivity had not done anything to her health, the music from the flute had immediately cured her.

"Who is that person, dear?" the king asked.

"He is Thạch Sanh, the one who saved me from the monster," the princess answered.

"But Lý Thông said he was your savior."

"He lied to you, dad. He abandoned Thạch Sanh in the cave to take all the credit away from him."

The king had Thạch Sanh brought to the palace. When she saw him in chains, she felt deeply sorry for him.

"Tell me your story, Thạch Sanh," the king said.

Thạch Sanh told him that he was an orphan who had learned some magical skills from a genie. He befriended Lý Thông and beheaded the snake, which Lý Thông took credit for; he wounded the eagle and saved the princess; he freed the son of the sea king; and the stolen jewelry was the work of the revengeful spirits of the snake and the eagle.

After hearing the whole story, the king ordered Thạch Sanh's chains removed. The fact that Thạch Sanh had killed the snake monster and the eagle made him a hero. The bravery, courage and dedication of the young man impressed the king. He had new clothes brought in for him and commanded a large banquet in his honor. He made him a duke and gave him his daughter in marriage as he had proclaimed earlier.

The king ordered the arrest and imprisonment of Lý Thông and his mother. He gave Thạch Sanh the power to judge and sentence them. Thạch Sanh, who had a good heart, pardoned the evildoers and told them to return to their old home. Relieved, both of them got out of town rapidly. On the way home, they were caught in the middle of a big storm and killed by lightning. Lý Thông was transformed into a cockroach spirit.

The wedding was celebrated with pomp and ceremony with the attendance of high officials and neighboring leaders. The princes who had unsuccessfully competed for the princess' hand were upset that she married a commoner. They raised an army and marched against the kingdom. Thạch Sanh, who replaced Lý Thông as commander of the royal army, easily defeated them.

Finding Thạch Sanh a good person, the king soon abdicated in his favor. Thạch Sanh, the new king, led a happy life with his princess. He made his country into a prosperous one.[62]

Comment The legend teaches us that gratitude is a natural feeling, for even trees have that feeling. The banyan was missing Thạch Sanh so much that its branches wilted away when he did not come back. The son of the sea king was grateful to his savior. He brought Thạch Sanh to his father, who rewarded him with a magic flute. Of course, the princess was also grateful to him. Although there are evildoers in life, the majority of people are nice enough to make life more enjoyable.

35. The Balance

A goldsmith once set up shop in a large city. No one knew where he came from. Since his craftsmanship was unique and beautiful, people flocked to his shop to buy or trade something of value. He was good and proficient in his business. People also liked him as a person and a businessman.

He soon expanded his business and built a large house for himself and his family. He had two nice boys who were the envy of the town. Although they were still young, people vied to have their daughters meet them with the thought of getting associated later on with the goldsmith's family.

The goldsmith, however, had a dark secret, which lay in his scale. He used a specially made scale that was composed of a beam with a string off its center. On one side was a counterweight and on the other a plate to hold the gold. The beam, however, was hollow and contained mercury. If he were selling something, he would tilt the mercury toward the plate adding extra weight to the merchandise. By selling less actual gold, he would pocket the difference.

If he were buying something, he would tilt the mercury toward the counterweight side. The gold therefore would weigh less than normal and he would pay less to the customer. The difference in weights was so minimal that customers did not realize they were being cheated.

XII. Southern Legends: Social

However, the little extra gold he made from each transaction added up with time. Over the years, his profits increased and fueled his business expansion.

Fifteen years later, the goldsmith had reached the top of his career. He had everything he could ask for: wealth, properties, and a large clientele. One day, he had a change of heart and told his wife, "We cannot go further like this, dear. I just hate to cheat people out of their money while they kept on trusting us. I am going to destroy this balance and buy a new and more accurate one. What do you think?"

"Sounds like a good idea. It suits me fine," she said.

"I am going to give some money to the Buddhist temple and the poor."

And he destroyed his balance and bought a new and accurate one. He helped the poor and the disinherited. He slept better each night for he was no longer tortured by his conscience. People somehow liked him better: instead of suffering his business picked up.

One day, following a freak accident, both his sons died. He was deeply wounded, and cried day and night. He had only two children, who were to take over his business. He blamed himself for having invited the disaster on his family and thought heaven had punished him for his misdeeds. He was sorry about his past and decided to be better in the future.

One night, a genie appeared to him in his dream. He told him that *Trời* had wanted to punish him in the past by giving him two boys. These were demons who, if they grew up, would only cause him problems and lead to his downfall. But since he had become a better person, it was decided to recall these demons by causing their deaths. He should no longer be concerned about the boys, but rather about living a good life. He would reach enlightenment if he kept on doing good work.

When he woke up, he told his wife about his wild dream. From that time onward, he became a better person by giving most of his wealth back to the community. He turned his house into a pagoda and settled in a smaller house. He spent most of his time in prayer and contemplation.[63]

Comments Vietnamese have the tendency to rationalize things by implying the law of karma or cause and effect.[64] When someone has suffered from a political, social or economical setback, people say that "*Trời phạt or Phật phạt*" (heaven or Buddha punishes him/her) uncritically, arguing that the victim might have done something wrong. In the story about the balance, the goldsmith, having cheated his customers, thought that Buddha punished him by taking away his two sons. The genie revealed to him that this was not the case.

Punishment had already been set for the father. The children—demons—would eventually make the father pay for his deeds. Luckily, since the father had already repented, the children were recalled in time. Children therefore could be a burden (punishment) or a gift (reward) for their parents. Vietnamese tend to rationalize that way all the time. They tend to find or make up a "cause-effect" meaning to anything. In that sense, they have made a judgment, right or wrong, about the person's intention or guilt.

This state of mind may be related to the fact that justice in Vietnam today, as well as in the past, has not been carried out strictly according to the laws of the lands. Unable to wait for social justice, which may take time to work or be deficient or ineffective, the public tends to rely on heaven's justice. Legends therefore tend to base their reasoning on empiric factors, which although not logical at all, reflect the popular mentality of the time.

The good thing is that a legend tends to connect the dots. There will always be a reward or punishment for any deed done. If the actor is not punished in his lifetime, his children will suffer the consequences. The saying "*Đời cha ăn mặn, đời con khác nước,*" which can be translated as "if the father eats salty food, his children will be thirsty," shows a clear connection between father and children.

In another story, Nguyễn Trãi—a national hero—was wrongly accused of regicide and condemned to death, along with three generations of his family.[65] Although he had not done anything wrong, a legend was circulated, explaining that Nguyễn Trãi had somehow killed a snake in the past. The snake transformed into Nguyễn Thị Lộ—his wife—to take revenge on him.

Nguyễn Trãi, after a brilliant career at the court, retired from office and took with him Nguyễn Thị Lộ, a lady of the court. King Lê Thánh Tôn, with whom Nguyễn Trãi had worked in the past, died and was replaced by his 20-year-old son, a playboy.

The new king one day decided to pay to Nguyễn Trãi a visit. Was he visiting Nguyễn Trãi, the hero, or Nguyễn Thị Lộ, who had been his mistress in the past? No one knew for sure, although it was rare for a king to pay a visit to a commoner. The king, after being feasted by Nguyễn Trãi, requested the services of Lộ for that night. Nguyễn Trãi kindly obliged. The next morning, the king left his host and took Nguyễn Thị Lộ with him. On his way back to his palace, he stopped at a local guesthouse. At six the following morning, Lộ ran out of the house crying for help. Soldiers came in and found the king dead. Nguyễn Thị Lộ and Nguyễn Trãi were accused of regicide and condemned to death.

Nguyễn Trãi, a national hero for having helped Lê Thánh Tôn get rid of the Chinese invaders, should not have been condemned to death. However, the regent and the queen, following the death of the young king, were afraid that Nguyễn Trãi might try to usurp the throne. They simply decided to get rid of him by condemning him of regicide. Years later, Nguyễn Trãi was fully rehabilitated.

This legend implies a third corollary: heaven (*trời*) is watching what we are doing and judging us. It is similar to the western "eye" that watched Cain after he killed his brother. This is the conscience that "is formed in early life by internalization of the standards of parents and other models of behavior." These standards in Vietnam are based on three religions: Buddhism, Taoism, and Confucianism. Confucianism stresses the pride of the individual and the respect of law and order. Taoism disregards material wealth and worldly privileges, while Buddhism teaches compassion, the law of cause and effect, and the impermanence of life. Catholicism is a recent introduction to the country: it was brought in by the French missionaries in the nineteenth century (although missionaries came earlier, their influence was negligible until the arrival of the French). *Trời* is nondenominational, since it is neither Buddhist, Catholic, Taoist, nor Confucian.

36. A Perfect Friendship

Two young friends took lessons from a private teacher. Since public schools were not available, people who had the means sent their children to a private teacher for schooling. In a land that prized learning, teaching was a highly regarded profession. It gave knowledge and opened new vistas to students. Teachers thus behaved like second parents to students. Educated students went on to become mandarins if they passed the final state examination.

Lưu Bình, who was the son of a mandarin, had all the material means to succeed. Intelligent and wealthy, he could afford the best teacher in the region. Dương Lễ, whose parents were poor, put himself through school, but had to work as a laborer on the side to make ends meet. Lưu Bình, seeing his friend struggling, brought him home and shared food and shelter with him. They both studied under the same lamp with the same teacher.

Dương Lễ, knowing the road to success went through education, studied laboriously day and night. Lưu Bình, overconfident because of his wealth, spent his time drinking and flirting. When the time came to take the exam, Dương Lễ passed it with honors while Lưu Bình failed miserably.

Dương Lễ thus became a mandarin who moved from one post to another. Lưu Bình, on the other hand, sank into depression. Dispirited, he wasted the rest of his fortune on drinking and womanizing. One day, swallowing his pride, he decided to look for his friend and ask for help. It took him some time to get to see the mandarin. The meeting was awkward. On one side was a well-dressed mandarin. On the other side, Lưu Bình was no longer an outgoing, frivolous young man but a time-battered person—a broken man.

The two old friends sat down to chat, and Dương Lễ told Lưu Bình to hit his books. Lưu Bình left dispirited.

"I helped this man when he went through difficult times. Now he turns me away. I will have the last word. I will show him."

Lưu Bình returned to his home depressed. A few days later, a lady knocked at his door and asked to see him.

"What can I do for you?" Lưu Bình asked.

"I am Châu Long. A friend of mine told me your tough situation, my lord. He has asked me to come and help you. I will do the household work while you study."

Lưu Bình, freed from the worries of everyday life, devoted himself to his studies. Châu Long cooked for him, took care of his house, and encouraged him whenever his spirit broke down. Three years was a long time to focus only on studying. When the time came to take the exam, he passed it with honors. When he told the news to Châu Long, she congratulated him.

"How could I thank you for all the things you have done for me?" Lưu Bình asked.

"You owe me nothing, my lord," Châu Long answered.

"You have helped me a lot. Without you, I could not have done it. You have given me hope and courage to study."

"Dương Lễ sent me to help and comfort you during your period of despair. Now that my job is done, please allow me to retire."

Lưu Bình finally understood the depth of Dương Lễ's friendship. His assistance was not direct and torrential; it was smooth, soothing, and gentle, like the flow of a small river.[66]

Comments There are many ways to help a friend in despair, material or moral. What would be the best approach? Since each case is unique, it should be individualized. While other people would have shunned friends who landed in difficult times, Dương Lễ took a unique approach. As Lưu Bình had helped him in the past, he too would help his friend, in a kind and friendly way, retake the exam. On the side, he would send his own wife—without letting Lưu Bình know about it—to help Lưu Bình. There was no better concrete way to help a friend in difficulty.

Although this legend is first and foremost about friendship, it is also about obedience and the dedication of a woman toward a man—who in his right mind would send his wife to serve another man? This shows that friendship could, in certain cases, transcend marital bonds.

When told repeatedly to young girls and teenagers in classrooms around the country, the legend reinforced in their minds the virtues of obedience and friendship. The greater the sacrifice, the higher would be the virtue. In a society that praises virtue, women soon equated sacrifice to duty and acted accordingly. They associated their worth within the society based on the degree of their sacrifice.[67]

37. The Lady of Stone

From National Highway One—that followed the coastal area and linked Saigon to Hanoi—one is able to see the tall and treacherous mountains on the western side and the wild blue sea on the eastern side. On this arid land of central Vietnam live tough and resilient people who struggle year in and year out against natural elements: the monsoon rains and the flooding that comes down the steep mountains.

One can look at the top of the mountains between Danang and Cam Ranh Bay and see the contours of a woman holding her son and looking at the horizon. People call it *Hòn Vọng Phu* or the Lady of Stone. No one built it. It just appeared there one day. Here is the story about this legend.

A fisherman's life is not always simple. If some days are beautiful, with blue skies and calm seas, others days can be fearsome, with hollering winds and angry seas. Life is therefore not easy between the bright and burning sun and the frightening sea storms. Some days, fish would be abundant; on other days, they are nowhere to be found. Making a living from the sea is tough and unpredictable, as is being the wife of a fisherman.

Văn was a young man who settled in a village in the central coastal region. Wanting to be a fisherman, he enrolled as a helper to elder fishermen. With time, he became a good one and made a decent living. He got acquainted with Hương, a girl from the area, and soon got married. They had a small boat and went out to fish together. They came home only when their boat was loaded with fish, lobsters, and shrimps. With time, they thought about saving money to upgrade their thatched-roof hut. When Hương became pregnant, she stayed ashore and took care of selling their catch. They soon had their first baby.

One day, as he helped wash the thick black hair that came down to her waist, he noticed a scar at the back of her neck. He had never paid attention to that area of her body before because she did not want anyone to mess around with her hair.

"How did you get that scar?" Văn asked.

"It was a long time ago. I was only three and my brother five. As we fought over something, he hit me hard, causing me to faint. I got a scar from the injury. He ran away and I never saw him again."

"What did you do next?"

"It took a long time to heal and ended up as a keloid. I helped my parents, who died at sea following a storm. I later got established here."

"Where were you born?"

"In a little village close to Phan Thiết."

Văn did not say anything; he went outside to take a deep breath. How could there be such a coincidence, Văn asked himself.

Fifteen years earlier, Văn was playing with his sister Hương. He hit her; she fell and injured herself. Scared, he ran away. He loved his sister a lot and had been looking for her all this time. He even went to see a medium, who stated that he would later marry his sister. He forgot about her but was careful about dating anyone who closely looked like her.

Văn spent a sleepless night. The events of yesteryear came back to haunt him—the fight over a piece of sugarcane, the wound on the head, the boy running away. What a coincidence. He did not want to tell her the truth because she would be filled with guilt and remorse.

The following morning, he took the boat out, but never came back. He had not said anything or left any message. His wife became worried when she did not see him coming home that night. Things did happen to fishermen: waves here, currents there... Life was so unpredictable for them.

One day passed by. She went to the beach to look for him but could not find him anywhere. Two days. Three days. She became worried. Finally, she led her son up to the mountain to scan the horizon. From there, she thought she would be able to see farther away than at sea level.

And every day, she went up there to scan the horizon to look for her husband, hoping the sea would release its hold on him. Rain or shine, people would see her up there every day. Heaven was touched by her faithfulness and one day transformed her into a stone statue that eerily looked like a widow waiting for her husband.

Fishermen would call out to her when they had trouble bringing their boat home. They asked her to blow the east wind that would not only push their boat to shore, but also give her husband a ride back home.[68]

Comments This legend deals with poor fishermen who live along the Vietnamese coastline and whose lives are often threatened by typhoons and sea storms. No one knows how many of them are taken away by rough sea storms.

It also tells the story of faithfulness, of a woman waiting for her husband to come home. She waited for him every day until she turned into a tone statue. In the old times, wars and sea storms were the main causes of widowhood.

This legend reminds us of Penelope in Homer's *Odyssey*. During the Trojan War, her husband, Odysseus, went to war against Troy. Although he succeeded, the gods punished him for having destroyed their temples. While other leaders returned home, Odysseus was condemned to sail around from one island to another. Penelope waited for one full decade to see her husband return home.

If the "Lady of Stone" is southern in origin, the northern equivalent is the "Lady Tô Thị."[69] The story is the same: the boy ran away after injuring his sister. They reunited and married each other. He realized she was his sister and enrolled into the army to avoid revealing an incestuous affair. Not knowing anything, she went to the Tam Thanh pagoda to pray. She sat on top of Lạng Sơn Mountain to wait for him. She ended up being transformed into a stone lady.

38. The Lady of Nam Xương

Vietnam is a warring country: throughout history, it has been at war against itself and the surrounding countries. If it was not a major war, it was a series of insurrections, large or small, against the state. Men had to go to war whether they liked it or not. It was the burden of citizens to serve their country.[70]

There was a jealous man, Trương, who once married a poor but beautiful wife. He followed her wherever she went and prevented her from meeting people. She never complained and remained a loving wife.

He went to war leaving behind his pregnant wife. A few months later, she delivered a beautiful boy. Time passed by; one year, two years, and three years went by without him returning. The son, who was almost four by that time, demanded to see his father. His demands were growing incessant and irritating. If in the beginning a toy or a tale could divert his attention away from the topic, later on nothing could. He wondered why all his friends had a father, but not him.

One night, as the mother walked past the lamp, her shadow was cast on the wall. She immediately had the idea of using it as the father.

"This is your dad."

"Is he there, mom?"

"Yes, he is."

"Can I see him every day? Why does he not talk?"

"He will talk to you if you are nice."

And every day, he wanted to see his father before going to sleep. Otherwise, he would not go to bed.

One day, his real father came back from the war. The child, having never seen him before, could not get used to him. As the father tried to hug him, he escaped. After a few attempts, he thought about giving his son time to get adjusted to his presence. One day, as he attempted to hold him one more time, the boy, "You are not my dad."

"How do you know?" his dad asked.

"My dad came only at night. When mom sat, he sat. When mom walked, he walked."

The father became suspicious. He thought his wife must have had an affair while he was away. In a Confucian world, having an affair was not an accepted behavior. A woman must be faithful to her husband.

He threw his wife out, although she vehemently denied having an affair. She argued for her case, but to no avail. Rejected, she wandered around town not knowing where to go. People began to shun her, since no one wanted to protect an unfaithful wife. A few people did help her, although local support was weak. Exhausted, she prayed to the river god.

"If I have been a faithful wife, please change me into a pearl in the river. If I have been unfaithful, let the fish eat me." Then she jumped into the river and drowned.

The husband became very upset upon hearing the news. He could not recover his wife's body.

At home, the father took care of the son. One night as he walked in front of the lamp, the child saw the shadow on the wall and yelled, "That is my dad." And he bowed to the shadow on the wall the same way his mother taught him.

"What did you say, son?" asked his father.

"Mommy told me the man on the wall was my dad."

The father realized he had made a big mistake. He had misunderstood her. She had just used the shadow on the wall to pretend the father was right there.

All he could do was to hold a ceremony with lit candles on an altar and build a shrine to remember her.[71]

King Lê Thánh Tôn later learned about the story of this faithful but unlucky lady. As he passed by the village one day, he stopped by the shrine people built to pay tribute to her.

Comments Indochina (Vietnam, Laos, Cambodia) has been a land embroiled in wars. From the 939 Vietnamese Independence from the Chinese to the 1858 French military action, no fewer than 62 significant wars and invasions have occurred in Indochina. Countless rebellions and police actions took place during the same period. War in Vietnam could take a long time to resolve. The 1627–1672 North-South War was one of the examples. This was accompanied by a complete separation between North and South for two centuries (1600–1802). Soldiers usually had to serve their country for the duration or until they were wounded or died.

The Lady of Nam Xương story occurred during the war against Champa in 1470. Vietnam at that time was localized to present-day North Vietnam, while central Vietnam was occupied by Champa, a Hinduized nation. It ended brutally after the Vietnamese sacked Vijaya, the Champa's capital.

39. A Brother's Devotion

A father died suddenly without leaving any will to his two sons, Hai and Ba. The eldest one, Hai, immediately took the largest share of the inheritance, leaving to Ba only a hut and a small piece of arid land.

Ba, a good-hearted person, did not seem to care: he accepted his brother's decision in good faith. Day in and day out, people would see him plough his brother's field. Over time, Hai's field became lush and fertile while Ba barely survived from his unfertile land.

Despite Ba's good will, Hai did not treat him well. He never invited his brother over to eat or rewarded him adequately. He, however, treated his friends differently. He feasted them on all occasions and helped them as much as he could. Hai's wife, who was a good-natured person, tried to convince him to treat his brother differently, but to no avail.

"Honey, should we treat Ba more nicely?" she asked.

"Why should I?"

"He is your brother, not your employee. He does many things for you, more than any of your friends. He is always there to help you out."

"I deal with him the way I like. Besides, my friends are good to me."

"Please be nice to him. He is closer to you than your friends. A brother's blood is always thicker than water."

Ba came to his brother's house only to celebrate festivals or anniversaries when his presence was required; otherwise, he would remain in his hut. He understood his sister-in-law's feelings as she tried to iron out the differences between the brothers and soften the rugged edges of her husband's behavior. Her attitude acted as soothing salve in Ba's wounds and helped him present a poor but dignified attitude. Ba never showed any resentment towards his brother. The sister-in-law, on the other hand, did not want to openly assist him because she did not want to hurt his feelings.

When Hai returned home one evening, his frightened wife ran toward him all in tears. He had never seen her in such a state.

Not knowing what had happened, he asked, "What is going on, honey?"

"Something terrible. This afternoon while you were away, a man came by and forced himself into the house. I ran in the kitchen and he pursued me there. I took the kitchen knife that was on the table and threatened him. He ran toward me and impaled himself on the knife. He died right away. I cleaned the house and wrapped him up in straw mats."

"Where is his body?"

"In the kitchen. It was an accident. We are not very friendly with the mandarin. Who knows what would happen if he ever heard about this case. I believe we need to bury him somewhere in the forest. You need someone close to help you out because he is heavy."

Distraught, he slumped in a chair, his head down. He stroked his hair in a pensive mode, trying to plan the steps he needed to make. Accident. A dead person. The mandarin. Bury the corpse. Helper.

"All right. Let me talk to my friends," he finally said.

Hai looked for ways to help his wife. He ran to his closest friend and was glad to find him at home.

"Could you do me a big favor?" he whispered to him.

"Sure. For you my friend, I would do anything," his friend loudly answered.

"I am involved in a difficult and embarrassing case."

"That is what friends are for."

XII. Southern Legends: Social

Reassured and energized by his friend's voice, Hai told him about the misadventure.

"Would you please help me bury the body," he asked him. The friend thought for a moment and immediately changed his demeanor. He said:

"Sorry, Hai. I would love to help you, but I have things to do tomorrow. I need to take care of an important problem. I cannot miss this appointment."

"Do not worry. I will find someone else."

He ran to his second friend, whom he had entertained a few times. The second friend, seeing Hai's face, enquired about his problem.

"It looks like you have seen a ghost, my dear Hai. What is going on? How could I help you? I would do anything for you, even if I have to sell my house."

As soon as Hai finished explaining about his problem, the friend happened to remember that his mother was sick and needed to go to the doctor. He would be glad to help him but had to care for his mother first. He sympathized with him and was sorry he could not help.

The third friend became worried at Hai's saddened look. He would help him if Hai could share his feelings and thoughts. Hai rejoiced at his friend's offer and warmed up to him. Frustrated by the refusal of the first two friends, he ventured to explain the details of his problem. On hearing the story, the third friend also backed out. At least he said that he shared his sympathy with Hai.

Dejected, Hai went to see other people. But all the doors closed on him, and finally he returned home worn-out and dispirited. All night, he sought for help from one friend to another. He thought they were good friends. Now he started realizing they were mere acquaintances who would never put their lives on the line to help him out.

He returned home very upset. His wife approached.

"It's late. If we need to dispose of this body, we could ask Ba. He would do anything to help us."

"Why should I call Ba?"

"Maybe you should ask him."

Exasperated, Hai went to see Ba. He told him about the need to bury someone fast and needed his help. Ba told him that he knew a place in the woods where they could safely dispose of the body. He grabbed his tools and went to Hai's house. The two brothers carried the body to the woods, dug a large hole and disposed of it. Working all night long, they completed their task in the early hours of the morning.

Hai was surprised when the mandarin called him to his office the next day. He did not know the reason, although he did suspect it. There he saw his three friends, who looked awkward when they saw him. He knew on the spot that they had betrayed him. The friends, feeling self-righteous, had gone to see the local mandarin.

"Hai's wife killed a man and Hai disposed of the body overnight. I would like you to know so that you could look into the matter," said the first one.

"I do not know if there was anything illegal or not. I just want you to know about the case," the second friend told the mandarin.

"I do not want to report a friend. But you might want to ask Hai about the illegal burial last night," the third friend told the mandarin.

The mandarin asked Hai to tell him about the body he had disposed, of the previous night. Hai truthfully reported that his wife had accidentally killed an intruder; he had asked for the help of his friends, who had excused themselves; and Hai and his brother had disposed of the body.

The mandarin then asked him to lead them to the burial site. At the site, after they unearthed the body and unrolled the mats, they found ... a dead dog. The mandarin asked Hai to explain what was going on. His wife asked for permission to talk.

"Since Hai mistreated his brother, I just wanted to show my husband that brotherly love is deep and holy. The day before, my dead dog helped me conceive the plan. I wrapped the dog up and asked him to bury it. And this is the result, o most righteous magistrate."

The mandarin turned to the three friends and scolded them.

"You are abusing Hai's friendship. Although he has treated you nicely, you have betrayed him. You each will be given 50 lashes."

Hai realized how good a brother he had. He sincerely apologized to Ba for his poor behavior and haughtiness. From that time onward, Hai and Ba became the best brothers on earth. He also thanked his wife for her realistic and good thinking.[72]

Comments In a land that has seen many wars, killings, and injustices, people tend to accept life the way it appears in front of their eyes. They accept what life gives them without asking for more. The younger brother accepts what he thinks of as "fate": a lesser share of the inheritance. He does not argue; he takes what life gives him and goes from there. Westerners have noticed this "passive" oriental attitude that allowed them to conquer Vietnam with a few thousand soldiers in the nineteenth century.

It is not always pessimism. The Vietnamese have fought hundreds of wars and won as well as lost many of them. They have realized that life repeats itself. They have taken down old governments and installed new ones, only to realize that new governments did the same old things as old ones have done in the past. Tired of this lack of change, they have turned to religion as a way to improve themselves. In Buddhism, they have found a way out of this karma. What the westerners see as passivity is just a different way of looking at the world. Asians want to improve themselves before trying to change the world. They are turning inward instead of outward.

This attitude is different from the western mentality where the majority would sue to get what they think they are entitled. They want more and fight for more. They end up getting more materially at the expense of lesser mental peace or spirituality. There is a price to pay for everything: either fight for material things and get less spiritually or get less materially and more spiritually.

The legend teaches us that nothing is above brotherhood, not even friendship. Although brotherhood sisterhood can invite a lot of envy and infighting, nothing supersedes blood bonds. Brothers and sisters who have grown up and gone through difficult or good times together tend to be very close to each other. They stick together through thick and thin. The same thing goes with workers within the same group or soldiers within the same regiment.

The Vietnamese have two expressions for friendship: *bạn* and *bè*. Bạn are the real friends or blood brothers who would defend you through thick and thin. Bè are similar to the ones in the story. They hang around when it is convenient or useful for them and disappear during difficult times.

By tradition, Vietnamese often use numbers to name their children. The eldest is usually called *Hai* (two) and the next one *Ba* (three), *Tư* (four) and so on. The number one (*một* or *nhứt*) is said to be reserved for the head of the household. They have the tendency to assign bad names to girls to ward off bad spirits that are attracted to girls with beautiful names. Of course, tradition has evolved a lot from the 1950s onward and people have been seeing more and more beautiful names given to girls. The eldest sister used to be a second mother to her siblings. She sometimes had to sacrifice her rights and, schooling to care for them.

40. The Sister-in-Law

Two brothers lived close to each other on land once owned by their parents. They were both married. The older one, Thắng, was very rich since he got the greatest share of the inheritance. The younger, Bình, was poor because his small plot of land barely allowed him to get by.

A drought that descended over the country made things worse for Bình and his family. Many families went hungry. After discussing between themselves for many days, the Bìnhs decided to swallow their pride and ask for help. Bình sent his son over to see if uncle Thắng would want to help them with anything. He thought it would be very difficult, for Thắng's wife was a stingy person.

The child came back sad and disgusted. He kept shaking his head.

"Uncle wanted to help us out, but auntie said that everyone should look out for himself as best as he could."

The following month, robbers came to Thắng's house. They beat the couple to find out where they kept their valuables. When he heard cries for help, Bình wanted to go but his wife stopped him.

"Everyone should look out for himself as best as he can, remember? When we were hungry, your brother and his wife did not give us any help."

Bình went over anyway. He chased away the robbers and saved the couple.

"We need to give him some rice," Thắng said to his wife. "He has saved both of us."

"Your brother did come and save us. Because he came late, robbers beat us. What thanks do we owe him?" his wife answered.

The drought got worse a few months later. Bình sent his son over to ask for help. He came back with a few handfuls of rice.

Very disheartened, Bình went to see his brother and said, "We are very poor. If you have some feelings for us, buy our house. This would give us some money to live on."

Thắng's wife was visibly happy.

"We are glad to buy your house, which, by the way, is not worth anything. But it will help us get rid of you so that you do not have to live off us any longer."

Bình and his family went away.

That year, robbers came back and beat Thắng to death. When Bình learned about the incident, he came back and raised his brother's children like his own.

Thắng's soul returned to see Bình one night.

"Thank you, brother. You have a good heart. I will make you rich from now on. The problem was not me, but your sister-in-law."[73]

Comments Sisters-in-law do play a major role in the relationship between brothers. If in "A Brother's Devotion" she could be nice and well meaning, in the present legend, she is mean and stingy. Introducing a woman into a family could therefore smooth or disrupt family bonds. For the Vietnamese, the family is not simply a cultural construct, but also a living entity composed of different people or groups of people. As family members grow, groups of people form to defend their own entities, roles, rights, and so on. Two or three different generations could live under the same roof, further complicating those relationships.

Blood brothers, even though separated by miles or years, form a unique bond. They protect themselves and help each other because "blood is always heavier than water," as the Vietnamese often say. The strongest ties are those of consanguinity. Blood brothers belong to the "insider" group. In-laws, although bonded by socio-economic factors or love, often remain strangers and competitors, "outsiders" in a sense. There will always be this struggle between insiders and outsiders, which could be latent and insignificant or wild and violent. If differences cannot be ironed out, they could lead to disruptive family feuds.

In the Vietnamese extended, multigenerational family, the dominant grandfather or grandmother usually kept the various competing units under control. But once that force disappeared, the units could break up and the family as a whole could disintegrate. Each unit, however, could become the nucleus for another extended family.

41. The Star Fruit Tree

Two brothers, Phát and Trọng, once lived on a farm with their parents. They helped plow the fields, plant rice seeds, and harvest the crop. Years passed by without any problems. When the parents died, they left everything—the farm, land, house and animals—to the elder son, Phát. The younger one, Trọng, received nothing except a star fruit tree.

Phát suddenly got rich. He worked part-time and hired his brother or others to farm for him. He wore fancy clothes and indulged in some of his pastimes. Trọng built himself a hut under the star fruit tree and began his new life. He took good care of the tree, watered it, and pruned it, since it was his unique belonging. The tree responded in kind and grew beautiful fruits, which he sold at the market. He also worked for his brother and other farmers in the neighborhood but barely made ends meet.

One day as he was working under the star fruit tree, he heard a big noise over his head and saw leaves and feathers falling down. He looked up and noticed a huge eagle standing on a branch on top of the tree. The majestic eagle sat there for a while, ate some of the fruits, and then flew away. He came back the day after and again on the third day.

Trọng got nervous as he lost more and more fruits. He did not know how to scare away a bird that was stealing his fruits. In despair, he spoke to the eagle one day.

"Dear bird, help yourself if you must. But leave some fruits for me. I need to take them to the market."

"Will do," answered the bird.

The next day, as the eagle swooped down again for his meal, Trọng told him again, "Please leave some for me, bird."

The bird, without saying anything, swooped down to the ground and regurgitated a small sized-diamond in front of Trọng.

"This is my payment," the bird said, and he flew away.

Surprised, Trọng did not know what to think. He took the diamond to the jeweler who paid him a good sum of money because of its size. With the money he got, he bought himself some food, clothing, and paid his debt. He still had some money left and considered himself lucky. Word got out that an eagle was paying in diamonds for his meal. Trọng's brother visited him in the afternoon and asked him about the eagle. He confirmed the story.

Phát then asked if he would like to trade the star fruit tree for his house and possessions. Trọng, who had no problems, acquiesced. After the deal was sealed, Trọng became happy: he could dedicate his time to working on the land and farm, which was his primary interest.

Phát, on the other hand, watched his star fruit tree closely. The bird did not come for many days. Then when he saw the eagle coming, he told him, "You need to pay me before you eat."

The eagle did not answer him. As the eagle was about to fly away after eating, Phát climbed up the tree and grabbed the bird's legs.

"You need to pay me now," he angrily yelled at the bird.

The bird got hold of him with the other leg and flew away. He flew high over the sea and released the man.

Phát did not know that greed would lead to strange things.[74]

Comments This is another story about greed, which does not pay. Over and over, children are exposed to these short stories that deal with life and good or bad habits acquired by men. They learn by osmosis through imitation of good habits and avoidance of bad ones. It is interesting to note the high number of stories dealing with greed.

In the present story as well as in "A Brother's Devotion," "The Sister-in-law," and "The Narcissus," the elder brother, despite getting the largest share of the inheritance, is still not happy with his lot. He either oppresses the younger one or tries to get hold of what the younger one owns—in this case a starfruit tree. There is always justice around the corner, for heaven is watching all of us. Heaven sent robbers to kill the elder brother in "The Sister-in-Law," and an eagle to take care of the bad brother in the present story.

42. The Narcissus

The narcissus is a hardy spring flower that is known in the U.S. as the daffodil. In Greek mythology, a boy was so fond of himself that he fell in love with his own reflection in the water. From where he died grew the narcissus. The Vietnamese legend of the narcissus is somewhat different.

Two brothers lived in the same family. The elder one was mean and always picked on the younger one. The latter did not want to fight, and therefore would often give up.

Both their parents died one day and the elder one took over everything, refusing to share with his sibling. He made the younger one work like a servant. Exasperated, the latter left home.

He aimlessly walked from one place to another, for he did not know anyone. Tired, he sat down by a pond to rest his feet. He felt sad, and lonely and wished he had a place to stay. While thinking about his fate, he saw a shrine close by and decided to take a close look. The place was dirty and had not been kept up for some time. Having nothing to do, he cleaned the altar, swept the floor, and bowed three times before leaving.

Sad and desperate, he did not know where to go and what to do. In his head whirled a flow of disjointed and incoherent ideas. He headed toward the pond and walked in. Water reached his knees, belly and then chest. His face was morose and his eyes vague.

Suddenly an old man appeared out of nowhere and grabbed him.

"What are you doing?" asked the man. "Trying to kill yourself?"

The young man seemed to wake up from a bad dream and shook his head.

"No. I was just thinking about my poverty-laden life."

"Don't worry. I will help you."

As soon as he finished talking, the pond turned into a field of white flowers that gave out a fragrant scent.

"Who are you? Where do you come from?" the young man asked.

"I am the spirit of the water. You have taken care of my shrine there a while ago. I am touched by your sincerity and your good will. All you need to do is work hard from now on. Grow all these flowers and sell them at the market. And you will be rich."

The spirit disappeared after saying these words. This was how the narcissus came about, a reward from the spirit of the water to a young man. The latter worked hard and within a short time became rich. His brother became jealous of him, fell sick and died.[75]

Comments This is another story about brothers. The naughty elder brother not only disinherited his sibling, he also harassed him. The younger one walked out in an attempt to find his own deliverance. He knew that as long as he remained in the house, he would be oppressed.

The legend teaches us about resilience and fighting back. When the young man was about to quit—being tired of life's struggles—the spirit of the water urged him to fight on. This is a different message from other legends: one needs to fight on in order to find salvation—riches in this case. The spirit told him to work harder, grow all these flowers and sell them at the market. Life is about fighting back and fighting despair and depression.

Inheritance rules under the Confucian system are different from western ones. Since the elder brother has the duty to keep ancestor worship rites alive, he would receive a major portion of the inheritance. However, he still has the duty to help his siblings. Girls do not receive anything or only a smaller portion of the inheritance. In reality, as shown in the legends, elder brothers tend to abuse the system and take almost everything for themselves. As dominant males, they make the rules once their fathers have passed away.

43. Peacock Hash, Phoenix Pie, and Dragon Whiskers

A rich couple once lived close to the imperial palace. Their house was one of the most beautiful in the neighborhood. They prided themselves on having almost everything and did not need anything. The husband, who was a good cook, lavished the most exotic dishes on his wife's taste buds.

One day, the husband tried to test his wife.

"We have tasted almost everything in this world, dear. Of the three most delicious things in the culinary world, peacock hash, phoenix pie, and dragon whiskers (*Nem công, chã phượng, râu rồng*) the only thing we have not tasted is peacock hash. I have heard that there is a peacock in the forbidden imperial garden. Would you like to taste it if we can get a hold of the peacock?"

Her eyes opened wide and she lustily said, "Definitely, dear."

Although it was not easy, the husband found his way into the imperial garden, snatched a peacock, and took it home. The wife was delighted to see the colorful animal and thought all day about tasting peacock hash.

He went to work, but instead of cooking the peacock, he hid it and used chicken meat instead. At dinnertime, he showed her his masterful work adorned with a few peacock feathers. She had never seen anything that beautiful in her life, and the sight of the exotic meal whetted her appetite. The wife tasted it and smacked her tongue.

"That was excellent, dear. I have never tasted anything that good. Could we have more?" She thought he was not only a good chef, but also someone who was interested in exotic recipes.

A day later, the mandarin sent out in the king's name a proclamation asking people to return the peacock. It was a crime to keep the king's property. Anyone who would denounce the thief would receive a position, if a man, and a royal title, if a woman.

The wife, after tasting the delicious peacock hash, had her sights set on the royal title—something she had always coveted. She went to the mandarin and complained.

"It is my husband who stole the peacock and ate it."

The mandarin had the husband come over for a talk. The latter brought the peacock with him and reported, "Although the peacock wandered into my yard, I have carefully taken care of it. I only wanted to test my wife's heart and asked her whether she would want to eat peacock hash. But I prepared chicken instead of peacock, for I would not want to kill the peacock. My wife now accuses me of stealing the peacock. Please investigate, dear mandarin."

The mandarin found the woman guilty of wrongdoing and appointed her husband as a royal official.[76]

Comments In this legend, the husband, wanting to test his wife's heart, enticed her to eat peacock hash. A masterful cook, he prepared a wonderful meal after snatching a peacock from the imperial garden. Not happy to savor the meal, she decided to turn her husband in for stealing the peacock.

This is another story of greed that turns wrong. Marital vows require that a wife stick to or protect her husband. Unable to control her greed, she turned him in expecting to receive a royal title. Her husband was able to detect her untruthfulness simply by testing her.

44. *The Grain of Rice*

After having created the earth, the Jade Emperor rested on his throne, which was nicely decorated with a dragon on each side. He was receiving the people who had just populated the different parts of the globe. Seeing a Vietnamese man, he asked him what he would like. The latter told him he wanted something to eat.

Since it was a reasonable request, he decreed that the Vietnamese should eat rice. Rice would be brought to their home every day; they would never go hungry. They would not even have to lift up a finger. The Vietnamese man returned home happy to have rice to eat. All he had to do was to hunt and fish and his meal would be complete.

Rice grains at the time were as big as coconuts and sometimes bigger. They arrived in single units every day before dinnertime. If the house was clean and neat, the grain would stop in front of the door. The family would pick it up and consume it; otherwise, it would go away and return another day.

The wife of the first Vietnamese man was not a neat person. She did not know how to care for and clean her hut. The leftover meals, the uncooked food, and the game piled up everywhere among dirty clothing, covers, and tools. Seeing the disorder in the hut, the grain stopped in front of the hut for a while, then moved away. It simply refused to enter the house.

The housewife became despondent. She told the grain to stop, but to no avail. The grain continued to go away like in a programmed show. She was afraid that her husband would later complain of not having any rice to eat. She took her broom and in a moment of anger took a swipe at the grain. The latter shattered into small pieces all over the ground. From that time onward, no more rice grains would stop at the hut.

People became hungry for a while. They gathered the tiny rice grains and ate them. Soon they ran out of rice. Desperate, they went to plead with the Jade Emperor.

"You did not respect the grain I sent you. From now on, you have to earn your own rice. I will send you rain and sunshine, but you have to grow rice through your labor. If you work hard enough, you will have enough to eat."

That is the reason why Vietnamese peasants had to toil in the sun, seed and plant rice grains, harvest rice stalks, and later thresh them. This was a time-consuming labor that required the whole family to pitch in in order to obtain rice.[77]

Comments This legend explains the origin of rice and how the Vietnamese ended up having to grow and eat rice. The Jade Emperor decided to punish them for not respecting the rice he had sent to them. Therefore, they had to labor hard to grow it.

Rice can be ground into flour and turned into rice cakes, rice wine or rice paper (*bánh tráng*). The latter is used to wrap meat and vegetables to yield *gỏi cuốn,* or meat rolls. It can be fried to make *chảy giò* (spring rolls). Vietnamese use boiled or fried rice. Sticky rice is used to make *bánh chưng* or *bánh tét*, a combination of sticky rice, meat and mungbean paste (see the Story of Bánh Chưng, southern tale # 22).

45. *The Two Tea Boxes*

Not all mandarins are greedy or abuse the villagers they are assigned to care for. The majority are decent and respectful of the laws they have vowed to uphold. Many are known to be outstanding government officials who conduct themselves beyond reproach. This is a story about one of them.

There was once a mandarin who lived modestly in a small village along the coastal area. He was known throughout the province for his strict probity. He refused to accept any gift whatsoever from his constituents. One day, a merchant for whom he had done many favors took him to the side and said, "Honorable mandarin, may I say something? I do not know how to express my gratitude toward you. Over the years, you have helped me a lot."

"Dear merchant, I have just done my duty," answered the mandarin.

"I agree. But I still have to express my utmost thanks to you."

"You do not have to give me anything. I would have done the same thing for any other citizen."

"May I just offer you a few bags of tea? This is modest and purely ritual."

The mandarin thought for a while.

"I do not want to make a precedent here. On the other hand, I do not want to offend you because you are a good member of society. Since it is just a small gift, I will be glad to accept it this time. But this is a onetime deal, do you understand me?"

"Of course, honorable mandarin."

The merchant brought him two bags of tea. When the mandarin lifted these bags up, he realized how heavy they were. He opened one of the bags and found gold in it.

Having accepted the gift, the mandarin found himself in a quandary. He had accepted a gift of tea and not gold. He therefore decided to return it to the merchant with a personal letter.

"I accepted your gift because I believed we had run out of tea. It turns out that I was wrong. We have more tea than we need at this time. I therefore must decline your gift and return it to you. Thank you for your thoughtfulness."[78]

Comments Mandarins, like today's government officials, were poorly paid for their services. They were given a small monthly wage and a piece of land to cultivate. The overall compensation barely allowed them to make ends meet. Many accepted gifts from villagers to pad their fixed income. From accepting little gifts here and there to accepting money in return for favors was not a big jump. Some, therefore, became corrupt.

Like all citizens, they had to live, and the only way to stay afloat was to accept bribes. This does not mean that taking bribes was tolerated. In fact, mandarins were taught to observe rules and regulations and not to abuse the system. They were told to protect their citizens. Many mandarins, like the one in the legend, were strict and straightforward. They could never be bribed. However, the regulatory system was so weak that it enticed weak mandarins to take bribes.

46. *The Jar of Gold*

A poor farmer and his wife lived on a small plot of land bequeathed by his parents. His parents and grandparents had worked on the same field before him. Unlike other people, he had neither grandiose ambition nor unfulfilled dreams. He was a simple man who believed in the power of hard work and sweat and the richness of the land.

One day as he was plowing with his constant companion, a brown buffalo he had owned for years, he hit something hard. The trauma shook him a lot, for he had never encountered this problem before. He had plowed and crisscrossed this field for a long time and knew it from right to left like he knew his ten fingers. Should there be any stone or rock in his field, he would have found it a long time ago.

He put a brake on his plow and went back to look. He dug the area up and found an old jar. How he could have missed it before, he did not know. It must have been lying a little bit deeper than the tip of his blade; that was the only explanation he could give to himself. On opening it, he found many gold coins. He had never seen that many coins in his life. Who could have left it there? He did not know. Perhaps someone had hidden the jar there and forgotten about it.

Since he was unconcerned about wealth, he dropped the jar back into the hole and marked it so that he could avoid it the next time. He continued to work like usual, as if nothing had happened. At night, he went home and took his supper. He then told his wife about it.

"I found some gold coins in a jar this afternoon."

"Did you bring it home?"

"No, I reburied it in the same place in the field."

"Someone will take it someday."

"No one knows. Since it is a gift from heaven, it will always be there."

While he was talking, two thieves happening by overheard the discussion. They eavesdropped on the couple as they discussed the location of the jar. The thieves later went to the field to retrieve it and brought it back to their lair. However, when they opened the lid, they only found ugly snakes. They swore loudly and threw the jar away.

The next day, the farmer went to work in his field again. He of course noticed the big hole in the middle of the field where the jar had been located. He went to check and found the jar missing. Undisturbed, he filled up the hole and went back to work. When he came home, he advised his wife about the missing jar.

"I told you so," the wife responded sarcastically. "You should have brought it home yesterday."

"Well. This was a gift from heaven. I can't help it if heaven takes back what it has given me."

The thieves, meanwhile, were planning to take revenge on the farmer. They thought the latter had played a game on them by replacing the coins with snakes. They collected the jar and placed it at the farmer's front porch, hoping the snakes would bite the farmer once he opened it. They then hid behind the bushes to watch his reaction.

As he walked out of the house in the morning, he noticed the jar. Surprised, he let out a big scream.

"There is my jar. How did it come here? Is it not heaven's intervention?"

"What did you say?" asked the wife, who showed up at the front door. The farmer held the jar up and showed it to her.

"You tell me you found it, lost it and now recovered it? What a weird story."

She took the jar from her husband's hands and opened it. Many gold coins dropped out. The thieves were perplexed: the other night, it was full of snakes and now full of gold coins. They realized there had been a divine intervention and ran away.

The farmer and his wife were now wealthy. She bought herself some fine clothes and spent time traveling here and there. The farmer continued to work in his field as if nothing had happened. He bought another plot next to his own and worked even harder than before.[79]

Comments This is another story about greed. The high number of legends dealing with this problem reflects its importance within society. Greed in all its forms—stealing, abusing power, taking over someone's property or rights—is never rewarded in these stories. In fact, the Confucian society prides itself on obeying law and order. A true Confucian person would rather remain poor than steal, illegally obtain a product, or beg for favor.

In "The Two Tea Boxes," the mandarin could have taken the gold inside the boxes; he decided that it was not right and returned it to its owner. In this legend, the farmer simply re-buried the jar of gold he had found on his own property. Even after finding it the second time, he was not affected at all by its discovery. He continued to work in his field like before.

To express the fact that greed is never rewarded, the legend presents two different outcomes. When thieves opened the jar, they only found snakes. This left them so disgusted that they threw away the jar. The same jar, however, yielded gold coins when opened by the farmer.

47. The Magic Gourd

A couple passed away following a short illness, leaving behind two sons. The eldest one, Lập, got married and took over the whole inheritance. He also managed to get his younger sibling, Tân, out of the house. The latter built himself a small hut at the base of a mountain, where he barely made ends meet. Whenever he was hungry, he came to town to ask for food. For three cold winters, he did not have much to eat and finally decided to ask his brother for help.

"How are you going to pay us back when you do not work? We would rather see you work for us," Lập retorted.

Tân agreed. He even built himself a shed on his brother's field to be close to his work. As he labored day and night, rice stalks were growing beautifully and harvest appeared to be promising. Seeing the rice stalks laden with golden grains, birds came by to feast on them. In the beginning, he let the hungry birds alone. As they began to destroy his harvest, Tân tried to chase them away. As they came back, he armed himself with a stick to get rid of them.

One day, he decided to follow the birds to take their nests. The chase somehow led him to the top of the mountain. There, he noticed a beautiful house, so beautiful that he thought he was dreaming. Forgetting his fatigue, he slowly made his way to the house. He could not figure out who could live in such a princely manner on top of the mountain. Driven by curiosity, he went around it, looked and found no one there. He gently opened the door, which was not locked, got in, and hid in one of the upstairs recesses.

As the sun was slowly setting, he heard noises at the front door. Two young maidens showed up, then three, four, five, six and seven people came in. They were all beautiful young women. They conversed joyfully and the house became as lively as a beehive. When they moved to the kitchen, one maiden held up a dry gourd, turned it back and forth, then said three times, "Dinner for seven."

A few minutes later, food magically showed up on the table. After the women dined, the plates magically disappeared and the table became clean and neat again like nothing had taken place. The maidens sat down and switched to sewing. Tired and hungry, Tân fell asleep without knowing it. When he woke up, the ladies were already awake. The youngest and most beautiful one rolled the gourd once again and breakfast was served. After eating, they left for work.

Tân came down from his hiding place. He took the gourd and like the maiden, rolled it back and forth and said three times, "Breakfast for one." Food became available in a few minutes. He was so hungry that he ate everything. He again dozed off until late morning. When he woke up, he found the magic gourd close by and figured that if he had that gourd with him, he could feed many hungry families back home.

Taking it with him, he ran back home and began inviting neighbors to his hut for dinner. They believed he was a thoughtful person who, despite his poverty, managed to provide neighbors with a free meal. Attracted by his unusual invitation, they came by and were surprised to see plenty of food on the table. They feasted on the sumptuous dinner and congratulated him for his generosity. Lập and his wife, despite being invited, did not show up. Lập thought his brother was using the excuse to borrow his money. His wife did not want to dirty her expensive outfit in Tân's small hut.

Rumors about the fancy dinner, however, had spread around. Piqued by curiosity, Lập wanted to find out how Tân had managed to feed so many people. He suspected him of stealing his grain and threatened to get rid of him.

Tân explained the whole story about the magic gourd. He also expressed his worry that the loss of the gourd would leave the maiden hungry. He therefore wanted to return it to its owners, but would use the gourd one more time to build up his strength before climbing the mountain.

Lập told him that he would like to go in his place. He proposed to exchange clothes with Tân and, dressed in rags, headed west toward the mountain. He struggled hard to climb the mountaintop. Sweat rolled down his temples and his hands and feet were sore. But the image of the magic gourd kept him moving. As expected, the beautiful house stood majestically at the top of the mountain. He made his way in and hid in the upstairs recess.

The maidens came home at the usual time. Seeing the door partially open, they suspected the presence of an intruder. Looking around the house, they were able to locate Lập.

"So this is the thief who stole our gourd," said the first maiden.

"Without it, we had to cook dinner every day," added the second one.

"We had to fetch water because of the loss of the gourd," argued the third one.

"We had to clean the dishes," continued the fourth one.

After making the accusation, each of them came around and pinched Lập's nose, which began to stretch out. After the last maiden had spoken, the tip of his nose was hanging down to his belly button. The maidens then chased him out of the house. Hanging on to his painful nose, he slowly walked home in the darkness of the night. By the time he reached it, it was morning and he was so exhausted and devastated that he fell on the ground. When he woke up in the evening, his nose was still swollen and painful. He could barely eat because he could not open his mouth. He looked tired and worried.

After thinking for a while, the couple decided to ask for Tân's help. The sister-in-law, despite her disgust, had to look for him. On hearing the request, Tân told her to go home and advised her he would visit Lập later. He did not want to see him right away because of the way he had been treated in the past. Not seeing him coming, the sister came back the second day, asking for help. By that time, she could barely control her tears. Tân explained that since he was not a medicine man, he did not know how to solve a medical problem.

He finally visited Lập on the third day. The couple had lost hope of seeing Tân. Lập, who could barely talk, promised that once he got well, he would share half of his fortune with him. Tân told him not to worry about it.

"If you are truthful, you will be cured of your problem," Tân said.

Tân returned to the house on the hill in an attempt to find a cure for his brother. He made sure he closed the door correctly. It was dark when he found a good place to hide for he was afraid the maidens could locate him. The latter came home by that time. They ate as usual and sat down for a long chat.

The first one said, "I feel bad for the guy. He must be very sore."

"That is his fault," answered the second one.

"If he cannot open his mouth, he will eventually die," added the third one.

"It is so simple. He only has to touch his nose with the gourd and say three times 'Live truthfully' and he would be cured," said the youngest one.

Tân had the answer he needed. He was happy to know the cure and silently thanked the maiden.

The maidens were talking through the night. Tired, Tân fell asleep. When he woke up, the house was empty. He quickly descended from his perch, grabbed the gourd and returned home. He hid the gourd before seeing Lập. Lập's nose was still swollen and his face was red. He looked tired and worn out. Tân told Lập he would be able to cure him. The couple once again reiterated their promise to give Tân half of the inheritance.

Tân went outside to grab his gourd. He stroked Lập's nose with the magic gourd and repeated three times, "live truthfully." Instantly, the nose shrunk down in size, and Lập, for the first time in many days, was able to talk and smile. The couple thanked Tân profusely and gave him what they had promised.

Tân took off to return the gourd. When he arrived at the destination, he found the maidens—who had taken a day off—at home. They became scared when they saw a stranger arriving at their door. Once Tân had explained the reason for his visit, they relaxed and thanked him for returning the gourd. Since he had lived truthfully, the maidens decided that he should take one of them for a wife. Tân chose the youngest and most beautiful one. They all celebrated the union with a big dinner. The following morning, the newlywed couple descended the mountain to begin their new life in the valley.[80]

Comments This is another nice story that finishes nicely. Tân, a poor but hard-working man, is rewarded for his good deeds. After finding a magic gourd and using it wisely, his brother gives him half of the inheritance and one of the maidens agrees to marry him. Lập, the bad brother who abused his sibling, was stuck with a long and painful nose. The moral of the legend is to "live truthfully." Like in many other stories, truthfulness is eventually rewarded.

48. A Devoted Daughter-in-Law

In the village of Phú Mỹ, there once was a widow by the name of Mã Ỗn. She had two grown-up sons, Mã Văn and Mã Võ. Mã Văn was a good student on his way to take the mandarinate examination while his brother Mã Võ, being a little slow, focused on business.

One day, the widow told Mã Văn,

"Son, it is time for you to think about getting married."

"Mother, I will do whatever you like." He bowed in front of her. "I, however, have three reasons for not getting married now.

"First, a good and devoted wife is difficult to find. If she is good, we will all be happy. Should she turn out not to be the right one, she will cause problems for you.

"Second, you have cared for me since I was young. To this day, I have not yet repaid my debt to you. Therefore, I would like to do something for you before getting married.

"Third, as a man I also want to be useful to my country before thinking about getting married."

"Son," Mã Ỗn yelled in an excited and angry voice, "stop arguing with me. I am getting old and both of you are still unmarried. Who will take care of you two if I happen to get sick? A daughter-in-law will surely help with the daily chores right now."

"Mother, I am sorry to upset you. Since we are poor, another mouth to feed would be a burden to the family. However, I am open to whatever you have decided."

Mã Ỗn held her tongue for a long time, then said, "I have asked someone to look for a bride for you. She has found Đào San Hô, who is nice, beautiful, and virtuous: she will fit you nicely. The asking for the bride will take place in five days. Get ready for the event."

Mã Văn bowed to his mother and began cleaning the house in preparation for the marriage. He had less than a week to get ready for the bride. Everything had been prearranged and he did not even know her.

The first year for the bride was uneventful. In the second year, for unknown reasons Mã Ỗn started yelling at Đào San Hô, calling her a prostitute. Whatever Hô did was wrong. The food she cooked was inedible and the way she cleaned the house was wrong. If she wore ragged clothes—because the family was poor—she was yelled at for depreciating the family status. Mã Ỗn screamed at and beat Hô almost every day.

The husband, seeing his mother upset with Hô, did not dare to look at her, talk to her, or protect her. Yet his mother still accused him of protecting her and siding with her; she told him to divorce her.

In the end, he said, "Mother, if I divorce her, you will have to find another wife for me. This can only cause you more worry in the future. If the next one turns out like Hô, she will upset you again. Could you just consider Hô like a servant and not a daughter-in-law, and she will be here to help you."

"Are you arguing with me? Are you trying to protect her? If so, you can hate me, live with her and make her your mother."

To soothe his mother's anger, Mã Văn decided to divorce his wife. He, however, could not help thinking that Hô was the ideal wife. She worked all day long from early morning until midnight and never argued against her mother-in-law. She did all the house chores, including feeding the chicken, and cleaning the pigpen. She made sure Mã Văn had everything he needed so he could concentrate on his studies. To her friends who complained that Mã Ỗn was a slave driver, she only said, "It is my entire fault. If my mother-in-law does not like me, it is because I do not know how to behave. I cannot blame my mother and my husband."

Đào San Hô was stunned to be told one day to leave the house. She cried and begged, but to no avail. Mã Ỗn, the matriarch, had made the decision to expel her, and it was final. Hô walked out, deeply hurt, lost and upset at the unfair treatment. She did not know where to go. She could have gone home, but knew she would only invite dishonor to her family. Her brothers would disavow her. In a land where face was important, being rejected by a husband was similar to receiving a death penalty. In everyone's eyes, she would be seen as a "bad" woman.

Hô wandered slowly and aimlessly; she seemed to walk on a cloud. She did not even realize she fainted. Was it because of despair, sadness, or hunger? In her dream, she met the lady of mercy, who told her that she, like everyone, has to go through her karma. In her past life, she had mistreated Mã Ôn and Mã Văn and now had to repay her debts toward them. She did not need to worry any longer because she had almost completed her karma.

Hô was thrilled on hearing the news. She, however, wondered where she could stay in the meantime. The lady reminded her that her aunt Châu Thị would be glad to house her in exchange for some menial work. In a few years, she would have the occasion to redeem herself.

When Hô woke up, she was lying by the side of the road. She gathered herself and made her way through winding, hilly and deserted roads to her aunt's house. She was tired, hungry, and alone on the road while thinking about her mother-in-law and husband.

When she knocked at Châu Thị's house, the latter asked, "Who are you, young lady?"

"Dear aunt, I am Đào San Hô, Mã Văn's wife."

"Is that you Đào San Hô? I did not recognize you. What can I do for you, dear?"

"Dear aunt," she said while kneeling in front of her, "the reason I am here today is because I have not behaved well according to my mother-in-law and husband. They have fired me. Without any other relative, I am forced to stop here and ask you to allow me to stay with you for a while. I will do everything that is needed to pay you back for your generosity."

"Hô, my dear, the relationship between mother and daughter-in-law is always challenging. You could be the nicest daughter-in-law and yet fail the test. Do not worry, make yourself at home here."

For the next two years, Hô struggled hard as she took odd jobs to feed herself. But her relationship with Châu Thị was perfect: the latter loved her like her own daughter.

In the meantime, Mã Ôn, after getting rid of Hô, proceeded to look for a bride for her second son, Mã Võ. The new bride was Túy Hoa, an ugly, ugly, fat and short girl who did not respect anyone. After the first few months during which she behaved well, she began taking control of the household. She yelled at Mã Ôn whenever she liked. If she was in a good mood, she fed mother and son; otherwise, she would eat alone and starved both of them.

She ordered Mã Võ around and told him to do all the hard work like milling the rice, cutting and gathering firewood, and feeding the chicken and pigs. She did not have to do anything but just lay around. If anyone dared say anything about her, she would pull the kitchen knife out and threaten to kill everyone in the house.

Where had the fiery Mã Ỗn gone? Where was that strong woman who constantly yelled at Đào San Hô? Facing Túy Hoa, she was only a diminutive woman in ragged clothes with saliva drooling from the corner of her mouth. Mother and son could not do anything but cry and swear in silence. As soon as Túy Hoa walked by, they straightened themselves out and became quiet.

As for Đào San Hô, she worked day and night. With whatever she could spare, she bought fruit and meat and asked Châu Thị to drop them at her mother-in-law's. She advised her to mention, when asked, that the gift came from Châu Thị's daughter-in-law.

Mã Ỗn, being starved by Túy Hoa, was always hungry. She was thrilled each time she received a gift from Hô and hid it in a corner. Then mother and son would eat it in the middle of the night without letting Túy Hoa know about it.

When Mã Ỗn one day fell sick, Châu Thị came to visit her.

"Why are you sick, sister?" Châu Thị asked.

"I have been hungry for the last two years," Mã Ỗn answered.

"Who has been starving you?"

Mã Ỗn pointed to the kitchen but did not say a word.

"Where are Mã Văn and Hô? Have they not been feeding you?"

"They were divorced a long time ago."

"But I understand Hô is such a good girl."

"They did not get along well. Do you have anyone good in mind?"

"Yes, Đào San Hô."

"She has the same name as my previous one."

"This is the same one. She has been with me the last two years. It is she who sent you all the food and fruit."

"Where did she get all this money?"

"She has been working hard for it. All her savings go into the gifts she sent you. She has been worrying about you lately when she heard that your new daughter-in-law has not treated you well. Why did you get rid of such a good daughter?"

"I did not know she has been thinking about and protecting us all this time. Is she still mad at us? How can we get her back?"

"She is not mad at you."

"In that case, could I send Mã Văn to bring her back?"

Mã Văn followed Châu Thị to her home. The former couple took some time to warm up to each other again. After bowing in front of Châu Thị to thank her for her generosity, they returned home.

Mã Ỗn greeted them at the front door. She tearfully said, "Daughter, I am sorry for what has happened and I beg for your pardon. Do not hold a grudge against me. There are many problems in the family at this time. Whenever you have time, I will tell you everything. Please come in."

Seeing Đào San Hô coming home, Túy Hoa suspected a plot, became angry and exploded.

"Why are you coming back after having been dismissed from this house? If you want to be a servant here and eat leftovers, you first have to ask and kowtow to me. This is my house now: if you will not ask for my permission, get out of here."

Recognizing Túy Hoa's wicked behavior, San Hô did not want to confront her, thereby causing more problems. She did whatever Túy Hoa asked her.

One month later, Túy Hoa made up her mind to build her own home and take whatever furniture Mã Ỗn owned to her place. San Hô comforted her mother-in-law and told her to keep quiet. She would work and buy her new furniture. Being an industrious person, she borrowed some money and bought poultry and pigs to raise and then sell later. The family survived, but remained poor. They were, however, closer than before.

San Hô one day decided to build a garden and grow vegetables in order to put extra food on the table. She cleaned the backyard, which was overgrown with bushes and weeds. As she dug holes to plant seeds, she hit hard rocks, which she removed. Underneath, she noticed some golden material. Surprised, she called the rest of the family to come and look at her new finding. Túy Hoa, seeing gold scooped, snatched up the largest piece and took it to the dealer. The gold somehow turned into brass, and Túy Hoa landed in jail for selling counterfeited material.

Mã Ỗn, on hearing the news, decided to let her rot in jail so she could learn her lesson. Mã Văn and San Hô had to talk to her day after day before she consented to bail her out. The gold they took from the backyard turned out to be real gold, which they used to get Túy Hoa out of jail. The latter, after having been imprisoned for a few months, learned her lesson. She changed completely and begged for Mã Ỗn's forgiveness.

From that time onward, the family's fortune changed for the better. Mã Văn passed his exam and became a mandarin. Mã Võ became a good army officer.[81]

Comments This legend reflects classic vintage Asian Confucian philosophy spiced with some Buddhist elements and explains very well the inner working of the Vietnamese family. The main wife is the *nội tướng* or the chief of the interior. As such, she controls everything that goes on in the house, from maids, concubines, children, cooking, and festivities that are given at home, to the investments and earnings of the husband. By controlling the purse, she controls everything.

If her husband—the household head—needs money to go for a drink with his friends, he has to ask her for money. If she refuses, he cannot go unless he has money stashed somewhere. Men usually brought all their earnings to their wives, who in turn allocated them some pocket money. He also could take any concubine, but only with the grudging consent of the first wife. If he did it anyway against her advice, conflicts would ensue between him and the concubine on one side and the main wife on the other side.

As the *nội tướng,* the first wife could abuse her power. Abused through rules and regulations by her parents and then her husband, she could turn her anger on her daughter-in-law, the outsider and the newest in the household. In Vietnam, where two or three generations live under the same roof, the power of the first wife can be absolute. A daughter-in-law's life can be a nightmare like in the above legend. As a corollary, men can also remain submissive to their own mothers. The latter could use the power of *hiếu* to control their children and force them to do whatever they want. In the legend, Mã Văn agreed with whatever his mother wanted: he married the girl she chose, and later divorced her.

Children are locked into submission by *hiếu,* which is a Confucian concept and has no good western equivalent. *Hiếu* means filial piety or love and respect for parents and ancestors. But since women do most of the caring for and nursing of parents, they carry the brunt of this rule. Kiều in Vietnamese literature is the well-known prototype of such a woman: she sold herself in order to raise money to save her father from jail time. In the present legend, the first daughter-in-law, San Hô, cared a lot for her mother-in-law. Even after her husband divorced her, she still managed to send food and presents to her mother-in-law.

There are also some Buddhist elements in this legend as exemplified by references to karma, reincarnation and the lady of mercy (Quan Âm Bồ Tát). Karma is a Buddhist concept that suggests that people need to purify themselves in the present life so that they will be re-born as a better human being in the next one (reincarnation). If a poor laborer behaves well, he could, for example be reborn as a wealthy landowner. Through successive rebirths, people eventually could "graduate" as buddhas, or enlightened sages. On the other hand, those who do not behave would have to go through continuous suffering in successive lives.

E. ETHNIC LEGENDS

Vietnam has more than 50 ethnic minorities who live in the western highland regions and have their own tales. As interaction with these people increases, the number of ethnic tales published has also increased. Here are two examples of these tales.

49. The Lush Valley
50. Ta-Po Chasing the Tiger

49. The Lush Valley

In the beginning of time when people still lived in caves, the Creator liked the Rhade so much that he sent his son Y Rim to teach them about rice cooking.

Lord Y Rim then taught them to make wine so everyone could enjoy it. Indeed, wine made people happy, and they spent all their time drinking and having fun, which led to laziness and other vices. Their gratitude, barely expressed, soon turned into anger.

They armed themselves and began looking for their benefactor. Among the crowd were two brothers Y Tong and Y Tang. Having fast legs, they ran after him before he disappeared behind thick bushes. They ended up in a deep cave, which they followed for two days.

When they reached the opening, a beautiful valley stood in front of their eyes. Trees were tall and beautiful, and there were birds singing, flowers blooming, deer frolicking near a river, and monkeys jumping from tree to tree.

The same thought hit them: this is their heaven. They ran back to their tribes and told them about the discovery. Everyone opted to move the new place, to which Y Tong and Y Tang gladly led them. The Ayan came first, followed by Eban, Hdrue, Hmok, Knul...[82]

50. Ta-Po Chasing the Tiger

The Ta-po are short with a fat belly, short neck, and strident voices. They hang around the highland falls, do not go far and often sit in one place. One day, a huge tiger came to the falls to get some water and in a threatening voice shouted, "Get out of my way, miserable animal."

"I may be small, but I bet you cannot beat me," answered the Ta-po.

"How dare you challenge me?"

"Show me what your meal looks like," said the Ta-po without showing any fear.

The tiger immediately sprang into the forest and killed a deer, a fox, and a boar and piled them in front of the Ta-po. The tiger said, "Although they are big game, they are not enough to satisfy my hunger. What is your meal like?"

"This is nothing compared to mine. Go back and look for some more game."

The tiger sprang up the hill unaware that the Ta-po had jumped on its back and started chewing on its hair. While the tiger was chasing an animal, the Ta-po kept eating the tiger's hair. When it returned, the Ta-po jumped down and sat at its usual place.

"You really took a long time to look for an animal. I've been waiting for you for too long and have completed my meal," said the Ta-po.

"Show me what you've eaten."

The Ta-po regurgitated some hair and answered, "My relatives and I mainly eat these animals."

Seeing only tiger's hair, the tiger began trembling.

"Do you have a lot of relatives?" asked the tiger.

"They are all over the hills. They can eat all the tigers in the area."

The tiger slowly backed out and mumbled, "Dear Ta-po."

"Po cap. Po cap...." The strident voice of the Ta-po resonated against the hills and the echo came back fast.

"With that many relatives, I'd better get out of here," said the tiger that quickly ran away.

The Ca-tu who live in the area recount that wherever the Ta-po live, no tiger dares to come by. They not only do not catch the Ta-po, because they chase away tigers, but they also don't settle where the Ta-po live.[83]

XIII. War and Postwar Legends

With the war going for more than two decades (1954–1975), followed by two other decades of "dark ages" (1975–1995) during which socialist oppression, suppression of all forms of freedoms, poverty, and fear reigned absolute in Ho's paradise,[1] it was not surprising to see the emergence of another type of legend. These are unique legends related to the war and postwar period.

They reflect unfulfilled human aspirations: these are the cries in the desert, cries for justice, freedom, and truth that were nonexistent under communist rule. Then there were cries for food, goods, and medicines in a socialist society that could not even feed its own people.

Private companies and the food industry were nationalized from 1975 onward. As a result, rice farmers did not want to work hard because they had to sell their harvest to the state at one tenth of its black market price. Fishermen did not want to work hard because their fish would be bought by the state at a tenth of the market price. Growers, producers, and farmers did not work, hard causing food production to plummet. The resulting hunger was seen everywhere, although it was worse in the concentration camps where prisoners tried to survive on two bowls of soup a day. It was so prevalent that inmates would eat any insect, snake, or rat that flew or crawled within their reach.[2] In the end, instead of transforming southerners into socialist people, reeducation often turns them against communism.[3]

Freedom and justice were nonexistent—to the point that South Vietnamese who had to endure a communist regime thought they lived in an exile land, an unreal world. Why call these stories legends, if lack of freedom, justice, equality, food, and goods existed in reality? Simply because they seemed so unreal that they could have only existed in a dream. The revolution was supposed to bring equality, freedom, food and accessible health care for everyone. It did not. Everyone became poor; only the leadership could get rich. The leadership took over any house in Saigon it wanted and moved into the best ones. It reserved for itself the best goods, fish, meat and the top positions in all state companies: private companies were also nationalized as part of the North taking over the South. While the people were supposed to be the "new owners," the real owner was the communist leadership. Which meant that if one was not a party member, one just had to get by with the leftovers, which was not much.

Southerners suffered in silence, trying to survive under the new regime and make ends meet first; gradually they left the country and became the boat people. Stories of the war became stories about the new rulers, stories of escape and survival, of getting out of the country by boat or on foot through Cambodia, of being terrorized by pirates, of living in refugee camps in other countries, and finally of landing in free western countries.

Huỳnh Sanh Thông edited and translated the first 16 tales of socialist reeducation in Vietnam in 1988. He titled it *To Be Made Over: Tales of Socialist Reeducation in Vietnam.* Since it has been 23 years since he compiled them, I have added nine new ones in this manuscript. There are many more out there, enough to fill up a few legend books about socialist reeducation, but since the majority of Vietnamese-Americans choose to write in their native language rather than in English, few of them are available to the American community.

All these legends reflect the personal experiences, pains, and miseries of the South Vietnamese who have harshly suffered under the communist regime.

1. The New Owners
2. The Man Who Dreamed of Spring
3. The Little Girl and Her Pebbles
4. Disarray
5. The Realtor
6. The Major
7. The Amerasian Girl
8. Lotus Flower
9. River Edges Are Still Wide Apart

1. The New Owners

They descended on Saigon like "swarms of locusts." Subjected to the bleak poverty of North Vietnam and decades of austere military life, they "seized voraciously on the opportunities" offered by the South. "They fought each other over houses, cars, prostitutes, and bribes."⁴ They grabbed everything they could put their hands on (watches, gold, jewelry, radios, television sets, motorbikes...) and sent them up north.

The *bộ đội* (soldiers) loved battery-powered watches that did not need rewinding and motorbikes that ran spontaneously without the need for pedaling. Not used to modern comfort, they either sat right on the floor of the house or pulled their legs up to sit cross-legged on chairs. Not used to sleeping on a bed, they hung hammocks right inside the house to rest for the night. In the process, they ruined many walls, if not the homes themselves. They strung wires in the front yards to hang their washed clothes: the black pajamas gently floating in the breeze sharply contrasted with the beautiful residences they occupied. They used the toilet bowl to clean vegetables, only to watch them disappear when they pushed the flushing lever. Children used to tease them by enquiring whether they had TV sets and other things in Hanoi. The *bộ đội* always answered by the positive because they did not want to be seen as backwards. But when pressed for details, they often gave evasive or incorrect answers.

Many *bộ đội* were so brain-washed by their government propaganda that they truly believed their siblings who left the North for the South back in 1954 were poor and did not have enough food to eat or decent dinner ware to use. When they met them back in Saigon, they were stunned to see the brick houses they lived in, the cars they drove and the nice silverware they used. The first question they would ask was whether their siblings worked for the CIA, for in their mind only CIA agents could afford all these luxuries.

Comments Northerners took whatever they liked—houses, cars, jewelry, ... and so forth—and called it "requisition."⁵ The real owners, however, never saw their properties or belongings again. Private property did not mean anything to those who wanted to steal.

As a result, people saw no good life or happiness when the revolution came, "only hunger, misery, suspicion, and hatred."⁶

2. The Man Who Dreamed of Spring⁷

In a reeducation camp in North Vietnam, Tính and Vân discussed life in the camp. Tính chastised the cadre who gave a talk about how a North Vietnamese pilot "turned off the motor of his fighter plane and ambushed an American bomber in the clouds." He felt sad for the stupidity of these revolutionaries who were deprived of thought and judgment: they were just automatons who regurgitated the Party's words.

Vân did not answer but asked him why he refused to divide the food to prisoners at mealtime. Tính responded that he had lost everything, including his freedom, prestige, and job, and now he wanted to preserve the last thread of his dignity. He did not want to be partial to any prisoner because dividing meant giving someone more and someone less.

Vân told him not to shirk the issue: if he did not do it, the others had to do the dirty work for him.

"Your human dignity will be shining bright and clear in how you respond to the challenge of this wretched prison, not in your refusal to dole out food."

On another occasion, Tính asked Vân why people in the North were angry toward the prisoners. When Vân responded that they might have had family members who died in the South during the war, he said,

"We were the ones who killed their last hope... They had counted on us to deliver them from slavery. Indeed we lost to these bastards in the end... People in the North are abject paupers ... they have been hungrier, more tattered and more wretched than at any other time. Why shouldn't they hold it against us?"

Throughout his life, Tính had only known war, death, and misery. He never had any time he could call spring. Never could there be blue skies in this cursed land, he thought.

One day, a tired Tính handed to Vân his food portion and said, "Please eat for me... This ration is not enough to keep you alive but enough to put off your death a while... The longer you delay your death, the better the chance you'll stand to see spring blossom." He hoped that one day people knew how to turn the brute force the enemy used against them and redirect it against the oppressive regime. "Spring would then come."

A few months later, Tính stumbled, knocked his head on some rocks and died.

Comments Life in the reeducation camps was about survival from beatings, illnesses, lack of food and medicines, isolation, depression, mosquitoes, and leeches. When they worked outdoors in the jungles, swarms of mosquitoes would descend on them and leeches stuck to their skin. Whoever had an extra piece of meat or one more spoon of rice could survive a few more days. Without food, their only thought was about eating ... eating.[8]

Having lived under the communist system, Nguyễn Long realized that "class struggle meant expunging by intimidation and that reeducation meant brain washing."⁹

3. The Little Girl and Her Pebbles

She was about six and came to the beach by herself every day. No one knew which part of the country she was from. She arrived on the island alone a week earlier on a drifting boat that had been attacked by pirates on many occasions. The rest of the passengers were in no better shape than her.

She played by herself on the beach and did not talk to anyone. She collected shells and remained there almost all day long without eating or drinking. When asked where her dad was, she answered, "Sea." Did she mean swept away by the waves? When asked where her mother was, she said, "Pirates." Did she mean taken away by the pirates? When asked about her brother, she murmured, "Blood." Was he killed by the pirates?

Sometimes, she looked at the sea as if to ask whether it would give back her parents. She then looked down at her shells and kept saying, "One for mom, one for me," after dutifully putting one shell on one side for her mother and another for herself.

"One for brother, one for me,

"One for mom, one for me," and so on.

If no one called her for lunch or dinner, she would stay there playing by herself. She never cried, maybe because she was stunned—stunned by the loss and the violence. She ran away from the communists with her family, and now she was alone by herself ... on the beach and in this strange world.

The little girl's world has stopped spinning around. It is not going anywhere and has left her staring at the nebulous and recent past. She would like to go back to the past but cannot. She wants to move forward but no one will help her. She wants life to go on so that she can follow it, but it will not move on. It somehow is mysteriously stuck right there and will not go any farther. It is like a carousel, the engine of which is broken: she wants the carousel to move around, but it just stands there, a contrary and unmovable piece of machinery.¹⁰

Comments This is the tale of a little girl who lost her family during a boat escape from Vietnam. She is one of the thousands of orphans who populate the refugee camps, alone among strangers in a strange new world.

4. Disarray

Two days after Saigon fell, Tuyết watched with horror as a group of *Công An* (security police) stormed into her parents' home with AK rifles and searched around the house, without warrant, before taking her father away. Since he had dealt with Americans (the latter were just guests in his Saigon hotel), he must be a spy, they said. Her mother cried without saying anything. It was hard to see her proud father being shackled and led away like a criminal.

The world suddenly collapsed before Tuyết's eyes. Months passed by without any news from him. The police was mum on this topic, until a year later when they advised the family about his death in a northern concentration camp. No one knew of the circumstances or the location of his demise. Two of her brothers were also sent to reeducation camps. Her younger brother picked up bad habits and did not want to go to school now that the household head was gone. Tuyết had to take care of her dad's business since her mother did not feel qualified to do it.

Tuyết's husband was sent to a reeducation camp. She went back to school while taking care of her father's business. She volunteered to dig dikes in the countryside so that her jailed husband could get a credit and go home earlier. It turned out to be a ploy by the *Công An,* because he still languished in the camps for three years before being released. But because she had done volunteer work, he was allowed to remain in Saigon instead of being sent to the new economic zones. Once released from the camps, he was sent to sweep the streets on the order of the section chief.

He then looked for ways to escape abroad, as many had done before him. As a matter of fact, she made all his travel arrangements, from connecting with handlers, buying a seat on a boat and getting a new identity card for him. The longer he remained in Vietnam, she thought, the higher the chance for him to be arrested again, for rules were unpredictable under the communist regime. Rules changed as fast as the monsoon rains. Although the first escape attempt failed, he successfully got out on the second occasion. She decided to stay back because of her pregnancy. Her mother-in-law forbade her to accompany him because it would bring "bad luck" to him, as fortune-tellers had suggested.

Tuyết stayed back and raised her son by herself. To make matters worse, her in-laws made her life harder once they knew their son had made it safely to Malaysia. That was just one way to snub a daughter-in-law. Tuyết struggled for six years on her own to raise her child before being able to get out of the country.[11]

Comments This tale shows the disintegration of a family: the father, two children, a son-in-law, and a nephew were sent to reeducation camps. The father and his son died in the camps, while another son perished during his boat escape.

Another story reveals how money was crucial in securing false papers necessary to escape abroad.[12] Those without money were doomed to stay back in the country.

5. *The Realtor*

He met her when he was an Army cadet and she a high school student. Touched by her grace and charm, he followed, got acquainted with, courted, and later married her, probably not in that order. For her, he was her first date. Did she love him? She was not sure. Why did she marry him then? Who knows? Women have their strange attractions and feelings that even they are not aware of.

When the war ended, he was shipped to various reeducation camps where he struggled under hardship and misery. There were eight to ten hours of daily hard labor followed by nights of self-criticism. Meals consisted of two bowls of rice a day with vegetables. He remembered these sleepless nights due to gnawing hunger. Since his letters remained unanswered and he received no visits from her, he realized she must have left the country with her family.

When he got out of jail four years later, he was sad and depressed to find an empty home.[13] He survived as best as he could with the help of his relatives, since former government officials and soldiers could not find any job under the communist regime. Then one day, he received a letter from her from the States. He reconnected with her, although he felt that the love was long gone. He applied for an HO (Humanitarian Operation) visa and, after a long process, flew to the U.S., where she picked him up and brought him to her house.

Over the years, she had become a successful realtor and bought herself a condo. On arrival, she gave him the basement room while she used the upstairs bedroom. He soon realized she had a life of her own and a boyfriend. The husband pondered his future in his small room and, not wanting to be a burden to his former wife, moved out one day.

Comments Life in the U.S. was difficult for males, especially those who had gone through reeducation camps. Having suffered hardships in the camps, they came to the U.S. many years after their wives had settled there, and realized that their wives had been breadwinners during that period. Unable to adapt to a new society, the men felt inferior to their wives. Family problems ensued, followed by divorces.[14]

6. The Major

Anh was a major in the South Vietnamese Armed Forces. He dutifully fought against the communists and, when Saigon fell in 1975, was hauled like one million other southerners to reeducation camps. Because he was felt to be a threat to the Hanoi regime, he was taken to a northern concentration camp to be watched more closely than others.[15] Anh endured hard work, hunger, weather changes, insults from his jailers, and misery from loss of pride and dignity. He worried about his wife and daughter Mai, whom he last saw on her sixth birthday. Years passed by at the concentration camp without any news from them.

Unbeknownst to him, his wife was facing hardship herself and decided to elope with another man. She left Mai to the care of a poor but goodhearted neighbor. The latter, "auntie," took Mai in and taught her to sell cakes for a living. She baked the cakes and Mai wandered around the streets to sell the goods. From a middle class family, Mai was suddenly thrown into the depths of society. The end of the war had made her an orphan who tried to survive as best as she could with another lady. Rain or shine, she had to go out and sell her goods; otherwise there would be no food to eat.

One day, she received a letter from her dad, who wondered how his daughter was doing. He wrote that he missed her and her mom. She cried but could not say anything. His father did not know that his wife had left him. She tucked her dad's letter in her pocket and resolved to make enough money to go up north to see him. She also missed him; at least, she knew she was not an orphan. With auntie's help, she forged ahead and made daily savings. Years went by fast... When it had been nine years since she had seen her dad, she told auntie she would go and see him.

Mai and auntie put together all their savings and booked themselves a pair of train tickets to Hanoi, then to the isolated camp in the countryside.

The reunion was tearful but warm. At least they had each other. A year later, Anh was released from the camp. He came home, saw the wretched life his daughter had been living and decided to dedicate his life to her education. He taught her every night, and gradually she picked up the basic education that she had missed for the past nine years.

When his application for an HO visa was granted, he and Mai flew to the U.S. She was placed in a remedial school and, after years of hard work and sacrifice from her dad, graduated from college.

Comments This legend ends up well although the girl's mother had left her a long time ago. Her father, once out of the reeducation camps, decided to put her through school. She graduated despite having no schooling for more than nine years. Many children were not that lucky.

7. *The Amerasian Girl*

Hương did not know why she was different from her siblings. She had white skin and golden locks while they had brown skin and black hair. She was the black sheep of the family and had to do more chores than her siblings. She wore the worn-out clothes they handed down to her. In her child's mind, she would have liked to ask her mother a lot of things, but a stern glance from her often shut off all questioning.

After Saigon fell, her condition became worse. She was pulled out of school because her mother said she could not afford to pay for her tuition, while her siblings continued school. Worse, she was told to go around the neighborhood to sell home made cakes and cookies. She struggled hard with this new life, but slowly overcame her fear. She sometimes felt sorry for herself because of her mother's rejection. Those who accepted her were street children.

Years passed by slowly and painfully for Hương. One day, after the U.S. agreed to repatriate Amerasian children, life became better for Hương. Her mother suddenly became nice to her; she no longer had to sell cakes and got new clothes instead of old ones. She was spoiled because she had become the "golden ticket" to America for the family.

After the family moved to the U.S., Hương was allowed to go to school, although catching up with the lost years was difficult. She joined the church choir, where she did well and was praised for her voice. She turned into a beautiful girl who soon gained many admirers among youths from the Vietnamese community. In one deciding move, she opted to get married to get out of the house. Although she loved her mother, she also resented her for mistreating her in the past. Her life became hectic as she conceived two children back to back. Confined to home by her jealous husband, she then decided to get out of the house and make new friends. Social life became more enjoyable for her, for she was born free and wanted to be free.

Comments Amerasians experienced prejudice and discrimination in Vietnam because they were the offspring of their enemy's collaborators. They were teased by their classmates, mostly children of communist officials. They withdrew from school, lacked education and ended up leading a poor life.[16]

8. Lotus Flower

Biên, a 16-year-old girl, had been behaving strangely during the last few months. She lost her way home a couple of times and claimed to have given a bike ride to a young girl, then an old man. A very active youngster, she unexpectedly and gradually became disabled with severe back pain that left her bedridden most of the time and unable to even perform house chores.

One day in 1991, she fainted — and a girl spoke through her with a strong Huế accent. That stranger turned out to be Lotus Flower, once the breadwinner of a poor family, who collected driftwood and sold it for a living. While working on the edge of the river, she suddenly lost her balance, fell into the water, and drowned. Her remains drifted and got lodged in the mud in the garden of Biên's father. She begged to be reburied as a normal person.

After getting adequate information from that voice, the family members ran to the garden patch, dug out Lotus's remains and reburied them in their family's burial patch. From that time onward, Biên spontaneously recovered from her disability, and Lotus and Biên became close friends. Other ghosts also manifested themselves through Biên, although she did not look for any of them. On another occasion, Biên was able to help neighbors locate the remains of three other orphan spirits, which somehow were buried one on top of the other.

As her notoriety increased, Biên was recognized as the province's girl shaman.[17]

Comment As the result of lengthy wars, dead and missing soldiers and civilians abound in Vietnam. That means that, for a country that believes in spirits, a lot of "lost" are wandering around and need the help of shamans to guide them back to their families. The above story shows that shamans may help some people.

9. River Edges Are Still Wide Apart

I was a South Vietnamese soldier who, on the night of 29 April 1975, was ready to step on a boat in Vung Tau to sail away. Because I was badly missing my old folks and helpless young siblings, I made the fateful decision to stay back. But the victorious northern soldiers shoved me into a reeducation camp without giving me the chance to see them.

Then, with deceitful lies and vengeful hate, they stole the best years of my life.

I once saw my cellmate reaching for a yam to satisfy his hunger. The warden swiftly crushed the bones of his hand with the butt of a rifle, leaving him disabled for life. When another cellmate swallowed a live frog he caught along the road, the warden hit him until he coughed up the animal, which turned from a grass green color to red when it came out.

When I was returned home following my release, the roof of my house was leaking and food was scarce. My father had died in a reeducation camp, my frail mother was selling yams for a living and my siblings were scattered everywhere. I, too, decided to leave the country to look for a new life.

Decades later, I returned back to Vietnam for a visit. From north to south, I have seen veterans from both sides: some on crutches, others in wheelchairs. Many have missing limbs, others painful scars. They pity themselves because they live in poverty, but no one blames them because anything could happen during the war.

When my wound occasionally flared up, I felt lancinating pain, which I could not get rid of even if I cut off an arm or a lung. That wound, northern countryman, was caused by your cruel hands and cruel heart.

After the war, of all the wicked ways to deal with southern countrymen, who are from the same race and skin color as you, you chose the worst one. You dug a river to divide the two sides. And now sitting imposingly on the river edge, you wave us to your side. But I am afraid that the river edges ... are still wide apart.

Comments This tale summarizes the feelings of a Vietnamese-American, which are published in a poem written on the internet.

XIV. A Tale of Deception and Failure

August 14, 2011, was Vu Lan (All Souls' Day), the Vietnamese Buddhist equivalent of the U.S. Mother's Day. In the U.S., overseas Buddhist Vietnamese flocked to pagodas to say prayers and thanks to their mothers. In Vietnam, the Liên Trì pagoda in Saigon organized a luncheon and gift-giving ceremony for hundreds of disabled southern Vietnamese veterans who have been neglected since the end of the war. The Công An, however, prevented the vets from joining the ceremony by taking away their invitations and by closely guarding the approach to the pagoda. Only a few vets have been able to get to the pagoda. The printed picture was worth the proverbial thousand words. It depicted four "dwarfs" along with a triple amputee. The dwarfs had lost both legs during the war and were sitting on their buttocks on the ground. They did not even have wheelchairs to help them move around. Nearby sat a triple amputee: he had a double-forearm and an above-the-knee amputation. He was not even fitted with prostheses.[1]

Thirty-six years after the war, communist officials still preyed on southern soldiers to exact their revenge. Why? Why not leave them in peace? These are disabled people who deserve medical and financial help, not more reprisal.

Greatness and deception are two entities that are entwined in Vietnamese culture through legends and history. Which one is true, which one is false? They are like the areca tree and the betel vine that hold each other in a deep embrace. They are never far from each other. Like day and night, they cannot be separated, for one depends on the other to survive. One fills in when the other goes missing. One explains the other. This is the image of Vietnam: an ambiguous state where truth and reality, legends and history, are also entwined together.

Vietnam has been searching for millennia without ever finding itself. One wonders which feature is she going to show next. Greatness or deception? War or peace? Wealth or poverty?

Vietnam had great and not-so-great leaders and kings. The great ones were there to compensate for the failed ones. The problem is that there were too few great ones to compensate for the many failed ones.

On the boat that took him from Saigon to France in 1911, Nguyễn Tất Thanh a.k.a. Hồ Chí Minh, worked as a cook and dreamed of liberating Vietnam from the French colonialists. In France, he helped the French found the French Communist Party. He then sneaked into Russia where he was trained as a hard-core communist. He developed a boundless and sickly admiration for Lenin. When the latter died in January 1924, Hồ shivered in temperatures under 40 degrees below zero, waiting to pay homage to Lenin because he could not wait until the next day.[2] Sent to China to represent the Soviets in Asia, he founded the Vietnamese Communist Party (VCP) and returned to Vietnam in 1941 to fight against the French.

During World War II, the Japanese upstaged the French in Vietnam and temporarily took over the country. Their loss to the Americans in 1945 caused a political vacuum, which Hồ used to his advantage to take over North Vietnam and make it a communist country.

The South remained under French and South Vietnamese control. The French tried to reconquer the North but lost at Điện Biên Phủ and retreated South in 1954. The Paris Accords divided Vietnam into two countries: the communist north under Ho and the democratic south under Bảo Đại, then Diệm.

The French took two extra years to get out of Vietnam, leaving in 1956. Diệm wanted to build a democracy in the south with U.S. support to fight back against the north. Hồ, with 50,000 to 70,000 dormant soldiers in the south, began a 20-year war to conquer the South.

To achieve that goal, he imposed a dictatorship over the North, starting with the ferocious Land Reform, during which 50,000 to 70,000 people were killed.[3] This was followed by suppression of all freedoms: anyone who opposed the party would be sent to reeducation camps or new economic zones (NEZ), virgin forested lands that they were forced to cultivate and live on.

Having imposed a martial rule in the north, he sent wave after wave of soldiers to conquer the south. In the end, 1.1 million young lives had been sacrificed to win the war.

In the south, he waged a brutal war that caused the death of 300,000 southern soldiers and more than half a million civilians. Overall, the Communist Party of Vietnam killed more than 1 million people to establish supremacy over the whole country.[4]

After the war ended in 1975, the CPV sent one million southerners to reeducation camps and another two million citizens to NEZ. Two million other people escaped abroad to form the Vietnamese expatriates (Việt Kiều). The economy was decimated because of communist nationalization of industry and commerce and collectivization of agriculture.[5] Southerners did not like it, and therefore, did not cooperate. They returned to their usual petty trading and commerce, which slowly lifted Vietnam out of its economic doldrums. To appease growing popular resentment against the CPV, it passed the đổi mới (renovation), opening the door to free commerce under strict state control. The economy improved, but greedy CPV leaders continued to divert money for their personal use. Corruption became rampant.[6]

Vietnam remains a poor country with no basic freedoms. The CPV is a one-party state. It mortgaged Vietnam's future by borrowing from the Soviets and Chinese to pay for war expenses, which the people are still paying.

History repeats itself. The Vietnamese communists turned out to be worse than the French colonialists they replaced, and the people remain poor and without freedom.

Hồ was a man who hid behind more than 50 aliases[7] and sometimes "faked tears" to get his point across, said his private secretary, Vũ Đình Huỳnh.[8] Hồ pledged that "all men are created equal,"[9] but those who have lived under Hồ's regime beg to differ.

Why would Hồ wage such a costly war only to end up with worse results than the French? "He must bear full responsibility for the consequences of his actions, for good or ill."[10]

Hồ introduced a foreign doctrine, communism, to give the CPV total control of the country: he brought the snake into the henhouse, and the people suffered as a result. Why would the CPV continue a "flawed" policy, when most countries around the world have run away from communism? Why would they continue to bleed the nation instead of shoring it up?

If Hồ gave some "pariahs of the world their true voices,"[11] as Duiker suggests, he also transformed half of the Vietnamese people, the southerners, into new pariahs—people who have no rights nor justice. He also forced three million Vietnamese to sail abroad aboard rickety boats. Tens of thousands of others drowned at sea during their escape.

Hồ turned out to be a consummate and Machiavellian politician for whose dangerous dealings the country still has to pay to this day. Behind the mask of a fatherly revolutionary, he ushered a reign of terror unlike any previous Vietnamese reign of terror and set the nation back three to four decades economically and politically.

Chapter Notes

Chapter I

1. Keith Taylor, "Authority and Legitimacy in 11th century Vietnam," in David G. Marr and Anthony Crothers, Milner, *Southeast Asia in the 9th to 14th Centuries* (Singapore: Institute of Southeast Asian Studies, 1986), 149.

Chapter II

1. In 1997, there were more than 15 million believers in a country of 90 million people, according to Minh Quang Nguyễn, *Religious Issues and Government Policies in Viet Nam* (Hanoi: Thế Giới, 1997), 259. The breakdown is as follows: Buddhists: 7,620,803; Catholics: 5,026,480; Protestants: 412,344; Cao Dai: 1,147,527; Hoa Hao: 1,306,969; Islam: 92,294; total: 15,609,417. The 2010 report can be found at http://www.gso.gov.vn/default_en.aspx?tabid=515&idmid=5&ItemID=10799. These figures give a gross idea of the variety of religions in Vietnam, most of them practiced in South Vietnam, because of multiculturalism and openness toward religions in this part of the country.

2. Alexander Soucy, "Re-establishment of the Truc Lam Thien Buddhist Sect," in Philip Taylor, *Modernity and Re-enchantment* (Lanham, MD: Rowman & Littlefield, 2007), 346–347.

3. Philip Taylor, *Goddess on the Rise*, (Honolulu: University of Hawaii Press, 2004), 3.

4. Đỗ Thị Hào and Mai Thị Ngọc Chúc, *Các Nữ Thần Vietnam* [The Goddesses of Vietnam] (Hanoi: Nha Xuat Ban Phu Nu, 1984). The number is higher today.

5. Philip Taylor, *Goddess on the Rise*, 49.

6. Heonik Kwon, *Ghosts of War in Vietnam*, (New York: Cambridge University Press, 2008), 39–41.

7. Léopold C. Cadière, *Croyances et pratiques religieuses des viêtnamiens*, vol. 2 (Paris: Ecole française d'Extrême-Orient, 1955), 59; Ann Unger and Walter Unger, *Pagodas, Gods, and Spirits of Vietnam* (London: Thames Hudson, 1997), p. 20.

8. Unger and Unger, 20.

9. Shaun Malarney, *Culture, Ritual and Revolution in Vietnam*, (Honolulu: University of Hawaii Press, 2002), 191.

10. Ibid, 199–204.

11. Seth Mydans, "Vietnam, an Convert Pursues Capitalism Devoutly," *New York Times*, April 5, 1996, A4.

12. Thành Khôi Lê, *Le Viêt-Nam: Histoire et Civilization* (Paris: Editions de Minuit, 1955), 105. Thành Khôi Lê differentiates the mysticism of Taoism from the rationalism of Confucianism. It is interesting to note that the latter would play an important and predominant role within many Asian societies while Taoism remains a marginal doctrine.

13. Kwok, Man-Ho, Martin Palmer, and Jay Ramsay, *Tao Te Ching: A New Translation* (Rockport, MA: Element Books, 1993), 38.

14. Ibid, 82.

15. Unger, 23–25

16. Ian Johnson, "The Rise of the Tao."

New York Times, November 5, 2010; http://www.nytimes.com/2010/11/07/magazine/07religion-t.html?hpw
	17. Danny Whitfield, *Historical and Cultural Dictionary of Vietnam* (Metuchen, NJ: Scarecrow Press, 1976), 264.
	18. Thành Khôi Lê, 148. The temple houses the statues of Confucius, his four main disciples and portraits of his 72 sages. It also served as a school for princes and the children of dignitaries.
	19. Unger, 28.
	20. Ibid, 29
	21. Stéphane Courtois, Mark Kramer, et al, *The Black Book of Communism: Crimes, Terror, Repression* (Cambridge, MA: Harvard University Press, 1999), x–xv.
	22. Ibid, 4.
	23. Robert Brigham, "Hô Chi Minh, Confucianism, and Marxism" in David Anderson and John Ernst, *The War That Never Ends* (Lexington: University Press of Kentucky, 2007), 119. Peasants flocked to communism on the promise it would get rid of an outdated and corrupt system. See also Nghia Vo, "Confucianism and Communism" in Nghia Vo, *The Men of Vietnam* (Denver, CO: Outskirts Press, Forum#4, 2008), 111–137.
	24. David Marr, *Vietnamese Tradition on Trial, 1920–1945* (Berkeley: University of California Press, 1981), 320.
	25. Quoted in Marr, *Vietnamese Tradition on Trial, 1920–1945*, 320.
	26. Whitfield, 51–52. Religious rites and offerings are made to both the god of the household and the spirit of the ancestor.
	27. Ibid, 17–18.
	28. Unger, 29–33
	29. Ibid, 38.
	30. Whitfield, 27–28
	31. Soucy, "Reestablishment of the Truc Lam Buddhist Sect" in Taylor, *Modernity and Re-enchantment*, 348–349.
	32. Unger, 14–15.

Chapter III

	1. Larry C. Thompson, *Refugee Workers in the Indochina Exodus, 1975–1982* (Jefferson, NC: McFarland, 2010), 29.
	2. Nhu Tang Truong. *A Viet Cong Memoir* (New York: Vintage, 1985), 282.
	3. Vo, Nghia, *The Bamboo Gulag: Political Imprisonment in Communist Vietnam* (Jefferson, NC: McFarland, 2004), 117–132, 151–156; James M. Freeman, *Hearts of Sorrow: Vietnamese-American Lives* (Stanford, CA: Stanford University Press, 1989), 244–247. Robert McKelvey, *A Gift of Barbed Wire: America's Allies Abandoned in Vietnam* (Seattle: University of Washington Press, 2002), 41–43.
	4. McKelvey, *A Gift of Barbed Wire*, 155.
	5. Tin Bùi,. *Following Hô Chi Minh: The Memoirs of a North Vietnamese Colonel* (Honolulu: University of Hawaii Press, 1995), 90.
	6. Mary T. Cargill and Jade Q. Huynh, *Voices of Vietnamese Boat People*, (Jefferson, NC: McFarland, 2000), 10–12. McKelvey, *A Gift of Barbed Wire*, 197–199.
	7. Tin Bùi, *Following Hô Chi Minh*, 95.
	8. Nhu Tang Truong, *A Viet Cong Memoir*, 289.
	9. Nghia Vo, *The Vietnamese Boat People*, 115–129.
	10. *Inhumane* was the word used by Tin Bùi to characterize the communist leadership: "lack of moral values, the inhumanity and blindness of a communist leadership which had become arrogant and lost touch with the people." Tin Bùi, *Following Hô Chi Minh*, 95.
	11. McKelvey, *A Gift of Barbed Wire*, 187.
	12. Ibid, 67.
	13. Karin San Juan, *Little Saigons: Staying Vietnamese in America* (Minneapolis: University of Minnesota Press, 2009), 68.
	14. Viet Thanh Nguyễn (2003) in San Juan, 84.
	15. After failing to mobilize the gentry to get rid of the French, Phan Boi Chau (1867–1940) decided that modernizing the country would reach the same goal. He therefore promoted the Dong Du (Eastern Travel) Movement to send students to study abroad, especially in Japan. The movement died down when the French

forced Japan to deport Phan in 1909. He then organized open rebellions against the French. Caught in 1925, he was sentenced to life in prison but the sentence commuted to a life under house arrest.

16. San Juan, 86.
17. http://en.wikipedia.org/wiki/Georg_Simmel, accessed 8-29-2010.
18. Thi Thu Lam Nguyễn, *Fallen Leaves* (New Haven, CT: Yale Southeast Asia Studies, 1989), 206.
19. San Juan, 88.
20. Nhu Tang Truong, 260. What his mother predicted became a reality a year later (1976), when Tang realized that the North Vietnamese ran South Vietnam like a fiefdom. "Communist officials fought over houses, cars, prostitutes, and bribes." Tang, a communist, escaped from Vietnam as a boat people and landed in France as a refugee. See Nhu Tang Truong, 289, 304-309.
21. Truong, 265.
22. Vo, *Saigon*, 249-256.
23. David Leeming, *The Oxford Illustrated Companion to World Mythology* (New York: Tess Press, 2005), 310.
24. Vo, "Vietnam and the Vietnamese," in Vo et al, *The Men of Vietnam*, 7-22.
25. Vo, "Confucianism and Communism," in Vo et al, *The Men of Vietnam*, 111-137.
26. Vo, "The Duality of the Vietnamese Mind," in Vo et al, *The Sorrows of War and Peace* (Denver, CO: Outskirts Press, Forum#2, 2008), 111-122.

Chapter IV

1. Thành Khôi Lê, 208. Among the books removed: books on rituals, penal codes of Lý and Trần, military treatises of Trần Hưng Đạo and collections of poetry and annals.
2. Jeannette Faurot, *Asian-Pacific Folktales and Legends* (New York: Simon & Schuster, 1995), 9.
3. Linda Degh. *Legend and Belief*, 97.
4. Royall Tyler. *Japanese Tales*.1987: lii
5. Linda Degh, *Legend and Belief: Dialectics of a Folklore Genre* (Bloomington: Indiana University Press, 2001), 322-329.
6. Ibid, 4.
7. Ibid, 362-387.
8. Ibid, 5.
9. Hue Tam Ho Tai. *Millenarianism and Peasant Politics in Vietnam* (Cambridge, MA: Harvard University Press, 1983), 69.
10. Lutz Rohrich. "The Quest of Meaning in Folk Narrative Research" in James M. McGlathery ed., *The Brothers Grimm and Folktale* (Urbana: University of Illinois Press, 1991), 1-15.
11. Ruth B Bottigheimer, *Fairy Tales: A New Story* (Albany, NY: Excelsior Editions, 2009), 4.

Chapter V

1. Philip Taylor, *Goddess*, 251.
2. Cited in Olga Dror, *Cult, Culture, and Authority: Princess Lieu Hanh in Vietnamese History* (Honolulu: University of Hawaii Press, 2007), 3.
3. Antony Landes, *Contes et Légendes Annamites* (Paris: Maisonneuves, 1886), 68-70.
4. Dror, 54, 83-84.
5. Ibid, 80-81.
6. Ibid, 200.
7. Philip Taylor, *Goddess*, 3.
8. Louis Malleret. "Cochinchine, Terre Inconnue." *Bulletin de la Societe des Etudes Indochinoises*, 18.3 (1943): 9-26.
9. Philip Taylor, *Goddess*, 65-66. The Vietnamese, similar to the Americans' western conquest, moved into the Mekong Delta in the seventeenth and eighteenth centuries.
10. Ibid, 75.
11. Stanley Karnow, *Vietnam: A History* (New York: Viking, 1983), 29-30; Văn Cảnh Nguyễn, *Vietnam Under Communism, 1975-1982* (Stanford, CA: Hoover Institution Press, 1983), 170-172. Even priests and Buddhist monks have escaped abroad.
12. Philip Taylor, *Goddess*, 85-89.
13. Ibid, 99-100.
14. Sir John Barrow, *A Voyage to Cochinchina* (London: Cadell and Davies

1806, New York: Oxford University Press, 1975), 303
15. Philip Taylor, *Goddess*, 104–106, 279; Vo, *Saigon*, 210–211. Without these women, the economy would have gone south under the communist system. There would have been no food to eat and no medicine to help sick patients and prisoners.
16. Vo, *Saigon*, 284–285, 292.
17. Choi Buynh Wook. *Southern Vietnam Under the Reign of Minh Mạng* (Ithaca, NY: Cornell University Southeast Asia Program, 2004), 54
18. Cited in Jules Silvestre, "L' Insurrection du Gia Dinh, la revolte de Khôi (1832–1834)," *Revue Indochinoise* 18, 7–8 (1915): 18
19. George Finlayson, *The Mission to Siam and Hue, the Capital of Cochinchina, in the Years 1821–1822* (London: J. Murray, 1826, New York: Oxford University Press, 1988), 319–320
20. Vo, "Roots of South Vietnamese Nationalism," in Vo et al, *The Sorrows of War and Peace*, 42–45.
21. V. Dang Chat, "General Lê Văn Duyệt," in Vo et al, *The Men of Vietnam*, 63.
22. Philip Taylor, *Goddess*, 212–213, 221. The revisionist Hanoi government believed that General Duyệt had been friendly to the French, which is an anathema for the communist government. It has gradually changed its view and now regards Duyệt as a patriot, although lingering doubts persist.
23. Ibid, 204.

Chapter VI

1. Faurot, 10.
2. Moss Roberts. *Chinese Fairy Tales and Fantasies* (New York: Pantheon, 1979), xviii.
3. Ibid, 70–73.
4. Ibid, 222–223, 224.
5. Ibid, xviii.
6. Faurot, 78–81.
7. http://en.wikipedia.org/wiki/Cinderella
8. Royall Tyler, *Japanese Tales* (New York: Pantheon, 1987), 35–37.
9. Ibid, 31–33.
10. Ibid, 30–31.
11. Ibid, 34–35.
12. Ibid, 29.
13. Ibid, 25.
14. Ibid, 115–116.
15. Ibid, 116–118.
16. Ibid, 56.
17. Ibid, 160–162.
18. Ibid, xix. Tyler called the Japanese "civilized."
19. Ibid, 85–86.
20. Ibid, 122–124.
21. A.K. Ramanujan, *Folktales from India* (New York: Pantheon, 1991), xxiii–xxx.
22. Ibid, 33–38.
23. Ibid, 79–81.
24. Ibid, 274–285.
25. Ibid, 293–296.

Chapter VII

1. Đồng Chi Nguyễn, *Kho Tàng Truyện Cô Tích Việt Nam* (Hanoi: Viện Văn Học, 1957; 5 vol. 1993 [reprinted]), 2417–2419.
2. Ibid, 22–23. He also discussed Marx and Engels' theories on p. 2419.
3. Ibid, 2445.
4. Ibid, 2475.
5. Ibid, 2499.
6. Ibid, 2580.
7. Ibid, 2563.
8. Ibid, 2564–2565.
9. Maurice Durand, "Trésor des Contes Vietnamiens," *Bulletin de l'École française d'Extrême-Orient* 52.1 (1964): 243–244, reprinted in Đồng Chi Nguyễn, 489–493.

Chapter VIII

1. Keith W.Taylor. *The Birth of Vietnam* (Berkeley: University of California Press, 1983), 352–353.
2. Tế Xuyên Lý. *Việt Điền U Linh Tập*, translated by Lê Hữu Mực (Saigon: Khai Trí, 1960), 9; hereafter referred to as VDULT.
3. Ibid, 13.
4. Thành Khôi Lê, 179–189. Vietnam

was one of the rare few countries that contained the Mongol invasions.

5. Keith W. Taylor. "Notes on the *Việt Điển U Linh Tập*," *The Vietnam Forum* 8 (1986): 28–29.
6. Dror, 16.
7. Tế Xuyên Lý, VDULT, 59.
8. Dror, 18–19; italics in original.
9. The fact that the Vietnamese were under Chinese rule from 42 A.C.E., (death of the Trưng Queens) to 939 A.C.E. (date of Independence), prevented them from writing any historical work to praise the Trungs.
10. See Southern Tale # 5.
11. Dror, 19. Had the Trưng won the war, they would have been remembered in a historical way. The loss and subsequent assimilation caused most people to only remember them through a cultish expression.
12. See reference 17 of Southern Legends.
13. Taylor, *The Birth of Vietnam*, 45.
14. Tế Xuyên Lý, VDULT, 41–44. It was considered a blessing by people in the thirteenth century, and in the middle ages in general, to last a long time in a position of leadership.
15. Daoist and Taoist are used interchangeably.
16. "King" is an honorific title that is used here to depict the awe that the people have for the spirits. Only a rare few of them are known to be actual kings.
17. Villagers first acknowledged him as a spirit, then prayed to him and built him a temple. As he was found to be responsive, the ruler(s) of the land bestowed him a title on various occasions.
18. Tế Xuyên Lý, VDULT: 49–50.
19. Ibid, 52–55.
20. Ibid, 59.
21. Ibid, 68–69.
22. Ibid, 70–71.
23. *Nam Quốc Sơn Hà* http://en.wikipedia.org/wiki/Nam_qu% E1%BB%91c_s%C6%A1n_h%C3%A0; author's translation.
24. Ibid, 73–74.
25. The future Hanoi area around the fourth century. In the ninth century Nguyễn Gia built a wall around it. Cao Biền built a new city at the same location.

Chapter IX

1. Vũ Quỳnh and Văn Nguyên Bùi, *Linh Nam Chich Quai*, 1492 (Dinh Gia Khanh: Nha Xuat Ban Van Hoc Hanoi, 2001 [reprinted]), 15.
2. Thành Khôi Lê, 195–196. The Chams attacked the southern Vietnamese provinces every year beginning in 1361. They sacked the capital Thăng Long in 1371 and 1377, and raided Vietnam in 1378 and 1380.
3. Ibid, 204–212.
4. Dror, 23.
5. Ibid, 25–26.
6. Ibid, 29–30.
7. Vũ Quỳnh and Văn Nguyên Bùi, *Linh Nam Chich Quai*, 29–33.
8. Shen Nung was an agricultural deity with roots in Tibetan culture. He was also connected to systems of agricultural settlement.
9. A constellation in the heavens thought to overlook northern Vietnam.
10. Although some authors have translated it as "the Land of the Red Devils," the correct meaning is "the Bountiful Land."
11. Đế Lai and Lạc Long Quân were cousins.
12. Although Âu Cơ is Đế Lai's wife, the *Đại Việt Sử Ký Toàn Tư* makes her his daughter; in that case, Lạc Long Quân would not be guilty of taking another man's wife.
13. The northern branch ended when Đế Du was defeated by Huang Ti, the "Yellow Emperor."
14. Vũ Quỳnh and Văn Nguyên Bùi, *Linh Nam Chich Quai*, 39–40.
15. One truong varies between 0.4 to 4.7 m depending on the object measured.
16. Vũ Quỳnh and Văn Nguyên Bùi, *Linh Nam Chich Quai*, 61–62.
17. "Tall" in Vietnamese.
18. Vũ Quỳnh and Văn Nguyên Bùi, *Linh Nam Chich Quai*, 50–54.
19. Ibid, 45–48.
20. Ibid, 64–65.
21. Bánh Chưng is a glutinous rice

cake containing meat and yellow bean filling and fashioned in a square shape. Bánh dầy is a whitish rice cake with pork filling.

22. Vũ Quỳnh and Vãn Nguyẽn Bùi, *Linh Nam Chich Quai*, 67–68; see Southern Tale # 25.

23. Ibid, 73–74.

24. Ibid, 76–81; see Southern Tale # 3.

25. Ibid, 86–88.

26. Cuong Tu Nguyẽn, *Zen in Medieval Vietnam: A Study and Translation of the Thiền uyển tập anh* (Honolulu: University of Hawaii Press, 1997), 71, 333.

27. Vũ Quỳnh and Vãn Nguyẽn Bùi, *Linh Nam Chich Quai*, 93–97; see Southern Tale # 2.

28. Ibid, 83–84. See southern tale # 5

29. Ibid, 89–90.

Chapter X

1. The French controlled Saigon in 1859 before conquering central then northern Vietnam in 1882.

2. Landes, *Contes et Legendes Annamites*, vi.

3. North and South Vietnam were divided into two regions from 1600 to 1802, the North being governed by the Lê/Trinh and the South by the Nguyễn. This two-century separation caused them to evolve different economic, social, cultural, and religious points of view.

4. Landes, vii.

5. Ibid, 1–2. This story is similar in reverse to Contemporary Tale # 35 (The Balance). In this story, the two good sons and spirits bestowed to a poor but good family were "recalled" because the mother wanted to take revenge on people who had treated her badly in the past. In The Balance, the two bad sons and spirits were "recalled" because the household head had behaved well in his present life.

6. Students who were often poor had to travel at their own expenses to the court (or other sites) to take the exam. If they succeeded, they were congratulated by the king and sent home with honor. Villagers had to pitch in to celebrate them.

7. Villagers used their own people as militia to stand watch around the villages. These duties often fell to the poor, while those who could afford it bought their way out of this responsibility.

8. All these legends offer the same moral viewpoint: if people behave nicely, they somehow will be nicely rewarded. In this story, this poor couple was given two laureate sons, which was a very rare feat. The mother, however, was so bent on taking revenge on those who had mistreated her in the past, that she lost all her merits and in the same token her sons.

9. Landes, 5–6.

10. Quan Võ was one of three friends who fought for Vietnam against the Chinese Yellow Turbans. He was taken prisoner and decapitated. He was made a hero In the 12th century, and elevated to the rank of "de" or "king" in 1594. From that time onward, he was known as the War King.

11. "Đình" means a communal gathering place.

12. Landes, 12–13.

13. Ibid, 49–51.

14. Ibid, 68–70. This is one of the many versions of this story.

15. Lê Thái Tổ (1428–1433) was the founder of the Lê Dynasty.

16. The "Eight Kim Căng" were eight generals created by the Buddha Quan Âm. They supposedly had divine powers.

17. Landes, 114.

18. Giao Cu Nguyễn, *Sự Tích Chim Cheo Beo* (Nhà Xuất Bản Tổng Hợp Đồng Nai: HCMC, 2005), 148–150; Landes, 142–144.

19. A chalk pot has an opening on top through which chalk can be introduced or removed.

20. Landes, 145–147.

21. According to ancient oracles, red spots (birth marks, telangiectasias, and other skin lesions) have different meanings depending on their location.

22. Landes, 151–153.

Chapter XI

1. Royall Tyler, *Japanese Tales*, liii; Fanny Hagin Mayer, *Ancient Tales in Modern Japan: An Anthology of Japanese*

Folk Tales (Bloomington: Indiana University Press, 1984).
2. Heonik Kwon, *Ghosts of War in Vietnam*, 39–41.
3. Unger, 18–20.
4. Philip Taylor, *Goddess*, 5.
5. Ramanujan, xxi.

Chapter XII

1. Keith Taylor, *The Birth of Vietnam*, 3–7, 303–305.
2. Ibid, 34–36.
3. Ibid, 24–26.
4. Vo, *The Trưng Sisters* (Bloomington, IN: AuthorHouse, 2000), 19–29; Thich Nhất Hanh, *A Taste of the Earth* (Berkeley, CA: Parallax Press, 1993), 3–10.
5. Alice M. Terada, *Under the Starfruit Tree: Folktales from Vietnam* (Honolulu: University of Hawaii Press, 1989), 50–53; Cam Nguyễn and Dana Sachs, *Two Cakes Fit for a King* (Honolulu: University of Hawaii Press, 2003), 27–32; Keith Taylor, *The Birth of Vietnam*, 6.
6. Keith Taylor. *The Birth of Vietnam*, 20–21.
7. See Nguyễn and Sachs, *Two Cakes Fit for a King*, 19–26.
8. Nguyễn and Sachs, *Two Cakes Fit for a King*, 53–59. The festival of the genie of Phù Đồng is celebrated from the sixth to the 12th of the fourth lunar month in Phù Đồng village, Hanoi.
9. Keith Taylor, *The Birth of Vietnam*, 4–5; Neil L. Jamieson, "The Traditional Family in Vietnam." *The Vietnam Forum* 8 (1986): 137–140. The North is full of shrines venerating heroes, gods and spirits. Being an ancient land, it reflects the period when people felt powerless and had to ask spirits, gods and genies to help them solve their problems. Time also accounts for the accumulation of shrines and temples. The South, being a new land conquered through their own strength and will, devotes less recourse to spirits/genies. Southerners seem to be less superstitious. If they are, they place their superstitions in Buddha and after 1990 in *Chuá Bà Xứ*, a goddess whose shrine is located on Sam Mountain close to Châu Đốc in Southwest Vietnam. See Philip Taylor, *Goddess*, 1–11.
10. Keith Taylor, *The Birth of Vietnam*, 37–41.
11. Ruth Ashby and Deborah Ohrn. *Herstory: Women Who changed the World* (New York: Penguin, 1995), 19.
12. Vo, *The Trưng Sisters*, 49–116, 125.
13. Sanh Thong Huỳnh, *An Anthology of Vietnamese Poems* (New Haven, CT: Yale University Press), 30.
14. Keith Taylor, *The Birth of Vietnam*, 334–339.
15. Vo, *The Trưng Sisters*, 117–122.
16. Keith Taylor, *The Birth of Vietnam*, 90–91.
17. Ashby and Ohrn, *Herstory*, 30.
18. Keith Taylor, *The Birth of Vietnam*, 6; George Coedès, *The Making of Southeast Asia*, translated by H.M. Wright (London: Routledge & Kegan Paul, 1967), 37; In the Funan culture—a Hinduized Mekong Delta culture of the first to fifth-century C.E.—Kaundynya encountered a naked woman in the Mekong Delta whom he married. He later founded the new Funan empire. This Funanese story is similar to *Nhật Gia Trạch*, but the man-woman role was reversed.
19. Hà Nguyễn, *Sử Tích Hồ Gươm*, 5–8, 25; Thanh Khôi Lê, *Le Vietnam*, 200–215; The Chinese invaded Đại Việt (Vietnam) in 1406 under the guise of restoring the Trần dynasty and took over the country the following year. All Vietnamese literary works were hauled back to China to be destroyed. Chinese culture and books were imposed on Đại Việt, which became once again the Chinese Giao Chỉ province. Tattooing, staining teeth black and chewing betel—Vietnamese tradition—were forbidden and hair had to be kept long according to the Chinese way. Literati were coerced into working for the new Chinese administration. Lê Lợi, one of the landowners in Lâm Sơn, refused to collaborate with the invaders. He spearheaded the revolt in 1418, which lasted until 1427. The legend of *The Lake of the Sword* marked the end of the revolt and the return of the sword to Lord Dragon.
20. Tu Trần and Mai Thi, *Sử Tích Loa*

Thành (Hanoi: Nha Xuat Ban Van Hoa, 2006), 105–112.

21. Unger,, 142–143; Quang Van Nguyễn, and Marjorie Pivar, *Fourth Uncle in the Mountain: A Memoir of a Barefoot Doctor in Vietnam* (New York: St. Martin's Press, 2004), 244–254.

22. This is a common saying; author's translation.

23. Nghia Vo, *Saigon: A History*. Jefferson, NC: McFarland, 34–39.

24. Daughton, "Recasting Pigneau de Behaine," in Nhung T. Tran and Anthony Reid, *Borderless Histories* (Madison: University of Wisconsin Press, 2006), 294.

25. Nguyễn and Sachs, *Two Cakes Fit for a King*, 71–76; George Schultz, *Vietnamese Legends* (Rutland, VT: Tuttle, 1965), 101–105.

26. J. Kluger, "Why Bosses Tend to Be Blowhards," *Time*, March 2, 2009, 48.

27. Nghia Vo et al, *The Lands of Freedom* (Denver, CO: Outskirts Press, Forum#5, 2009), 37–54.

28. Terada, *Under the Starfruit Tree*, 7.

29. Hà Nguyễn, *Sữ Tích Hồ Gươm*, 158–161.

30. Ibid, 162–167; Schultz, *Vietnamese Legends*, 106.

31. George Schultz. *Vietnamese Legends*, 153.

32. Ibid, 56.

33. Hà Nguyễn, *Sữ Tích Hồ Gươm*, 122–124.

34. Terada, *Under the Starfruit Tree*, 37; Giao Cư Nguyễn, *Sự Tích Con Dã Tràng* (Nhà Xuất Bản Tổng Hợp Đồng Nai: HCMC, 2005), 5–19.

35. Schultz, *Vietnamese Legends*, 86.

36. Vo, "Confucianism and Communism," in Vo et al, *The Men of Vietnam*, 111–120.

37. Hà Nguyễn, *Sự Tích Hồ Gươm*, 57–59; Terada, *Under the Starfruit Tree*, 109.

38. Hà Nguyễn, *Sữ Tích Hồ Gươm*, 60–62.

39. Vo, "Confucian Women," in Vo et al, *The Women of Vietnam* (Denver, CO: Outskirts Press, Forum#3, 2008), 4.

40. John C. Shafer, "Lục Văn Tiên: Its Relation to Prior Texts," *The Vietnam Forum* 1.1 (1983): 62.

41. Vo et al, *The Women of Vietnam*, 9–12.

42. Hà Nguyễn, *Sự Tích Hồ Gươm*, 27–29; Terada, *Under the Starfruit Tree*, 105.

43. Hà Nguyễn, *Sự Tích Hồ Gươm*, 37–39; Schultz, *Vietnamese Legends*, 31.

44. Clotilde Chivas-Baron and E.M. Smith-Dampier, *Stories and Legends of Annam* (London: A. Melrose, 1920), 71–74; Schultz, *Vietnamese Legends*, 39–41.

45. Nguyễn and Sachs, *Two Cakes Fit for a King*, 87–94; Hà Nguyễn, *Sự Tích Hồ Gươm*, 51–56.

46. Sanh Thong Huỳnh, *An Anthology of Vietnamese Poems*, 353.

47. Ibid, 43.

48. Vo, "Roots of South Vietnamese Nationalism," in Vo et al, *The Sorrows of War and Peace* (Denver, CO: Outskirts Press, Forum#2, 2008), 37–38; Keith Taylor, "Nguyễn Hoang and the Beginning of South Vietnam's Southward Expansion," in Anthony Reid, *Southeast Asia in the Early Modern Era* (Ithaca, NY: Cornell University Press, 1993), 42–65.

49. Tú Trần and Mai Thi, *Sự Tích Loa Thành*, 159–165; Nguyễn and Sachs, *Two Cakes Fit for a King*, 33–41.

50. Giao Cư Nguyễn, *Cá Hoa Long* (Nhà Xuất Bản Tổng Hợp Đồng Nai: HCMC, 2005), 95–101; Schultz, *Vietnamese Legends*, 48–55.

51. Nghia Vo, *The Việt Kiều in America: Personal Accounts of Postwar Immigrants from Vietnam* (Jefferson, NC: McFarland, 2009), 3.

52. Schultz, *Vietnamese Legends*, 60.

53. Ibid, 93.

54. Ibid, 29.

55. Schultz, *Vietnamese Legends*, 90.

56. Alexander Woodside, *Vietnam and the Chinese Model* (Cambridge, MA: Harvard University Press, 1971), 170–172.

57. Ibid, 195–199.

58. Jamieson, "The Traditional Family in Vietnam," *The Vietnam Forum* 8 (1986): 135–136.

59. Nguyễn Du, *The Tale of Kieu* (New York: Vintage, 1973), 142.

60. Vo, "Kieu's Karma," in Vo et al, *The Lands of Freedom* (Denver, CO: Outskirts Press, Forum#5, 2009), 164.

61. Terada, *Under the Starfruit Tree,* 23–34; Schultz, *Vietnamese Legends,* 143.
62. Giao Cư Nguyễn, *Thạch Sanh,* 5–15; Schultz, *Vietnamese Legends,* 106.
63. Ho Hien, "The Mercury Balance Syndrome," in Vo et al, *Remembering Saigon* (Denver, CO: Outskirts Press, Forum#1, 2008), 165–171.
64. Vo, "Kieu's Fatalism," in Vo et al, *The Lands of Freedom,* 164.
65. Thành Khôi Lê, *Le Vietnam,* 221.
66. Landes, 268–271; Schultz. *Vietnamese Legends,* 125–127.
67. Vo, "Confucian Women," in Vo et al, *The Women of Vietnam,* 1–15; Vo, "Confucianism and Communism," in Vo et al, *The Men of Vietnam,* 111–120.
68. Terada, *Under the Starfruit Tree,* 115.
69. Tú Trần and Mai Thi, *Sử Tích Loa Thành,* 186–193.
70. Arthur Dommen, *The Indochinese Experience of the French and the Americans: Nationalism and Communism in Cambodia, Laos and Vietnam* (Bloomington: Indiana University Press, 2001), 1.
71. Terada, *Under the Starfruit Tree,* 10.
72. Schultz, *Vietnamese Legends,* 136.
73. Jamieson, "The Traditional Family in Vietnam." *The Vietnam Forum* 8 (1986): 94–94.
74. Terada, *Under the Starfruit Tree,* 3.
75. Jamieson, "The Traditional Family in Vietnam." *The Vietnam Forum* 8 (1986): 96–97.
76. Ibid, 105–106.
77. Ibid, 107–108.
78. Schultz, *Vietnamese Legends,* 72.
79. Ibid, 80.
80. Giao Cư Nguyễn, *Sự Tích Con Dã Tràng,* 147–158.
81. Ibid, 55–96.
82. Ibid, 97–100.
83. Ibid, 101–105.

Chapter XIII

1. Sanh Thong Huỳnh, *To Be Made Over: Tales of Socialist Reeducation in Vietnam* (New Haven, CT: Yale Southeast Asia Studies, 1988), x. Violations of human rights have been perpetrated against southerners.
2. Vo, *The Bamboo Gulag,* 122–125. Hunger was so pervasive that they would eat anything—lizards, mice, centipedes, birds, grasshoppers, snakes.
3. Huỳnh, *To Be Made Over,* x.
4. Nhu Tang Truong, *A Viet Cong Memoir,* 289.
5. Võ Kỳ Điền, "The Old Man Who Believed Only What He Saw" in Huỳnh, *To Be Made Over,* 23.
6. Ibid, 25.
7. Nguyễn Ngọc Thuần, "The Man Who Dreamed of Spring" in Huỳnh, *To Be Made Over,* 114–121.
8. Tri Vu Tran, *Lost Years,* 38, 167–168, 227.
9. Long Nguyễn and Harry H. Kendall, *After Saigon Fell: Daily Life Under the Vietnamese Communists* (Berkeley: University of California, 1981), xv.
10. Vo, "The Tale of the Girl and the Seashells," in Vo et al, *The Sorrows of War and Peace,* 167–171.
11. Vo, *The Viet Kieu in America,* 101–109.
12. Nguyễn and Kendall, *After Saigon Fell,* 124–125.
13. McKelvey, *A Gift of Barbed Wire,* 95. Most of the prisoners came home with moderate to severe depression.
14. Ibid, 128–129.
15. Freeman, *Hearts of Sorrow,* 224–254; McKelvey, *A Gift of Barbed Wire,* 84–94; Edward P. Metzner et al, *Reeducation in Postwar Vietnam: Personal Postscripts to Peace* (College Station: Texas A & M University Press, 2001), 24–27.
16. McKelvey, *The Dust of Life: America's Children Abandoned in Vietnam* (Seattle: University of Washington Press, 1999), 47.
17. Heonik Kwon, 109–116

Chapter XIV

1. "TPB VNCH và tù nhân chính trị tôn giáo bị cấm nhận quà," August 14, 2011, accessed at http://www.rfa.org/vietnamese/in_depth/fmr-pol-pris-proh-to-receive-gifts-dhieu-08142011134414.html

2. William Duiker, *Hô Chi Minh: A Life* (New York: Hyperion, 2000), 97. Ho got frostbite that night.

3. Courtois, Kramer et al. *The Black Book of Communism*, 569. Numbers could be as high as 100,000; Robert F. Turner, *Vietnamese Communism: Its Origin and Development* (Stanford, CA: Stanford University Press, 1975), 143.

4. Ibid, 4.

5. Duiker, 568.

6. Ibid, 575.

7. Turner, 3.

8. Duiker, 572.

9. Ibid, 323. Statement made at Ba Đình Square on September 2, 1945, when Hô engineered a coup to take over North Vietnam.

10. Ibid, 576.

11. Ibid, 577.

Bibliography

Anderson, David L., and John Ernst. *The War That Never Ends*. Lexington: University Press of Kentucky, 2007.

Ashby, Ruth, and Deborah Ohrn. *Herstory: Women Who Changed the World*. New York: Penguin, 1995.

Barrow, Sir John. *A Voyage to Cochinchina*. London: Cadell and Davies 1806, New York: Oxford University Press, 1975.

Bottigheimer, Ruth B. *Fairy Tales: A New Story*. Albany: State University of New York Press, 2009.

Bùi, Thị Ngọc Diệp, and Đồng Chi Nguyễn. *Sữ Tích Hồ Gươm*. Hanoi: Nhà Xuất Bản Văn Hóa, 2007.

Bùi, Tin. *Following Hô Chi Minh: The Memoirs of a North Vietnamese Colonel*. Honolulu: University of Hawaii Press, 1995.

Cadière, Léopold C. *Croyances et pratiques religieuses des viêtnamiens*. Paris: Ecole française d'Extrême-Orient, 1955.

Cargill, Mary T., and Jade Q. Huynh. *Voices of Vietnamese Boat People*. Jefferson, NC: McFarland, 2000.

Chivas-Baron, Clotilde, and E.M. Smith-Dampier. *Stories and Legends of Annam*. London: A. Melrose, 1920.

Coedès, Georges. *The Making of Southeast Asia*. Translated by H.M. Wright. London: Routledge & Kegan Paul, 1967.

Courtois, Stéphane, Mark Kramer, et al. *The Black Book of Communism: Crimes, Terror, Repression*. Cambridge, MA: Harvard University Press, 1999.

Degh, Linda. *Legend and Belief: Dialectics of a Folklore Genre*. Bloomington: Indiana University Press, 2001.

Đỗ, Thị Hào, and Thị Ngọc Chúc Mai. *Các Nữ Thần Việt Nam* [The Goddesses of Vietnam]. Hanoi: Nhà Xuất Bản Phụ Nữ, 1984.

Dommen, Arthur J. *The Indochinese Experience of the French and the Americans: Nationalism and Communism in Cambodia, Laos and Vietnam*. Bloomington: Indiana University Press, 2001.

Dror, Olga. *Cult, Culture, and Authority: Princess Lieu Hanh in Vietnamese History*. Honolulu: University of Hawaii Press, 2007.

Duiker, William. *Hô Chi Minh: A Life*. New York: Hyperion, 2000.

Duong, Van Quyen, Jewel Reinhart Coburn, and Nena Grigorian Ullberg. *Beyond the East Wind: Legends and Folktales of Vietnam*. Thousand Oaks, CA: Burn, Hart & Co, 1976.

Faurot, Jeannette L. *Asian-Pacific Folktales and Legends*. New York: Simon & Schuster, 1995.

Finlayson George. *The Mission to Siam and Hue, the Capital of Cochinchina, in the Years 1821–1822*. London: J. Murray, 1826, New York: Oxford University Press, 1988.

Freeman, James M. *Hearts of Sorrow: Vietnamese-American Lives*. Stanford, CA: Stanford University Press, 1989.

Ho Tai, Hue Tam. *Millenarianism and Peasant Politics in Vietnam*. Cambridge, MA: Harvard University Press, 1983.

Huỳnh, Sanh Thong. *An Anthology of*

Vietnamese Poems. New Haven, CT: Yale University Press, 1996.
Huỳnh, Sanh Thong. "Folk History in Vietnam." *The Vietnam Forum* 3.5 (1985):66–80.
Huỳnh, Sanh Thong, *To Be Made Over: Tales of Socialist Reeducation in Vietnam*. New Haven, CT: Yale Southeast Asia Studies, 1988.
Jamieson, Neil L. "The Traditional Family in Vietnam." *The Vietnam Forum* 8 (1986): 91–150.
Johnson, Ian. "The Rise of the Tao." *The New York Times Magazine*, November 5, 2010.
Karnow, Stanley. *Vietnam: A History*. New York: Viking, 1983.
Kluger, J. "Why Bosses Tend to Be Blowhards." *Time*, March 2, 2009.
Kwok, Man-Ho, Martin Palmer, and Jay Ramsay. *Tao Te Ching: A New Translation*. Rockport, MA: Element Books, 1993.
Kwon, Heonik. *Ghosts of War in Vietnam*. New York: Cambridge University Press, 2008.
Landes, Antony. *Contes et Légendes Annamites*. Paris: Maisonneuves, 1886.
Lê, Thành Khôi *Le Viêt-Nam: Histoire et Civilization*. Paris: Editions de Minuit, 1955.
Leeming, David. *The Oxford Illustrated Companion to World Mythology*. New York: Tess Press, 2005.
Lý, Tế Xuyên. *Việt Điền U Linh Tập, 1329*. Translated by Lê Hữu Mực. Saigon: Khai Trí, 1960.
Malarney, Shaun. *Culture, Ritual and Revolution in Vietnam*. Honolulu: University of Hawaii Press, 2002.
Malleret, Louis. "Cochinchine: Terre Inconnue." *Bulletin de la Societe des Etudes Indochinoises* 18.3 (1943).
Marr, David G. *Vietnamese Tradition on Trial, 1920–1945*. Berkeley: University of California Press, 1981.
Marr, David G., and Anthony Crothers Milner. *Southeast Asia in the 9th to 14th Centuries*. Singapore: Institute of Southeast Asian Studies, 1986.

Mayer, Fanny Hagin. *Ancient Tales in Modern Japan: An Anthology of Japanese Folk Tales*. Bloomington: Indiana University Press, 1984.
McGlathery, James M. *The Brothers Grimm and Folktale*. Urbana: University of Illinois Press, 1991.
McKelvey, Robert S. *The Dust of Life: America's Children Abandoned in Vietnam*. Seattle: University of Washington Press, 1999.
McKelvey, Robert S. *A Gift of Barbed Wire: America's Allies Abandoned in Vietnam*. Seattle: University of Washington Press, 2002.
Metzner, Edward P. et al. *Reeducation in Postwar Vietnam: Personal Postscripts to Peace*. College Station: Texas A & M University Press, 2001.
Mydans, Seth. "Vietnam, a Convert Pursues Capitalism Devoutly." *The New York Times*, April 5, 1996.
Nguyễn, Cam, and Dana Sachs. *Two Cakes Fit for a King*. Honolulu: University of Hawaii Press, 2003.
Nguyễn, Cuong Tu. *Zen in Medieval Vietnam: A Study and Translation of the Thiền uyển tập anh*. Honolulu: University of Hawaii Press, 1997.
Nguyễn, Đồng Chi. *Kho Tàng Truyện Cổ Tích Việt Nam*. Hanoi: Viện Văn Học, 1957; 5 vol. 1993 (reprinted).
Nguyễn, Du. *The Tale of Kieu*. New York: Vintage, 1973.
Nguyễn, Giao Cư. *Cá Hoa Long*. Nhà Xuất Bãn Tổng Hợp Đồng Nai: HCMC, 2005.
Nguyễn, Giao Cư. *Sự Tích Chim Cheo Beo*. Nhà Xuất Bãn Tổng Hợp Đồng Nai: HCMC, 2005.
Nguyễn, Giao Cư. *Sự Tích Con Dã Tràng*. Nhà Xuất Bãn Tổng Hợp Đồng Nai: HCMC, 2005.
Nguyễn, Giao Cư. *Thạch Sanh*. Nhà Xuất Bản Mỹ Thuật: HCMC, 2004.
Nguyễn, Khoa Thai Anh. "The Lady of Nam Xuong." *Nhà Magazine*, Dec 2003.
Nguyễn, Long, and Harry H. Kendall. *After Saigon Fell: Daily Life Under the*

Vietnamese Communists. Berkeley: University of California, 1981.
Nguyễn, Minh Quang, *Religious Issues and Government Policies in Viet Nam*. Hanoi: The Gioi, 1997.
Nguyễn, Quang Van, and Marjorie Pivar. *Fourth Uncle in the Mountain: A Memoir of a Barefoot Doctor in Vietnam*. New York: St. Martin's Press, 2004.
Nguyễn, Thi Thu Lam. *Fallen Leaves*. New Haven, CT: Yale Southeast Asia Studies, 1989.
Nguyễn, Văn Cảnh. *Vietnam Under Communism, 1975–1982*. Stanford, CA: Hoover Institution Press, 1983.
Nhất Hạnh, Thích. *A Taste of the Earth*. Berkeley, CA: Parallax Press, 1993.
Ramanujan, A.K. *Folk Tales from India*. New York: Pantheon, 1991.
Reid, Anthony. *Southeast Asia in the Early Modern Era*. Ithaca, NY: Cornell University Press, 1993.
Roberts, Moss. *Chinese Fairy Tales and Fantasies*. New York: Pantheon, 1979.
San Juan, Karin. *Little Saigons: Staying Vietnamese in America*. Minneapolis: University of Minnesota Press, 2009.
Schultz, George F. *Vietnamese Legends*. Rutland, VT: Tuttle, 1965.
Shafer, John C. "Lục Văn Tiên: Its Relation to Prior Texts." *The Vietnam Forum* 1.1 (1983): 59–66.
Silvestre, Jules, "L' Insurrection du Gia Dinh, la revolte de Khôi (1832–1834)." *Revue Indochinoise* 18, 7–8 (1915): 1–37.
Taylor, Keith W. *The Birth of Vietnam*. Berkeley: University of California Press, 1983.
Taylor, Keith W. "Notes on the *Viet Dinh U Linh Tap*." *The Vietnam Forum* 8 (1986): 26–59.
Taylor, Philip. *Goddess on the Rise*. Honolulu: University of Hawaii Press, 2004.
Taylor, Philip. *Modernity and Re-enchantment: Religion in Post-Revolution Vietnam*. Lanham, MD: Rowman & Littlefield, 2007.
Terada, Alice M. *Under the Starfruit Tree: Folktales from Vietnam*. Honolulu: University of Hawaii Press, 1989.
Thompson, Larry C. *Refugee Workers in the Indochina Exodus, 1975–1982*. Jefferson, NC: McFarland, 2010.
Tran, Tri Vu. *Lost Years: My 1,632 Days in Vietnamese Reeducation Camps*. Berkeley: University of California Press, 1988.
Trần, Tu, and Thi Mai. *Su Tich Loa Thanh*. Hanoi: Nha Xuat Ban Van Hoa, 2006.
Truong, Nhu Tang. *A Viet Cong Memoir*. New York: Vintage, 1985.
Truong Vinh Ky. Chuyen Doi Xua. 1909. See text p. 89
Turner, Robert F. *Vietnamese Communism: Its Origin and Development*. Stanford, CA: Stanford University Press, 1975.
Tyler, Royall. *Japanese Tales*. New York: Pantheon, 1987.
Unger, Ann Helen, and Walter Unger. *Pagodas, Gods, and Spirits of Vietnam*. New York: Thames and Hudson, 1997.
Vo, Nghia M. *The Bamboo Gulag: Political Imprisonment in Communist Vietnam*. Jefferson, NC: McFarland, 2004.
Vo, Nghia M. *The Trung Sisters*. Bloomington, IN: AuthorHouse, 2000.
Vo, Nghia M. *The Viet Kieu in America: Personal Accounts of Postwar Immigrants from Vietnam*. Jefferson, NC: McFarland, 2009.
Vo, Nghia M. *Vietnam: A History*. Jefferson, NC: McFarland, 2011.
Vo, Nghia M. *The Vietnamese Boat People, 1954 and 1975–1992*. Jefferson, NC: McFarland, 2006.
Vo, Nghia M., V. Dang Chat and V. Ho Hien. *The Lands of Freedom*. Denver, CO: Outskirts Press, Forum#5, 2009.
Vo, Nghia M., V. Dang Chat and V. Ho Hien. *The Men of Vietnam*. Denver, CO: Outskirts Press, Forum#4, 2008.
Vo, Nghia M., V. Dang Chat and V. Ho Hien. *Remembering Saigon*. Denver, CO: Outskirts Press, Forum#1, 2008.
Vo, Nghia M., V. Dang Chat and V. Ho Hien. *The Sorrows of War and Peace*. Denver, CO: Outskirts Press, Forum#2, 2008.
Vo, Nghia M., V. Dang Chat and V. Ho

Hien. *The Women of Vietnam*. Denver, CO: Outskirts Press, Forum#3, 2008.

Vũ, Quỳnh, and Văn Nguyễn Bùi. *Linh Nam Chich Quai*, 1492. Dinh Gia Khanh: Nha Xuat Ban Van Hoc Hanoi, 2001 (reprinted).

Whitfield, Danny J. *Historical and Cultural Dictionary of Vietnam*. Metuchen, NJ: Scarecrow Press, 1976.

Woodside, Alexander B. *Vietnam and the Chinese Model*. Cambridge, MA: Harvard University Press, 1971.

Wook, Choi Buynh. *Southern Vietnam Under the Reign of Minh Mang*. Ithaca, NY: Cornell University Southeast Asia Program, 2004.

Index

ả đào 180; *see also* songstress
A Man 49; *see also* Man Nương
Amerasian 242
An Dương Vương (An Dương King) 53, 69, 103; *see also* Thục Phán
An Hạt 54
ancestor worship 7, 13
Annam (center) 21
animism 6
áo dài 189
areca tree 61
aristocracy 13
anti-communism 20
Âu Cơ 20, 59–60

Bà Chiểu 33
Bà Chúa Kho 6
Bà Chúa Xứ 6, 31–32, 93
Bà Đen (Black Lady) 93
Bạch Đằng 52
balance 198
bàn thờ gia tiên 14
bàn thờ tổ tiên 14
bánh chưng 67, 155
bánh dầy 67
bánh tét 67, 155
bánh tráng 219
banyan 157, 193
Barrow 32
Bernard Fall 20
betel 61, 148
Bishop de Behaine 125
Bố Cái Đại Vương 52; *see also* Phùng Hưng
bộ đội 236
bravery 50
bribe 37
brotherhood 150
Buddhism 6, 14–15, 39, 49, 78, 84, 199
buffalo 130

Cải 125
Cam Ré 7
candidate 183
Cao Lỗ 71
capitalism 20

capriciousness 92
cause-effect 200
Celestial Lake 80
Chaigneau 33
chalk pot 84
Cham 31, 55, 164, 182
Châu Đốc 31, 93
chày giã 219
Chế Củ 55
China 183
Chinese tales 35–38
Chivas-Baron 44
Chu Điền 53
Chủ Đồng Tử 29, 63
Chùa Quán Sứ 7
Cổ Loa 72, 92, 104
Cô Tuyết 7
Coburn Jewell 93
Cochinchina (south) 21
cockfighting 33
cocoon 139
Communism 13
Côn Sơn 124
concubine 37
Confucianism 6, 11–14, 36, 147, 154, 231
Công An 6
công dã tràng 145
corruption 36
courtship 39
Cox, Marian 38
crab 131, 141
crime 20
criminal totalitarianism 13
crocodile 83
crossbow 103; *see also* An Dương Vương
cử nhân 183
cult 50
Cuội 157

Dã Tràng 141; *see also* crab
Đại La 56; *see also* Hanoi
Đại Việt Sử Ký Toàn Thư 99
đàng ngoài (north) 21, 164
đàng trong (south) 21, 164
daughter-in-law 41, 226

Đế (emperor) 57
Đế Minh 58
deception 245
Degh 24
destitute 85
devotion 207
đình 9, 79
Dinh Cô 93
Đinh Tiên Hoàng 15
disarray 239
distrust 15
divine 48–49
division 16
Đồ Lê (or Gia La Đồ Lê) 72–73; see also Khẩu Đà La
Đoàn Thị Điểm 30
đổi mới (renovation) 7
Đông Hải (eastern Sea) 61
Đồng Sơn 100
Dror Olga 50
Đức Thần Gióng (Spirit of Phù Đổng Village) 29
Đức Thần Tản Viên (Spirit of Mount Tản Viên) 29; see also Mountain spirit
duck 146
Dương Lễ 201
Dương Văn Quyền 93
Durand, Maurice 45

egg 90
emotional intelligence 137
enlightenment 14
enslavement 16
evil 48
examination 36

face 160
fairy 97, 170, 172
fairy tale 26, 45
faked tear 247
fate 12, 41, 185
Father Lý 17
Faurot 35
fidelity 150
fisherman 164, 203
flute 164
fly 135–136
fortune 135
fox 40
freedom 16
friendship 207, 211
frontier 32

gambling 135
gecko 133
Genie (spirit) of Phù Đổng 26, 104; see also Ông Gióí
ghost 6, 40
Gia Long 32
Giáng Hương 170, 174
Giao Chỉ 54, 100

Giáp Tự 10
girl 238
God/goddess 89–90, 92–93, 147
goddess worship 7, 15
gold 220
goldsmith 199
gourd 220
greed 214
guardian 79

Hà Long Bay 99
Hà Nguyên 46
Hall of Mirrors 127
Hanoi 20, 46; see also Thăng Long
hát bội 33
Hậu Thổ 49
heaven 126
heaven's mandate 12
heaven's will 64
herdsboy 38
heroism 48–49, 90
hiếu 231
highlanders (Thượng or Mường) 20
Hinduism 57
history 47, 90
Hồ Chí Minh 246
Hồ cult 10
Hồ Gươm (Hồ Hoàn Kiếm) 121
Hồ Xuân Hương 118
Hoàng Phi Yến 124
Homer 205
Hòn Vọng Phu 203; see also Lady of Stone
Hồng Đức 113
Hùng king (Hùng Vương) 57, 60, 62, 66, 74, 98, 150
Huyền Không 124
Huỳnh Sanh Thông 235

impoverishment 17
incarceration 16
independence 57
Indian tales 40–42
inheritance 207, 216
initiative 163
intelligence 48

Jade Emperor 10
Japanese tales 38–40
Joan of Arc 116

karma 185, 211
Khẩu Đà La 49, 73
Khmer 31
Kiều Phú 57
Kim Căng 82
Kim Quy 69–70, 104
Kipling, Rudyard 145
kitchen god 11, 151; see also Ông Táo
Kwon 7

Lạc 100

Index

Lạc Long Quân 20, 58–59, 61, 96–100
Lạc Việt 181
Lady of Nam Xương 205
Lady of Stone 203
Lady Tô Thị 205
Lady Triệu (or Triệu Ẩu) 115–116
laissez-faire 145
land of bliss 168
land reform 246
Landes Antony 29, 44, 77
Lang Bạc 54
Lang Liêu 66, 155
Lăng Ông 33; see also Lê Văn Duyệt
Laotzu 11
laureate 78
Lê Lợi 26
Lê Thái Tổ 29, 121
Lê Thân 120
Lê Thánh Tông 163
Le Thi Răm 124
Lê Văn Duyệt 32–34
Lê Văn Hữu 114
legend 26
Leopold Cadière 15
Liễu Hạnh (princess) 11, 29–31, 81
Lĩnh Nam Chích Quái (LNCQ) 57–76
literati 57
Little Saigon 19
lộc 31
locust 235
Lông Đỗ 56; see also Hanoi
Long Hải 93
lowlanders (Kinh) 20
loyalty 48
Lưu Bình 201
Lưu Sinh 181
Lý 6
Lý Ánh Tông 50, 54
Lý Bôn 52
Lý Nhân Tông 55
Lý Ông Trọng 54, 68–69; see also Lý Thân
Lý Phật Tử 52; see also Southern Emperor
Lý Tế Xuyên 23, 47
Lý Thái Tông 55
Lý Thân 68; see also Lý Ông Trọng
Lý Thánh Tông 13, 55
Lý Thông 191
Lý Thường Kiệt 48, 55

Mã Viện 54
Mahayana 14
Mai An Tiên (or An Tiên) 67
major 241
male-centered 40
Malleret Louis 31
Man Nương 72
mandarin 36, 148, 183, 220
Marble Mountains 122; see also Ngũ Hành Sơn
marsh boy 63; see also Chử Đồng Tử
matriarchy 13, 118

Mê Linh 113
mê tín dị đoan 33
medium 8
Mekong 32
Ming 57
Minh Mạng 33
misunderstanding 145
Mongol 48
monk 39
moon 159
moral authority 57
moral virtue 48
mosquito 137–138
Mother Buddha 72; see also A Man
Mountain spirit 74; see also Đức Thần Tản Viên; Sơn Tinh
Mowgli 145
Mường 99; see also highlander

Nam Quốc Sơn Hà 56; see also Lý Thường Kiệt
narcissus 215
Nation 113
ngày giỗ tổ 14
Nghệ An 78
Ngô Đình Diệm 114
Ngô Đình Nhu 114
Ngô Quyền 52
Ngô Sĩ Liên 99, 114
Ngọc Hoàng Thượng Đế 9, 153; see also Jade Emperor
Ngọc Nhân 137
Ngũ Hành Sơn 124; see also Marble mountain
Nguyễn Ánh 124
Nguyễn Cầm 46
Nguyễn Công Trứ 164
Nguyễn Đồng Chi 44
Nguyễn Du 185
Nguyễn Gia Cư 93
Nguyễn Hoàng 164
Nguyễn Kỳ 175
Nguyễn Thị Lộ 200
Nguyễn Trãi 200
Nhật Dạ Trạch 119
Như Nguyệt 55; see also Lý Thường Kiệt
Night Marsh King 53; see also Triệu Quang Phục, Việt King
nightmare 17
nội tướng 231
nothingness 11

Odyssey 205
Ông Giỏi 26; see also Genie of Phù Đổng; Phù Đổng Thiên Vương
Ông Táo (kitchen god) 11
overseas Vietnamese 20; see also Viet Kieu; Vietnamese American

pariah 247
Paris Accords 19

patriarchy 13
peacock 216
peasant 92
petty commerce 32
Phan Bội Châu 18
Pháp Điện 73
Pháp Lôi 73
Pháp Vân 73
Pháp Vũ 73
Phù Đổng Thiên Vương 64–66
Phùng Hưng 52; *see also* Bố Cái Đại Vương
Phùng Thị Chính 113
pig king 84
pragmatism 130
preserved body 51
princess 167; *see also* fairy
prudish 39
P'u Sung-lin 34

Quan Âm (goddess of mercy) 11
Quan Đệ 79

rain maker 50
Ramanujan 40, 94
responsiveness 6, 49, 51, 75
Rhodopsis 38
rice 218

sacrifice 90
Saigon 16
salvation 11
Sam Mountain 31
San Juan 17
scholar 181
Schultz, George 93
Sea spirit 61, 74; *see also* Thủy Tinh
Shiva 31
shrine 90; *see also* temple
Sĩ Nhiếp 49, 51
sĩ, nông, công, thương 163, 180
Siddhartha Gautama 14
silkworm 139
Simmel, Georg 18
sisters-in-law 211
snake 141
Son of Heaven 36
Sơn Tinh 101; *see also* Mountain spirit
songstress 175
sorcery 12
Southern Emperor 53; *see also* Lý Phật Tử
spirit 6, 8, 9, 47–48, 92, 196
spiritual resolution 10
starfruit 213
statesman 170
stepmother 131, 186
stone dog 183
storytelling 24
submissiveness 154
superhuman 47
supernatural 47

tailor 159
tale 94; *see also* fairy tale
Tấm Cám 132, 186
tam tòng 154
Tản Viên Mountain 74
Taoism 7, 11–12, 37
Ta-po 232
tattoo 99
Tây Ninh 93
Tây Sơn 33, 125
tea box 219
temple 49, 52; *see also* shrine
Terada Alice 93
Tết 156
Thạch Sanh 191
Thạch Sùng 133
Thần Nông 57
Thăng Long (Hanoi) 13, 48; *see also* Hanoi
Tháp Rùa 121
Theravada 14
Thi Sách 54
Thích Nhật Hạnh 93
Thiên Thai 138
Thiên Y A Na 31
Thiệu Trị 33
Thục Phán 69; *see also* An Dương King
Thủy Tinh 101; *see also* Sea spirit
Tiên Du 170
Tiên Dung 62–63
Tiên Hậu (Mother of the Realm) 31
tiến sĩ 183
tiger 129
title 49
To Định 54
Tô Lịch 49, 56, 75
toad 126
Tống (Song) 55
Tonkin (north) 21, 77
Trần Thuận Tông 168
Trần Tú 46
Triệu Đà 53
Triệu Quang Phục 52; *see also* Night Marsh King, Việt King
Triệu Thị Minh 115
Trời 163, 199; *see also* heaven
trúng gió 8
Trưng Nhị 54
Trưng Thu 158
Trưng Trắc 54
Trưng Sisters 49, 54, 75, 112–115
Trương Chi 165
Trương Như Tảng 16, 19
Trương Vĩnh Ký 93
Tứ Bất Tử (Four Immortals) 29
tú tài 183
Từ Thức 168
Từ Uyên 172
turtle 86; *see also* Kim Quy
Tyler, Royall 89

Unger 13
unity 128
upright conduct 48

Văn Lang 60
Văn Miếu (Temple of Literature) 13
Văn Tiến Dũng 20
Văn Xuân 52
Việt Điền U Linh Tập (VDULT) 23, 47–56
Việt Kiều 129, 171, 247
Việt King 52; *see also* Triệu Quang Phục
Vietnamese-American 18; *see also* Việt Kiều

Vĩnh Phú 10
Vu Lan 245
Vũ Quỳnh 57
Vương (king) 57

watermelon 67–68, 161
wisdom 129
women-centered 40
worship 47

Zen 15

www.ingramcontent.com/pod-product-compliance
Ingram Content Group UK Ltd.
Pitfield, Milton Keynes, MK11 3LW, UK
UKHW041931140426
5217IPUK00014B/424